"What's wrong? Aren't yo

"What's wrong?" She tossed the remainder aside and jumped up to face him squarely. He was tall, but then so was she. Tilting her head back a fraction, she glared at him. "Oh, let me see… I'd intended to go shopping but instead interrupted a robbery. I had a gun held to my head. I was forced to ride for hours with a stranger to an undisclosed destination. To put it in simpler terms—you kidnapped me. Tackled me. Threatened me. Tore my favorite dress." She indicated the hem with a sweep of her hand. "And worst of all," she added, her voice wobbling, "you made me miss my mother's birthday."

One rogue tear slipped down her cheek, and she blinked fast to dry her eyes.

Before she could comprehend what he intended, he lifted his hand to her face and ever so gently wiped the tear away with the pad of his thumb. His touch was as delicate as a butterfly's wing.

It confused her. There was more to this outlaw than she had anticipated.

Karen Kirst

The Reluctant Outlaw
&
The Bridal Swap

LOVE INSPIRED
INSPIRATIONAL ROMANCE

LOVE INSPIRED®

INSPIRATIONAL ROMANCE

ISBN-13: 978-1-335-45481-2

PLEASE RECYCLE · THIS PRODUCT IS RECYCLABLE ·

Recycling programs for this product may not exist in your area.

CONTENTS

Karen Kirst was born and raised in east Tennessee near the Great Smoky Mountains. She's been a lifelong lover of books, but it wasn't until after college that she had the grand idea to write one herself. Now she divides her time between being a wife, homeschooling mom and romance writer. Her favorite pastimes are reading, visiting tearooms and watching romantic comedies.

Books by Karen Kirst

Love Inspired Suspense

Explosive Reunion
Intensive Care Crisis
Danger in the Deep

Love Inspired Historical

Smoky Mountain Matches

The Reluctant Outlaw
The Bridal Swap
The Gift of Family
His Mountain Miss
The Husband Hunt
Married by Christmas
From Boss to Bridegroom
The Bachelor's Homecoming
Reclaiming His Past
The Sheriff's Christmas Twins
Wed by Necessity

Visit the Author Profile page
at Harlequin.com for more titles.

THE RELUCTANT OUTLAW

For God has not given us a spirit of fear,
but of power and of love and of a sound mind.
—*2 Timothy* 1:7

To my husband, Marek—
thank you for your endless support and
encouragement. You are my voice of reason.
Without you, there would be no laughter in my life.

To my parents, Richard and Dorothy Kirst—thanks,
Mom, for all those trips to the library. I wouldn't be
living this dream today had it not been for you. And
Dad, your generosity is what I love most about you.

To my critique partners—
my sister Shelly Benson, niece Jessica Price
and best friend, Danielle Mattson—
thank you for your insights and encouragement
on this journey to publication!

A big thanks to my editor Emily Rodmell! You
took a chance on me and I'm so thankful you did!

My ultimate thank-you goes to
my Heavenly Father, God, and His Son, Jesus Christ!

Apart from Him, I can do nothing.

Chapter One

Gatlinburg, Tennessee
June 1880

Blocking the entrance to Clawson's Mercantile, Evan Harrison tried to blend in with the overhang's shadows. He'd dressed in head-to-toe black, his hat pulled low to shade his eyes. Leaning against the glass-paned door, arms crossed and one ankle slung carelessly over the other, he could've been waiting for someone or simply watching the morning rush of people. What passersby couldn't see was his heart's sharp tattoo against his rib cage and the sweat sliding between his shoulder blades to trickle down his spine.

His narrowed gaze flicked to and fro, his muscles bunched and ready to spring should anyone head his way. *Hurry up, Fitz.* He wondered how Art was doing in the back alley.

This wasn't his first holdup, so why the unease? He scanned the crowd again, and the burning in his gut grew worse. He was worried about Fitz. The outlaw inside the mercantile was a wild card. Lenny Fitzgerald had proven time and again that he wasn't afraid to spill innocent blood. And he wasn't particular about his victims.

Evan had done his best to prevent the violence, but he could only do so much without arousing suspicion. He couldn't take a chance of blowing his cover. He'd worked too hard and waited too long to have that happen now.

He closed his eyes, wishing he could put off the inevitable. Then he remembered the reason he was there and his resolve hardened. He was on a quest for justice, and he *would* get it. No matter what.

He snapped his eyes open at the sound of someone approaching. Shifting his head to the right, he caught sight of a young woman striding down the boardwalk in his direction, her boots clipping the weathered planks with determination. She was on a mission, it seemed.

Please let her be headed anywhere else but here, he thought.

As she neared, he couldn't help but notice her bold beauty. Sleek red hair peeked out from beneath a navy-and-cream floral-print bonnet framing an oval-shaped face. He admired her ivory complexion, so rare in redheads, and the pert nose, regal cheekbones and generous mouth. Her sturdy navy dress outlined a pleasing female form, tall yet graceful.

She must've noticed him staring, for she quirked a cinnamon eyebrow, her lips firming in disapproval. Her eyes raked him before meeting his gaze head-on. One jerk of her chin hinted of a stubborn streak.

"Excuse me." She speared him with her gaze. "You're blocking the entrance."

Her eyes were green, not the expected blue. Deep green, the color of spruce trees streaked with sunset gold.

Straightening, Evan plucked the hay from his mouth and tossed it to the ground.

"You can't go in there."

A line of confusion formed between her fine eyebrows. "Why not?"

"Mr. Clawson had to step out for a few minutes. He asked me to tell any customers who happened by that he'd be right back."

Annoyance flickered in those gorgeous eyes. "That's impossible. Mr. Clawson is dead. His son-in-law, Larry Moore, is the owner now."

Swallowing his frustration, he struggled to maintain an air of indifference. Could she see the vein throbbing at his temple? "My mistake. Guess I mixed up the names."

A loud shout, followed by a heavy thump, sounded through the door. Evan cringed, resisting the urge to turn and look. She craned her neck to peer beyond his shoulder, and he sidestepped to block her line of sight.

"Someone is in there," she snapped, her eyes narrowing. "What kind of game are you playing?"

"Trust me, I'm not playing—"

"Is there a problem, Miss O'Malley?" a male voice interrupted from the street.

This situation was going from bad to worse. Evan turned to see a well-dressed man observing them, his curious gaze shifting from the young woman to settle on him. As a stranger in town, Evan would naturally be regarded with a certain amount of suspicion. He had to fix this. Fast.

"Good morning, Lane," the young lady greeted the man with a slight smile. "This *gentleman* and I were just discussing—"

"How rude I was for not opening the door for her,"

Evan finished. Grabbing the door handle, he made a slight bow. Surprise flashed across her face. "I do apologize for the oversight, ma'am." Evan pulled the door open and with a light hand on her elbow ushered her inside, calling over his shoulder, "I apologize for the misunderstanding. Good day, sir."

"Yes, goodbye, Lane."

The door closed with a final whoosh, cutting off her farewell. Through the window, Evan watched the man hesitate a moment before planting his hat back on his head and walking away. One problem taken care of. One to go.

"What was that all about?" she demanded.

Evan scanned the room. Fitzgerald was nowhere to be seen, which meant he was probably in the back, tying up the owner.

He took hold of her arm, speaking in low, urgent tones. "You're in a situation way over your head, lady. I need you to walk back out that door and as far away from this mercantile as you can. Talk to no one. I can't guarantee your safety if you alert anyone to what's happening here."

She stared at him. "What—"

"No questions. There isn't time—"

"What's that girl doing in here?"

Evan stiffened at the sound of Fitzgerald's cold voice behind him. "Keep quiet," he murmured in her ear. Without releasing her, he faced the outlaw whose features were concealed by a red bandanna.

"She was determined to do her shopping," Evan drawled. "Looks like her impatience has earned her a stint in the storeroom with the owner. I'll tie her up."

"You will do no such thing!" she cried, attempting to pry his hand loose.

Fitzgerald shook his head. "Forget it. She'll have to come with us."

"No." Her chances of survival were slim to none if she went with them.

"She's seen your face. We can't leave her here."

"I thought we agreed—no hostages. I don't like this—"

"Then you should've done your job and kept her away," Fitzgerald snapped. "Let's go."

Evan hesitated in order to give Fitzgerald a few second's head start.

"A hostage will only slow you down, you know," she argued, her eyes large in her pale face. "Leave me here. I'll tell the sheriff I didn't get a good look at you. You have my word."

He didn't reply. What could he say at this point? His mind was whirling with too many scenarios—all of them unpleasant—to attempt rational conversation.

"You're making a huge mistake! As soon as people realize what's happened, they'll organize a posse and come looking for you."

He sensed her mounting desperation, but was helpless to do anything about it.

"Isn't the cash enough? Do you really want to add kidnapping to your list of crimes?"

Ignoring her questions, he forcibly led her past the stockroom and the floor-to-ceiling shelves overflowing with goods, past the storekeeper's office and, finally, to the private quarters. At the rear entrance, he warned her to keep quiet.

"Where's Mr. Moore?" she demanded. "Is he okay?"

He slipped the Colt Peacemaker out of his holster, making sure she got a good look at it. He wasn't above intimidation to keep her in line. Her life depended on it. "Whatever you do, stay close to me."

For once, she didn't utter a word. Evan hoped that she wasn't too strong-willed to do as he said. He didn't know what Fitz would do if she made a scene.

He grabbed the bandanna bunched around his neck and tugged it up to cover his face. Opening the door a crack, he checked the alleyway. Fitz and Art were already saddling up. He hurried her down the wooden stairs to where his horse, Lucky, was hitched, prodding her forward with a hand on her back.

"Get on the horse."

She dug her heels in the rocky dirt. "Uh-uh."

"Do it or I'll toss you up there myself," he growled from his position directly behind her, letting her feel the tip of the gun barrel near her shoulder. Her resistance irritated him—didn't she have the good sense to be scared?

With a huff, she grabbed the saddle horn, placed her foot in the stirrup and hauled herself up. He replaced his firearm and swung up behind her.

Art's eyes bulged when he spotted her. "Who's that?"

Fitz barked, "Never mind. Let's ride."

"Might as well relax," Evan told his hostage, signaling Lucky to head out. "It's gonna be a long ride."

Juliana O'Malley seethed with anger. As the miles between her and Gatlinburg stretched endlessly into the distance, she passed the time dreaming up ways to get even with the man holding her captive—everything from pushing him off a cliff to hog-tying him and leaving him at the mercy of wild animals.

It was either that or succumb to mind-numbing fear.

She was familiar with firearms all right, but never in her life had she had one waved in her face.

Lord Jesus, please help me, she prayed. *I'm in a bit of a situation here.*

If only she'd heeded her instincts. The moment she became aware of the man in black's blatant scrutiny, she'd known that he was no gentleman. Her cheeks burned even now as she recalled how his intense gaze had taken in every inch of her. Scandalous!

She squirmed in the saddle. His muscled arms tightened in response, imprisoning her against his rock-hard chest. His warm breath stirred the hair at her nape and prickles of awareness danced along her skin.

Juliana squeezed her eyes tight and tried not to dwell on his disturbing nearness. At least he smelled pleasant enough, she consoled herself. Beneath the smell of horse and sweat, she detected the clean scent of soap.

They would have to stop soon, she reasoned. They'd ridden for what seemed like an eternity, yet her kidnappers had given no sign of slowing the horses. She was hot and thirsty, her mouth gritty from the dust clouds stirred by the horses' hooves.

As desperately as she wanted to get off the horse, however, she wasn't eager to find out what they planned to do with her once they reached their destination.

As she saw it, she had only one option. Escape. She'd have to try to outrun him, because she was no match for his physical strength. Luckily, she was a fast runner. Just two weeks earlier, her cousin Caleb had challenged her to a footrace and she'd won. Not by much, but she'd won fair and square. He'd been hoppin' mad—

She gasped. Her mother and sisters would be wondering why she hadn't returned with the supplies. It was her mother's birthday, and they had a full day of work to get ready for the big celebration dinner that night. They wouldn't worry too much at first, but with each passing hour their concern would grow until finally someone would go looking for her.

The horses in front slowed and their mount did the same, veering off the trail into the dense woods. She straightened, nerves taut, thoughts of home scattered. What now? Would the brute release her? Here in the middle of nowhere to fend for herself? Or did he have something more sinister in mind?

"Where are we?" she demanded. They'd used the trail along Baskins Creek heading southeast out of Gatlinburg, but she was in unfamiliar surroundings now. "What are you going to do with me?"

The man dismounted without a word. Reaching up, his hands spanned her waist and swung her down as if she weighed no more than a sack of feathers. The imprints of his fingers against her rib cage were like branding irons. Fear shot through her, leaving her dizzy and weak.

He stepped away long enough to take hold of the horse's bridle. He tugged his bandanna down and gestured toward the other men already entering the forest. "Now we walk."

Juliana resisted, unwilling to blindly follow him. "I'm not moving from this spot until you answer me."

He spun on his heel and brought his face close to hers, his grip on her arm firm but not bruising. She'd noticed his eyes right off. A brilliant shade—dark, almost purple-blue—put her in mind of the poisonous larkspur blooms that dotted the meadows each spring. Beautiful yet deadly.

"Do as I say, Miss O'Malley," he said in a near whisper, "and I just might be able to get you out of this mess."

"You need help, Harrison?" The man who'd robbed Mr. Moore had stopped and was watching them. Something about him disturbed her. "Looks like a handful to me."

Her captor, apparently named Harrison, didn't turn around. His eyes never wavering from her face, he drawled, "Good thing I like my women feisty."

Juliana stiffened. She opened her mouth to protest, but faltered at the almost imperceptible shake of his head. Strangely, his suggestive words were at odds with the grim light in his eyes.

"Not me," the other man snorted. "I like mine submissive."

Harrison's mouth flattened, his features hardening to granite. He was angry, perhaps even disgusted, by the other man.

To Juliana, he said, "There's a stream straight ahead and some shade. We'll rest long enough to eat a bite before heading back out."

Juliana felt a spark of hope. "You can leave me here. We're not so far from Gatlinburg, after all. Might take me a while, but I can make it back before nightfall. I don't mind walking—"

He held up a hand. "That's not an option. Come on, I'm parched and so is my horse."

"But I want to go home! My mother and sisters will be desperate to find me!"

He glanced over his shoulder. The others had disappeared into the woods, leaving them alone. His eyes bored into hers. "Trust me. I'm going to think of a way to get you home."

Trust *him?* A common thief? He was the one who'd forced her from the mercantile and ordered her onto his horse. No, his words were empty, as substantial as a fist-ful of air.

This was her chance. It might be her only one.

Grateful that she'd chosen to wear her brand-new, hard-soled work boots, Juliana did what she'd done as a child tousling with her cousins—nailed him in the shin with the toe of her boot and with her free arm elbowed him in the ribs. He grunted in surprise and relaxed his hold.

Juliana slipped out of his grasp and sprinted away, uncertain which direction to take. She found herself fol-lowing the hard-packed dirt trail on which they'd just traveled.

Her bonnet hung by its strings around her neck, and her hair, loosened by the jarring ride on horseback, un-coiled now to stream down her back.

Heavy footsteps sounded close behind and a small scream escaped her lips.

Faster! She pushed her legs to take longer strides. Her temples throbbed. Her side ached. The chase was over as suddenly as it began.

Bands of steel encircled her waist and down she went. Her captor twisted beneath her and she landed on top of him, his body a cushion against the rocky ground. The wind was knocked from her lungs. His arms locked around her.

"That," he puffed angrily, "was a stupid stunt."

Using her hands on his chest as leverage, she arched away from him, trying to break free of his hold. Her struggles were useless against his brute strength. He held fast. With a grunt, he rolled over so that he hovered above her, hands pressing her shoulders into the dirt. His face was inches from her own, his breath mingling with hers.

"Listen to me," he warned through gritted teeth, "if you want to survive the night you'd better do *exactly* as I say."

His dark blue eyes turned stone-cold and the look on his rugged face bordered on menacing. She trembled involuntarily.

"*I'm* not the one you need to worry about. Fitzgerald and the others will not have patience with your antics. They would've shot you dead the instant you bolted. In fact, I'm going to have to do some fancy talkin' to explain why I didn't."

At her swift intake of breath, his voice gentled somewhat. "I'm not trying to scare you into cooperating. I'm trying to keep you out of trouble. Understand?"

Juliana nodded.

"No, I wanna hear you say it."

"I understand," she managed.

"No more stunts?"

"No more stunts."

"I sure hope you mean that, lady."

He stood and pulled her to her feet. Then he marched her back to where his horse stood grazing and guided them both into the woods.

Twigs cracked beneath their boots. Far above them, birds twittered a cheerful song in their nests. Juliana was grateful for the shade. Her neck was damp from the weight of her hair, and the bodice of her dress clung to her skin. Her heart thumped against her rib cage. He'd frightened her there at the last, more even than when he'd aimed a gun at her. His forbidding expression still burned in her mind.

When she finally saw the stream up ahead, she resisted the urge to run and lie down in it.

Two of the bandits turned to stare at them. The skinny one seemed nervous, his gaze shifting between her and the other two. The man she assumed was Fitzgerald looked hard at her. He was not an unattractive man, average really, and built like a bull.

Juliana resisted the urge to hide behind Harrison.

"I thought you said you could handle her." The words came out as an accusation.

"She didn't get away, did she?" Harrison shot back.

"We'll have to get rid of her at some point, you know. She knows too much."

The cruel words, spoken so casually, washed over her like a wave of icy water.

"Not yet." Harrison stole a glance at her. "I want some time alone with her first."

Juliana faltered, suddenly sick to her stomach. After all his promises to get her to safety, she hadn't expected *that*. She lowered her gaze to the ground.

Fitzgerald barked a laugh. "Good for you, Harrison. I was beginning to wonder about you. Six months on the trail and you never once joined us at the saloon."

"Yeah, well, I've always been a sucker for Irish beauties."

Juliana's head shot up, but he kept his face averted from her searching gaze. A red flush climbed up his neck, indicating what? Embarrassment? No, that would mean he possessed a conscience.

Moving to dig in his saddlebags, he brought out a small tin cup and held it out to her without sparing her a glance. It chafed to have to accept anything from him, but thirst drove her. Careful to avoid his fingers, she grabbed the cup and hurried to the water's edge to fill it. The cold, crisp water washed away the film of dirt coating her throat.

"Take this." He appeared beside her with a bulging handkerchief. "We're only going to be here about fifteen minutes, so if I were you I'd eat fast."

"I don't want it." She stood abruptly and stepped back, wary of his intentions.

"Take it." He closed the distance between them and loomed over her. "You'll need your strength."

She *was* hungry. Snatching the bundle from him, she marched over to the nearest tree and, moving beneath the branches into the shade, sank down in the soft grass and smoothed her dress to cover her pantaloons.

She watched Fitzgerald and the young outlaw, who were crouched downstream and cramming food into their mouths as if it were their last meal. Harrison didn't join them. With clean, precise movements, he crouched and dipped his canteen into the stream. Lifting it to his mouth, he swallowed long and deep, his corded neck muscles visible. After refilling and capping the canteen, he retrieved his lunch from his horse's saddlebag and ate standing up. His hat hung on the saddle horn, providing Juliana with a clear view of his profile.

She noted his strong jawline, stubborn chin and grim mouth.

He wore his sleek, ebony hair short. The conservative style suited him. His clothes weren't of the finest quality but were in good condition. No missing buttons in the black cotton shirt, no patches or holes in the black pants. The fact that he was dressed in black from head to toe seemed to fit his personality.

He was, in a word, formidable. Impenetrable. Hard. Callous.

He glanced her way and caught her studying him. Juliana felt her cheeks flame, and she immediately dropped her gaze to the food in her lap.

Her lavish breakfast seemed so long ago, although in reality it had only been about five hours. The sun was almost directly overhead, so she guessed it was nearing noon. Unexpected tears came to her eyes as she ate the slabs of ham and hard biscuits, and she had a difficult time swallowing.

Today was to have been a day of celebration. Instead, it was a nightmare!

Why, Lord? I don't understand. What is to become of me?

Her mother's birthday was ruined. Ruined!

Certainly there would be no celebration now. All that hard work wasted! Fifteen-year-old twins Jessica and Jane had put in more hours than anybody, preparing various meats, pies and, of course, the birthday cake. How disappointed they must be!

She wondered if Megan had gone into town to search for her. Of her four sisters, Juliana was closest to nineteen-year-old Megan. She was the quiet, thoughtful one. The bookworm, her head filled with all sorts of romantic notions Juliana liked to tease her about. Poor Megan. Even she'd have a hard time putting a romantic spin on this situation.

What if Sheriff Timmons had sent someone out to the O'Malley farm to relay the awful news? They would be frantic with worry!

If it hadn't been for this trio of wastrels, especially Harrison, the scoundrel…that greedy, no good—

Dusty black boots appeared in her line of vision, and she looked up to find the blackguard staring down at her, his brow furrowed in question.

"What's wrong? Aren't you hungry?"

"What's wrong?" She tossed the remainder aside and jumped up to face him squarely. He was tall, but then so was she. Tilting her head back a fraction, she glared at him. "Oh, let me see… I'd intended to go shopping but instead interrupted a robbery. I had a gun held to my head. I was forced to ride for *hours* with strangers to an undisclosed destination. To put it in simpler terms—you kidnapped me. Tackled me. Threatened me. Tore my favorite dress." She indicated the hem with a sweep of her hand. "And worst of all," her voice wobbled, "you made me miss my mother's birthday."

One rogue tear slipped down her cheek, and she blinked fast to dry her eyes.

Before she could comprehend what he intended, he lifted his hand to her face and ever so gently wiped the tear away with the pad of his thumb. His touch was as delicate as a butterfly's wing.

"I'm sorry."

Juliana couldn't move. Was that regret darkening his eyes? All coherent thought evaporated. She hadn't a clue what to think or say. Him? *Apologize?*

He didn't give her a chance to respond. The next moment he pivoted on his heel and strode away, making her wonder if she'd imagined the tender moment.

"Time to go," he called over his shoulder. Apparently he was confident she wasn't going to try to run away again. And why shouldn't he be? He'd already proved she didn't have a chance of escaping him.

She eyed his holster. Her cousin Josh had taught her a lot of useful skills, one of them being how to shoot.

With the gun in his possession, *he* had the upper hand. But if she should ever get her hands on it…

Juliana determined right then and there to stay alert and watch for her chance to get that gun. It was her only hope of escape.

Chapter Two

"I've never understood why some people choose to live on the wrong side of the law," Juliana said. "Doesn't it bother you that you're harming innocent people?"

Harrison didn't acknowledge the question. No surprise there. Her attempts at conversation had been met with stubborn silence all along.

They were moving deeper into the Smoky Mountains, in the opposite direction of Gatlinburg and the larger towns of Pigeon Forge and Sevierville. The foursome had traveled through lush forests and meadows, beauty she would've appreciated in other circumstances. The air here beneath the soaring canopy of tree branches was cooler than in the open countryside, and for that Juliana was thankful. Midsummer temperatures in East Tennessee could quickly become unbearable.

It was late now, though, and the sun's heat had lost its bite. A soft breeze teased her hair and cooled her skin, rustling leaves whispering secrets above her. The forest was darkening, the shadows lengthening as they trudged on.

Juliana was having a hard time keeping up with Harrison. The trail had long since disappeared, and they were dodging trees and gnarled roots poking out of the ground. Twice she'd stumbled but managed to catch herself before hitting the dirt face-first.

"Poor Mr. Moore," she said. "I can't imagine how he reacted to being robbed at gunpoint. I hope he doesn't have a heart attack."

"Has he had one before?"

"No, but he isn't well. Don't tell me you're actually concerned?" When he didn't respond, she continued, "You *did* steal all his money, you know. What if he's forced to close the mercantile? I know for a fact he doesn't have any living relatives, so there's nowhere for him to go. He's such a kind, generous man, too. I don't want to even *think* about what he would do if he lost the store."

"If he's such a fine human being, then I'm sure someone would be willing to take him in."

"That's it?" she demanded, her breath coming in puffs. "That's your solution? You take away a man's livelihood and the best you can come up with is to let someone else take care of it? What about all the other people you've hurt? Do you ever stop and think about the damage you've caused?"

The skinny outlaw, whom she now knew was called Art, slowed to match their pace. "I think about it all the time. Even see some of the folks' faces I've robbed in my dreams."

Harrison's lips turned down at this, but he remained silent. Juliana studied Art's features. "Aren't you a bit young to be keeping company with ruthless criminals?"

"I'm seventeen," he said matter-of-factly. "Old enough to make my own choices."

The same age as her sister, Nicole. "Don't you have a family? Brothers? Sisters?"

"Yes, ma'am, I do," he responded softly, resignedly. "But my momma ain't got no idea where I am. Better if she thinks I'm dead than knows the truth. She'd never forgive me…"

Her heart ached for him. "Oh, Art, I'm sure you don't mean that. Were you and your mother close?"

His chest puffed out. "Yeah. I'm her oldest boy. She always said how proud she was to have me for a son."

"You know what I think? Your mother won't care what you've done as long as you're home, living an honest life."

Art was silent a moment, his brown eyes troubled. "You really think she'd take me back? And forgive me for up and leaving and joining this gang?"

"Yes, I do. But more than your mother's forgiveness, you need God's."

"My momma believes in Jesus. She read aloud from her Bible every morning and prayed with me before bed. But I—" He shook his head in shame. "I didn't always listen. I daydreamed a lot. Thought I was too young for religious stuff."

"And what about now?"

His earnest expression startled her. Here was a young man searching for the truth.

"More than anything, I want peace. I haven't had that in a long time." He lowered his voice. "I hang with a dangerous crowd. Ain't no tellin' when a bullet might find me. I've been thinkin' a lot lately about death. Trouble is, I don't know where I'm headed when I die."

"Art, I—"

"Enough yakking." Fitzgerald scowled over his shoulder. "Harrison, if you don't shut her up, I will."

With a shrug, Art moved away. Beside her, Harrison shot her a warning glance.

Frustrated with the interruption, she prayed for another opportunity to speak with Art about Christ. She couldn't help thinking perhaps *he* was the reason she'd been placed in this situation.

"How much farther?" she whispered.

Harrison wiped his brow with a handkerchief. "A quarter of a mile. Maybe more."

Ugh. While her new boots were great for defense, their stiffness tortured her feet. Blisters were already forming. She sighed.

"Take a drink." He paused to lift a canteen from the saddle. "I don't want you passing out from dehydration."

He made it sound as if he was more worried about her possibly holding him back than her health. Scoundrel. Her thirst overrode her distaste at sharing a canteen with a stranger. She took a long swallow of the cool liquid and handed it back to him.

"Watch your step," he advised. "The last thing we need is a twisted ankle or worse."

Juliana noticed he slowed his pace after that. When full darkness enveloped them, he lit a lamp to light their path.

God, I don't understand why You've allowed this to happen. I know You love me, but I'm having a hard time believing I'll ever get home. Please keep me safe. And comfort poor Mr. Moore. Somehow give him his money back. And my family, Lord, give them peace.

In all likelihood, every person in Gatlinburg had heard the news of her abduction. No doubt many of the church members were even now gathered at the church to pray. The thought brought her a small measure of comfort.

Had Sheriff Timmons already organized a posse to pursue her kidnappers? Her uncle and cousins were surely taking a lead in the mission to rescue her. But how long had it taken for someone to discover Mr. Moore?

Since she had no way of knowing what was going on back home, she comforted herself with the fact that at some point her captors would let down their guard, and she would be ready to spring into action.

Time passed more slowly than a snail in a windstorm. Juliana tried not to dwell on her bruised toes or aching calves. Nor did she attempt to start another conversation. What was the point? She would only be rebuffed.

"We're here."

The sound of Harrison's deep, no-nonsense voice in the darkness startled her. In the distance a tiny yellow light flickered. The cabin?

Juliana's steps slowed as reality slammed into her. There would be more outlaws in that cabin. She was alone. A single, unprotected female at the mercy of a gang of hardened criminals. A relentless procession of unhappy scenarios flashed through her mind, churning up the acid in her stomach. Every cell in her body screamed at her to flee.

She glanced at the enigmatic man walking beside her, recalling his vow to get her to safety. Had he meant it? Or had he said that to keep her from running again?

Her face flamed as she remembered his comments about liking feisty women and being attracted to Irish beauties. What were his true intentions? She was having trouble deciding what to believe.

Harrison must've sensed her unease, because he curled his fingers around her wrist and held fast. She glared at him but didn't try to free herself. Her muscles were weak from fear.

Fitzgerald and Art reached the cabin first. After securing their horses beneath a nearby tree, they waited for her and Harrison.

"Art." Harrison stopped before the young man. "I want you to stay out here with the lady."

Art's eyes bulged, his mouth flopping open like a dead trout. "Me?" His Adam's apple bobbed up and down. "I don't know—"

"It's simple," Harrison interrupted, his tone meant to instill confidence. "Stand right here beside her and whatever you do, *do not* let her out of your sight."

He released her wrist but didn't move away. Tucking his thumb beneath her chin, he eased her face up. "I'll be back in a few minutes," he reassured her in a surprisingly gentle tone. "Don't try anything foolish."

Juliana stared mutely at his rugged face, wreathed in shadows. So immobilizing was her fear at this point that stringing two words together seemed like an impossible task.

The cabin door banged open then and half-a-dozen men spilled into the yard, their greetings tapering to a deafening silence when they caught sight of her.

Evan stepped in front of Miss O'Malley to shield her from the men's predatory gazes. Young, innocent and beautiful, she was a lamb amid ravenous wolves. As they strained to get a glimpse of her, he could almost see them salivating in anticipation.

God, please help me get her out of here.

He stilled, stunned by the spontaneous prayer. He

hadn't prayed in months, not since the day his brother had been gunned down in cold blood.

"It's about time you boys got back." Cliff Roberts, the gang's leader, separated from the rest of the group. The middle-aged man held up his kerosene lamp, casting a muted circle of light about him. "Got the loot?"

"Right here, boss." Fitzgerald held up two bulging sacks.

"Good." His steely gaze bore into Evan. "Who's the girl?"

"There was a situation at the mercantile." Evan held the man's gaze.

Fitzgerald snorted. "Harrison wasn't doin' his job."

Roberts arched a brow in silent question.

Evan clenched his teeth. "It was either get her inside or risk a scene on the front steps. I figured the mission was more important."

He heard her sharp intake of breath and wished he hadn't phrased it quite that way. She didn't know it yet, but it was about to get worse.

"I'll take care of her, boss," Fitzgerald challenged, his leer making Evan's skin crawl.

"No," Evan's tone brooked no argument. "She's mine."

"I'll wager two dollars Harrison can best Fitz!" one of the men hollered.

Murmurs rumbled through the group. "Yeah, fight!"

"Winner gets the girl!"

Ignoring Miss O'Malley's outraged sputter, Evan settled a heavy hand on his weapon. "No contest. If any of you wants her, you'll have to kill me first."

Thick silence settled over the group. Crickets' buzzes swelled to fill it, as did the odd horse snuffle. His senses on high alert, Evan waited for someone to challenge his claim. He'd meant every single word. She was there through no fault of her own. He would guard her with his life.

John Hooper held up his hands. "Whoa, Harrison. No use gettin' touchy."

"Yeah, we didn't know ya done fell in love!" Another man snickered.

Roberts studied him. "Enough! Everyone inside. Now."

Mumbling and laughing, the men filed back through the door. Evan's breath left his lungs in a whoosh. He held back until he and Miss O'Malley were the only ones in the yard.

"You're not taking me in there, are you?" she demanded in a strangled whisper, her fingers clutching his forearm.

"Not for long, I promise."

"I'm supposed to believe you?" Her voice went shrill. "After all the foul—"

"Harrison!" someone inside called. "Let's go."

"Come on," Evan said.

Placing his palm against her lower back, he pressed her forward into the small, musty cabin. The smell of unwashed bodies and cigar smoke assaulted his senses, but he quickly masked his distaste.

Most of the men were seated at the table, and at their entrance, their bold gazes locked onto the lady at his side. She hung back, no doubt frightened out of her mind. And for good reason.

Fitzgerald stood in the corner near the door, his lips curled in a menacing smirk and his dark eyes challenging.

"Harrison." Roberts motioned him toward the cabin's only bedroom. "We need to talk."

Evan started forward with Miss O'Malley.

"No, she stays here."

No way was he leaving her side. Evan opened his mouth to protest. "But—"

"Ten minutes. Gauging from your proclamation just now, I figure she'll be safe enough."

Evan changed direction and, leading her to an over-turned carton in front of the fireplace, motioned for her to sit. Her wide green eyes begged him not to abandon her, and he almost caved. But he couldn't defy the gang leader's wishes without placing her in even greater danger. With a light squeeze to her ice-cold hands, he crossed the room with leaden steps.

Juliana watched him walk away, her heart frozen in fear. Her only ally, if he was truly that—and she had serious misgivings—was leaving her to face the enemy alone. Suddenly she understood a fraction of what Daniel must've felt as the guards sealed him in that lions' den and he awaited the advance of roaring, ravenous lions.

She began to pray in earnest, and to her surprise, the men largely ignored her as they took up their poker game. She kept her eyes downcast, thinking to defer their attention by being as immobile as a statue.

When their conversation faltered a few minutes later, she lifted her head to find out why. All eyes were on Art as he approached and crouched down beside her.

"Oh, go on about your business." He gestured toward the group. "I just wanna chat with the lady."

One by one, they turned their attention back to the game.

Art spoke in low tones, and she had to incline her head to hear him clearly.

"You don't have to be afraid of Harrison, ya know." His brown eyes appealed to her. "He ain't like the others."

"Why are you telling me this?" she whispered. She half wished he'd go back to his corner and let her go back to being invisible.

"I know you must be terrible scared," his voice dipped even lower, "but if I know Harrison, he'll try to get you to safety."

Interesting. Here was one outlaw urging her to trust another outlaw.

"Why would he do that?"

"Can't rightly say. But I ain't never seen him harm a living soul. Goes out of his way to avoid bloodshed." He dipped his chin. "And he's real respectful of the ladies. Harrison's a gentleman through and through."

Juliana smothered an unlady-like snort of disbelief. Gentleman? Hah. Her kidnapper resembled no gentleman she'd ever known.

Thinking perhaps this might be her last chance to broach the subject of faith, she leaned in close. "Remember what you said earlier about peace? And about not knowing where you're headed when you die?"

His face grew solemn. "Yeah."

"Jesus loves you, Art. He wants to free you from this life of sin. All you have to do is ask for forgiveness."

"I ain't never gonna be perfect."

She placed a hand on his arm, willing him to understand. "He doesn't expect us to be. We're only human, after all." She rushed to add, "But if we put our trust in God, He'll help us when we're weak and forgive us when we mess up."

"What are you two whispering about?" a gruff voice interrupted. "Hatching an escape plan?"

Art clambered to his feet. "N-no, nothing like that."

Catching Fitzgerald's hot glare at the young man, Juliana's temper took hold and she bolted to her feet.

"Leave him alone," she cried, "he was just trying to be nice."

With his bear paw of a hand, Fitzgerald seized her arm in a painful grip. "You watch how you speak to me, you good-for-nothing—"

"Don't, Fitz," Art protested. "Harrison won't like it if you roughhouse his girl."

Juliana could feel the bruises already starting to form where his fingers buried into her flesh. She winced in pain.

Where was Harrison?

Chapter Three

Evan was having trouble focusing on the conversation. He couldn't shake Miss O'Malley's stricken expression. He could only hope that with his challenge fresh in their minds, the men would think twice before approaching her. His ears strained for any sound of distress, but he could hear only the steady hum of voices and the occasional bark of laughter.

"What's the story with this girl? Why did you bring her here?" Roberts propped an arm on the windowsill.

"Things got out of hand. She was making a scene right there in plain view, and then a gentleman friend of hers approached us. I had to think fast. Defuse the situation."

"You like her," he accused.

Evan gave a noncommittal shrug. "I've always been partial to redheads."

Where was Roberts going with this line of questioning?

The older man's gray eyes narrowed slightly. "She's a witness. You know what that means."

Ah. Roberts was probing his motives and trying to decide if he had the stomach to do away with her. With a deep breath, Evan set out to convince his leader that he didn't have a conscience.

"I've been alone too long," he said, forcing a lusty sigh. "A man needs female companionship every now and then, if you know what I mean. A few nights with her are all I need."

"Like 'em unspoiled, I see." The other man straightened. "Just don't get attached, Harrison. You understand what you'll have to do before you head back?"

Swallowing back the bile rising in his throat, he spoke without emotion. "I remember. Dead witnesses can't testify."

A malicious grin split Roberts's bearded face. "Exactly."

A high-pitched scream pierced the air. Evan's heart plummeted to his knees. He jerked open the bedroom door in time to see Fitzgerald's fist connect with Miss O'Malley's cheek, the force of the blow knocking her to the floor.

White-hot fury shot through Evan, and he unsheathed his weapon. "Outside now," he growled. "Just you and me."

"Gladly." Fitz took a step toward the door.

"No." Roberts stepped between them. He threw Evan an exasperated glance. "Remember your job, Harrison. Or do I need to leave it to someone else?"

"No." Evan fought for control over his emotions. So much was riding on the next few moments. "I'll do it," he ground out.

Deciding that it was high time to get out of there, he strode to the corner and hauled her up, ignoring her whimpers when all he wanted to do was comfort her. When he spoke, he made sure everyone heard him.

"Come on, sweetheart," he forced himself to say in as lewd a tone he could manage, "Let's go have some fun."

She shivered at his words. Evan felt nauseated, but he kept his expression blank. He looked at Roberts. "Give me a few days. I plan on takin' my time."

"Remember, Harrison, don't come back until the matter's taken care of."

Evan tugged the brim of his hat in response, half dragging her out the door and down the steps. Sweat dotted his brow. Adrenaline surged through his body. He had to get her out of there before Fitz talked Roberts out of letting her go.

Her breaths were coming in pitiful gasps. Walking with her body tucked against his side, he kept one hand on each of her arms as he propelled her through the darkness. Her steps were halting, as if trying to slow their progress. He hoped she wouldn't try to bolt again.

When he heard the cabin door slam open, he urged her to go faster. He didn't waste a second glancing back. He would *not* fail her as he'd failed his brother, James. He would get her to safety or die trying.

Reaching his horse, he pushed her up into the saddle and swung up behind her, digging his heels into Lucky's sides to jolt the big black into action. One hand holding the reins, he wrapped his free arm around her middle and held her snugly against him. They rode out in the opposite direction of the way they'd come. He wasn't sure of their exact destination at this point. All he wanted was to put as many miles as possible between them and that cabin.

He felt her trembling. In response, he tightened his hold.

He despised what he'd had to do back there. He'd given his word that he wouldn't hurt her, and look what he'd done. No doubt she believed what he'd said to the others and was scared out of her mind.

As soon as he felt confident that no one was following them, he'd stop and explain everything.

Juliana couldn't stop shaking. The stark terror flowing through her body rendered her weak and limp. She had no power to fight her fate.

Her captor held her in a steel grip, as if afraid she'd jump from the horse's back.

She resolutely focused on the movement of the horse's muscles beneath her, the heavy night air rushing past her face, the sense of light and darkness as they moved between shadows and moonlight. She refused to let herself wonder where he was taking her.

He'd promised not to hurt her. Why had she thought for an instant that she could trust him to keep his word? He was a criminal, for goodness' sake. How naïve could she be?

He'd seemed to want to keep her out of harm's way, though. He'd hinted at the cruelty of the men he associated with and had warned her not to try and escape. Had that just been a sly ploy to get her to trust him? Maybe he'd wanted to keep her all to himself, so that after they dropped off the money he could sneak off and do whatever he wanted with her.

Her stomach clenched into a hard, tight ball. She wondered how she would survive the coming hours.

The entire right side of her face ached where Fitzgerald had hit her. The blow had been unexpected—she'd had no time to brace herself or move away. The pain was excruciating.

When he slowed the horse to a walk, she stiffened

her back and tried to hold herself away from him. He didn't seem to notice. Pulling his arm away, he slid off the horse and tied the reins to a low-slung tree branch. Then he was standing there with one hand on the saddle horn, waiting for her to dismount.

"Please," she pleaded, unable to look at him, "don't do this." She was not above begging.

"Come here," he said in a voice as smooth as velvet.

"I can't." She stared straight ahead, refusing to go willingly.

He moved closer, his chest pressing against her thigh. "Look at me."

Angling her head down, she obeyed, fearing that if she didn't he'd yank her out of the saddle. Standing in a patch of moonlight, his face was clearly visible except his eyes.

"I'm not going to hurt you. I've never in my life laid a hand on a female, and I don't aim to start with you." He spoke each word slowly and distinctly, as if addressing a small child. "Please get down. We need to talk."

Juliana hesitated. She'd always thought of herself as a good judge of character. Now she wasn't so sure. His manner was straightforward enough. But he'd handled her roughly and had insinuated vulgar things in front of the other men.

"I know I scared you back there." He grimaced, his white teeth glinting in the pale light. "Please believe me—it was all for show. I had to convince them that I meant business. I didn't want to take the chance of one of them challenging my claim on you."

"Your *claim?*"

"I'm the new guy. They don't know me, and they don't trust me. They have seniority. If any one of those men had decided he wanted you, Roberts would've sided against me. I would've had no say in the matter." He watched her for a moment, then dropped his hand and stepped back. He held his palms up in front of his chest. "If I promise not to touch you and not to come within three feet of you, will you come down?"

He certainly seemed to be telling the truth. If not, he was an accomplished actor. There was the other matter of his weapon. He didn't have to waste his breath being polite. He could've pulled his gun on her and ordered her down.

Juliana dismounted. When her feet hit the ground, her knees buckled. He moved to steady her, only to freeze midstep when he remembered his promise. She sagged against the horse's side for support. To his credit, the large animal didn't sidestep or flinch, just swished his tail at her.

Harrison passed a weary hand down his face, drawing in a deep breath. "Can I at least help you sit down?"

She shook her head. "No."

Straightening, she managed to walk, albeit unsteadily, to what looked like a good spot before sinking to her knees. She didn't take her eyes off him as he kneeled in the grass opposite her, his forearm resting across one bent knee.

She clasped her hands and remained silent, her eyes lowered to her lap. Her heartbeat was beginning to settle into a more natural rhythm. Surely if he intended to hurt her, he would've done so by now.

"This is going to sound dumb, but how is your face? I can't see it—that's why I'm asking."

Her first instinct was to examine the area with her fingers, but she was afraid to touch it. "I don't think my jaw is dislocated, though it hurts when I talk."

"And the pain? Is it bearable? Unfortunately, I don't travel with whiskey, but I can make a poultice in the morning that will draw out some of the sting."

At this point, the pain was so great that Juliana would've gladly accepted whiskey if he'd had any. Her cheek throbbed in time with her heartbeat, and each time she opened her mouth to speak, it felt as if she was being punched all over again.

He spoke before she had a chance to respond. "It's that bad, huh?" He dropped his head. "This wasn't supposed to happen." Then he looked at her. "I'm sorry. If I'd known—" He broke off midsentence, standing to his feet in one fluid motion. He began to pace.

"What happened with Fitzgerald? Why did he hit you?"

"You mean, what did I do to provoke him? You think I deserved this, don't you?"

Juliana gasped when he dropped to his knees before her. "Never." He raised his hand as if to touch her. Instead, he let it drop back to his lap. "You are not to blame for what happened."

Staring at the man before her, she struggled to reconcile his gentle concern with the harsh intensity he'd displayed earlier in the day. Her mind flashed back to the moments before the other outlaws tumbled out of the cabin, and she remembered his reassuring words, his tender touch. Who was he, really?

"Art and I were talking," she said softly. "Fitzgerald didn't like it."

His jaw hardened, his hand curling into a tight fist. "He tends to lose his temper on a whim."

"Actually, I lost my temper first."

"What?" Harrison's gaze sharpened. "Why?"

"He was bullying Art. I couldn't sit by and watch him do it when Art had done nothing wrong except befriend me."

He said nothing. Just stared at her as if she had suddenly sprouted an extra head.

"Aren't you going to say anything?" she queried at last.

"Frankly, I'm at a loss for words. I don't know whether to compliment you or give you a good scolding. Standing up for Art was a sweet gesture, Miss O'Malley." He cocked his head to one side. "On the other hand, it was an extremely foolish thing to do, given your situation."

Juliana couldn't argue with that. Still, she wasn't sure she'd do anything differently given the chance to do it all over again. Art struck her as an impressionable young man who'd been caught up with the wrong crowd.

"He's awfully young. How did he come to be with a gang of outlaws?"

"He's been with them longer than I have. Nearly a year, I believe. He was a good friend of Roberts's son, Randy."

"Was?"

"Yeah. About a month after I arrived, Randy and his father had an argument. A very loud, very contentious argument. Rumor has it Randy wanted Fitzgerald gone, but the old man wouldn't go for it. So Randy left."

"Why didn't Art go with him?"

"I can't answer that."

"Answer me this, then. Why are *you* with them?"

"Ah, that's a story for another time," he stood abruptly. "We need to get going."

Her heart lurched. "Where?"

He glanced away. "Home."

Home. How she longed to see her family, to feel their

comforting arms about her. She knew instinctively it would be a long time before she felt safe again.

"How do I know you're telling me the truth?"

His expression was unreadable. "I guess you'll just have to trust me."

Juliana realized she didn't have a choice. She didn't like it one bit that he was in total control of her fate.

No. That wasn't true. God was in control.

Evan appeared uncertain as he stood next to the horse, waiting for her to approach. He was obviously debating whether or not he should help her up. His behavior led her to believe he'd been taught to treat women with respect and that, despite his descent into criminal activity, he adhered to some ingrained habits.

Juliana made the decision to accept his help. Holding out her hand, she didn't miss the way his black brows shot up as he boosted her into the saddle. After untying the reins, he swung up behind her and spoke to Lucky in encouraging tones.

At first, Juliana sat ramrod straight in the saddle. Then her shoulders began to ache. And the horse's gait over the uneven terrain kept knocking her into Harrison. When her head bumped his chin, he curled an arm around her waist and tugged her back against him.

"Relax, Miss O'Malley."

His low, mellow voice washed over her, and very slowly the tension left her body.

Her lids grew heavier with each swaying step, until they fluttered closed and she surrendered herself to sleep.

Relaxed now against his chest, her head tucked against his shoulder, Miss O'Malley was a warm weight in his arms. The heady scent of lavender tickled his nose. Captivated, Evan lowered his face to her hair and inhaled her sweet fragrance. He sighed. How long had it been since he'd been in the company of a female? He'd certainly never courted one.

After his parents' sudden deaths weeks after his nineteenth birthday, he'd funneled all his energy into running the farm. His brother, James, just seventeen at the time, had put in the same grueling hours as he had. Side by side, they'd worked long and hard, determined to make a go of their father's homestead. Then the day came that changed everything. The news of James's murder had driven all thoughts of the future from Evan's mind. At twenty-five, he was long past the typical marrying age. Still, settling down and starting a family seemed about as likely as a fish sprouting legs.

Evan shifted in the saddle. His neck and shoulder muscles burned from overuse, and his lower back was stiff. Knowing it was past time to give his body a break, Evan decided to stop for the night. They'd spent most of the day in the saddle or walking, and tomorrow would be no different. They both needed rest.

Heading off the trail, he searched for shelter. He settled on a protected spot tucked in the midst of a stand of mature trees. The night air was comfortable enough that he wouldn't need to build a fire. The blankets in his bedroll would provide ample warmth.

Careful to balance Miss O'Malley's sleeping form, Evan slid off the stocky horse's back. It wasn't easy, but he managed to get her off Lucky and into his arms. Stepping carefully through the low grass, he lowered her to the ground. Then he returned for the bedroll.

Tucking the thickest quilt he owned around her body, he made certain every inch of her was cocooned in the material. Crouched beside her, he paused when she began to mumble words he couldn't quite make out.

With unsure fingers, he smoothed the silky strands away from her forehead. The action caused her to smile in her sleep, and she turned into his touch. Evan sucked in a breath. Her cheek, soft and cool, rested against his open palm. What now?

He didn't dare move a muscle. What if she woke and found him like this?

She'd panic, that's what!

With the steadiness of a surgeon extracting a bullet, Evan slid his hand free.

Then he bolted.

Relief flooded him when, looking back over his shoulder, he saw that she remained oblivious to her surroundings. Great. He'd avoided an awful scene. If she'd awoken to find him hovering over her, well, she surely would've assumed the worst.

Evan crossed the meadow and sank down at the base of a tree. The nervous energy surging through his body made him restless, edgy. Jerking off his hat, he slapped it against his thigh.

His mission had hit a major snag. Ten months with the gang and he had nothing. No leads and no suspects. While his brother lay in a cold, lonely grave, his murderers were living full and fancy-free. Bitterness left a bad taste in his mouth.

A wave of loneliness washed over him. How he wished he could turn the clock back to that fatal night and force James to abandon the trip! Maybe if he'd been more convincing in his arguments or outright refused to let his brother leave, James would still be alive today.

Evan had made the decision last night to go through

with the robbery and then head to Knoxville on his own. James had been killed near the Tennessee River, on the outskirts of downtown. He planned to visit each and every saloon and tavern until he found the information he sought. No matter how long it took, he would never stop searching.

He glanced at the beautiful lady asleep in his bedroll. For now, though, his plans would have to wait until she was back with her family.

He gripped the rifle lying across his lap. He'd get little sleep this night. If Fitz or any of the other outlaws intended on coming after them, he would be ready.

Juliana woke shortly after sunrise to the smell of frying salt pork and coffee. Disoriented, she stared up at the patchwork of green leaves and blue sky. Where was she? Her sisters' animated chatter had been replaced by birdcalls and her comfortable bed by dewy grass and unyielding earth.

Then it all came rushing back. The mercantile. The kidnapping. The cabin.

Her stomach rebelled, and she thought she might retch. Holding very still and taking even, shallow breaths, she waited until the sensation passed.

Her cheek throbbed. She gingerly probed the area with her fingertips and winced at the pain. She didn't need a mirror to tell her what it must look like.

Propping herself up on her elbows, her hair falling in waves about her shoulders, she surveyed her surroundings. Her gaze locked onto Harrison, so intent on his task of tending the fire, and apprehension skittered down her spine. Should she trust this enigmatic stranger to stand by his promise to see her safely home?

Watching him now, she had to admit that under ordinary circumstances she would be curious about him. He was one of those men who commanded attention based on his calm self-assurance, the unleashed power in his muscular form and his dark, forbidding good looks. He was like no other man she'd ever known.

He looked up then from the cast-iron skillet and caught her staring.

"Good morning," he said matter-of-factly, as if they were old acquaintances.

He loaded up two trenchers with the pork and hoecakes. He rose in one fluid movement and approached her with long strides. Crouching beside her, he offered her one. "Can you eat something?"

His nearness intensified the queasiness in her stomach. Still, they'd skipped supper last night. "I'll try."

Juliana sat up, self-conscious about her disheveled appearance. When he didn't move away, she lifted her head. She read the displeasure in his expression.

"What?"

"Your cheek," he stated darkly. "It looks pretty bad. Is the pain worse this morning?"

Was that remorse in his voice? Surely he hadn't developed a conscience overnight.

"Not very." She wasn't being exactly truthful, but she wasn't about to admit to him the pain she was in. What was the point?

His eyes narrowed. "I don't believe you."

"Believe what you want." She shrugged, lifting her trencher of untouched food. "Can we please eat now?"

"Be my guest." He hesitated a moment before turning to his own breakfast.

Stubble darkened his jaw, and his eyes were bloodshot.

Had he not slept? She quelled the urge to ask. What did she care whether he'd slept or not?

They ate in silence. Juliana nibbled at the slightly sweet hoecake, thankful that her stomach didn't protest. One taste of the salty meat was one too many, however, and she tossed it back on the plate. Gulping down coffee to rid herself of the aftertaste, she grimaced. She didn't like black coffee. Her mom had made sure to always have cream and sugar on the table for Juliana, the only one of her five daughters who drank coffee.

"Is something wrong?" he asked midchew.

"I'm not used to the strong stuff."

He swallowed. "You'll get used to it."

"Considering I'll be home in a few hours, I doubt it matters."

He didn't meet her eyes as he stood to his feet. "I'm going to rinse these off," he said, gathering the dirty utensils. "If you're done eating, you can come with me. You'll have a chance to wash up if you'd like."

What a difference a day makes, she thought. She supposed he felt guilty for what had happened and that was the reason he was acting kind. Rising to her feet, she tried in vain to smooth her wrinkled dress. "I don't suppose you have a brush in those saddlebags, do you?"

"There's a comb." He rifled through the leather bags and produced a simple black comb. "Will this do?" he asked, his eyes raking her mass of auburn hair.

Her cheeks warmed at his inspection. "Yes."

Falling into step beside him, she ventured a side glance. "How long have you been living like this? I mean...have you always been a thief?"

One black brow quirked up. "Yeah, it all started when

I was three. I just had to have that lemon drop at the mercantile, so I swiped it."

"Ah, a sense of humor. I'm surprised, Harrison."

"Harrison is my last name. Call me Evan."

"Oh. Okay… Evan."

Her gaze drifted down to where the top two buttons of his cotton shirt were undone. His tanned neck shone with a fine film of perspiration, his steady pulse visible in the hollows above his collarbone.

Juliana wondered at her absence of fear in his presence. His close proximity made her feel unsettled, even nervous. But she didn't believe he would harm her.

"And your name is…" he prompted. His blue eyes, so distinctive and intense, were fastened onto her face in open scrutiny. His dark hair and clothes only made his eyes seem brighter.

"I don't believe I'll tell you, Evan Harrison."

"Why not?" his brow furrowed. "*Miss O'Malley* is a bit formal, don't you think?"

"Why should I? You and I will never again clap eyes on each other after today."

Chapter Four

Bone-weary from passing the night drifting in and out of sleep, Evan was in no mood to argue. So he clamped his mouth shut and continued down the path.

Contrary woman! He could only imagine how she was going to react when he told her the bad news—that she wasn't going home today or any day soon. His mind was made up, though. She could get angry, cry or throw a fit. Didn't matter. She would not sway his decision.

Leaving the cool shade behind, he stepped out into the bright sunshine. A wide ribbon of shimmering green meandered through the clearing, the sound of rushing water filling his ears. While not deep enough to bathe in, the stream was adequate for a quick wash.

He glanced back at Miss O'Malley, his eyes drawn to her sleek red hair glinting in the sun. Then he caught sight of her discolored cheek and winced.

He reached into his back pocket and pulled out his bandanna. He rinsed the black material in the cool water, wrung out the excess and folded it in a neat square.

He went to stand before her and, lifting the compress, lightly placed it against her cheek. For a moment she didn't blink. He lost himself in her impossibly green eyes. There was a flash of apprehension which she quickly masked. That he'd caused her unease made him feel ill. He pressed the compress into her hand and stepped back abruptly. Of course she would be wary of him. He was her kidnapper, after all.

"Keep that on for a few minutes," he murmured. "It probably won't help much with the swelling, but the cold will feel good. As soon as we get washed up, I'll make you a poultice."

His concern for her, a stranger whose name he hadn't bothered to ask until a minute ago, was a foreign emotion. He'd been consumed with his own needs for so long—his desire for revenge and his well-thought-out plans to get it.

Evan felt ashamed. Selfish. Hard-hearted. Almost like an entirely different person than he'd been before his brother's murder. His cousin certainly had tried to convince him to let the authorities handle it, had warned Evan of the hazards of settling old scores.

The faith he'd grown up with and cultivated as an adult—the same faith he'd considered the foundation of his existence—had splintered beneath him in the space of a day. He'd fallen into an abyss of suspicion and inner turmoil.

"How long will it take to get back to town?" she asked, interrupting his thoughts.

Evan weighed his words carefully. "We're not going to Gatlinburg. I've decided it's too risky to take you back there. For now, anyway."

"I don't understand." Although her voice remained calm, he sensed the brewing storm.

"I'd planned to take you straight home to your family, but since the men know about you…we can't risk it. I figure the safest spot for you right now is my place—"

The hand holding the compress against her cheek went limp, and she looked at him in horror. "*Your* place? The home of a thief and kidnapper? No! I am not sleeping one night under your roof!"

Goodness, but she was stunning when riled up. A faint blush stained her cheeks, her pink mouth puckered in disapproval and graceful hands propped on her slim hips. She looked eager for a fight.

"You'll be safe there. That's what matters."

"Safe?" Her expression turned disbelieving. "With the man who held a gun on me, forced me from my family and is currently planning to whisk me away to parts unknown?"

"Why don't you calm down so we can discuss this rationally?"

"When it comes to my freedom, I don't feel particularly rational!"

"I brought you here. It's my duty to get you home safe and sound—"

"Oh, I see…" she scoffed. "You've got it all planned out. The triumphant return! You deliver me to my front doorstep and my family will fall to their knees in gratitude—a true hero."

"I'm no one's hero," he shot back. "Remember that."

Bitter regret rose in his throat like bile. He'd failed to protect his only brother—tried and failed.

He lowered his voice. "The men go into town once or twice a week for supplies. With your flame-colored hair, you might as well wear a sign around your neck. If I take you back now, I'd be risking your life and mine."

"I'm not the only redhead in town, you know."

"Gatlinburg isn't exactly a big town." He paused, trying to think of a way to make her see reason. "What about your sisters?"

She stilled. "What about them?"

"Suppose one of the men—let's say Fitzgerald—spotted you in town and followed you home. You wouldn't be the only one in danger."

She looked away, evenly spaced white teeth worrying her lower lip. He could see that she was torn. At last, she crossed her arms. She didn't appear pleased with the change in plans.

"Do you realize the anguish my mother must be feeling right now? And my sisters? I'm the oldest. They depend on me."

"You haven't mentioned your father."

Her eyes darkened. "He died four years ago of a heart attack."

"I'm sorry." Evan understood the pain of losing a parent. "We can send a telegram from Cades Cove, let them know you're safe and will be home soon."

She closed her eyes, distress twisting her lovely features. "This is a nightmare."

"A nightmare that will soon be over."

Resigned, she sighed. "What do you have in mind?"

"We'll pass by Gatlinburg and make our way to Cades Cove. My farm is there. We can make the trip in about three days if the weather holds. You'll have the place to yourself while I ride back to the hideout and convince the men I got rid of you. They'll be heading out in a week or so. Then I'll come back for you and escort you home."

"Why would you do that? Why go to so much trouble on my behalf when you're partly responsible for my kidnapping?"

He deserved that. "That's right. I'm responsible." He jammed a thumb in his chest. "As I said before, I got you into this mess and I intend to get you out of it."

"Something's not right." She studied him, a speculative gleam in her eye. "Little details about you that don't quite add up."

Intrigued, he crossed his arms and waited. "Such as?"

"Well, for starters, you talk funny."

He hadn't expected that. "Excuse me?"

"No, no, that's not the right word." She began to pace, and he could practically see the wheels in her brain whirling. She snapped her fingers. "Educated! That's it! You don't use foul language. And you don't speak as if you were raised in a saloon, as one would expect from a common criminal."

"And you're acquainted with common criminals, I take it?"

"Thanks to you, I am now."

"Yes, that's unfortunate. I apologize."

"There." She pointed a finger at him. "That's the other thing. You shouldn't be apologizing to me."

"I shouldn't?" This woman was beginning to confuse him.

"You treat me as if I have value. Those other men…" She shuddered. "What I mean to say is that, for the most part, you've treated me with respect. A truly hardened criminal would've done as those men suggested and gotten rid of me."

"Wait just a minute—"

"Shh! Don't try to distract me. There's one more thing, and it's a doozy."

A no-nonsense expression stole across her face and, straightening to her full height, she focused her entire attention on him. He felt like a witness under cross-examination.

"Well? What is it?"

"Money."

"What about it?"

"Where is the money you risked your life *and* mine for? You walked out of that cabin without a moment's hesitation. Have you even given it a second thought?"

"I've been kinda busy plotting our next move."

"Exactly."

Uncomfortable with her astute observations, he sought to distract her. "Is that all, Irish?"

"Yes, that's all." Her eyes narrowed. "What did you call me?"

"Fits, doesn't it? Or would you prefer *Red?*"

"Absolutely not!"

"I suppose I could try to guess your name," Evan made a show of studying her, and he gained much satisfaction at seeing her squirm. "How about Matilda?"

Her finely arched eyebrows shot up. "You think I look like a Matilda?"

"Hmm…no, that's not quite right, is it?" He stroked his chin thoughtfully. "I know. Bertha."

"Bertha?"

"That's not it, either, huh? Okay, a Bible name. Rachel. I like that one."

"Me, too, but it's not mine."

"Can you give me a hint? Tell me what letter it starts with?"

She bit her lip, and he could tell that she was beginning to find some humor in the conversation. A thrill shot through him. Trying to make her smile could become addictive.

"That would make it too easy. Besides, you don't deserve the help."

"In the meantime, then, I'll stick with *Irish*."

"What? That's not a proper name!"

"It's yours until you decide to quit being stubborn." He shrugged, tossing her a washcloth. "See those trees over there? I'll be right on the other side washing up while you do the same here. You'll have plenty of privacy, but if you need anything just call out."

Juliana watched him stride away, her eyes fixed on his broad back. She noted the way the smooth material stretched across his powerful shoulders and biceps. A wall of solid muscle, he moved with purpose and confidence. On the outside, he was every girl's dream.

A pity he spent his days terrorizing innocents and taking what didn't belong to him.

His horse moved into her line of vision, his majestic black head low to the ground as he nibbled a clump of red clover. He was a fine specimen. Glossy coat, firm flesh, strong legs. Probably a fast runner...

Juliana clapped a hand over her mouth. Lifting his head, Lucky stared at her blankly for a second or two before resuming his snacking. No...she couldn't. *Or could she?*

She spoke in low, soothing tones as she approached the animal and tried to convey an air of calm she didn't feel. What would Evan Harrison do if he came back and caught her trying to steal his horse?

"You're a fine-lookin' boy, aren't you?" she crooned softly, taking hold of his studded bridle and rubbing her palm down his side. He was already used to her scent, and he seemed to welcome the attention. "Would you care to give me a ride somewhere, Lucky?"

She'd have to ride bareback, since she wasn't strong enough to lift the saddle with all the gear attached to it. While she preferred a saddle, riding without one was doable. If Lucky would let her, that is.

"I have to try, right, boy?" She continued to rub his soft coat, her heart thumping in her chest. "I need my freedom." She laid her forehead against his neck. "Will you help me?"

Juliana searched the woods where Evan had disappeared. Nothing. Now was her chance. She prayed Lucky wouldn't throw her.

Still speaking soft words of encouragement, she led him to a fallen log, where she stepped up, grabbed hold and vaulted up and onto his back. Half lying on her stomach, she scooted closer to his neck, her inner thighs pressing into his sides for balance. She signaled for him to move out.

The big black obeyed without a moment's hesitation. She glanced over her shoulder and again saw no sign of Evan. She was sweating—not from exertion but from sheer nerves. Her stomach, already upset, was now a hard knot. Her hands shook.

As she got farther from the campsite, however, Juliana felt like shouting for joy. Freedom was in her sights. God had surely presented her with this chance at escape.

The going would be tough, no doubt. She had no supplies of any kind. Her cousins, she thanked God, had taught her many skills that would help her find food and shelter. The only problem, in her mind, was figuring out which direction to go. But even if she couldn't get all the way back to Gatlinburg, she figured she'd come across a town eventually where she could get help.

She took note of the sun's position and rode in the opposite direction. They'd been traveling east, so it made sense that home was to the west.

"Mr. Evan Harrison is in for one big surprise." She grinned, ignoring the nudge of conscience. He's strong and healthy, she reasoned. Wouldn't hurt him a bit to hike to civilization.

What she would do with the horse once she got home, she hadn't a clue. She couldn't keep him—he didn't belong to her. She couldn't very well return him, either. Evan knew she lived in or near Gatlinburg, and it wouldn't be difficult for him to find her. Although her time with him had been brief, she had a gut feeling that he would come looking for what was rightfully his. The thought of meeting him face-to-face at this point unnerved Juliana.

Pushing that disturbing thought away, she focused on her surroundings. She couldn't afford to daydream. Not only did she need to keep Lucky headed in the right direction, she also had to keep a lookout for snakes or wild boars that might spook him.

She was vulnerable out here alone, she knew. If only she had a weapon.

I will never leave you, nor forsake you. The words from the book of Joshua reassured her. *I know, Father, and I thank You for reminding me.*

After a mile or so of the beautiful yet monotonous terrain—wide-spaced hickory, spruce and sugar maple trees—her thoughts strayed again to Evan Harrison and his concerns about Lenny Fitzgerald and the others. He didn't have her completely convinced of the danger. If they only planned to be in the vicinity for a week or two, all she had to do was stay home and not venture into town.

And of course she planned to give Sheriff Timmons a detailed description of Lenny Fitzgerald. Wanted posters would go up all over town. That should send the criminal running in the opposite direction!

But what about Mr. Harrison? Would she give a description of him, too? William Timmons would want the man who'd kidnapped Juliana. In the sheriff's eyes, she realized, tracking down Evan Harrison would take precedence over capturing any of the others.

Juliana wanted justice. Evan deserved to be punished for what he'd done, of course, but somehow she couldn't place him on the same level as those other men. There was something different about him…she just couldn't put her finger on what that something was.

She had a knack for puzzles, though. It might take a while, but she was confident she'd figure it out sooner or later.

Evan dried his face and neck and wondered if Miss O'Malley was finished. He'd decided on a whim to give her some privacy. She'd already endured enough on account of him, and to be honest, she was handling the situation with unusual grace. It wouldn't kill him to show her a little kindness.

Deciding he'd been gone long enough, he ambled back toward camp. The weather was fine for travel, he noted with relief. Not a cloud to be seen in the pale blue sky. The temperature was climbing—it would be a scorcher— so they would stick to the forest as long as possible. He hoped they made good time. The sooner this whole mess was behind him the better.

When he emerged from the trees into the clearing, it didn't at first register that anything was amiss. A few seconds was all it took for him to realize his grave error.

He stood there slack-jawed for the space of a full minute.

She was gone. Gone! And so was his horse!

"Why that—" He clamped his mouth shut. He'd learned his childhood lessons well, and his mother had taught him not to disrespect women. Still…the woman had stolen his horse!

What did she expect him to do? *Walk* to Cades Cove?

He let out a low growl. Who did she think she was? Didn't she know the punishment for stealing a horse was a hangman's noose?

He set about packing his gear, only what he couldn't live without. His eyes fell on the saddle. She was riding his horse bareback? How had she managed to mount him?

She couldn't have gotten far, he reasoned. Irritation warred with concern. This was mostly uninhabited country—no place for a woman alone. How did she plan to feed herself? He checked the canteens. They were all there, which meant that she was traveling without water. In the height of summer. In the heat of the day. Great. He kicked a tin cup and it arced through the air. Just great.

He'd promised to return her home safe. It was his attempt at righting a wrong. If he failed at this, it would be like losing James all over again. Maybe worse.

Chapter Five

Juliana was thirsty. And hot. Her throat was so dry it hurt to swallow. In her haste, she hadn't thought about the need for water or protection from the sun's rays. Her bonnet was probably where she'd left it—tossed on top of her blanket. Her fair skin felt tight and was sensitive to the touch, especially her cheeks and forehead.

Gauging the sun's position, she guessed it to be near eleven o'clock. She'd left the forest behind about two hours into the journey and had been traveling through open fields ever since. In the distance, she saw another forest and hoped it wouldn't take long to get there.

Her stomach was empty and urgently protesting that fact. If she didn't find a place to fish, she would stop and search for berries and nuts. An apple tree would go a long way toward filling her stomach. Lucky's, too.

In all likelihood, Evan would laugh at her situation. After what she'd done, there'd be no room in his heart for compassion. It was an unwritten rule of their society—a man simply didn't mess with another man's horse. She supposed that rule applied to women, too.

While Juliana was thankful that she'd been able to

escape her kidnapper, she couldn't deny that men came in handy sometimes. Especially out on the open trail.

At long last, when Juliana was near to the point of falling off the horse, she reached the trees. She heard the sound of rushing water and sagged with relief. Past the point of all care, she ran to the water, flopped down on her stomach and submerged her face. Her unbound auburn hair floated on the surface like an intricate spiderweb.

Rolling over on her back, she lay there half-in, half-out of the water, arms spread wide. Lucky was there nearby, noisily drinking his fill.

"What a sight we must be." She chuckled, reveling in the cold wetness and blessed relief from the relentless sun. *Thank You, Lord. I was about to suffer a sunstroke, I do believe.*

Reluctantly she sat up to survey her surroundings. Water sluiced down her back, but she didn't mind. It felt divine. Nothing about her surroundings triggered a memory. Of course she'd slept in the saddle last night, so it stood to reason that she wouldn't recognize the landmarks.

Butterflies filled her stomach at the memory of being held in Evan's strong embrace. She'd fought to keep her eyes open, but between Lucky's loping gait and Evan's warmth enveloping her it had been an impossible battle. The fact that he'd carried and settled her in for the night made her face flame with embarrassment. Disgusted at herself for letting the outlaw affect her, she addressed his horse.

"Are you hungry, Lucky?"

The black had already searched out a patch of green grass and was chomping away.

Juliana scanned the brook, disappointed to find only minnows in the shallow depths. There weren't any frogs, either. Not even a turtle. A flash of white caught her eye, and she glanced up to see a cottontail hopping past. "You sure are a cute little guy. I hate to say this within your earshot, but if I had a gun I'd be having you for lunch."

Squeezing the excess moisture out of her hair, she used Evan's comb to smooth the long locks.

Lucky didn't protest when she led him deeper into the woods. He was such a sweet horse. A prize, really. Evan must be heartsick at having lost him.

Well, if he hadn't kidnapped her in the first place, she reasoned, he would still have the horse in his possession.

They came upon a blueberry patch, but someone or something had beaten them to it. Few berries remained, which only seemed to amplify her hunger. It also brought to mind her mother's birthday cake, piled high with blueberries and strawberries. She'd never gotten a taste of that magnificent dessert.

When I get home, she promised herself, *I'm gonna ask the twins to make another one just for me.*

Daydreaming about her homecoming, Juliana thought her mind was playing tricks on her when she caught the scent of meat roasting over an open flame. Her mouth watered. Someone was nearby—with food.

As much as she longed to go crashing through the underbrush and demand to be fed, she decided not to announce her presence before getting a look at whomever was out there. A woman alone had to be cautious or risk serious harm.

With Lucky following close behind, she ventured closer to where she believed the scent was coming from. Unexpectedly, a raucous male voice broke the silence.

She halted midstep and goose bumps skimmed along her skin. He was singing a ditty unfit for a lady's ears.

Juliana continued her approach, however, determined to see for herself what he looked like. Dense weeds and bushes provided cover so that she could get close without him spotting her. Looping the reins around a tree limb and issuing a command for Lucky to stay, she crawled into the bushes.

The pop and sizzle of meat made her mouth water. A fat brown spider landed on her hand and, gasping aloud, she flung it away. She *detested* spiders. Once, when she was a little girl, she had been playing in the hayloft when she disturbed a whole nest of them. Tiny spiders—hundreds of them—scurried in all directions and, of course, some of them crawled over her shoes. Screaming at the top of her lungs, she ran to climb down the ladder and, in her haste, fell to the hard dirt floor below. She suffered a broken arm and spent half the summer confined to the house.

Juliana searched the branches above her head and the grass below for more of the wretched things. Satisfied that she was safe, she crept deeper into the bushes. A dark form was visible through the leaves, and as she neared she saw that his back was to her. Unfortunately, he was still singing in a loud, off-key voice, sitting cross-legged before the fire and guzzling whiskey from a half-empty bottle. His clothes were wrinkled and stained and the edges ragged.

He looked harmless enough. Probably a down-on-his-luck drifter. And the demands of her empty stomach were starting to override her hesitation. What could she offer him in exchange for a share of the meal? All she had was the comb in her pocket, and from the looks of him, he wouldn't be interested. Did she dare hope he would help her out of the goodness of his heart?

All he could do is say no, she supposed.

Her mind made up, she retraced her steps and approached the campsite.

Rounding the bushes, she collided with a tall, thin body. She jumped back with a startled gasp.

"Miss O'Malley!"

Juliana glanced up into Art's shocked face. "Art! What are you doing here?"

"The boss sent us. Didn't trust Harrison—" His gaze skittered away for a brief second before returning to her face. "I'm mighty glad you're okay, miss. 'Course, I never believed any of that stuff Harrison said. Where is he anyhow?" He glanced over her shoulder at Evan's horse.

"He, um..." She stalled, racking her brain for a plausible story.

"Oh, miss." Art groaned, brown eyes going wide, "You didn't give him the slip, did ya?"

"Well, I—"

He slapped his head. "This ain't good at all! He'll be hoppin' mad! And there's no telling what Fitzgerald will do."

Juliana took an automatic step back. "Fitzgerald? He's here? With you?"

"Yep, that's him singin' like a drunk bullfrog."

Oh, no. What now? Harrison was right!

Her pulse skyrocketing, she pivoted on her heel and strode toward Lucky. "I have to find Evan!"

She had one foot in the stirrup when she heard the click of a gun hammer.

"Stop right there."

Juliana froze. Dread settled like a leaden weight on her shoulders.

"Step away from the horse," Fitzgerald ordered with a wave of his pistol.

She was in big trouble, and Evan was miles away. Too far to rescue her this time. Not that he would after what she'd done to him. Silently, she did as she was told.

"Where's Harrison?" he demanded, all joviality of a few moments ago gone.

"He's not here." She looked him straight in the eye, refusing to give him the satisfaction of seeing her fear.

"I can see that," he snapped. "Where is he?"

"A few miles back at camp."

Juliana jerked when he barked a harsh laugh.

"Harrison underestimated you, I see. I'm beginning to understand his preference for spirited women. Maybe I'll keep you around for a while." His full lips curled into an insolent sneer. "See for myself what all the fuss is about."

Art spoke up. "What are you planning, Fitz?"

Juliana squelched the urge to squirm beneath the outlaw's lewd stare. She clasped her hands together to stop them from shaking.

"Give me time." He looked over at the young man. "I'll come up with something. For now, nature calls. Make sure she doesn't escape. Or else."

Art gulped. He watched Fitzgerald disappear into the woods. Then he approached with eager strides.

"You have to go *now!*" He urged her in Lucky's direction.

Staring up at his boyish face, years away from manhood, Juliana felt like weeping. Here was her chance at escape, and she couldn't take it.

She placed a restraining hand on his arm. "I can't," she whispered. "Who knows what he'll do to you?"

Art shook his head, his fine blond hair sliding into his eyes. "Don't you worry about me. Go back to Harrison. He'll help you—I just know it."

Evan's handsome face swam before her eyes, and she wished with all her being that she'd trusted him.

"I'm not so sure about that," she choked out. "In any case, I can't leave on your watch."

Straightening to his full height, Art gave her a stubborn glare. "And I say you *can*. And you will."

Unaccustomed to seeing the awkward teen so sure of himself, Juliana's jaw dropped. He was maturing before her very eyes. Too bad it was a wasted effort. She could not in good conscience leave him to the mercy of Fitzgerald's wrath.

"I appreciate what you're trying to do, Art. But I just can't do it."

"Do you know what Harrison will do when he finds out Fitz has you?" he demanded. "I'd almost rather face Fitz. Please. Go."

A loud whistle threaded through the trees, and they jumped apart as Fitz strolled back into the clearing. He looked from one to the other.

"I'm starved. Let's eat."

Evan hated to admit he'd been outsmarted by a female. He'd gone over the morning's events a couple of times, drawing the conclusion that he'd gone soft. Give her some privacy, he'd told himself. Be a gentleman!

The kicker was he'd left his horse in the care of a stranger. When was that ever a smart thing to do? He had let his guard down, and now he was minus one first-rate horse. It was a costly mistake in more ways than one.

Where was she?

He'd seen horse droppings and broken shrubs, even spotted some fresh tracks in the soft earth. He was confident he was on their trail, so why hadn't he found them yet?

He'd been walking for hours. What he needed was a cup of coffee to perk him up. With the little sleep he had to go on, he was dragging. His feet hurt. There was a permanent dent in his shoulder from the saddlebag strap. He had every right to be irate. Somehow…he wasn't. Not at her. If anything, he blamed himself for getting her into this situation in the first place.

If only she had waited a little longer to do her shopping yesterday.

If only he hadn't been too ill to take his brother to Knoxville ten months ago.

There were too many twists and turns in life that could lead a man down the wrong path.

Especially when the man was doing the leading and not God.

Evan stopped walking, one hand on his hip and the other hanging on to the strap. Where had that thought come from? He'd been running from the Lord for a while now—since James's death. Evan's faith had shattered the moment he heard the news. Guilt was his constant companion these days, not the Lord.

Tilting his head back, he watched tiny robins hop from branch to branch, singing merrily to each other. Squirrels darted up the broad, grooved tree trunks, searching for acorns. Buttercups and dandelions dotted the forest floor.

God's touch was evident in every insect, every petal, every leaf.

Oh, Father, I miss You so much sometimes it hurts.

Evan shook his head, wondering how much longer he could take living like this.

He scanned the forest, noting that the trees were beginning to thin and that it appeared brighter in the distance. He was headed for a clearing. Lifting his hat, he wiped his forehead with his sleeve, too lazy at this point to dig in his pocket for a hanky.

Where was she?

He took a long swallow from his canteen, screwed the lid back on, and started walking again.

Ignoring Art's sidelong glances, Juliana stared into the fire. What now?

"Sit down." Fitz motioned with his half-empty whiskey bottle.

Her appetite had fled at the sight of him. Now bile rose up in her throat at the thought of having to share a meal with the outlaw.

When she hesitated, he leaned over and seized her upper arm, forcing her to sit down hard. Ducking her head, Juliana swallowed an anguished groan. Surely any sign of weakness would only stir his anger.

Art was silent. Still, she sensed his frustration as he plopped down beside her.

Fitz sat opposite her. With his bare fingers, he snatched the meat from the still-sizzling skillet, tore off a big hunk and dropped it on a flat green leaf. "Enjoy it." He leered viciously. "Might be your last."

Juliana ignored him. She pulled off tiny bits and somehow managed to swallow without choking. Nauseous from the rush of adrenaline, her stomach protested but she managed to keep it down.

Lord Jesus, please help me think of a way out of this mess. Give me wisdom and courage. I need You desperately.

"Did you leave Harrison alive or dead?" Fitz grunted, wiping his sleeve across his greasy mouth.

She lifted her eyes to meet his and was shocked by the coldness and hatred there. This was a person with absolutely no morals, a person who wouldn't think twice about hurting or even killing another human being.

How foolish she'd been to leave Evan Harrison's protection! He was an outlaw, yes, but he hadn't harmed her. He had even promised to escort her home!

With Lenny Fitzgerald calling the shots, her life could be over in the blink of an eye.

"Last I saw him, he was alive and well," she said.

"How did you manage to steal his horse?"

"He let his guard down."

"We won't do that, will we, Art?" Fitzgerald shot Art a warning glare.

Juliana swallowed hard. This conversation was going nowhere fast. Her gaze darted around, looking for a weapon of some kind. If she could delay him just long enough for her to get a head start, she was sure Lucky could outrun his mount. Besides, the man was half-drunk. He'd be slower than normal.

Her gaze landed on the cast-iron skillet resting above the flames. Melted fatback popped and hissed. An idea seized her, and she acted on it before she could change her mind.

Leaning forward, she reached out a hand. "Mind if I help myself to some more meat?"

He eyed her a moment, then shrugged his beefy shoulders.

Inhaling deeply, she grabbed the handle and slung the skillet upwards, the burning hot liquid spilling out to splatter across his face and neck. He yelped in pain, his hands clawing at his face.

Panicked, Juliana let the skillet fall to the ground. She jumped to her feet and sprinted to Lucky's side, vaulting onto his back with more speed than she knew she possessed.

"You'll pay for this!" he bellowed in a fit of rage. "You won't get away—"

Hearing him hollering for Art to follow her, she glanced back and saw him pretend to stumble and twist his ankle.

She silently praised Art's quick thinking.

Juliana urged Lucky into an all-out gallop. Her heart throbbed in time to the horse's hoofbeats against the hard earth as they dodged trees and fallen logs. Within moments, they left the forest behind for the wide, open plain. Juliana held on tight as the black lengthened his stride—heading back the way they'd come, back to where she'd started from, back to Evan Harrison.

Chapter Six

Finally emerging from the trees, Evan paused to take in his surroundings. Before him lay miles and miles of grassland. The forest behind him covered the hills to the right and curved around in front of him far in the distance. It would've made sense for her to have stayed with the tree line, but he could clearly see the trampled grass leading into the empty field.

He thought of the bonnet she'd forgotten back at camp, now tucked safely in his pack. He could only imagine her discomfort traveling in the direct sunlight without the benefit of shade. If she hadn't found water… No, he wouldn't allow his thoughts to go there. She was smart. Resourceful.

About a quarter of a mile later, he caught sight of what looked to be a horse and rider. To be safe, he unsheathed his gun. Too slow for his liking, the figure neared, and he saw that the animal was dark in color, although whether brown or black he couldn't tell. The rider was slumped over, using the horse's neck for support.

Evan stiffened, his muscles primed to spring into action. Something was wrong. In the instant he realized that it was *his* horse carrying Miss O'Malley, he slid his gun back into the holster and started running.

When he came alongside Lucky, she fell into his arms, her unexpected weight and forward motion knocking him to the ground. Evan pushed up into a sitting position, his arms locked around her slender form.

"Irish! What happened?"

"Oh, Evan." She sobbed into his chest, her fingers clutching his shirt. "I'm so s-sorry—"

His anger evaporated at the sight of her tears. "Are you injured? Ill?"

"N-no."

Relief filtered through his soul like soothing rain. She was safe.

"Shh," he murmured, resting his chin against her head. "Everything's all right now."

Comforting her, holding her, felt so right. His eyes drifting closed, he inhaled her sweet lavender scent and smoothed her hair with gentle strokes. The strands felt like pure bliss to his fingertips…thick and heavy and silken. His hands drifted lower to rub circles along her back. He felt her sigh as she settled her weight more firmly against him, the wetness from her cheeks seeping into his shirt. He didn't mind.

He tightened his hold, aware of the need she was stirring within him. The need to connect, to *matter*. To share life's joys and burdens. To love and be loved.

Irish lifted her face to gaze at him, her tear-filled eyes looking like forest ferns sparkling with dewdrops. His eyes dropped to her pink lips, the lower one full and inviting. It would be so easy to angle his head down and—

"Evan, I stole your horse. And Fitzgerald found out—" She broke off, a shudder racking her body.

"What?" His heart skidded to a halt, and his gaze jerked upwards to meet hers. Evan gripped her shoulders and held her away from him. "You saw Fitzgerald? Where? What happened? Did he hurt you?"

"No, but he threatened me. And after what I did to him—" She clutched his biceps, "Evan, we have to go! We have to get out of here before he catches up to us."

"What did you do, Irish?" He tensed.

"I threw hot grease in his face."

"You *what?*"

"It was my only option at the time." Her chin came up in defense, a spark of her usual spirit flaring in her eyes. "I had to distract him…somehow get a head start. It worked, didn't it?"

Evan dropped his hands and sat back, his mind numb with the implications. There was no question now as to whether or not Fitzgerald would follow them and watch for a chance to strike. After what she did to him, he would be out for blood.

"Art was with him."

"Art?" Evan repeated. "Did he say why?"

Her eyes dulled. "Your boss sent him and Fitzgerald to make sure you held up your end of the bargain."

He couldn't say he was surprised. After the way he'd reacted to Fitz's treatment of her, Roberts was bound to have his doubts.

"I didn't mean a word of it, remember?" he said softly, reaching out to stroke her cheek. She looked so lost just then. And vulnerable. It made him all the more determined to get her home safe.

"You realize, don't you, that you absolutely can *not* go back to Gatlinburg until he leaves the area."

A worried crease appeared between her brows. Her

hair was tousled, her skin sunburned, her dark dress streaked with dirt and grass stains. In his opinion, she couldn't have looked more beautiful.

"I should've stayed with you." She swallowed hard. "I didn't believe you when you said he might be following us. I'm sorry I abandoned you."

After her run-in with Fitzgerald, Evan was confident she wouldn't try another stunt like that again. No reason to make her feel worse than she already did.

"Would you have kept Lucky?" he said.

"I figured you'd come looking for him. I planned to take good care of him until you found us."

"Good answer." He stood and helped her up, resisting the urge to pull her close. He couldn't believe he'd almost kissed her a moment ago. Bad idea. The worst. No matter how beautiful or alluring she was, he could not allow himself to be distracted from his mission. Nor could he afford to forget the immeasurable pain that love ultimately cost a man. He was better off alone.

"Come on. Let's go back to camp and get the rest of my stuff."

She placed a hand on his forearm, her expression somber. "Can you forgive me?"

Her humble request shamed him. Brushing her aside, he picked his hat off the ground and thumped it against his thigh to dislodge the dirt. "You kidnapped my horse—an animal that's happy as long as he has food and a kind word now and then. I had a part in kidnapping you—a woman with feelings and needs and family you care about." He put on his hat and pulled the brim down low. "Think on that and then tell me who needs to ask for forgiveness." He turned his back. "It's time to go."

Irish appeared to sense his need to be alone with his

thoughts because she didn't say anything else. He helped her mount before hauling himself up behind her.

He pulled her bonnet out of his bag and handed it to her, waiting until she put it on to signal Lucky. He would've liked to urge him into a full gallop, but he knew his horse's limits. They traveled instead at a moderate pace, stopping now and then for a drink of water and a short rest.

Evan could tell that she was nervous. She searched the woods continually, as if expecting Fitzgerald to jump out from behind the nearest tree.

He gave her arm a squeeze. "Relax, Irish. You have my word that I'll do everything in my power to keep you safe."

She responded by resting against him. "I'm glad I have you to protect me."

Again her words hit him like a punch in the gut. Guilt gnawed at his insides. He certainly didn't feel like a hero in all this.

Evan tried to recall what life had been like before James's murder. Plowing the fields, feeding the animals, repairing tools and broken-down equipment. Hard work that brought satisfaction at the end of the day. Going to church on Sundays. Attending town picnics.

Those days of normalcy were long gone. He was living a nightmare…forced to do things he'd never dreamed he'd do. If someone had told him a year ago that he'd be robbing banks and keeping company with a nest of vipers, he would've laughed his head off. If someone had told him that he would kidnap an innocent young lady, Evan would've punched him square in the face and spit on him to boot.

Goodness, but how life could take twisted turns.

* * *

By the time they arrived back at camp, the brilliant yellow-orange sun hung low in the sky. The intense rays blended into the horizon, painting the pale expanse in swirls of pastel pink and orange.

Evan was eager to dismount and put some much-needed space between himself and his lovely riding companion. She filled his senses with her scent and softness. He was aware of her every sigh. He imagined that he could even detect her heartbeat pulsating in the creamy skin near the base of her throat.

Get a grip, Harrison. Yanking on the reins, he slipped to the ground before Lucky could come to a complete stop. He helped her down, breaking contact as soon as her boots touched the ground. "Why don't you rest a spell? I'll rustle up something for us to eat."

"I'd actually prefer to help if you have something for me to do."

He hesitated. "You can gather wood for the fire, if you'd like, but I don't want you to overdo it."

"I'm fine."

"Okay." He stepped away, only to halt midstep to glance back at her. "Oh, and Irish?"

She met his gaze with an unreadable expression, cinnamon eyebrows raised in question.

"Don't disappear on me this time."

A ghost of a smile crossed her lips. "I'll be here, I promise."

"Good."

As Evan tended to Lucky, he reminded himself that he was better off alone. Loving someone left a man vulnerable and open to heartache. God had seen fit to take away everyone who'd ever mattered in his life—first his parents, then his only brother. No way was he going to let anyone else get close. He simply could not face another loss.

Feeling irritable, he went in search of his saddle and other belongings. They were exactly as he'd left them, which should've pleased him. Walking back and seeing Irish's flushed countenance as she worked sparked his ire. He strode to her side and took the bundle of wood from her arms.

"I thought I told you not to overdo it," he growled. "Go sit down."

"And I told you, I'm fine. I think I'm smart enough to know my own limitations." Her glare dared him to challenge her assertion.

His gaze took in the damp tendrils clinging to her temple and nape and the fine sheen of moisture on her forehead. "You're short of breath, and your face is redder than a strawberry patch. With all the layers you're wearing, it's a wonder you haven't passed out standing still in this heat."

Her mouth fell open. "Gentlemen do not discuss ladies' undergarments."

Oddly amused by her discomfiture, he smirked. "I never claimed to be one." He placed a hand on her shoulder and gently turned her in the direction of the nearest shade tree on the bank. "Humor me. Go sit down."

Shifting the wood, he watched as she did his bidding. Once settled, her skirts arranged about her just so, she speared him with her dark gaze. "Happy now?"

"Yes, thank you. Rest while I fetch you some cold water."

She was silent, offering only a simple thank-you when

he handed her the cup. Evan gathered his fishing gear and settled on the bank beside her.

His gaze on the shimmering water, he asked, "So who taught you to ride bareback?"

"My cousin, Joshua."

He glanced over at her. She appeared at ease, her legs tucked to one side and her graceful hands clasped in her lap. Her green eyes seemed to miss nothing.

"And he thought that was necessary because…" Evan prompted.

"Oh, I don't think he had any particular reason. We did it for fun and, like everything else, it turned into a competition. He's two years older than me and more like a big brother than a cousin. He lives next door with his folks and two younger brothers, Nathan and Caleb. We see each other almost every day."

"Did he teach you how to shoot a bow and arrow, too?"

"Now you're teasing me." Her lips curved in a most intriguing smile.

An answering smile on his face, he held up his hands. "No, honest. I'd like to know what else your talented cousin taught you."

"Let's just say that because of his patient instruction, I'm more skilled in manly pursuits than the average woman. And severely lacking in those skills necessary to make a comfortable home."

Evan felt a tug on his line. He eased it up out of the water, pleased to see a medium-weight trout dangling on the end. He made quick work of unhooking the fish and getting his line back in the water. "So let me guess, while your sisters were learning to make biscuits and crochet, you were gallivanting about the countryside with your cousins."

Her soft trill of laughter warmed his insides. "That about it sums it up, yes. I do my share of chores, of course. I like to work in the garden and oversee the care of the animals."

"You don't look like a tomboy," he offered over the rim of his cup.

He was rewarded with a soft pink blush along her cheekbones. She shot him a wry glance. "I'm not as particular about my appearance as some of my sisters, but I do like nice clothes. Of course, this dress is sadly ruined."

"I'll replace it."

Irish shook her head. "I could never accept such a personal gift from a stranger."

He lowered his gaze to the creek. Odd, he didn't consider them strangers. Not friends, certainly. What then? Two people whose lives intersect for a fleeting moment, like two leaves floating on the breeze, colliding, twirling together in a delicate spiral, only to drift apart and land in separate spots?

He sighed. This line of thinking could only lead to trouble.

"You must be tired after all that walking," she said, obviously interpreting his sigh as a sign of physical exhaustion instead of the emotional upheaval it reflected. "Am I allowed to help at all? I can get the fire going and make coffee, at least."

"Can you fish?"

"Yes, of course."

He handed her his pole and a small collection of worms. "These don't bother you?"

"Nah."

"Okay, then. You catch our dinner, and I'll cook it. Deal?"

"I think that's a wise solution." She laughed again, a

delightful, enchanting music that washed over him and made him long for impossible dreams. He bolted to his feet to keep from doing something rash, like kissing her sweet mouth.

"I'll leave you to it then."

As Evan lit the fire and set the coffee to boiling, he forced all thoughts of Irish from his mind. He had to get a grip. Focus. Fitzgerald was out there somewhere. Evan couldn't afford to let down his guard, not even for a second.

When she presented him with four fish half an hour later, he praised her efforts but didn't attempt conversation. He cleaned, gutted and cooked them in silence while Irish stowed his fishing rod and spread out a blanket for them to sit on.

Evan noticed that she bowed her head to pray silently before eating and found himself doing the same. As they ate, darkness slowly swallowed the last fingers of light. A soft breeze rustled the leaves and water trickled over mossy stones.

"I can't recall the last time I ate a meal outside." Her honeyed voice was subdued. "There's a spot on our land similar to this." She gestured to the surrounding meadow. "It's so peaceful. Reminds me of the Psalm, 'He makes me lie down in green pastures, He leads me beside still waters.'"

"He restores my soul," he finished almost without thought.

Her head came up. "Evan, is God a part of your life?"

Evan hesitated. "He used to be, but now…let's just say I've long since lost sight of Him."

"I'm sorry to hear that." She was quiet, absently plucking blades of grass. "You know, He hasn't lost sight of *you*. His Word says that *nothing* can separate us from the love He has for us."

His mood turned somber. "I remember. It's just that there's some things I need to do before I can fix my relationship with Him."

"I think you've got that backward, Evan. Think about it." She stood and gathered the dishes. "I'm going to wash these and repack them."

He watched her walk to the water's edge, relieved that she'd dropped the subject. He wasn't eager to talk to her or anyone else about his failures.

By the time she returned, he had the bedroll laid out near the fire. "You'll sleep here." He pointed to a cluster of trees across the way. "I'll be over there standing watch. If you need anything just call out."

"You don't plan on sleeping at all?"

He held his cup of steaming coffee aloft, his third since supper. "Not if I can help it."

"But," she hesitated, "you need rest just as much as I do."

"I'm used to living on little sleep."

"I've slept outside a number of times, but always close to home." Her voice was hushed in the darkness. "Do you think we're safe here?"

Evan wondered if her mind was on the wildlife or their pursuer. In his opinion, Fitzgerald would've had to tend to his injuries before setting off after them. Animals were another matter.

"Yes, I do. Try not to worry."

He couldn't see her features, but he caught the slight shake of her head. "Fear is a foreign emotion for me. I hadn't realized until this moment how predictable my life is. Since every day is much the same, there's never any reason to feel insecure or frightened. If my sister, Megan, were here, she'd know just the right verse to make me feel better. She's memorized the most of any of us."

He was quiet a long time. Finally, he spoke. "I will lie down and sleep in peace, for You alone, O Lord, make me dwell in safety. Psalm 4:8."

"Thank you, Evan," she whispered softly. "I needed that."

"Sweet dreams, Irish."

Evan tried to get comfortable, but it was next to impossible. He gazed up at the velvet black sky, his thoughts on the lady across the way. He hoped she was able to get some rest.

He'd never met anyone like her. She was sweetness and spice. Unafraid to speak her mind, yet wise enough to know when not to. With her to worry about, thoughts of James's death and the need for revenge no longer dominated his every waking moment.

He found himself longing to be in his own cabin, sleeping in his own bed. Longing to live simply once again—tending his crops and cows and goats and chickens—not living in the shadow of danger, keeping company with amoral, ruthless outlaws.

Evan wondered what Irish would think about his spread. It certainly was no stretch to picture her on his front porch, rocking in the chair he'd carved with his own hands, her red-gold hair fluttering in the breeze.

He didn't even know her name. On impulse, he left his post and went to crouch beside her sleeping form.

"Irish?" He placed a hand on her shoulder and squeezed.

"Mmm?" Eyes closed, she smiled in her sleep.

"Irish, what's your real name?"

"Mmm?"

"Your name."

"Juliana, silly," she mumbled before turning on her side, her back to him.

"Juliana," he breathed softly, testing her name on his lips. "Beautiful, just like you."

Chapter Seven

A heavy hand covered her mouth, startling her out of a deep sleep. Her foggy brain couldn't make sense of the rapid-fire words assailing her ear. Panic swelled in her chest. Whimpering, she tried to pry the fingers away.

"Hush," a low, familiar voice murmured against her ear. "It's me, Evan."

His clean scent reached her nose, and the tension left her body. He dropped his hand and helped her sit up.

"There's something out there. Follow me and be quiet."

She stuffed her feet into her boots without bothering to tie the laces. She took hold of his outstretched hand, taking comfort in the warmth of his touch. That connection was her lifeline as he pulled her quickly through the darkness. She was breathless by the time he stopped.

He settled both hands on her shoulders and leaned in close. "Stay here. I'm going after Lucky."

All she could think was that Fitzgerald had found them, and the possibility struck terror in her heart. He would surely kill her after what she'd done. "Do you think he's found us?"

"I don't know," he said. "But I want you to promise me you'll stay right here."

"I promise."

"Right here," he reiterated, "in this very spot."

"I won't move an inch."

He hesitated. Was he wondering whether or not he could trust her?

"Do you know how to shoot a gun?"

Juliana hid a smile. If he only knew. "As a matter of fact, I do."

He dropped his hands and reached for his holster. Then he pressed a gun into her hands. "Here. Whatever you do, take care where you aim this thing."

She took it, oddly touched by his gesture. "Why are you doing this? Considering that I stole your horse, how can you trust me with a weapon?"

"Am I wrong to trust you, Juliana?"

Her name on his lips was a soft caress. It had a strange effect on her. "How do you know my name?"

"Simple. I waited until you were half-asleep to ask. You gave it up readily."

"You don't play fair," she said, heat rushing to her face. What else had he learned?

"And you do?" His black brows winged up.

He had a point. He'd been very forgiving yesterday when he met up with her and Lucky. Why, he hadn't even scolded her for stealing his horse and stranding him in the middle of nowhere! She'd deserved a good tongue lashing at the very least. Instead he'd been gentle, soothing her as she wept in his arms.

A high-pitched whinny pierced the night air.

Evan flinched. "I have to go."

"Be careful."

His gave a brief nod. Then he was gone.

Juliana watched the dark path where he'd disappeared, her fists clenched so tightly her nails pinched her palms. *Maybe it's just a deer,* she told herself. *Or a razorback.*

She looked down at the gun he'd given her, turning it over in her hands. With this one act, he'd made it clear that he no longer saw her as his hostage but an equal. He trusted her not to turn on him or, worse, shoot him.

After yesterday, Juliana wouldn't even consider using his weapon against him. Lenny Fitzgerald's presence had changed everything. With that madman in pursuit, she wasn't about to try to make it on her own.

She flipped open the chamber to check for bullets. Five and an empty. But wait. There was something jammed into the empty chamber. A small piece of paper. A banknote, perhaps? She'd heard of men doing that. After all, no one was going to get to it unless you were dead.

Juliana bit her lip. Should she or shouldn't she? It wasn't like she was going to steal it. She just wanted a peek.

Unfurling the paper, she moved into a patch of moonlight in order to read the bold words:

WANTED:
$100 REWARD
For the Arrest and
Conviction of Evan Trey Harrison.
Sheriff Aaron Tate
Cades Cove, Tennessee

She gasped and clapped a hand over her mouth. It couldn't be!

Why was she so shocked? He'd never denied being an

outlaw. Now she held the hard evidence in her hands. Her disappointment felt like a dull blade jabbing her skin.

She'd glimpsed tenderness in Evan. And goodness. He was responsible, intelligent, and, yes, even charming when it suited his purposes. The crazy part was that she was attracted to him.

Face it, Juliana. Deep down inside you wanted this whole thing to be a mistake. You wanted him to be a normal man with a reasonable explanation for kidnapping you.

Lucky's protests reached her ears, reminding her that Evan could return at any moment. No way did she want him to find her with this. She rolled it up with unsteady fingers and shoved it back in place.

Her promise not to move forgotten, she crept through the darkness toward higher ground. She needed to see what was happening. Spying a fallen log at the base of a sycamore tree, she stepped up and braced herself against the trunk. The extra height gave her a clear view of camp. The flames had died down, but there was enough light for her to make out Evan's tall form and that of his horse.

Evan was trying to calm him and lead him in her direction. He wasn't having much success—whatever was out there had Lucky spooked. The horse pranced sideways, the whites of his eyes showing. Not a good sign.

Watching Evan, Juliana couldn't help but admire his ability to control the large animal. His shoulder and arm muscles bunched as he held firm to the bridle. He didn't get angry and lash out. Instead, he held his ground and used quiet tones to soothe the horse's nerves.

The wanted poster fresh in her mind, she reminded herself not to forget that he was a common thief. And kidnapper. She couldn't stop the sigh of relief, however, when they finally began to walk in her direction.

Backtracking, she reached her prior spot just as Evan and Lucky rounded the corner. He gave her a measuring look but said nothing.

"What now?" she said, adrenaline pumping. Would her nervousness give her away? He knew, after all, what was hidden in his gun.

"We find a place where we can watch the campsite without being detected."

"How about up there?" She pointed to the place she'd just been, trying for an even tone of voice. "Looks like a good place."

Again, he studied her. Then he dipped his head. "Let's go check it out."

He led the way, guiding Lucky. Juliana followed at a close distance. Within minutes they were standing side by side, sheltered by the thick foliage.

While she felt protected in his presence, she wasn't entirely at ease. Standing so close to him, she was aware of the hardness of his body, the unleashed power of his muscles. When his shoulder brushed hers, her skin heated. The darkness cloaking them only added to the sense of intimacy.

He stiffened and sucked in a breath.

Juliana scanned the forest, but didn't see a thing. "What is it?" she whispered.

"Bear."

Her heart sped up. Hopefully it was a male. There was nothing more dangerous than to come between a momma bear and her cubs. She searched the area again, paying attention to the dark shadows near the fire. One of the shadows separated from the rest.

Even from this distance, the black bear looked menacing. On all fours, the animal was short but stout with a wide block-shaped head, massive shoulders, rounded stomach and legs the size of tree trunks. The bear's long snout swayed to and fro, sniffing the air.

When Evan lifted his rifle and took aim, she seized his forearm. "Don't shoot him!" she hissed. "He'll leave as soon as he doesn't find what he's looking for."

"I'm not going to shoot him," he said without taking his eye off the bear. "I'm going to shoot *at* him. There's a difference."

"Why?"

"I don't want him coming back."

"We're not staying here, are we? I won't be going back to sleep, I assure you."

He was silent. Then he said, "It's nearly dawn anyway. We can head out once I retrieve our things. Still, I want to know for sure he's long gone while I do that."

The blast of the firearm startled her, and she almost lost her footing on the log. She glared over at him. He could've given her a warning! He didn't seem to notice her irritation.

The bear lumbered back in the direction from which he'd come. Evan lowered his rifle and, curling his fingers around her upper arm, helped her down. "Let's get out of here."

She waited until he'd strapped the rifle onto the back of the saddle to return his six-shooter.

"Here." She held it out to him.

He didn't immediately take it. "You can hold on to it if you want."

Didn't he remember the wanted poster? "No, thanks."

He swept off his hat and plunged his fingers in his

hair. "Juliana, you realize I'm not holding you here, don't you? All I want is to get you home safe and sound. Do you believe me?"

The logical part of her urged her to remember that he was a crook. A man unworthy of her trust. Her heart sent out a different message—*trust him.* Straightening her shoulders, she looked him square in the eyes. "I do."

"Good. I'm glad." He looked relieved.

Again she held out the gun. This time he took it and slid it in his holster. They walked back in silence. As they gathered the bedroll and saddlebags, Juliana kept glancing over her shoulder to check the woods. She couldn't help but be glad when they were finally back in the saddle.

It didn't occur to Juliana to wonder why she wasn't bothered by the fact they were heading in the opposite direction as her home, putting more miles between herself and her family. Or perhaps it did, and she just wasn't brave enough to face the truth.

By midmorning, Juliana was famished. Last night's fish was a distant memory, and she'd been up since before dawn. She wondered if Evan was planning to skip breakfast altogether. Surely he craved his coffee.

Her mouth watered in anticipation at the sight of a berry patch not far off the trail. "Evan, look! Can we stop?"

He tugged on the reins. "Are you a fan of blackberries?"

"I am. What about you?" She shouldn't care about his likes and dislikes. Remember the wanted sign!

"I prefer blueberries," he said, dismounting, "but these are good, too." He helped her down. "Sorry I didn't stop sooner. I was trying to put as much distance between us and that bear as possible."

Juliana figured he was more concerned about Fitzgerald than the bear, but didn't want to worry her by saying so.

"Would you mind if I left the picking to you while I get a fire going? I can't wait a minute longer for a cup of coffee."

She couldn't hold back her grin. "Not at all."

He cocked his head to the side. "What's so funny?"

"You're addicted to that stuff," she said with a soft laugh.

"I admit it. I am," he said in all seriousness. "Are you gonna join me?"

Juliana realized that they were becoming familiar with each other's habits. She wasn't sure if that was a good thing or not.

"Yeah, sure."

"That's what I thought." He arched a brow at her, a hint of a smile playing around his mouth, before turning on his heel and striding away to gather firewood.

Her grin widened, pleasure rippling through her.

She instantly quashed it. Why did the first man to stir her interest have to be a criminal? With a sigh, she bent to pluck enough ripe berries for the both of them. For every handful she dropped into the empty tin, two went into her mouth. She couldn't help it. Fresh fruit was a rare treat. Besides, she was starving!

When she'd filled the tin, she walked over to where Evan was crouched beside the small fire. The brim of his hat hid his face.

"Want some?" she said, extending the tin to him.

He lifted his head, his gaze shifting from the fruit to her face. His eyes went wide, and his mouth went slack.

Juliana was instantly on guard. "What is it?" she demanded, her hand going to her hair. "Is there a bug on me?"

Clamping his lips together, he shook his head. A merry twinkle entered his eyes, and she guessed that he was trying not to laugh.

"Have you been snacking on the job?" He couldn't disguise the tremor of amusement in his voice.

Planting one fist on her hip, she retorted, "What if I have?"

Unable to contain his mirth, Evan threw back his head and laughed—a deep, hearty sound that rumbled through his chest. She would've appreciated the sound of it if she wasn't so irritated.

"Oh, Juliana," he breathed, his hand splayed across his flat stomach. "You should see yourself. Your lips are stained dark red! Your teeth, too."

"What?" Mortified, she covered her mouth with her hand.

He popped one of the berries in his mouth. Then he flashed her an impish grin. "Mmm. I can see why you couldn't wait. Very tasty."

Indignation rose in her chest. "You've been out of polite society far too long, Evan Harrison. A true gentleman wouldn't dare make fun of a lady."

His expression sobered, but his eyes continued to dance. "You're right. I'm sorry." Scooping up a few more berries, he chewed slowly as if to savor the taste. His smile was a mile wide. "Are my teeth red now?"

Juliana didn't want to let go of her irritation, but it was hard not to in light of his good-natured teasing. Seeing him this way was a welcome change from his normally serious manner.

She dropped her hand from her waist. "Not as red as mine, I imagine."

"Hey." He caught her wrist. "I didn't mean to insult you."

A small smile touched her lips. "I know. I shouldn't have gotten so riled up. Guess I'm a bit touchy about my appearance right now. I don't remember ever going without a bath and a change of clothes before."

She could only imagine what she must look like. Wisps of hair had escaped her untidy braid to trail down her neck. Her injured cheek was no doubt a mottled purple and yellow, and now her lips and teeth were red. Her dress was torn and stained and missing a button. Her new boots were scuffed and dirty.

She was a mess! While she wasn't fashion crazy, like her sister, Nicole, she liked to look nice and neat. That Evan should see her like this bothered her. That she cared bothered her even more.

His indigo eyes bored into hers. "Let me be frank, Irish. You are the most beautiful woman I've ever met. A little dirt can't hide that fact."

Juliana's lips parted in disbelief. Her knees went weak. The heat of his fingers burned into her wrist and moved up her arm.

She couldn't speak. Evan thought she was beautiful? Did that mean he was as affected by her nearness as she was his?

Gazes locked, silence stretched between them.

When he released her and turned back toward the fire, she swallowed back regret.

Admit it. You want him to kiss you.

No! It was wrong to want anything from this man. He made a living stealing from honest people. His friends were thieves and possibly murderers. And while he admitted that he was once close to God, he certainly wasn't now. Everything he stood for went against her beliefs.

"Evan."

He looked up at her, his expression guarded.

"Have you ever killed a man?"

A veil came down over his eyes, but not before she glimpsed a spark of anger. "No, I have not."

"Have you shot a man?"

His lips thinned. "No," he ground out, "I have not."

He was angry, but her questions were legitimate. She simply *had* to know.

"I guess your next question is whether or not I've kidnapped a person before. The answer is, no, I have not. You're the first. Anything else you'd like to ask?"

Actually, yes. But she wasn't about to push her luck. "No."

"Good," he said in a clipped voice. "Let's eat and get back on the trail. We've wasted enough time here already."

Chapter Eight

He was wet, cold and miserable. Exhausted, too.

Gray clouds had rolled in about an hour earlier, spitting rain off and on. In the last twenty minutes the rain had come down more steadily. Didn't look like it was going to stop anytime soon. He'd kept his eye open for shelter, but hadn't spotted anything.

He was getting desperate.

His hat kept his head and face dry, but water dripped off the brim to slide down the back of his neck and under his shirt collar. Juliana's bonnet, made of less sturdy material, was saturated and provided little, if any, cover from the rain.

She shivered and his arms tightened around her.

"What's that?"

His gaze followed the direction of her outstretched finger to a dark structure nearly covered by vines. Whatever it was, it was old and had probably been abandoned a long time ago. But with the storm nearing, it wasn't as if he had much choice.

He leaned in close, his face pressed close to her cheek.

"Good eyes, Irish. With a little work, it might be just the thing we need."

Evan dismounted and turned to help her down. He noticed that her face and lips were pale, and beneath the bonnet her hair was plastered to her head.

"I'll work as fast as I can," he promised, determined to get her warm and dry as quickly as possible.

He searched for the oversize knife he packed for emergencies and began cutting away the vines and undergrowth. It was muddy, backbreaking work. He kept his eye out for snakes and others critters. Of course, he was more concerned about the condition of the inside of the cabin. No telling what he'd find there.

A bolt of lightning split the sky, followed by a deafening crack of thunder. Juliana let out a small cry, but had the peace of mind to grab his horse's bridle and calm him with soft strokes. Evan worked faster.

Fifteen minutes later, sweating and out of breath, he stood back to survey what he'd uncovered. "What do you think?" he called over the noise of the rain.

"Great job." The admiration on her face made all the hard work worthwhile.

"Thanks. Wait on the porch while I check the inside."

She followed him up the steps and onto the porch, standing off to the side as he pushed on the door. It didn't budge, so he threw his shoulder against the weathered wood. It scraped along the floorboards. An unpleasant musty odor hit him in the face and he drew back, giving his eyes time to adjust to the dim interior. As he scanned the square room, he noted a rough wooden table and four chairs in one corner and a cot along the far wall. A large stone fireplace took up the wall opposite the door.

He shoved the door open wider to let in more light.

Vines had squeezed through the floorboards and climbed up the walls, and spiderwebs hung suspended in the corners. He tested the floorboards with his weight as he went farther inside. There were a couple of soft spots, but all in all he thought it was sound.

"Not the best of accommodations, but it'll do," he told Juliana, who stood in the open doorway. "Come in. I'm going for my bags."

She scooted past him, her eyes wide as she looked around the small space. "Please don't let there be any spiders in those webs."

"That's what I'm here for, remember?"

She shivered again.

"I'll be right back." He bounded down the steps. His boots splashed through the mud as he ran to retrieve the saddlebags.

Back inside, he held up one of the bags. "There's a shirt and pants in here. Put them on. They're clean and dry."

"I couldn't possibly—"

"You're soaked to the skin. Trust me—you don't want to catch pneumonia."

Sighing, she reluctantly accepted the clothes. The bill of her bonnet drooped over her eyes and she pushed it back up with one finger. "What about you?"

"I've got another change in this one."

"I don't have any other choice, do I?"

"Not if you want to stay well. I'll be outside working on some sort of shelter for Lucky."

He tugged the door closed behind him and went to work hacking out an overhang. By the time he was finished, his palms were raw and bruised. His shirt and pants were plastered to his skin. Although it was the middle of July, he was beginning to feel chilled. He longed for hot coffee and a fire, but at least he had a change of clothes. With the big horse blocking him, Evan peeled off the wet garments and slipped into the dry clothes. Holding the satchel over his head, he sprinted to the cabin.

Juliana was perched on one of the chairs, her arms wrapped around her middle to ward off the cold. She looked like a young girl with her wet hair hanging loose around her shoulders. She was clearly uncomfortable wearing his clothing, but trying to make the best of it.

He moved closer, removed his hat and placed it on the table. Staring at her in the faint light, he noticed the swelling in her cheek hadn't gone down.

"Does it hurt worse?"

She lightly trailed her fingertips across the purplish-yellow skin. "About the same."

When she didn't elaborate, he got the feeling she was trying to spare him more guilt. He had no idea why she would do such a thing. She owed him nothing. After all he'd done, he deserved nothing less than her contempt.

"I was afraid of that," he murmured, frustrated at his inability to help ease her discomfort. If only he had some alcohol on hand... He kept some at home for medicinal reasons, of course, but he didn't travel with the stuff. "A poultice would help, but with this rain it will be a while before I can make one."

A shiver coursed through her body. She began to briskly rub her hands up and down her arms. No doubt her wet hair wasn't helping. He was cold, too.

"Do you have a ribbon or string to tie your hair back with?"

"No. And in my haste last night, I misplaced the last of my hairpins."

Evan thought for a moment. "Let me braid it for you, and I'll tie it with a strip of cloth." He rifled through his bag for a cloth and his knife.

"I can braid my own hair," she protested.

"Oh, really?" He paused in what he was doing to look at her. "Hold out your hands."

She stopped rubbing her arms and held them out. "So?"

"So?" He closed his hands over hers, resolutely ignoring the pleasure he felt at the simple touch. "You're trembling. And your fingers are like ice."

She dropped her gaze and gasped. "Evan, you're bleeding!"

He looked down and noticed the angry red scratches crisscrossing the tops of his hands. One in particular was deep and oozing blood. Only after he spotted it did the stinging set in. He pulled his hands away.

"It's nothing."

"It isn't nothing," she countered. "We have to wrap this up tight. Give me that clean cloth."

"Hang on." With one quick movement he cut a long strip from the cloth and laid it on the table. "That's for your hair."

She gave him a look but didn't comment, only motioned for him to sit next to her. She cradled his injured hand in her lap and pressed the material against the wound to stanch the flow. Her touch was gentle, calming. Evan stared at her bent head. He wondered what she was thinking as she wrapped the material around his hand and secured it with a knot.

"There. It's the best I can do."

"Thank you." He didn't know why, but Juliana's fussing over him made him feel lonely. "Now for your hair."

"What about your hand?"

"I can still move my fingers, see?" He wiggled his fingers.

"Don't tell me you've done this before." Her eyes searched his expectantly.

"No, but it can't be that hard, can it? Face the other direction so I can reach." When she only stared at him, he leaned forward. "Don't be stubborn, Irish." He deliberately kept his tone light so as to put her at ease. "I'll be quick, I promise."

With a doubtful expression, she presented him with her back. He realized his mistake the moment he plunged his fingers in the silky tresses. Her scent enveloped him, awakening his senses to her sweetness. The warmth of her body beckoned him. He wanted to hold her, to discover if her graceful form would fit against his as well as he suspected. When his fingertips raked across her nape, he heard her swift intake of air. His hands stilled.

He spotted the blush staining her cheek and leaned forward an inch. He would press a kiss against her smooth skin.

"Evan?"

The uncertainty in her voice stopped him. Juliana would not welcome his attentions. Of course she wouldn't. And why was he thinking such thoughts, anyway? He wouldn't allow himself to feel anything for her.

He straightened. He made quick work of her hair, then moved back to put as much space between them as possible. When she reached up to touch her hair, he noticed her fingers trembling. So. She was not unaffected by him. Evan tried not to be pleased, but failed.

Clearing his throat, he pulled a compact tin can out of his bags. "Have you ever eaten smoked oysters?"

"N-no, not that I recall."

"Hooper couldn't get enough of these, so he swiped a few cans from each mercantile we came to. I'd forgotten I had it, actually, but it's our good fortune. Without a fire, I've little to offer in the way of food." He worked to get the lid open.

"I'm hungry enough to overlook the fact I'm eating stolen property," she said dryly, the tension between them easing.

"You first."

Scooping one up with her fingers, she popped one in her mouth and chewed. "It's good."

"Yeah? I think so, too." He ate slowly, savoring the taste.

The rain intensified suddenly. It sounded like a hundred men stomping on the roof. Juliana looked around him to peer out the one dirt-caked window. "Do you think we'll be able to travel tomorrow?"

"Hard to say." He shrugged. "I know you're eager to get to Cades Cove and send that telegram. I'll do my best to get you there as quickly as possible."

Her expression grew troubled. "The longer my family has to wait for news, the tougher it will be. If I can't be there in person, I can at least put their minds at ease…" Her words trailed off, her lashes lowering to hide her eyes. She plucked absently at her sleeve.

She was obviously thinking of her family, missing them, and he felt awful about what he put her through. Maybe talking about them would lift her spirits. Besides, he was curious about Juliana and her life back in Gatlinburg.

"Why don't you tell me about your sisters?"

Her expression turned affectionate. "Megan is nineteen, two years younger than me. She's the bookworm."

So Juliana was twenty-one. He couldn't imagine why she was still unmarried. Were the men of Gatlinburg blind?

"Some nights we gather around the fire and listen to Megan read aloud. All sorts of books…poetry, historical documents, adventure novels. And after Megan is Nicole." An indulgent smile lifted her lips. "She's seventeen. Ah, it seems that Nicole's sole purpose in life is to be beautiful. I'm not certain which she deems more important—bonnets or ribbons. Momma still holds out hope that she will turn her attention to more worthwhile matters, but I'm not convinced."

"Give her time."

"I'm afraid it will take something drastic to change her ways." She pushed the too-long sleeves back up. "After Nicole are fifteen-year-old twins, Jessica and Jane. And, before you ask, yes, they're identical." It was obvious that she adored her sisters, and that they all shared a special bond.

"Do all your sisters have red hair?"

She touched a hand to her hair. "I'm the only one, although the twins' hair does have an auburn tint. Mother says I inherited this hair from my father's side. A great-grandmother, I believe."

"Were you teased a lot growing up?"

"Actually, no. There may have been a few comments, but I didn't let it bother me. I was happy to be different."

"It's beautiful," Evan blurted, his voice hushed in the still air.

She ducked her head. "Thank you."

"I'm glad you told me about your family. You're lucky to have them."

Her gaze searched his face. "What about you? Don't you have any family?"

The question sparked sad, bittersweet memories. No, he didn't have family. Not anymore.

"My parents died six years ago," he admitted. "I was nineteen, old enough to be on my own but still a kid in many ways. I was devastated. Lost. Confused…but I had James—" He stopped, unwilling to continue lest he spill the whole sordid story. Juliana was too easy to talk to.

"How did they die?"

"Hmm?"

"Your parents?"

"Cholera outbreak. It happened so fast there wasn't time to say goodbye."

He remembered the shock of it all, how his mother and father fell ill that fateful spring morning. By nightfall they were dead. In a flash, responsibility for the homestead—their very livelihood—was thrust upon him. And his brother…

"I'm so sorry." Her voice, soothing and heavy with compassion, interrupted his thoughts. "I know what it's like to lose someone you love dearly. My father died when I was ten. He and I were close."

Evan was silent, not trusting himself to speak just then. How long had it been since someone, *anyone*, had cared how he felt? Had showed him an ounce of compassion?

"Who is James?"

"My brother."

"And he's where now?"

Gone. Dead. "He died almost a year ago. I'm alone now."

"Evan." She leaned closer and placed a cool hand on his arm. "Are you familiar with the verse promising that God will never leave us nor forsake us?"

"Yes, of course." At his mother's insistence, he and his brother had memorized many verses from the Holy Scriptures.

"God's Word tells us Jesus is a friend who sticks closer than a brother. If you have Jesus, rest assured that you are *never* alone."

"I appreciate your kind words, Juliana. After what I've put you through, I don't deserve your compassion."

"I'm simply speaking the truth. All you have to do is trust Him."

"I'm not ready," he admitted with regret. The grief inside him was too fresh, too deep to ignore. Suddenly he was exhausted, both physically and mentally. Unfortunately, he doubted that he'd get much sleep that night.

He rose to his feet. "Would you mind if I turned in early?"

"Where exactly do you plan on sleeping?"

"The front porch."

Her gaze slid to the cot with its ratted cover. "How about I take the porch and you take that thing?"

A smile touched his lips. "Sorry."

"How do you expect me to sleep with spiderwebs hanging above my head? And who knows what sort of filth is embedded in that blanket? I'd rather sleep standing up!"

"I would make you a pallet on the floor, but the bedroll is soaked."

"Whatever. I'll think of something."

Lightning flashed, illuminating the room for a brief second, followed by a low growl of thunder directly above them. The window glass shuddered. "It could be worse, ya know. We could be out in that."

Her brows drew together. "Are you sure you'll be okay on the porch?"

Her worry about his safety touched him. "I'll be fine." If he didn't get struck by lightning. "Try to get some rest."

He'd opened the door when her voice halted him. "Good night, Evan."

He didn't turn around. "Good night, Juliana."

Chapter Nine

The quiet woke her. The storm had raged through the night, gusts of wind shaking the walls of the little cabin until she feared they would collapse. Her thoughts never strayed from Evan, out there in the elements simply to give her privacy and protect her reputation. She doubted he got even a minute of sleep.

She was eager to see how he'd fared.

Lifting her arms above her head, she stretched, trying to loosen the kinks in her muscles. Her back and shoulders were in knots. In the end, she'd been unable to bring herself to sleep on the cot, so she'd chosen to sit in a chair and rest her arms and head on the table. It was a miserable way to sleep.

Juliana touched a hand to her hair, grimacing as her fingers encountered her untidy braid. She longed for a bar of soap, a tub of hot water and especially a clean dress. Reaching across the table, she checked to see if hers had dried overnight. The shirt and trousers Evan had loaned her billowed about her body like a tent, and she felt undone.

Her dress was still damp, so she turned her attention

to her hair. As it had been braided wet, her hair now fell in soft waves about her shoulders. She pulled a comb through the strands and tied the mass back. It was the best she could do under the circumstances.

A glance out the window told her it was daylight. Time to check on Evan.

She hurried to the door and tugged it open, a little anxious about what she might find. What if he'd been struck by debris tossed about by the wind? Or, worse, struck by lightning? Breathing a little faster than normal, her gaze sought his familiar form.

What she saw melted her heart.

He was huddled on his side, his arm thrown over his head in a protective pose, his knees drawn up toward his chest. His breathing was deep and even. His clothes were wet, which she didn't like, and he wasn't wearing his boots. Odd.

She looked around and saw them at the edge of the porch, near the steps. Why would he take them off, she wondered. Maybe they were new, like hers, and rubbing his feet raw in places.

Noticing water from the roof splattering down, she reached for them. Her fingers brushed against a rigid bulge beneath the lining in one of them and she paused. What in the world? Curious, she picked it up for a closer inspection.

The material was smooth all around the top of the boot except for that one spot. Raised bumps felt like tiny stitches of thread, as if someone had made a small slit in the lining and later sewed it closed.

She glanced at Evan, relieved to see that he hadn't stirred. Had he hidden something in his boot? After finding the wanted sign stashed in his gun, she wouldn't be surprised.

Prodding the area, she felt a small, round object with ragged edges. What could it be? Not a gold or silver coin. The edges weren't smooth. She racked her brain for clues but couldn't imagine what he would want to hide.

Too bad she didn't remember where he put his knife.

She put the boots back where they'd been, and with another glance at Evan, tiptoed back inside and shut the door as quietly as possible. She sat back down at the table and plotted her next move. One way or another, she would eventually uncover his secrets.

One very long hour later, she heard him stirring. He jerked his head up in surprise when she threw open the door.

"Morning," he greeted, his voice husky from disuse. His brilliant blue eyes fastened on her face. In her mind, he looked much too fresh for just having spent a cold and miserable night in the rain. "Did you get any rest?" he asked, bending to tug on his boots.

She watched closely, noting their snug fit. Surely the hard object would chafe against his leg.

"Juliana?"

He straightened, his expression questioning.

"Oh." She realized that she hadn't answered him. "Yes, well, I managed to get a little. What about you? Was it awful?"

He folded his arms across his chest and stared at her. "I've slept in worse conditions."

"Worse than this?" Her brows shot up to her hairline. "I don't think I want to hear about it."

He smiled then. "No, you don't."

She glanced beyond his shoulder. The sky was a clear, robin's-egg blue this morning, the greens and browns of the forest crisp and vibrant as if the rain had washed away a film of dust from the tree leaves, the grass, the flower petals, the rocks.

"Is it too muddy to travel?"

He twisted around to look over his shoulder. "Not if we're extra careful." He turned back. "I want coffee first, though. And breakfast. The first order of business is finding dry wood for a fire. I'll probably have to break apart one of the chairs. Maybe two."

Juliana's stomach rumbled at the mention of food. She held out her hand. "Give me a gun and I'll rustle up breakfast."

His mouth went slack. "What?"

She grinned at his dumbfounded expression. "You heard me."

His dark brows slashed together. "Let me get this straight—you can't cook but you can shoot small animals?"

"I thought I explained about my cousins. They taught me a lot of things, one of them being how to shoot a gun."

He studied her a moment, then shook his head no. "I'll do it. I'll get a fire going and you can be in charge of the coffee." He brushed past her on his way inside.

"Which is it?" she demanded, her humor fading. "You don't trust me with a weapon or you don't believe I have enough skill to bag our breakfast?"

Evan shot her that look of his that said he thought she was acting foolish. "If I didn't trust you, I wouldn't have given you my gun the other night. And I believe you can do whatever you set your mind to. You're a very resourceful woman."

His words erased her irritation. All that was left was bewilderment. "Then why?"

He paused with his hand on the chair back, his mouth set in a stubborn line. "I can't let you go alone. Fitzgerald is still out there. He won't give up until he gets his revenge."

Her stomach quivered at the thought. "It's because of what I did back there, isn't it? I mean, he despised me before—"

Evan was suddenly right in front of her, his fingers gently tipping up her chin, forcing her to look at him. His blue eyes blazed at her. "None of this is your doing, Juliana. You're in this situation because of a decision I made—a foolish one. Fitz hates my guts. That hatred extends to anyone associated with me. Understand?"

Juliana simply nodded. He held her gaze a moment more before dropping his hand and taking a step back.

"What does he have against you?"

Evan was quiet, weighing her question. "He considers me a threat because I'm not afraid of him. I don't cower at his rantings and ravings. And Roberts likes me, which makes Fitz worry that someday I could become the second in command instead of him."

Juliana stared at Evan. The words coming out of his mouth did not accord with the man she knew him to be. No, she corrected herself, the man she desperately *wanted* him to be. Frustration bubbling up inside, she fisted her hands at her sides. She decided that she did not want to hear anymore about his lawless life. If by that she was hiding her head in the sand and ignoring reality, so be it.

"I'm going outside," she announced. At his intake of breath, she added sardonically, "to answer the call of nature."

"Fine. Take this with you." He pressed a gun in her hand. "And keep your eyes open."

"Yes, sir."

He cocked an eyebrow. Before he could respond, she whirled around and stalked out.

Evan watched her hasty retreat, hoping she'd calm down and pay attention to her surroundings. He didn't have a clue what had sparked her ire. One minute she'd been cool as a cucumber and the next she'd looked as if she'd like to throttle him.

He couldn't stop the grin tugging at his mouth.

Juliana O'Malley was one amazing woman. One in a million. His initial instincts had been on the mark—she was no simpering wallflower. She was spirited. And brave. Smart. Witty. *Don't forget beautiful.*

"How can I?" he muttered to himself, pulling his small axe out and beginning to hack the chair into pieces.

Every time she turned those wide, luminous eyes his way, the cracks in the walls around his heart fractured another inch. And that smile...at times sweet, at times teasing, at all times harboring secrets he'd like to explore...made him want things he'd never have. Love. Laughter. Marriage.

He brought the axe down with more force than necessary. No. He couldn't afford to dream dreams. He'd made his decision to go it alone and he would stick by that.

Twenty minutes later, the fire was roaring and coffee was made, yet Juliana had not returned.

Evan wore a trampled trail in the grass, his gaze searching the woods for a glimpse of her fiery hair. He strained for any sound at all that might mean she was nearby or, God forbid, in trouble.

She has the gun, remember?

True, but if she'd been caught by surprise…

His gut twisted as his mind flashed back to the cabin and Fitz's assault, then to the moment she'd fallen into his arms after escaping the outlaw's clutches. The abject terror in her eyes had stirred within him a fury at the other man like nothing he'd experienced before. Not even the news of James's murder had evoked such a reaction.

Evan scanned the woods again. Surely she wouldn't have gone so far as to get lost.

What if Fitz had her even now? The thought made his blood run cold. If anything happened to her—

There. A rustling to his right. Unsheathing his weapon, he crept toward the sound, all senses on high alert.

The flash of red hair glinting in the sunlight made his limbs go limp with relief. It was her. Then he spotted what she carried in her hands, and his blood pressure skyrocketed. She'd blatantly disregarded his order to stay close. Stuffing his gun back into his holster, he marched back to the fire.

Juliana strolled back into camp feeling extremely satisfied with herself. She could only imagine Evan's surprise—

"Where have you been?"

She halted in her tracks, her gaze flying upward to find him standing near the fire, arms crossed across his chest and feet braced apart, the brim of his black hat shielding his eyes. Eyes she supposed were as blistering as the flames spitting and popping near his feet.

Holding up her bounty, she gave him a smile meant to cool his ire. "These two crossed my path, and I wasn't about to let them get away. I don't know about you, but I'm ravenous."

His gaze flicked to the rabbits dangling from her fingers then back up to her face. His expression remained inscrutable.

"One more minute and I was coming to look for you. From now on I'll be accompanying you on all your calls of nature."

Juliana opened her mouth to utter a retort, then bit her lip. Arguing wasn't going to improve his mood. She simply shrugged. "So are you going to ready them or shall I?"

Surprise registered, but he didn't comment. "I'll do it."

He held out his hand, and she crossed to where he stood. He took her burden from her without a word. When she started to move away, his hand shot out and imprisoned her wrist. Startled, she gasped at the severity of his expression.

"Promise me you won't do that again."

"Evan, I—"

"You've no clue what's been going through my mind the last half hour."

Frustration edged his generous lips. Worry was there in the line between his dark brows. Concern darkened his eyes to that beguiling purple-blue.

She sighed, truly repentant for causing him trouble. "I'm fine. Nothing happened."

"This time. Juliana, I don't think it's registered just how dangerous this man is. I've watched him gun down men for no other reason than the thrill of shedding blood. He has a reason to despise you now as much as he does me. If he catches you, he will kill you."

Her blood ran cold at the conviction in his statement.

She'd seen the cold emptiness in Fitzgerald's eyes, had known instinctively that he wouldn't hesitate to hurt her.

"I'm sorry. You have my word I won't do it again."

With a terse nod, Evan turned away. She stood quietly by as he dressed the rabbits and readied the spits, unable to think of a single thing to do. By the time he had breakfast started, she couldn't handle the silence any longer.

Juliana settled herself on a fallen log near the fire, a cup of coffee cradled in her hands.

"How much farther until we reach Cades Cove?"

He glanced at the sky. "If the weather holds we should arrive late tomorrow."

"Tell me about your town. Is it large?"

The tension left his features as his thoughts turned to home. "What it lacks in size, it makes up for in charm. It's nestled in the most picturesque, most fertile valley in East Tennessee. You'll see for yourself soon enough."

"What about the people? Are they friendly?"

"Friendly enough, I suppose. Why do you ask?"

"Just curious." She shrugged. "I've never traveled outside of Gatlinburg."

His brows lifted in surprise. "You're in for a treat then. I guarantee you'll be impressed."

"How long have you lived there?"

"Since I was fifteen. We lived just over the mountains in North Carolina before that."

"I've heard that North Carolina rivals Tennessee in beauty."

"I'd agree with that." He turned the skewers so the meat would cook evenly. He propped his arm on one knee in a half-kneeling position. "We were happy there. Then one day my father met up with an old acquaintance who had traveled through East Tennessee. He filled my father's head with stories of rich farmland, rivers teeming with catfish and trout, forests and abundant wildlife. Land was selling for a fair price, so my father convinced my mother to leave her home for a new one."

It wasn't a new story. Hundreds, if not thousands, of families living in the East had given up everything in search of a new and better life in the West. So far, Evan Harrison's childhood sounded typical. What had gone wrong? Why had he chosen a life of crime?

"Was she difficult to convince?"

A rare grin crossed his lips, and Juliana's breath hitched. He was solemn so much of the time that when he smiled the effect was mesmerizing.

"At first she was adamant about staying in North Carolina, but when she realized how important it was to him she agreed to come."

"Do you think she ever regretted the move?"

"Mother loved the valley, but I think she was lonely. She missed her friends. Since she was an educated lady, she assumed responsibility for our lessons. Of course, James and I weren't too pleased. Neither one of us were that interested in learning."

Juliana watched as Evan's attention turned inward, obviously remembering better times. She tried to imagine him as a carefree and happy young teenager. His parents sounded like such nice people. Perhaps their untimely deaths, combined with the loss of his brother, were the reasons Evan had turned to a life of crime.

Rising to her feet, she approached the fire and sat across from him. His blue eyes, darkened with sorrow and regret, fastened onto her face. He seemed a million miles away.

"Evan, do you have any living relatives? Grandparents? Aunts or uncles?"

Her question brought him back to the present, and he nodded. "My aunt and uncle live in Raleigh, and their son Lucas owns the land that adjoins mine. He's watching over my place and tending to my animals while I'm gone."

Surprise rippled through her. "That's wonderful! Are the two of you close?"

"Yes, of course. He's a good man."

"You're not alone then, Evan. You should be thankful that he lives nearby. He sounds trustworthy, too, considering that you've left your home in his care."

"I am thankful," he retorted, removing the meat from the fire and setting it aside to cool. "We'll stop by his house on the way home."

She digested that information. Did he know about Evan's illegal activities? "And where does he think you've been all this time?"

"Luke respects my privacy," he said without meeting her gaze. There was an unspoken warning for her to do the same. She watched his nimble fingers carefully remove the meat and place it in their trenchers. She admired his strong, capable-looking hands.

Adding a couple of biscuits, he handed the plate to her.

"Don't burn yourself. It's still hot."

"Thanks."

Sensing his reluctance to continue the conversation, she ate in silence.

When they finished, she wiped the grease from the trenchers and wrapped them in a towel while Evan cleared their belongings out of the shelter and readied the horse for travel. Determined not to wear his clothes any longer than necessary, Juliana went inside the cabin and changed into her damp dress.

His look was questioning when she stepped out. "Is it dry already?"

"Not completely, no."

He stood next to Lucky, watching her approach. "Are you sure you want to risk getting sick?"

She stopped in front of him. "In this heat and humidity, I'm sure it will dry soon enough."

He studied her before lifting a shoulder. "It's your decision."

He helped her into the saddle and, vaulting up behind her, grabbed the reins and signaled Lucky. Without conscious thought, Juliana leaned back against Evan. In response, his arms tightened around her waist. She could feel his heart beat through the thin material of her dress. It took all her concentration to keep her breathing even. She could not deny that she was thrilled to be close to him once again.

Juliana, a voice inside her head warned, *guard your heart. Evan Harrison may be attentive and attractive, but he's not for you. If he's ever captured, he could very well spend the rest of his life behind bars.*

The prospect sickened her, and she knew without a doubt that her heart was in danger. She had to wonder where her good sense had gone. Attracted to a criminal! What would her mother say?

Despite everything, he mattered to her. His future mattered.

"How long have you been living like this? And don't sidestep the question, as you did before."

A sigh rumbled through his chest, stirring her hair.

"This isn't a career choice, if that's what you're worried about. It's simply a means to an end."

"I don't understand."

"I have no other choice," he asserted, his voice hard.

Juliana sensed the heaviness in his spirit. "Everyone has a choice—a choice to do right or to do wrong. There is no joy in a life of sin."

"I can't expect you to understand," he said, guiding Lucky around a rotten log blocking their path.

"Enlighten me," she implored, twisting her face around. "I want to understand."

"Why do you care?"

"Because I—" She hesitated, reluctant to admit her feelings. "I don't want to see you spend the rest of your life in jail."

"I don't plan to."

His complacency stirred her irritation. "Surely you don't believe that you can dodge the law forever! Aren't you tired of running? From your past? The law? God?"

He was quiet a long time, and she wished she could see his expression. "Don't worry about me. Concentrate on getting home to your family. Once you're home safe and sound, you won't spare me another thought."

Juliana knew that would never happen. Evan Harrison wasn't a man easily forgotten.

"I've heard it said that you can run from God, but you can never *outrun* God," she said quietly. "One of these days you'll grow tired of all this."

"You might be right," he quipped. "For now, why don't we agree to have this conversation another time?"

Far from ready to end the conversation, Juliana quashed her irritation.

Since she couldn't talk to Evan, she talked to the Lord.

As the pair rode through the forest, she poured out her concerns to God. The tension gradually eased.

God is in control, she reminded herself. *In the heavens above He hung the moon, the stars, the planets. He created the Earth in six days. Working a miracle in one outlaw's heart was by no means out of reach. With God, all things were possible.*

Chapter Ten

Evan's thoughts were not as upbeat. If he were completely honest, he'd acknowledge his growing attachment to Juliana O'Malley. She was beautiful, yes, but it was her sweet spirit and compassion that touched his soul.

The knowledge that she cared about him while thinking he was an outlaw both thrilled and frightened him.

Of course, he told himself, her only concern was for his spiritual welfare. She couldn't possibly be interested in him as a man. And even if she were, his hands were tied. Evan had a job to do—self-appointed, as it were—to bring to justice the men responsible for James's death.

Vengeance is mine, saith the Lord.

The still, quiet words crept into his mind, catching him by surprise. There it was again. The Lord's voice, so long silent. *But, Father,* he argued, *those murderers took an innocent life—my only brother. They must pay.*

Then Evan remembered another verse he'd learned at his mother's knee.

Let all bitterness, and wrath, and anger, and evil speaking be put away from you. Be kind and compas-

sionate to one another, forgiving each other, just as in Christ God forgave you.

Forgive those monsters? Impossible!

And yet, deep down, he knew if he would but ask, God would help him do just that. Question was, did he really want to? He held on to his anger so the grief wouldn't bury him.

With each passing day Evan missed James a little more. Instead of lessening, his grief only deepened with time. More than brothers, they'd been best friends.

From his earliest memories, their mother had encouraged teamwork. Margaret Harrison had instilled in her sons a sense of responsibility for one another. If Evan needed help milking the cows, James was expected to pitch in. If James was having trouble learning his letters, Evan tutored him.

Left alone after their parents' death, he and James had relied on each other even more. Four years of pouring all their sweat, energy and resources into the farm had paid off—it was now a profitable, well-kept spread.

But because of a senseless act of violence, James was no longer around to enjoy the rewards of their labor. Dead at twenty-one. Evan's saddest moments were when he allowed himself to think about all the wonderful experiences James would miss. Falling in love. Getting married. Babies.

No, he couldn't dwell on that now. Juliana's safety took top priority.

Straightening in the saddle, he focused once more on their surroundings. Juliana was so quiet she must have dozed off. He allowed himself to enjoy her closeness, knowing it would soon be over. He dreaded leaving her.

He'd miss her and worry about her every minute they were apart.

She might be able to forget him, but he knew without a shadow of a doubt that he'd never forget her. Evan sucked in a swift breath, amazed suddenly at how quickly she'd turned his life upside down.

Four days ago, he'd been consumed with thoughts of revenge and strategy. All his energy went into maintaining his masquerade as a low-down thief. He'd ignored the Holy Spirit's subtle nudges.

Then Juliana walked into his life.

Not only had his quest for revenge been pushed aside, his mind was consumed with thoughts of her. And he'd actually talked to God. A little.

A flash of white darted across the dirt path, spooking Lucky. The horse sidestepped. Tightening the reins, Evan spoke in low, soothing tones in an attempt to calm him. Juliana gripped the saddle horn.

"What was that?"

"Probably a rabbit. Whatever it was, it's gone."

She kneaded the back of her neck. "Can we stop at the next stream? I don't care how deep it is. I need to get clean somehow. I feel as though I haven't bathed in a month." She twisted her face so that he was presented with her profile. "I suppose it isn't proper to speak about such things in front of you. You'll have to excuse my frank speech—I'm used to being in the company of women."

"I'm not so easily offended. Besides, it's only you, me and the animals out here. I figure the rules of proper society don't apply."

"That's a relief." She laughed. "Because I believe I've broken almost all of them."

* * *

Juliana thought she might melt. The humid air pressed against her, and her clothes clung to her damp, sticky skin. A cloud of gnats hummed about her head.

They'd been hiking for miles, it seemed. Her calves and thighs were burning with exertion, and of course her toes ached from rubbing against the inside of her boots. Her way of coping was to clamp her mouth shut and focus on placing one foot in front of the other.

Evan wasn't speaking, either. His lips pressed in a harsh line, he didn't appear to be any happier than she was with the situation. When they crested the largest of the hills and Juliana spotted a patch of sparkling blue in the valley below, she wanted to jump for joy.

"Is that a lake?" she huffed.

He paused beside her, his gaze following the direction of her outstretched finger. "Sure looks like it." He tipped his black hat up. "Let's go check it out."

Two hours later, they stood on the grassy banks of Lake Restawhile. Someone had erected a rough, hand-made sign proclaiming the name. The name fit.

Weeping willows spilled their trailing pale green branches onto the water's crystalline surface, and larger, more massive oaks rose majestically to the sky. Clusters of bright red poppies dotted the fields. Cheerful blue and yellow forget-me-knots brightened the water's edge. Swans glided in serene splendor across the water.

Juliana glanced at Evan. "I'm going in."

He grinned boyishly. "Me, too."

Her heart leapt at the eagerness in his eyes. Gone were the shadows and weariness.

"I'll unload our stuff over there." He pointed to a

nearby oak. "While I'm doing that, you can go on in. I'll keep my eyes averted while you ready yourself."

Juliana felt her face heat. Her sisters would be scandalized…it wasn't proper for her and Evan to swim together unaccompanied. Nor spend the night in each other's company without a chaperone, but it wasn't as if they'd had a choice. Under normal circumstances, they would be expected to marry. However, she wasn't there of her own volition. And he was a criminal. Not exactly normal circumstances at all.

The reminder darkened her mood a bit. If she wasn't careful, she was going to start thinking of this as an adventure with Evan as the dashing hero.

Marching over to the nearest weeping willow, she swept aside the thick veil of branches and stepped inside the natural enclosure. The branches fell back into place with a soft swoosh, effectively cutting off her view of the pond and the surrounding trees.

She undid the buttons on her bodice, stepped out of the dress and folded it in a neat square. Underneath she wore a white cotton camisole, nipped in at the waist with a drawstring, and white knickers trimmed with lace ruffles. They were dingy from dust and sweat. A dip in the pond would take care of that.

Untying her boots, she set them beside her folded dress and hurriedly peeled off her knee-high stockings. The moist, cool dirt felt good against her bare feet, and she wiggled her toes. A sigh escaped her. Finally, release from those stiff boots! Peering through the leaves, she monitored Evan's movements.

His back was to her, his attention on his horse. Praying that he wouldn't turn around and see her unmentionables, she sprinted to the shallow end and waded in. The cool water enveloped her body in a soothing embrace. She dove underwater, darting down deep and back up again for air. After about five minutes of this, she came up for a rest and stifled a scream when she bumped into something solid.

Warm fingers closed over her shoulders.

"I didn't mean to startle you," Evan's husky voice sounded above her. "Are you all right?"

She shoved her hair out of her eyes and stared at him. He was too close for comfort, water droplets clinging to his golden skin. His jet-black hair was slicked back away from his forehead. All that was visible above the water were the tops of his powerful shoulders.

Juliana's mouth went dry. Evan's dark blue eyes roamed her face before zeroing in on her lips. Water gently lapped their bodies. The air hummed with electricity. In a desperate act of self-preservation, Juliana splashed water into his face and slipped free of his hold. As she darted in the opposite direction, a spray of water rained down on her head.

His deep-throated laughter broke the tension. They splashed each other until, tired and lazy, they agreed to a cease-fire. Floating in the water, Juliana couldn't recall the last time she'd had so much fun. Evan had enjoyed himself, too. His laughter made her heart soar.

"Can we camp here for the night?" Juliana asked hopefully.

Evan scanned the area. "We can stay until after supper, but we'll bed down a ways out. I don't want to be here after dark. That's when animals will come looking for a drink."

"You're suited to this life, aren't you?" she said. When

he looked at her askance, she amended, "I meant you're at home in the outdoors. You were a farmer, right?"

"I *am* a farmer," he insisted, "always will be. I'm just…sidetracked at the moment."

She really wanted to ask him about that wanted poster. And the mysterious object in his boot. Instead, she said, "Do you like being a farmer?"

He thought for a moment, bobbing up and down in the water. "It never occurred to me to do anything else. I like caring for the animals. I like workin' with my hands. I have an area in my barn where I tinker with tools. I'm always trying to figure out new ways to do things."

"So you're an inventor of sorts."

"I guess you could say that." He nodded. "I've come up with a few handy gadgets over the years—even sold a few to the neighbors."

"That's impressive. Have you thought about selling your gadgets in the mercantile? You could pay the owner a small percentage in exchange for shelf space." And it's legal, she added silently.

He shrugged. "I don't have time to make many extra. It was hard enough to keep up with all the chores when James was alive. After his death, I decided to hire someone to help. Before I could do that, I went to see the sheriff—" He stopped and clamped his lips together.

"And?" she prompted.

"Forget it." He pushed his fingers through his damp hair, and Juliana tried not to stare at his carved biceps.

"Have I given you any reason not to trust me?"

One black eyebrow quirked up. "Hmm, wasn't it just yesterday that you stole my horse and left me stranded in the middle of nowhere?"

"*Stole* is such a strong word." She adopted an innocent expression. "I prefer the word *borrowed* and only for a short time."

He tilted his head to study her. "You're something else, Irish."

"Don't try to distract me, Evan. It won't work."

"I'm trying to protect you."

"From what?" She threw her hands up. What was he hiding?

"From information that could get you into trouble. Let's face it—the less you know about me, the better."

"I don't agree."

"You don't have to." He straightened to his full height and stared down at her. "Doesn't change anything, though."

Juliana averted her eyes from the sight of all that male skin. She was beyond frustrated—why did he have to be so stubborn?

"Juliana." Evan's hard, low voice snagged her attention. "Go and get dressed this instant."

Her head snapped up, alarmed at the urgency in his voice. "Why? What—"

"We're about to have company." He was already striding to the shore. "Do it now," he barked over his shoulder.

Juliana hesitated for an instant, her eyes scanning the fields. There, in the distance, she spotted the approaching riders. There were at least three horses. Evan and she were outnumbered. Her heart leapt into her throat.

In her haste, her legs seemed sluggish in the water. At last she reached the shore, and she dashed to her hiding place behind the curtain of branches. Loosening the drawstring, she ripped her wet camisole up and over her head and pulled off the knickers, not taking the time to dry herself before hurriedly pulling on her navy calico.

The sound of horses' hooves grew louder. Her trembling fingers fumbled with the buttons. Stuffing her feet into her boots, she burst out of her hiding place in time to see Evan withdraw his weapon.

Evan assumed an air of calm. Not an easy task considering that he was sopping wet and half dressed. He had no idea what to expect from the approaching trio. Could be normal folks. Or they could be outlaws like Cliff Roberts and his gang. If that was the case, he was at a disadvantage.

Gripping the revolver, he kept his gaze on the riders. When they got close enough, he was able to see that the lead horse carried a clean-shaven male, the second, a female, and the third a young boy. A family. Evan relaxed his stance, but his gaze remained sharp.

Thank You, God. The thanks were heartfelt and spontaneous. He admitted to himself that he couldn't protect Juliana without help from God.

"Howdy," the man greeted cautiously. He appeared to be older than Evan, possibly in his mid-thirties. All three horses halted. "Mind if we stop and rest awhile?"

Evan smirked, thinking of the handmade sign Juliana and he had seen on the other side of the lake. "Fine with me."

The man's attention volleyed between Evan and Juliana, who stood waiting by the trees. He was assessing the situation, of course, just as Evan had done. With instructions to the woman and boy to stay put, he dismounted and approached with an outstretched hand.

"The name's Henry Talbot."

Evan shook the man's hand. He'd learned to distinguish honest men from the corrupt over the course of the last few months. This one appeared to be on the up and up. "Pleased to meet you. I'm Evan Harrison."

Mr. Talbot's gaze slid to Juliana once more, then to Evan's haphazard attire. "I hope we aren't disturbing you."

Knowing what he must be thinking, Evan felt heat creep up his neck. "No, no…we were swimming, is all."

The man hooked a thumb over his shoulder. "My family and I've been traveling since this morning. We need a break, especially the little ones."

"Yeah, well, this looks like a fine place to camp. Don't mind us."

"Great. I'll go tell my wife."

While Mr. Talbot went to assist his family, Evan holstered his weapon, made quick work of his shirt buttons and tucked the ends into his waistband. He strode over to Juliana. Her face was pale.

He gave her shoulder a reassuring squeeze. "There's nothing to worry about."

Her gaze was on the newcomers. "Who are they?"

"Henry Talbot and family." He threaded his fingers through hers, pleased with how well her hand fit into his larger one. "Come on, let's go meet everybody."

"Wait." She held back. "What are we going to tell them about us?"

Evan met her questioning gaze. "Nothing. Most likely they'll assume we're husband and wife." Her green eyes lit with emotion he couldn't identify. "Does that bother you?"

"I hate the thought of deception."

In the not-so-distant past, Evan would've felt exactly the same way. After months of living a lie, however, he'd pushed aside his conscience enough times to weaken its effect. He felt ashamed.

"I'm sorry I've put you in this position, but that doesn't change reality. A single man and woman traveling alone together—well, it simply isn't done. We don't want them asking questions we can't answer."

"I know."

The look in her eyes made it clear that she trusted him. Juliana humbled him in so many ways. She thought he was a wanted man and yet, she trusted him. Juliana O'Malley was a rare woman.

He leaned in close, so that their foreheads nearly touched. "Why aren't you married, Juliana?"

He heard her swift intake of breath. Her cinnamon-colored eyebrows drew together. "Why are you asking me this?"

"I'm curious, that's why."

"I haven't met anyone I wanted to marry, I guess."

"Have you ever been asked?"

Her chin came up. "You're getting awfully personal, Mr. Harrison."

"Is that a yes?"

"I'm not answering any more of your questions." Her green eyes blazed in bold defiance.

When he spoke, his voice was as smooth as velvet. "Remember, Irish, you're my wife for the next twenty-four hours. As hard as it may be, try to act like you're crazy about me."

On a whim, Evan pressed his mouth against hers. A jolt of lightning-swift heat surged through him clear down to his toes. In that instant, he knew he was lost. Soft and sweet with a hint of honey, her lips were like a cool drop of water to a man dying of thirst.

Of their own volition, his hands crept up to cradle her face, his thumbs stroking her satin cheeks. A tide of unfamiliar emotion welled up within him and threatened to carry him away. He fought the urge to crush her to him and never let go.

He tore his mouth from hers, his breathing ragged. She stood stock-still, her eyes a maelstrom of emotion. Accusation. Longing. Confusion.

"Juliana, I—" he began, his voice gravelly.

"Mr. Harrison?"

Evan dropped his hands and pivoted to find Henry Talbot and his family standing a few feet away. The boy's eyes were wide as saucers, which meant they'd probably witnessed the kiss. His ears burned with embarrassment.

He eased Juliana forward. "Excuse me, Mr. Talbot. I didn't hear your approach. This is Juliana."

Juliana didn't spare a glance his way as she bestowed a welcoming smile on the couple.

"This is Rose." He indicated the small, dark-haired woman by his side, "and this is our son, Matt."

"It's nice to meet you," Juliana offered in a friendly manner. "What's the little girl's name?"

Confused, Evan glanced around to see whom she was referring to. Then Rose Talbot turned sideways, and he glimpsed the sleeping toddler snug in her wrap. He hadn't noticed the material harness strapping her to her mother's back.

"Her name is Joy." Mr. Talbot smoothed her dark hair with a gentle hand and shared a smile with his wife. "We waited a long time for this little treasure."

"She's adorable," Juliana said in a soft voice, clearly enchanted with the curly-headed tot. "How old is she?"

Rose spoke up. "She'll be two next month."

Evan turned his attention to the boy. "You must be about twelve."

Matt's face relaxed into a gap-toothed smile. "Naw, mister, I just turned nine in March."

He feigned disbelief, rocking back on his heels. "I can't believe it. By the way you handled your mount, I thought for sure you were older."

Matt shrugged, his eyes downcast as he toed the dirt with his boot.

"Your pa must be really proud," he added.

Mr. Talbot nodded. "I am at that. Matt's a quick learner."

Evan clapped his hands together. "How about I start a fire and put on some coffee?"

"We'd be much obliged, Mr. Harrison," Mr. Talbot agreed. "Matt, come and help me with the horses."

"Yes, sir." Matt straightened to attention.

"Please, call me Evan."

"And you can call me Henry." He wrapped his arm around his son's small shoulders and led him away.

Juliana stepped forward. "Can I help you, Mrs. Talbot?"

"That's sweet of you, thanks."

While Juliana helped the other woman, Evan went in search of firewood. His mind was not on the task—it was on the kiss. The experience had rocked him to the core. The touch had been so intimate, so sweet…he couldn't imagine kissing anyone else besides Juliana. Just the thought of another man touching her made his stomach clench in anguish.

Face the facts, Harrison. You have no claim on her.

It was true. Besides, he couldn't afford to get sidetracked now. He was on a mission to find James's killers and bring them to justice. Too much was at stake.

He'd have to watch his step from here on out. A couple of days—three at the most—and he'd drop her off in Cades Cove. Leave her in his cousin's capable hands. Time away would help him get perspective on things. He and Juliana had simply spent too much time alone together. What normal, red-blooded man could hold himself aloof from her for very long?

Juliana was beautiful and graceful and sweet, with a little spice thrown in for good measure. He liked her spirit. She kept him on his toes.

Stop it. Listing her attributes won't help matters.

Evan pushed thoughts of her out of his mind and focused instead on the mundane task of finding firewood.

Chapter Eleven

Juliana sat cross-legged in the grass, her arms cradling the petite toddler. The girl's mother was taking a few moments to stretch and refresh herself. Joy's body was a warm weight in her lap, her chubby hands clasped together as if in prayer. Brown curls framed a heart-shaped face. Impossibly long, sooty eyelashes rested against pink cheeks. Her rosebud mouth was parted to form a small *O*.

Unfamiliar feelings stirred in Juliana's chest. Would a daughter of hers look like this precious treasure? Or would she have red hair and pale skin like her? She wondered what Evan's offspring would look like. Glossy black hair, deep indigo eyes and golden skin?

Rose approached carrying a bulging leather satchel and sat across from Juliana. "Is she getting too heavy?"

"Not at all."

"Joy doesn't normally sleep this long, but she's been ill. I didn't want to travel until she'd fully recovered, but we need to get home."

The poor baby. "What was the illness?"

Rose pushed wayward strands out of her eyes, her weariness evident in the way she arched her back and kneaded the back of her neck. "I'm not sure. We've been visiting my sister the last few weeks, and her husband and sons came down with a high fever and chills. Joy was the only one of us to get it." She reached out and smoothed her daughter's hair. "I was worried sick about her. I lost a child to sickness a few years back, and it nearly buried me. Just the thought of losing Joy or Matt..." Her voice trailed off and her brown eyes grew wet with moisture.

The grief in the other woman's voice spurred Juliana to reach over and squeeze her hand. "Are you a believer, Rose?"

She gave her a quivering smile. "I am."

"Would you mind if I said a prayer for Joy?"

"I'd appreciate that, Juliana."

Still holding the other woman's hand, Juliana closed her eyes and uttered a simple prayer. "Dear Lord Jesus, thank You for loving us. Your Word says that You have a plan for each of us, a plan for a future and a hope. Please restore little Joy's health and give the Talbots a safe trip home. We know that You are in control, and You will never abandon us. In Jesus's name I pray, Amen."

Her intent had been to encourage the other woman, but remembering God's promises aloud boosted her own flagging spirits. God had allowed Evan to kidnap her, and He'd been with her every moment since. He hadn't lost sight of her. She didn't understand His reasons, but she recalled reading somewhere in His Word that His thoughts were above her thoughts and His ways above her ways. That made sense, considering that He created the entire universe, and He created her.

"Thank you." Rose sighed and smiled. "Not everyone would take the time to pray for a stranger."

The other woman's face grew serious once more. Her

eyes were sharp as she scanned their surroundings in a deceptively casual manner. Seeing no one about, she spoke in urgent tones. "I can help you, too. I know it's none of my business, and my Henry would say I'm putting my nose where it doesn't belong, but I simply have to ask where you got that shiner."

Juliana's hand went to her mouth in surprise. She'd forgotten all about the bruises. What could she possibly say? Certainly not the truth! She couldn't bring herself to outright lie to this kind woman, however. Think, Juliana, think!

"I know it looks bad—" she held Rose's concerned gaze. "You must believe me, however, when I say that Evan would never hurt me. He's a good man."

And she realized that she meant it. Deep down, Evan *was* a good man. He was guilty of making bad choices, of course. But he had admitted to being a Christian and was even familiar with the Holy Scriptures. At some point he'd lived a normal life. How she wished she'd met him back then. Maybe they would've had a chance.

Rose was waiting for her to continue, uncertainty etched in her features.

"There was another man." Joy stirred in her lap and rubbed her eyes with her fists. "Evan rescued me from him."

"Oh." Rose looked at a loss for words, but she appeared to accept Juliana's assertion. "Well, then, I'm glad he was there to protect you."

"Yes," Juliana murmured, dropping her gaze, "me, too."

She hadn't thought about it in quite that way. In an ironic twist, Evan was now her protector.

"Momma."

Juliana looked down into eyes the color of melted chocolate and smiled. The little girl popped her thumb into her mouth and started sucking, content to stay in Juliana's lap. Her wide, curious eyes stared unblinking up at her. Juliana must have passed the inspection, for Joy's lips curled up in an impish grin. Her heart melted at the sight. What a treasure!

A movement at the edge of her vision snagged her attention. It was Evan, returning with an armful of kindling. His intense gaze was centered on her, but he was too far away for her to catch his expression. He was probably wondering what they were discussing so intently.

Juliana watched him drop the sticks and broken branches in a heap before heading their way. Dusting the dirt from his shirt and pants, he walked with long, purposeful strides. There wasn't an ounce of fat on his muscular frame.

"Ladies." He tugged on the brim of his hat, his larkspur blue eyes unreadable as his gaze scanned Juliana's face and dropped to the child in her lap. "Juliana, may I speak with you for a moment?"

"Up!"

All three adults turned their gazes to the little girl, who'd extended her arms in Evan's direction.

Lifting her head, Juliana bit her lip to ward off a grin. Evan looked stricken.

Before he could respond, Joy scrambled off Juliana's lap and tugged on his pants leg. "Up! Pwease!"

"Joy, Mr. Harrison is busy—" Rose began.

"It's all right," he said. Reaching down, he scooped her up and held her against his chest. The toddler and outlaw stared at each other, taking each other's measure. Then, to everyone's shock, Joy slapped a noisy kiss on his cheek and giggled. His low rumble of laughter mingled with hers, a delightful sound to Juliana's ears. She and Rose shared a smile. They watched as Joy laid her head on his shoulder, her tiny arm curling around his neck.

Serious once more, Evan's gaze found Juliana's. The look was full of questions she couldn't answer.

She closed her eyes and relived the moments leading up to his kiss. He'd been talking in that honeyed voice he reserved for those times he wanted to charm her. His breath had fanned out across her mouth, teasing her. His lazy caress had driven all rational thought from her mind. Unable to move, she'd stood mesmerized by his touch and the promise in his eyes.

Evan Harrison might not pose a threat to her physical well-being, but he was downright dangerous to her heart. He had pledged to protect her, yes, but he didn't care about her. Getting her home safe was all that mattered to him. He considered it his duty and his responsibility. He regretted having played a part in her kidnapping and was trying to make things right.

The fact that he'd taken such liberties with her when he had no intention of furthering their relationship angered her. How could he be so casual with his affection…so careless with her heart? Juliana decided then and there to keep him at arm's length. If she allowed him continued access to her body, her heart would no doubt succumb and she'd find herself in love with an outlaw.

She opened her eyes to find him still watching her. Her lungs suddenly seemed devoid of air. He held her captive without laying a hand on her! No. She was through being toyed with.

Jumping to her feet, Juliana murmured an excuse to

Rose and strode away, her head held high. How dare he toy with her?

"Juliana, wait!"

Ignoring him, she continued walking away from camp.

"I'll take her," she heard Rose say.

Gritting her teeth, she fought to keep the tears at bay. Why did she allow him to affect her? Her inexperience with men, perhaps? Or was it him in particular?

"Juliana, please stop and talk to me." Evan was right behind her, following closely but making no move to stop her. "I'll follow you back to Gatlinburg if I have to. You know I'm stubborn enough to do it."

Stopping abruptly, she whirled to confront him. "Can't I have a few moments alone?"

He stood a foot away, hands on his hips, boots planted wide as if braced for a fight. "Not out here, you can't. It isn't safe."

"Being with you isn't safe," she retorted, instantly wishing she could call the words back.

"What's that supposed to mean?" He dropped his hands to his sides, confusion written all over his face.

At the appeal in his eyes, the fight went out of her. Juliana chose to be upfront with him. "I'm not experienced in matters of the heart, Evan. I have a handful of male friends and acquaintances, but I haven't experienced a serious courtship. When you kissed me, I—" She closed her eyes and blew out a breath. "I thought that my first kiss would be with a man I love. A man I intended to marry."

"And instead it was with me," he stated flatly, an odd glint of hurt in his eyes. "I think I understand now why you're angry. I apologize, Juliana. I overstepped my bounds. It won't happen again."

Instead of bringing satisfaction, his words tore at her.

It's for the best, a quiet voice reminded her. If they kept their distance from each other, she would be able to get through the next few days with her heart intact. Then she could return to her old life with no regrets.

Squaring her shoulders, she pushed the words through her lips. "Thank you, Evan. I knew you'd understand."

He tugged the brim of his hat down low, his manner all cool formality. "We'd better start back. Mr. Talbot will be wondering what happened to that coffee I promised him."

He motioned for her to go in front of him, which she did with reluctance. Conscious of his eyes upon her as they walked through the ankle-high grass, she kept her back stiff and shoulders straight. The exposed skin at her nape prickled as if his gaze was a physical touch. When the pond came into view, Juliana sprinted to reach the edge, leaving Evan behind.

She scanned the rocks and sandy soil for a long, smooth stick. When she'd found one, she crossed the field to where Rose and Joy sat on a blanket sharing a canteen of water.

"Do you know how to fry frogs' legs?" Juliana asked.

Shading her eyes, Rose grinned up at Juliana. "I do. Do you think you can catch enough for all of us?"

"I could if Matt helped me. Would Mr. Talbot mind my borrowing him for an hour?"

The dark-haired woman's head bobbed. "Henry's fond of anything battered and fried. I can fry up some hush puppies, along with some taters and onions my sister insisted on giving us."

"If I have time, I'll hunt for berries to serve as dessert."

"Sounds good to me." Rose tickled the little girl's tummy. "What do you say, Pumpkin?"

Joy nodded. "Yum!"

Juliana smiled down at them. "I'd better get started if we want to eat before dark."

She found Matt in the shade of poplar trees, brushing down the horses. His father was nearby, sorting their supplies. Once she explained her plan, Henry gladly gave his permission. While Matt didn't jump up and down for joy, she sensed his eagerness. He offered to use the knife his pa had given him to sharpen their sticks. Juliana could tell he was proud of that knife. He was a sweet boy, caught in the awkward transition from a child to a young man.

While she and Matt gigged for frogs, Evan started a fire and made coffee. Determined not to glance his way, she kept her head down and eyes on the water. But her ears strained for the sound of his low-timbered voice. To the casual observer, she no doubt appeared to be relaxed and happy. Nothing could be further from the truth.

Juliana was tense, her stomach as jumpy as the frogs leaping about trying to avoid their spears. Her head ached from holding back the tide of tears. Her emotions were a raw, jumbled mess.

"Dear Lord," she whispered, "I need wisdom."

"Did you say something, Miss Juliana?" Matt balanced on a rock nearly submerged in the water. His pants legs were rolled up to his knees, and he was barefoot. His hair was dark and wavy like his sister's, but instead of brown eyes, his were green. Henry and Rose Talbot had been blessed with adorable kids.

"I was praying out loud."

He held his spear aloft. "My ma does that a lot."

"What about you?"

"Nah. I do it mostly in my head." His brows shot up,

and he pointed to a spot near her foot. "Look—there's a five-pounder!"

Juliana looked down and spotted the fat frog. While five pounds might be a stretch, three wouldn't be exaggerating. Moving slowly so as not to frighten it off, she lifted her weapon and, with a swift, sure stroke, plunged it down.

"You got him! You got him!" Matt whirled his arms and nearly fell into the water.

Depositing her latest catch into the pail, she said, "I think we have enough, Matt. I'm going to get these ready for your momma."

Awe filled his eyes. "You mean you're gonna skin them yourself?"

"I'd planned on it. Would you rather do it?"

"But you're a girl!" he blurted out.

She paused in the midst of pulling on her stockings and flashed him an indulgent smile. "And?"

He hesitated. "I thought girls didn't like that sort of thing."

"I don't particularly like the task, but I've done it often enough to get used to it. If I want to eat it, I have to know how to prepare it, right?"

"Right."

She could see that he was mulling this information over. Rising to her feet, she asked, "Would you like to help me?"

"Yes, ma'am." He scrambled onto the bank and started tugging on his socks and boots.

"Carry the pail for me?"

"Yes, ma'am!"

As they searched for a place to work, Juliana couldn't

resist a glance at the fire. Evan was nowhere to be seen. Frowning, she wondered where he had gone.

Rose was peeling a mound of potatoes. Joy was amusing herself by tossing the peelings in all directions. Henry sat on the other side of his daughter, drinking a cup of coffee and listening to her chatter.

An hour passed. Then another. Evan was nowhere to be seen. Juliana was worried. Just because it was daylight didn't mean there weren't wild animals roaming the woods. Their encounter with the black bear flashed through her mind. What if he'd stumbled across another one?

Or worse, what if Lenny Fitzgerald had caught up to them? The thought of Evan in danger made her heart race. By the time she and Matt were finished, she was trembling with apprehension.

"Are you all right, Miss Juliana?"

Washing her hands in the shallow water, she looked over her shoulder at the concerned boy. "Why do you ask?"

"You're awful pale," he said in a serious tone. "And you got quiet all of a sudden."

Juliana felt bad about causing him alarm. She mustered up a fleeting smile. "I'm sorry, Matt. I guess I was thinking too hard about something." She walked over to where he was crouched down and placed a hand on his shoulder. "Thank you for your help this afternoon."

He beamed up at her. "You're welcome."

With a squeeze and a pat, she picked up the pail containing the frogs' legs and took it over to Rose. Her legs were unsteady, and she felt as if she might lose her lunch.

"Juliana!" Rose scrambled to her feet and took the pail

from her. "Sit down right here in the shade while I pour you a drink of water. You look parched."

Juliana sank to her knees, accepting the tin cup pressed into her hand and sipping the cool liquid. She untied her bonnet with her free hand, slipped it off and placed it in her lap.

"I hope you didn't get too hot," Rose commented as she resumed her task. "Would you like a cool compress for your forehead?"

"No, thank you. The water is helping." She met Henry's gaze. "Do you know where Evan went?"

"He went looking for berries," Henry's eyes twinkled. "Heard you had a hankerin' for dessert."

Juliana didn't know what to think. Evan was out there searching for berries in order to please her? That meant that, in a roundabout way, it was her own fault she was sick with worry.

"He's been gone a long time, don't you think?" She brushed a black ant off the corner of the blanket.

"Your husband should be along shortly," he assured her. "Don't worry, he's got protection."

She didn't respond, merely sipped more water. A weapon wouldn't do him any good if he didn't have time to draw it.

Father God, my thoughts are spiraling out of control. You know exactly where he is and what he's doing. Keep him safe. I ask this in Jesus's name, Amen. Oh, and please help me not to worry.

Evan stared down at the smoldering fire pit with dismay. Next to it lay an empty whiskey bottle and the remains of someone's supper. Whoever had been there hadn't taken the time to clean up after themselves.

He picked up the bottle and examined it more closely. The label was partly worn off, but he could make out enough of it to know that it was the cheap brand Fitzgerald preferred. Tossing it to the ground, he searched for more clues, but came up empty.

If Fitzgerald was nearby, he'd have to warn Henry Talbot.

The Talbots' arrival had proved to be a blessing. Before now, he hadn't been able to backtrack and check for signs that Fitzgerald was indeed following them. He hadn't wanted to leave Juliana alone and unprotected. With Henry to watch over her, however, he'd felt that he could leave her for a while.

He figured he'd been gone about two hours, enough time to relive their last conversation about a hundred times. Her words had seared him clean through to his soul. He'd never been shot, but he figured the pain of a bullet hole couldn't compare to the wound she'd inflicted.

Juliana hadn't wanted him to kiss her. She said she didn't feel *safe* with him.

Burying his face in Lucky's coarse neck, he groaned. What a mess he'd made of things! Her mistrust dealt a harsh blow to his honor. Evan would die before forcing himself on a woman.

Slamming his hat on his head, he swung into the saddle and turned Lucky in the direction of camp.

Memories of the kiss resurfaced. Juliana had been irritated with him beforehand, but she'd responded to his touch. Hadn't she? Had he imagined the longing in her eyes?

His grip tightened on the reins. One thing was for certain—he would not kiss her again unless she asked him to. And, knowing Juliana, that day would likely never come.

* * *

Juliana paced before the fire, stopping every few moments to search the darkness and listen for the sound of a rider approaching. Her nerves were stretched to the limit. If Evan didn't show up soon, she would borrow one of Henry's horses and go search for him herself.

Her imagination was running wild, dreaming up all sorts of reasons why he hadn't returned. Fear taunted her, robbing her of peace.

Supper had turned out to be a huge disappointment. The food Rose worked so hard to prepare hadn't tempted her a bit. For Rose's sake, she'd managed to eat a portion of her meal. Even with that small amount, her stomach had cramped up and she'd resorted to sipping coffee.

The other couple had done their best to keep her mind off Evan. They entertained her with stories of the children's antics. They were kind people who shared her love for the Lord. She was thankful for their companionship.

Throughout the evening, Henry hadn't appeared at all concerned over Evan's absence, but Rose hadn't been able to hide her unease.

"Juliana?"

Stopping short, she shot the other woman a hopeful look. "Anything?"

With a sympathetic smile, Rose shook her head. Black curls framed her face and spilled over her shoulders, making her appear ten years younger. Juliana thought she was a handsome woman.

"Would you like for me to pray with you?" Rose asked.

"That would be nice."

Rose approached and, clasping Juliana's hands, she began to pray for Evan's safety and swift return. For Juliana, she prayed for peace and faith in God's goodness.

"Thank you, Rose. I've only known you a day but I already consider you a friend."

Rose's face lit up, warming Juliana. "Not only are we friends, but sisters in Christ."

The weight of her and Evan's deception weighed heavily on her conscience, but she couldn't tell Rose the truth. Not yet. Perhaps someday, when the time was right, she would confide in her new friend and ask for forgiveness.

"The children are already asleep, but Henry and I will be up awhile longer. Just so you know, Henry plans on staying awake until Evan shows up."

"I'll be awake, too. I doubt I'll sleep this night."

"Try not to worry, Juliana." She spoke with conviction. "From what I've seen, it's obvious that Evan loves you dearly. He'll fight to get back to you with everything in him."

Juliana bit her lip. If only he truly did love her. If only he wasn't an outlaw. If only...

"I hope you're right," she sighed, her heart heavy.

"According to Henry, I'm always right," Rose grinned and patted her arm. "Wake me if you need to. I won't mind."

"I'll do that," she agreed. "Good night."

"Good night."

Juliana watched her walk back to where they'd bedded down on the far side of the fire. She spoke to Henry, who turned and waved. Juliana lifted her hand in a limp wave and resumed her pacing.

Chapter Twelve

Exhaustion threatened to overtake Evan. His lower back ached from sitting in the saddle for hours on end, and his head pounded from lack of food. At this late hour, hunger was the only thing keeping him awake. He tried to remember what he'd eaten for lunch and realized he and Juliana had skipped it. He wondered if she'd thought to save him a plate from supper, or if she'd thought about it and decided to let him fend for himself.

The light from the fire was a welcome sight. Sensing water and rest were within reach, his horse cantered into the campsite, arriving winded and nearly tossing Evan to the ground with his abrupt stop.

"Whoa there, big boy." He spoke in low tones so as not to wake the others. He balanced his hat on the saddle horn and ran his fingers through his hair.

Sliding out of the saddle, he jerked at the unexpected sound of Juliana's voice directly behind him.

"Where have you been?"

He turned to face her, taken aback by her undisguised anger. Her eyes were enormous in her colorless face.

Tendrils had escaped the once-tidy bun, and there was a smudge of dirt on her chin. She looked fit to be tied.

"Do you realize how worried I—*we* have been?"

Evan stared down at her. The desire to hug away her worries was strong, but he knew she wouldn't welcome it. As hard as it was, he turned his back on her and began to see to his horse, speaking over his shoulder as he worked.

"I'm sorry about that, but I had my reasons."

Silence greeted his remark. Then, "And what might those be, may I ask?"

"Fitzgerald," he grunted, lifting the saddle and dropping it on the ground nearby. His glance flicked to her face, then away. "He's on our trail." He removed the saddle blanket from Lucky's back.

"Did you see him?"

"Nope."

"Then how—"

"Whiskey bottle." He brushed the black's coarse hair until it shined in the low light. "I know the brand he drinks. That, and the place was a mess. Typical of him."

When she didn't respond, Evan paused. Heaving a sigh, he slowly turned around. Fear was written all over her. When he noticed her trembling, his willpower took a nosedive. Still, he managed to hold back.

"Please try not to worry, Juliana." He gazed deep into her eyes, trying to impart comfort without actually touching her. "He'll have to go through me to get to you."

"That's what I'm afraid of," she whispered.

Evan's fists clenched. He swallowed hard. How much was a man supposed to take? He wasn't made of steel.

"I don't plan on losing, darlin'," he drawled, his voice a soft caress.

"Evan, I—"

"Glad to see you made it back." Henry strode up and clapped him on the shoulder. "Everything all right?"

"Actually, I need to speak with you." He glanced at Juliana. "Do you happen to have any leftovers? I'm starving."

She stared at him. "I'll get a plate ready for you. How about coffee as well?"

He flashed her a grateful smile. "I'd like that, if you're not too tired."

"I'm too wound up to be tired."

"You can keep me company while I eat then."

With an arched brow, she whirled away and went to ready the food. He stared after her, content simply to watch her move about. Henry cleared his throat, and, pulling his gaze away, Evan began to lay out the facts.

After stoking the fire, Juliana set the coffee on to heat. The night air was fresh and sweet and pleasant. Crickets chirped. The fat, luminescent moon cast a glow over the land as mist rolled in across the pond.

Her eyes drank in the sight of Evan, safe and sound in her presence. In the pale moonlight, she could make out his profile as he spoke with Henry. Wide forehead, straight nose, angled jaw, determined chin. His short black hair lay smoothly against his head.

His bearing spoke of self-assurance and resolve. Did he fear nothing?

Her own battle with fear had left her limp and worn out. It had taken her on a wild ride that day—from the heights of worry to the depths of despair. She knew that God had not given her a spirit of fear, but of power and of a sound mind. Instead of trusting in Him, however, she'd allowed herself to become consumed with the emotion.

Now there was new reason to fear—Lenny Fitzgerald was hot on their trail.

God, I'm so confused. I'm falling in love with one outlaw and being hunted by another. Where are You in all of this? How will I find my way?

Juliana missed her family, especially her sister, Megan, and her cousin, Josh. Megan was a good listener, and her faith was solid. As roommates, it was their habit to confide in each other while everyone else slept. In the comfort of their beds, they often talked long into the night. Megan would surely have something constructive to say concerning Juliana's growing attachment to Evan. Josh was a good listener, too. He gave sound advice from the male perspective.

She wondered what they were doing at that moment. No doubt her entire family was in turmoil over her disappearance. She wondered if there were men still searching for her. She knew Josh would never give up. Her cousin would search until he found her.

Josh and Evan were alike in that they were both determined men. Once their purpose was set, they would do anything to accomplish it. If the circumstances had been different, she had no doubt the two would've been great friends. As things stood, she would have a hard time convincing her cousin not to shoot the man who'd kidnapped her.

Evan was saying good-night to Henry, who looked tense. Evan would've warned him of the danger without telling him the whole truth about their situation. She prayed that no harm would come to the Talbot family. She wouldn't be able to live with the guilt if Fitzgerald harmed her new friends.

Lowering his tall frame to the ground, Evan propped

his arms on his bent knees and stared intently at her. "Are you all right?"

"I'm fine." She focused on pouring them each a cup of coffee, all the while avoiding his direct gaze.

"Are you still angry at me?"

As she handed a cup to him, his fingers closed over hers. A jolt of awareness shot through her. Her gaze flew to his face. Carefully releasing her fingers while still holding onto the cup, his expression became guarded and his eyes watchful.

"Well?" he prompted. "Are you?"

"I'm not angry. I reacted out of fear, I suppose."

His dark gaze roamed her face. "Does that mean you care what happens to me, Juliana?"

She stiffened, her mind scrambling for a proper response. Had she been that obvious? "Of course I care for your safety," she stammered. "If something happened to you, who would take me home?"

He winced as if she'd inflicted physical pain. "That's right. I'm your ticket home."

For the second time that day, Juliana wished her words had been left unspoken. She'd hurt him. "I didn't mean that how it sounded, Evan. Really—"

He held up a hand. "You don't have to explain. I understand."

"Evan, please—"

With a feather-light touch of his finger, he lifted her chin. "I wasn't expecting a declaration of love, Juliana."

Dropping his hand, he turned his head to stare into the fire.

Juliana squeezed her eyes shut. She'd led him to believe he was merely a means to an end. Her ticket home, as he put it. That was a lie. Against her better judgment, she had begun to care deeply for him. Worrying and fretting about his whereabouts all evening had brought that fact to light.

"Why do you associate with men like Fitzgerald?" she said suddenly. "You're nothing like them."

He sipped his coffee. "As I said earlier, it's a temporary thing."

"Is it the money?"

He shot her a look of dismissal. "I don't need money."

"What is it you need, Evan?"

He didn't speak for the span of a few seconds. The smile he summoned up bordered on a grimace. "I need to eat, Irish. That's it."

Frustration bubbled up deep inside, and she bit back a retort. Why couldn't he trust her? If he didn't do it for the money—and she'd seen the evidence of that back at the cabin where he'd left the money from the mercantile heist—then what was his motivation? Was he a thrill seeker? Or was it something else entirely? What had driven Evan Harrison to leave his farm for a life of crime?

Juliana wanted desperately to press the issue, but the circles of exhaustion under his eyes and the weariness in his posture aroused her compassion. He was spent. And hungry. This conversation could wait until later.

Grabbing a square cloth, she lifted his trencher from the coals and handed it to him. "I hope you like frogs' legs. Matt and I caught them."

"Sure do." He accepted the trencher with eagerness. "I'll bet Matt had a great time." He bit into one and heaved a contented sigh. "This is the best meal I've had in a long time. Thank you."

"Rose prepared it—not me."

"Yes, but you helped catch the critters. Something else Josh taught you?"

"Yes." She smothered a yawn, and he looked up.

"You're tired," he stated. "Go to bed."

"I can wait until you're finished."

"I'm gonna be up awhile, so you go on ahead. It's been a long day."

She brushed the escaped tendrils away from her face. "Aren't you tired?"

His mouth full of food, he swallowed and wiped his mouth with his handkerchief. "I am, but considering Fitzgerald is out there, I think it's wise if someone stands guard."

"But you've been in the saddle all day!"

"It's just for a couple of hours. Henry's gonna take the second shift."

"I suppose you'll want to sleep in tomorrow morning."

"I was planning on it, yes," he said wryly. "Is that okay with you? Or do you have plans for me that can't wait until after breakfast?"

"No, no plans." She yawned for the second time in five minutes.

"Good night, Juliana." His tone left no room for argument.

"Good night, Evan."

Juliana hadn't been able to sleep for thoughts of Evan. The long night of tossing and turning had left her feeling out of sorts. What was driving him? What was he hiding? Frustration with him, his refusal to trust her and her own wayward heart bubbled up within her.

With jerky movements she scrubbed the pots clean, but her attention was not on the task at hand. Like a magnet, her gaze was drawn repeatedly to his sleeping form and the black boots propped a few feet away. Her thoughts turned to the paring knife she'd slipped in her pocket at breakfast. Could she really do this?

After all she'd been through, Juliana felt as if she deserved some answers. And if Evan refused to give her the information she sought, then she'd just have to take it upon herself to find it. Her mind made up, she wiped her hands dry and checked to see whether or not the others were watching. They seemed to be sufficiently occupied.

She didn't give herself time to change her mind. She approached Evan with cautious steps, her gaze on his relaxed features. He didn't stir. He was so handsome, perhaps even more so now that he was unguarded and peaceful. Her heart gave a painful twinge. She felt horrible doing this, as if she herself were a criminal. The last thing she wanted to do was hurt him. If only Evan would confide in her...

Fat chance. Ignoring the warning voice inside her head, she scooped up the boots and hurried to an area of tall grass near the water's edge and sank down, her back to camp. The knife poised in midair, she hesitated. Was this really the right thing to do? After all, she was about to destroy his property. There would be no repairing the lining, so he would know it had been tampered with. And who else but her would do such a thing?

Juliana worried her bottom lip, debating. No matter the consequences, she *had* to know. Perhaps this *thing,* whatever it was, would give her some insight into what he was hiding.

Her mind made up, she sliced through the stitches. Her hands were unsteady as she explored the lining with her fingers. It took a few tries, but she eventually managed to retrieve the object.

A sheriff's badge. She faltered, her stomach tightening. No. It couldn't be.

"What do you think you're doing?"

Her heart slammed against her chest at the sound of Evan's deep voice directly behind her. She clutched the star in her fist and bolted to her feet.

He looked grim. Dark brows winged low, his mouth was turned down in intense displeasure.

"I—I—" she stammered, her mind a complete blank.

His hands on his hips, he waited for her answer. There was no avoiding the issue. He could plainly see what she was doing. She stuck her hand out, palm open, the gold star shining in the light.

"How did you get this, Evan?" she demanded, suddenly angry. Had he lied to her? "Please tell me you didn't kill a lawman and then hid the evidence."

She held her breath as she waited for his response, half-afraid to hear it. She couldn't tell by his expression what he was thinking. That frustrated her.

"I've never killed a man," he said slowly, his eyes narrowing, "I thought I made that clear."

"So why are you carrying a badge around in your boot? Whose is it?"

"I'd like to know how you found it. Do you make a habit of examining men's footwear?"

Her cheeks heated. "Absolutely not. I was trying to move your boots out of the rain yesterday when I discovered it. You were asleep at the time."

With a backward glance over his shoulder, he advanced toward her. He held his hand out. "May I have that back now?"

Reluctantly, she relinquished it. He brushed past her and, scooping up the knife, shot her a look of exasperation before dropping it in his pocket. Then he bent to tug on his boots. When he straightened, his jaw was set.

He came to stand directly in front of her. "I understand your need to know the truth. I'd do the same thing if I were in your position. But let me make myself very clear—" his blue eyes skewered her "—don't put your nose where it doesn't belong. My business is just that—mine."

His words hurt. "Are you threatening me?" she asked incredulously.

His mouth firmed. "Call it whatever you want, Juliana."

Spinning on his heel, he strode away without another word.

Juliana watched him leave, her mouth hanging open. What in the world? She'd expected his anger, but threats? It didn't make sense. He hadn't been that abrupt with her since the first day.

She was no closer to the truth. In fact, the badge had only sparked more questions.

She stamped her foot in frustration. Why did he have to be so stubborn?

Evan tried to smother the annoyance roiling in his gut. She had some nerve! Why couldn't she leave well enough alone?

The badge was safe in his pants pocket. For now. He shook his head in disgust. He'd thought he'd found the perfect hiding place. Either he was that bad or she was that good.

He strode back to camp and quickly rolled his bedroll

into a tidy bundle. What he really wanted to do was go back to sleep. He'd gone to bed with a raging headache. The long rest hadn't helped this time. It felt like an axe was being driven into the base of his skull.

Retrieving his shaving kit, he walked to the opposite side of the lake to shave. As soon as he was finished, he would get a cup of coffee and a plate of food. Maybe that was the reason he felt out of sorts this morning.

His thoughts strayed again to Juliana. He could tell her everything, he supposed.

Yet something inside him resisted. If she knew the truth, there would be no more barriers. No reasons to keep her distance. No more defenses.

The walls protecting his heart were not rock-solid. Against his better judgment, he already cared more than was wise. If he told her the truth now, he wasn't so sure he could remain detached. And falling in love was *not* an option.

By the time he finished shaving, Evan realized that breakfast would have to wait. He needed to lie down again or risk collapsing in a heap. He just barely made it back. As it was, he didn't have the strength to fix his blankets, so he stretched out in the grass and promptly fell into a dark oblivion.

A feather brushed over his nose. Lifting a limp hand, Evan batted it away and turned onto his side, his arm cushioning his head. Sleep sucked him back down.

A feather tickled his ear. Grumbling at the disturbance, he swatted again. All he wanted was to sleep in peace. He felt as if he'd been flattened by a runaway wagon.

"Baba!"

A child's voice interrupted his dreams and a warm weight plumped down onto his rib cage. Jerked awake, he opened his eyes in time to see a curly haired moppet tumble sideways into the grass. Unfazed, she scrambled on top of him once more, her chubby hands clutching his blue cotton shirt for balance. Leaning in close, her brown eyes were large with curiosity as she gazed at him.

"Fafa!"

Careful not to dislodge her, he maneuvered himself onto his back. She picked up a broken willow branch and waved it in the air.

Studying the little girl, he was struck by her sweet face and wide-eyed curiosity. Her sunny yellow frock combined with her large, heavily lashed brown eyes and coffee-colored curls put him in mind of the tall sunflowers growing along the far edge of his property.

Ah, to be a child again, innocent and free of the worries of this world.

She slid off his chest and toddled in the direction of the water. Evan sat up and pushed a hand through his rumpled hair. He had no idea how long he'd been out.

He tracked the little girl with his gaze. She was headed for the wildflower patch, no doubt drawn by the rainbow of bright colors—blue, red, yellow, pink and purple blossoms swaying in the wind.

The girl's mother was hunched over the fire, stirring the contents of the iron kettle. Henry sat nearby sharpening his knives. Matt wasn't in sight, nor was Juliana.

He stood and ambled after the child. She wasn't near the water, but snakes liked to hide in tall grass and he didn't want to take any chances.

On her knees in the midst of the wildflowers, she buried her nose in the fragrant blossoms. Occasionally, her tiny pink tongue jetted out to lick a petal. He shook his head in amusement. When she reached for a pale pink, bell-shaped flower, he hurried to warn her.

Squatting to her level, he said, "Hey, princess, don't mess with that one," pointing to the cluster of foxgloves. "These flowers will make your tummy hurt real bad. Don't touch them and don't put them in your mouth."

"Fafa?" She quirked her head, her tiny brow wrinkled in dismay.

Flower? He pointed again. "Fafa no good."

A shadow fell across his body.

"When did you learn baby talk?"

Despite his irritation with her, pleasure curled through him at the sound of her lyrical voice. "How long have I been asleep?"

"A long while."

When he rose to greet her, black spots danced before his eyes and he swayed. He squeezed his eyes shut in hoping that the light-headed sensation would pass.

"What's wrong?" Juliana moved closer. Her slender hand closed over his wrist, thrilling him despite his discomfort.

"Probably stood up too fast," he muttered, pinching the bridge of his nose between his thumb and finger. His head throbbed.

He opened his eyes and was relieved to find his vision clear. Juliana's face was within touching distance, her forehead puckered in concern. Pale eyelashes framed dark green irises, tiny flecks of gold reflected by the shafts of sunlight peaking through the puffy clouds overhead. A breeze picked up, teasing strands of hair from the neat bun at her nape.

"Are you okay now?"

"I'm fine."

A tug on his pants leg had him looking down. The little girl held her hands up to him. "Up!"

"I guess that means she wants me to hold her again, huh?" he said, bending to pick her up.

"Wait, Evan," Juliana cautioned, "are you able to carry her? She may look light, but she's not."

With the girl perched in his arms, he turned to Juliana. "I'm fine, really. Let's deliver this bundle to her parents. My morning coffee is long overdue."

Gauging from the expression on her face, Juliana wasn't convinced. She walked beside him without speaking. The gusts of wind took the edge off the humidity. He eyed the darkening sky. They were likely in for a squall.

"I see you finally decided to roll out of bed, Harrison," Henry called out, his ready smile in place. Evan liked the man and would be sorry when they parted ways.

"I found something that belongs to you." He set the girl down. She hurried to her father's side. Henry set aside his tools to pull her into his lap. Evan nodded to Talbot's wife. "Good morning, Mrs. Talbot."

"I told you to call me Rose," she scolded in a light tone. "Would you like your breakfast now? We saved a plate for you. Bacon, beans and corn bread."

His stomach revolted at the notion of food. "Thank you kindly, ma'am, but I believe I'll just take a cup of coffee if you have any."

Her brows rose in surprise. "Sure, we have plenty."

"I'll get it." Juliana moved to fill a tin cup with the dark brew. When she handed it to him, she lowered her voice. "Are you sure you're okay? It's unusual for you to skip a meal."

He accepted the cup with a nod. "I'm just feelin' a

little off today." He sipped the steaming liquid. "Probably a combination of not eating all day yesterday and not enough sleep."

"Maybe we should stick around here another day," she suggested. "We could leave early tomorrow morning."

She had a point. With the way he was feeling, hitting the trail in this heat held little appeal. Still, he didn't like the idea of sitting in one place with Fitzgerald on their trail. And time was an issue—he needed to get her settled in Cades Cove and then report back to Roberts and the gang.

"Your idea is tempting, but we need to get home." He tried to convey with a look what he couldn't say aloud.

"What's your hurry?" Henry joined them, his daughter on his hip. "Stay with us one more night. It'll give us a chance to visit a bit more before we say our goodbyes."

Evan couldn't think straight, what with the sledgehammer pounding away in his skull. The coffee tasted bitter going down, so he threw it out. Juliana gave him an odd look. He shrugged.

"I can't think…" The edges of his vision went black, and he stumbled back.

"Evan!"

Juliana calling his name was the last thing he heard before he lost consciousness and slid to the ground.

Chapter Thirteen

Juliana reached for him, but wasn't fast enough. He hit the ground hard, his head glancing off a fallen log. A thin stream of red trickled from his temple down past his ear and into his hair.

Alarm spiraling through her, Juliana fell to her knees. "Evan!" She cradled his face in her hands. "Speak to me."

Stepping over his prone body, Henry kneeled, held Evan's wrist and checked his pulse. "Does he have any health problems?"

"No." Evan hadn't mentioned a thing. He seemed so strong and healthy. But she'd only known him a few days. "At least, none that I know of."

Rose rushed up and placed a hand on Juliana's shoulder. "What can I do?"

Her thoughts scattered, Juliana's only focus was on Evan himself.

Henry spoke with utter calm and authority. "We need clean water and bandages for his head wound." Letting go of Evan's arm, Henry placed a hand on his forehead. "His pulse is thready. And he's burning up." He looked at her. "Does he have a tent among his gear?"

"I don't think so."

"You can borrow ours." He gave instructions to his wife. "Have Matt empty the tent of our things and ready a pallet for Evan."

"All right," Rose said before Juliana could protest. "I'll be right back."

With a squeeze of Juliana's shoulder, she left, taking Joy with her.

"You really don't have to do that," she said.

"Evan's ill. He'll need cover if it starts to rain."

"Thank you." She paused. "What do you think is wrong with him?" She tore her gaze away to look at Henry.

Henry's dark eyes were somber. "Could be any number of things. Did he get bit by anything recently?"

"Like a spider?"

He nodded. Her eyes drifted back to Evan's still form. "He didn't say. But he was really tired last night. We didn't talk long before I went to bed."

Rose brought the bandages and a bowl of clean water. She offered to clean the wound, but Juliana declined, preferring to perform the task herself. With great care, Juliana cleansed the gash and wrapped long strips of cloth around his head, tying it off tight enough to stem the flow of blood. She was thankful the wound wasn't deep and wouldn't require a sewing kit. She was in no mood to sew his skin back together. She was worried by the fact that not once during her ministrations did he flinch or flutter an eyelid.

"I have an idea." Henry's voice broke into her reverie. "Once we get him inside the tent, why don't you undress him and look for marks or spots that look suspicious."

Dread filled her as his words registered. Setting the bowl aside, she looked over at him. "I can't do that."

"Why not? You're his wife."

"Well, I—" She scrambled for a solid reason for her refusal and came up blank. As much as she wanted to help, she couldn't bring herself to do as he suggested. "Could you do it, Henry? You probably have a much better idea of what to look for than I do."

He studied her a moment, and Juliana felt a flush creep up her neck.

"Yes, of course." He moved to rise. "Will you stay here with him while I help Matt?"

"I won't leave him."

"Holler if there's any change."

"Okay."

She scooted closer and gently took his head in her lap, smoothing his hair with trembling fingers. Against the dark material of her dress, his face was deathly pale. His skin was dry and hot. His chest rose and fell in shallow, rapid breaths.

"What's wrong with him, Lord?" she whispered, brushing aside the wetness on her cheeks. "I'm scared."

She checked the bandage. So far, there was no sign of blood soaking through the thick cotton. A small blessing.

Juliana racked her brain, trying to think if Evan had eaten anything odd in the last day or so. As far as she knew, he'd eaten the exact same food as she. Unless he'd eaten something on the trail he'd failed to mention.

The wind picked up, tugging at her skirt and whipping strands of hair across her face. Slate-gray clouds swirled in the sky overhead, blocking out the sunshine. Henry and Matt worked with quick, efficient movements to ready the tent. She prayed the rain would hold off.

Rose brought Juliana a bowl of clean, cool water and strips of cloth with which to bathe Evan's face and neck. With a light touch, she swabbed his forehead, cheeks, chin and neck. She unbuttoned the top buttons of his sky-blue shirt and spread the material wide so that she could access more skin. Curiosity overriding common sense, she slipped her hand beneath his shirt and flattened her palm against the hard muscles, the light covering of hair teasing her fingers. His heart thumped an angry rhythm, his skin fiery to the touch. Yanking her hand back, she ignored the flare of heat in her middle.

"Miss Juliana?"

She jerked at the sound of Matt's voice behind her, the sudden movement jarring Evan's head. He groaned but didn't open his eyes. "Yes, Matt?"

"The tent's ready."

Henry rushed over. Between the three of them, they were able to lift his body off the ground and carry him to the tent beneath a magnolia tree. With the thick, inter-woven branches, it was a good choice. Rainwater would sluice off the outer leaves and flowers onto the ground, leaving the inner circle of ground beneath the branches relatively dry. They settled him inside the cozy interior on a soft pallet.

Juliana stopped Matt's departure with a hand on his arm. "The water is already tepid. Would you mind re-filling it?"

His dark eyes were wide with uncertainty. "Yes, ma'am."

"Thanks."

The sound of Evan's labored breathing stirred fear in Juliana's soul. Whatever was ailing him was serious. Miles from the closest town and doctor, they would have to depend on herbs or plants to provide a remedy.

"Mrs. Harrison." Henry spoke as he untied Evan's bootlaces. "I'm going to check him now. Do you plan to stay or would you rather wait outside?"

"I'll go speak with Rose." With a last caress of Evan's cheek, she scooted outside and looked up at the dark sky. She thanked God for holding off the weather until Evan was settled. She headed toward the fire where Rose sat with Joy, who was apparently unhappy with the choice of beans for lunch.

"No!" Crossing her arms, the little girl averted her face.

Rose held the spoon aloft, encouraging Joy to eat. She looked up at Juliana's approach. Her black hair was damp with sweat from cooking over the fire. Lowering the spoon to the bowl, she waited for Juliana to speak.

"He's not doing well," she said, discouraged. "I'm worried, Rose. We're out in the middle of nowhere, and we haven't a clue what's wrong with him. He's so hot. If the fever gets out of control—"

"Let's hold off on the what ifs, okay?" Rose held up a hand. "Someone very wise once told me that what ifs open the door to fear. We don't need that. We need clear-headed thinking."

"Of course you're right."

"What's the first thing we need to do?" Rose asked, thinking aloud. She tugged on Joy's shoe. "Come sit next to me, Joy baby." The child obeyed. Intent on watching them, she ate the beans her mother again offered her.

"We have to get that fever down," Juliana uttered on a shaky breath.

"Right. My grandmother used coneflowers for pain and fevers. Have you noticed any growing around here?"

"No, but I haven't been on the lookout for them."

"Why don't you search in this area while I finish feeding Joy? If you don't find any, Henry can look farther out."

Careful to keep the camp in sight, Juliana combed the area for the large purple flower. Her gaze swept across the prairie. With its thigh-high grasses and sparse tree cover, she didn't hold out much hope that she would find what she was looking for. The coneflower was a woodland plant, preferring the shady forest floor to direct sunlight.

In the distance, she spotted Henry leaving the tent. She sprinted toward him and arrived winded.

He was the first to speak, his eyes kind as he looked at her. "I didn't see a thing. Nothing at all that would call for suspicion. He must have some sort of sickness."

"How is he?" Her gaze darted to the opening.

"The same. Fever, shallow breathing." He touched her elbow briefly. "I need to speak with Rose. While I do that, why don't you try to get some water into him?"

"Tell her I didn't find the coneflower."

His mouth drooped. "I will."

Stooping over, she entered the tent and waited for her eyes to adjust to the faint light. He was dressed in his white undershirt. A cheerful red, blue and yellow patchwork quilt covered him to his chest, adding a dash of color to the dim space.

She settled on the pallet and brought his hand to her lap. With her fingertip, she traced the blue veins beneath his tan skin. Testing the weight of it, she took comfort in the strength and capability she knew he possessed. These hands had caught her when she stumbled, comforted her when she cried, held her close when she was afraid. She lifted his hand and pressed her cheek into his palm.

His eyes remained closed, shutting out the rest of the world.

When had his face become so dear? Five days ago, she would've passed Evan Harrison on the street without a second thought. How had he come to mean so much to her in such a short time? A better question would be how had she allowed herself to fall in love with an outlaw? A man who courted danger?

Alice O'Malley had raised her daughters to fear God and live upright, godly lives. She expected her daughters to choose men of moral character and good standing in the community. Her mother would be horrified if she knew that her eldest daughter had fallen in love with the very man who'd kidnapped her.

What was the secret he guarded so closely?

"What are you hiding?" she whispered softly.

The flap lifted, and a stiff wind circled through the space. Henry ducked his head in and beckoned her outside. With reluctance she left Evan's side. Henry and Rose stood side by side waiting to talk to her, while Matt played with his baby sister. Their grave expressions gave her pause.

"Mrs. Harrison," Henry began, "I'm inclined to believe that Evan has contracted the same sickness that swept through my sister-in-law's house. Joy had similar symptoms, but as you can see she's almost recovered."

"Remember I mentioned it yesterday?" Rose prompted.

"Yes, I remember." She kneaded her stiff neck muscles. Dread flooded her entire being. "But she and the others were given medicine to control their fevers, right?"

Husband and wife exchanged a look. "Yes. And the adults fared slightly worse than the children. Took longer to recuperate."

Her heart hammered against her rib cage. "Tell me directly, Henry. Without the medicine, what do you think Evan's chances are of surviving?"

He didn't flinch at her words. "He's young and healthy. If we can bring the fever down and get him to drink plenty of fluids, I believe he has a fighting chance."

A tiny bud of hope burst forth in her heart.

"How are you with a gun?" he asked.

"Me? I know my way around a firearm."

"Good." He lifted a weapon from his left holster and gave it to her. "Don't be afraid to use it."

"What about Matt?"

"Matt has his own rifle."

Her gaze strayed to the boy playing peekaboo with his sister. She prayed he wouldn't be forced to use it. "Evan told you about Fitzgerald, didn't he?"

His lips flattened. "Yes." He shifted, his arm going around his wife's shoulders. "I wouldn't be leaving if it wasn't absolutely necessary. As it is, I'm not going far. I figure it's about an hour's ride to the forest edge. Once there, I'll travel on foot until I find the coneflower. Pray I find it soon, for everyone's sake."

Rose lifted her face to his. "I'll be praying every minute you're gone."

His expression softened, and he dropped a kiss on her cheek. "Thank you, my dear."

"Me, too," Juliana added. "I appreciate all you're doing for Evan."

Settling his hat on his head, he returned, "I know he'd do the same for me."

Juliana recognized the truth of his words. Evan would be quick to help a man in need. She watched the pair walk arm in arm toward the horses, turning away when they embraced. The clouds overhead rushed past without releasing a single drop of water. While the wind was still brisk, it had lessened in the last ten minutes or so. It seemed as if the storm would pass them by. Praise the Lord!

"Oh, Father God, please protect Henry. Again, stay the weather as he searches. Bring him back swiftly, and protect us while we wait. In Jesus's name, Amen."

Juliana headed for the fire, determined to get some broth into Evan. She would do everything in her power to help him get well. The alternative didn't bear thinking about.

Juliana spoke in soothing tones as she coaxed Evan to sip the lukewarm broth. He'd drifted in and out of consciousness as the afternoon wore on, at times mumbling random words she couldn't make sense of. It was suppertime now, around five o'clock or so, she guessed, and the fever still raged through his body.

Holding the cup to his parched lips, she managed to get a bit of the broth into him. She set the cup aside and gently lowered his head back down to the pillow. Then, as she'd done countless times, she dipped the cloth into the water bowl and, wringing out the excess, began to wipe his face. Not that it appeared to be helping.

Outside the tent, the constant wind had given way to occasional gusts. While the sun still hid behind a thick layer of clouds, it hadn't rained. Every now and then, she lifted the flap and peeked out to see if Henry had returned yet. She hoped he hadn't run into bad weather.

Evan couldn't seem to lie still. Restless, he moved his head from side to side. His low moans tugged at her heartstrings. Watching him suffer while she sat helplessly by made her want to weep with frustration.

She leaned in close. One bright spot in this whole ordeal was that she was free to look at him and touch him and speak without reservation. "Evan, darling," she murmured, smoothing his damp hair, "hold on a little while longer. Henry will be back before you know it with that coneflower and you'll soon be on the mend."

She prayed that her words would prove to be true.

The nightmare was back.

James was driving the wagon, minding his own business, when six masked men on horseback emerged from the woods with guns drawn. A mix of anger and disbelief marked his expression. With no choice, he halted the team and faced his enemies with courage. True to his character, he didn't give in. He didn't go down without a fight.

The scene distorted into chaos, and James was lying facedown in the dirt. Evan was there, tugging on his shoulder to turn him over. James flopped over and his hat slipped back. Instead of his brother's dear face, an eyeless skull with a gaping mouth stared up at him.

"James!" His brother's name was ripped from his lips. "Where?"

"Shh," a familiar voice close to his ear soothed, "You're all right. I'm here."

Juliana. At the sound of her sweet voice, the horror of the dream slipped away. Evan tried to say her name, but he couldn't. Blackness overtook him once again.

Henry rode into camp about an hour after supper. She ducked outside as soon as she heard the sound of an approaching rider. Rose walked swiftly over with Joy in her arms. Matt followed close behind.

He dismounted near the tent. One glimpse of his expression was all it took for Juliana's hopes to fly away on the wind.

"You couldn't find it, could you?" Hands clasped at her waist, she braced herself for his answer.

His eyes held a wealth of regret in their dark depths. "I'm sorry, Mrs. Harrison." His gaze flicked to his wife at her gasp of dismay. "I stayed away as long as I dared. I think it may be too late in the season for that particular wildflower, because I didn't see a single one."

"I don't understand," she heard herself saying. "We all asked God to lead you to it. Why didn't He answer our prayers?"

"God always answers our prayers," Henry said kindly, "it's just that sometimes His answer is no."

"Then what are we supposed to do?" she demanded, a single tear sliding down her cheek. "If his fever doesn't break soon, he could—" She clamped her lips shut, her eyes darting to Matt. She couldn't say it in front of the boy.

"One thing we're going to do is continue to pray and ask God to spare Evan's life."

Juliana buried her face in her hands. *Dear Father, I don't understand why You didn't allow Henry to find that flower. Based on Your word, I know in my mind that You love Evan and have a plan and a future for him. But my heart is rebelling, Lord. Help me to trust You, God. Please spare Evan. I love him.*

And now she might not have a chance to tell him. She'd led him to believe that he meant nothing to her. In trying to protect herself, she'd hurt him.

Henry and Rose stepped closer and took turns praying out loud. Her heart heavy, Juliana couldn't stop the tears from coursing down her cheeks. Their heartfelt words of petition humbled her. These relative strangers were pouring their hearts out to God, requesting healing for a man they didn't know. A man they thought was her husband.

Juliana hated that they'd deceived this dear couple. She was tempted to tell them the truth, but felt like she'd be betraying Evan's trust if she did. After all, how would they react when they found out he'd kidnapped her?

Of course, she could tell them the truth without giving them all the details. She made up her mind that if— no, *when*—Evan got well, she would discuss the matter with him.

"Mind if I take a look?" Henry splayed a hand toward the tent.

"Please do."

"Juliana." Rose placed her arm around her shoulders and steered her toward the fire. "You've been in there with him all day. Come and sit in the fresh air awhile. Eat something. It will do you good."

"I don't like to be away from him," she protested.

"Henry will sit with him until you return. He won't be alone."

"Momma." Matt's quiet voice halted their progress. "Can I take Joy to the water's edge and show her the frogs?"

"Yes, you may." She bent to put the girl down. "But don't take your eyes off her."

"I won't, I promise." He held out his hand. "Come on."

Grinning, Joy placed her tiny hand in his.

"Mind your brother, Joy," Rose called after them. "And try not to get wet."

At the fire pit, she pressed a cup of coffee into Juliana's hands. "Have a seat."

"No, thanks. I'd rather stand awhile." Her legs and back were stiff from sitting in that cramped space most of the day. The coffee tasted fresh and strong. She was finally learning to appreciate black coffee.

"So what now?" She faced the other woman. "Do you have any suggestions?"

Rose chewed on her lip. "I know this sounds crazy, but we could try putting him in the shallow end of the pond. Having most of his body submerged in the water might bring his temperature down."

Juliana looked over at the placid water drenched in muted hues of orange-gold. In the distance, the sun was an orange ball hovering above the horizon. Above their heads, the clouds had finally dispersed. The sky was a pale, whitish-blue color. "At this point, I'm willing to try just about anything."

"We'll ask Henry, but not until you've eaten." She passed Juliana a bowl and spoon. "It's not much, but it will fill your stomach."

The aroma of rabbit stew teased her nose and her stomach growled in response. She was hungrier than she'd realized. Eating standing up, she savored every bite of the tender meat, wild mushrooms and ramps.

"Thank you." She licked her lips. "Very tasty. You're a great cook."

"Would you like more? There's plenty to go around."

"I'm tempted, but I think I'll pass for now. Have you eaten yet?"

"Not yet." She tucked a curl behind her ear and blew out a breath. She looked tuckered out. "I was waiting for Henry."

"Why don't you take a couple bowls over there." She hooked a thumb over her shoulder. "Discuss your idea with him while you both eat. You'll be near enough to hear Evan if he calls out." Juliana began gathering the dirty dishes and utensils. "Meanwhile, I'm going to wash the dishes. I feel horrible about leaving all the work for you to do."

"Don't. You've been exactly where you should be—at your husband's side."

Ignoring the twinge of guilt, she paused in the midst of stacking the dishes. "I'm so glad you both are here. I don't know what I would've done if Evan had taken ill when we were alone on the trail. I wouldn't have been able to tend to his needs while trying to hunt for food and cook and wash dishes. I have that much to be thankful for, at least."

Rose sent her a tired smile. "I'm happy God worked it out so that we could be here. I've been in your position before. I know what it's like to be on the receiving end, and it's nice to be able to give back for a change."

"Well, I appreciate all you've done. Now go eat," Juliana insisted. "I'll watch out for the kids."

After a moment's hesitation, Rose dipped a portion for herself and her husband into two bowls. "I'm sure he'll want coffee, too, but it can wait until after we eat."

"I'll leave it, then. Don't rush. Enjoy some time alone with your husband."

"Thank you."

Juliana watched her walk away before turning to her task.

Crouched at the water's edge, Juliana inhaled the fresh air. Although she wanted to be near Evan, it was nice to be outside doing something useful with her hands. The tent was a small, confined space, made smaller by Evan's wide shoulders and long legs.

The children's laughter reached her, followed by sounds of splashing water. Resting her hands on her knees, she watched the brother and sister toss pebbles into the pond. Joy's high-pitched squeals mingled with Matt's carefree laughter. Watching them interact, her thoughts drifted to her own siblings.

In her mind's eye, she summoned a picture of each of her sisters. Jessica and Jane in the kitchen preparing supper, their faces smudged with flour. Megan curled up on the couch with a book, oblivious to everything around her. Nicole sewing in her favorite chair by the window, the picture of a prim and proper young lady.

She missed them   plain and simple. Longed to see them face-to-face. Her heart ached at the fear and worry and pain they must be enduring on account of her disappearance. Her family had no idea whether she was alive or dead. And now that Evan was ill, delaying their arrival in his hometown, they would have to wait and wonder even longer.

The fact that she would see them again in the near future brought her immense comfort.

Evan, on the other hand, wouldn't see his brother again this side of heaven. From the depth of the grief she'd glimpsed in his eyes whenever the subject came up, the two had been extremely close. Considering they'd lost their parents as young men, she could imagine how they'd leaned on each other during that time of loss.

He'd obviously been dreaming about his brother. Could his death be the reason behind Evan's current situation? Juliana realized that she didn't know the details surrounding his passing. She'd neglected to ask.

Clearing her thoughts, she checked on the children and, spotting them chasing a butterfly, continued with her task. By the time she was finished, dusk had settled around her. She called for Matt and Joy to join her, which they promptly did. Upon reaching the fire pit, she noticed the flames had died down so she added a couple of logs to the heap.

"Juliana." Henry and Rose approached. "He's asking for you."

"He's awake?"

"He's groggy. His communication is fuzzy, but he's very clear about his wish to see you."

Her heart skipped a beat. "And the fever? Has it broken?"

"I'm afraid not."

"Rose, I hate to ask…" She indicated the clean dishes.

"I'll put everything away." She gave Juliana a gentle shove. "Go. Be with him."

Gathering her skirts, Juliana jogged across the narrow field. His eyes were open and searching for her when she reached him.

"Juliana?" he rasped, his head turning toward her. His ebony hair was slicked back, his forehead wet with sweat. The strips of cloth holding the bandage in place were twisted from so much movement. She would need to redress the wound soon.

"I'm here." She hurriedly kneeled at his side, her water-splotched skirt a cloud about her knees. She sandwiched his hand between hers.

In his larkspur-blue eyes she saw regret and pain. "I'm sorry."

"Evan," she whispered, her vision blurring with tears, "don't do this."

He licked his dry lips before continuing. "I never should've—" He broke off, too weak to continue, his frustration evident. "Taken you."

Juliana leaned closer, smiling tenderly through her tears. "I'm not sorry."

His lids fluttered closed, and she thought that perhaps he'd drifted back to sleep. Disappointment skittered through her. She wanted, no *needed,* to talk to him.

"You're not?" he grunted after a moment, leveling a look at her.

"You asked me if I care about what happens to you." She dipped her head, focusing on the rapid rise and fall of his chest. "And I led you to believe something other than the truth." Taking a deep breath, she gazed down into his eyes. "I don't regret going to the mercantile that morning. I don't regret our kiss. And, yes, I do care about you."

I love you. But she couldn't say the words aloud. Not yet.

A tiny spark of hope lit in his eyes. "You…forgive… me?"

"Yes, of course," she rushed to say, the corners of her eyes crinkling as she smiled.

His gaze roamed slowly across her face, as if memorizing her features. "You're…beautiful… Irish."

The nickname brought a fresh wave of emotion, and she blinked to dry her eyes. She'd shed more tears in the last several days than she had her entire life!

Scooting closer, she reached for the tin cup. "Try to drink some water, okay?"

His eyes never left her as she cradled his head and helped him drink. "Good nurse," he murmured.

With trembling fingers, she touched his stubbly jaw. "You should rest now."

His fingers gripped hers, his expression turning urgent. "Something I need…tell you." His voice faded and his eyelids drooped. "I'm not…"

Juliana moved closer. "You're not what?" she prompted softly.

When he didn't respond, she realized that he'd fallen asleep. She sat there, watching and waiting for him to stir again. What had he been about to say? Whatever it was would have to wait until he regained consciousness. And by that time he would've probably already forgotten.

Fatigue weighed her down, and she couldn't resist stretching out on the blanket next to him. Just for a few minutes, she told herself, and then she would go and talk to Henry.

Chapter Fourteen

Juliana awoke some time later to the sound of Evan's moans. Through the slim openings in the tent, she could see that it was night. Though exactly how long she'd slept she had no idea.

"C-cold." His teeth chattered, and, because of her close proximity, she felt the tremors that racked his body.

Pushing her unkempt hair out of her eyes, she scrambled to her knees. The kerosene lamp in the corner cast a faint glow across the small interior. She thought his face appeared paler than normal, but it was hard to tell.

His body trembled beneath the single blanket covering him. "P-please…"

"I'll go for more blankets," she reassured him. "I'll be right back."

Outside, she waited for her eyes to adjust before starting across the field to where the Talbots slept near the fire. When she had just about reached them, a tall figure stepped out from behind a tree.

She stopped short, her loud gasp splitting the silence.

"It's me, Henry." He whipped off his hat, but with no

moon in the cloudless sky, his features remained indistinguishable. She recognized his voice, however.

"Henry!" Her hands went to her throat. "You scared the life out of me!"

"I'm sorry," he said, "I didn't mean to startle you. I thought it best to keep watch, considering. Are you all right?"

"I'll be fine," she said, though her heart continued to race. "Evan has the chills. I've come for extra blankets, if there are any to be had."

"Good thing for us, Rose likes to be prepared. She insisted we bring every last one."

"I imagine that when traveling with children, one must expect the unexpected."

He chuckled in the darkness. "Yes, ma'am."

He quickly gathered up the extras while trying not to disturb his slumbering family. He carried the bundle back to the tent for her and helped her cover Evan.

"I don't understand," she said, tucking the material beneath him, creating a cocoon. "How can he be so cold and yet so hot at the same time?"

Resting on her haunches, she looked over at Henry.

"It's his body's way of trying to cool itself. Same thing happened with the others."

"Did Rose talk to you about her idea?"

"She did. I don't think it's wise at this point, what with the chills and all."

Frustration at the whole situation sharpened her tone. "I hate seeing him suffer like this."

"I understand," Henry commiserated. "If it were my Rose lying here sick, well, I don't know if I would've handled it as well as you."

"I don't like feeling helpless." She sighed.

"You're taking care of his needs as best you can, and even though he's unconscious much of the time, I'm certain he senses your presence. That must be a huge comfort to him."

Her gaze slid to Evan's shivering form. "I hope so."

"I'm going to make some sassafras tea." He turned to go. "Maybe that will help."

"It certainly can't hurt. Thank you."

"I'll be back in a jiff."

Juliana scooted next to Evan and tugged the layer of blankets up so that they nearly reached his chin. Placing her palm against his forehead, she found it damp and clammy.

"God in heaven above," she prayed with her eyes shut tight, "I ask You to please spare Evan's life. Give him another chance. Give *us* a chance, if it is Your will. Drive the fever from his body and restore his health. In Jesus's name I pray, Amen."

Time passed slowly. The tremors began to come quicker and harder than before. She hugged him tighter, trying to ease the violence of them. His lips quivered with cold. His moans became low pleadings for the pain to stop.

Juliana cried in earnest, her heart ripping in two. He was getting worse. She feared that she was losing him.

Voices penetrated the fog surrounding his brain. Hushed, worried voices. He tried to concentrate on what they were saying, but his mind wouldn't cooperate.

He couldn't seem to stop shaking. So cold. And weak. He doubted that he could lift his little finger, he was that exhausted.

Where was Juliana? He needed to talk to her. There was so much to say...

The voices were louder now. He focused on the words, stunned to discover that they were praying for him. Begging God for his life. His heart hitched within his breast, unease skittering through his limbs. Was he hovering near death?

He didn't want to die. He wanted to live! Not the way he had before, bent on revenge and consumed with hatred. More than anything, he craved peace. He understood now that God could handle his anger and his grief, but He would not tolerate his rebellion.

It was hard to put his thoughts together, but he prayed as best he could.

Forgive me, Lord, for blaming You for James's death. Forgive me for holding on to the hate in my heart. Help me. I want to be near You as I was before.

At the completion of his prayer, he felt at peace for the first time in almost a year. How he'd missed that sense of calm and comfort only the Lord could bestow. He was forgiven, and that's all that mattered.

Feeling his deep sigh, Juliana lifted her head. His tremors eased.

"What's happening?" Rose asked, in part fearful, in part hopeful.

Juliana felt his forehead again. "Hotter than ever." Disappointment weighed her down.

"We could try willow leaves," Henry said quietly. "I don't know why I didn't think of this before, but my sister used them to make a concoction once when my mother became ill and there wasn't a doctor available. There were weeping willows on our property just like the ones here."

Juliana had never heard of that particular remedy. "You know as well as I do that a homemade remedy can be tricky. Too little and it has no effect. Too much can be deadly. Do you remember if she used the leaves and bark together? And what about the quantity?"

"I was just a boy. I don't remember much about it."

"Are you certain it was a willow tree?" Rose said.

"Absolutely."

"I don't know. It's risky." She looked at Rose. "What do you think?"

"It appears to me he's getting worse, not better. We can either wait and hope he can fight this on his own or try the willow leaves. Henry is positive that's what was given his mother, so we could try a small amount at first."

Juliana studied Evan's still form. The decision was ultimately hers, she knew. She was torn between the need to act and the fear of things going horribly wrong. What if they gave him too much? Or if he had some sort of adverse reaction? She would never be able to forgive herself. On the other hand, if they did nothing and he got worse…

"Let's do it," she blurted before she could change her mind.

Henry moved to get up. "I'll go."

"I'll brew the tea," Rose added.

Needing reassurance, Juliana stopped Rose with a hand on her arm. "Am I doing the right thing?"

"I believe so, yes." She placed her hand over Juliana's. "Remember, God is watching over him."

"I know," she breathed, her attention already on Evan. She hoped she wouldn't regret this decision.

That night was one of the longest in Juliana's life. Despite Henry's urging to get some rest, she refused. Since she'd slept much of the day, she wasn't at all sleepy.

And even if she was, she couldn't leave him. Not until she knew whether or not the willow leaves were going to work.

They managed to get a few cups of the brew into him. While he didn't appear to have a reaction, neither did his condition change. Juliana was growing more frustrated by the minute.

Rose ducked her head in. "Juliana, I made coffee. Why don't you come outside for a little while? You need a break. Fresh air will do you good."

Henry nodded. "Go on. I'll be here."

Evan was sleeping peacefully, so she decided it wouldn't hurt to leave him in Henry's care for a bit.

"It's nearing daybreak." Rose moved back to give her room to exit. "We could start breakfast."

"Hey," Henry spoke up, "both of you stay alert."

Juliana didn't want to think about Fitzgerald, not with Evan lying here so ill. But Henry was right. There was a very real possibility that Fitzgerald would find them. They couldn't let their guard down simply because they were worried about Evan.

"I'll take the gun you loaned me, Henry."

Outside the tent, Rose handed her a cup of steaming hot coffee. "Let's go sit by the pond."

"We'll get eaten up by mosquitoes," she objected. "How about here on this old log?" She indicated a spot not far from the tent. "We'll be close by but still able to see the children."

"That's fine."

They sat and sipped their coffee in companionable silence. Around them the animals began to stir as the darkness slowly lifted.

"How are you holding up?"

Cupping the warm mug in her hands, Juliana turned her head to look at the other woman. "I've been better."

"You're very devoted. You two seem to share a special bond."

The corners of her mouth lifted a fraction at the irony of that statement. "Yes, I guess you could say that. How did you and Henry meet?"

Rose spoke at length about how they'd been neighbors and she'd fancied Henry, but he'd hardly seemed to notice her. Absorbed in Rose's story, Juliana lost track of the time.

"Do you mind my asking how you met?" Rose asked.

At Juliana's uneasy expression, Rose continued, "You seem so well suited is all—that's why I asked. Don't feel as if you have to answer—"

Henry poked his head out, his expression urgent. "Juliana! He's awake!"

In her haste, she toppled her mug, spilling most of the contents on the ground. Her heart in her throat, she rushed to Evan's side. Her sole focus was on Evan, so she didn't notice when Henry left to speak with his wife.

"Juliana?" His deep voice was rough from disuse.

"Oh, Evan, you're awake!" Her first thought was to check his temperature, and she pressed her palm against his forehead. Cool and dry. Thank God! All the stress and worry of the last few days drained from her body.

"Your fever's gone," she whispered.

His clear gaze clung to hers. "What's wrong with me?"

Suddenly self-conscious, she removed her hand and let it fall to her lap. "You've been ill. Do you remember anything at all?"

A wrinkle formed between his brows. "The last thing

I remember is holding Joy. What happened? Did I pass out?"

"Yes, Evan. You've been in and out of consciousness for the last two days."

"Two days?" His eyes widened. When he tried to sit up, Juliana put restraining hands on his shoulders.

"Don't try to sit up. You don't have the strength—"

"We've lost a lot of time." He struggled a moment then fell back with a grunt. "Why am I so weak?" As was to be expected, he was irritated and confused.

She smoothed the blankets across his chest out of habit. He watched her every move. "Your body has been fighting this sickness. On top of that you haven't eaten anything."

"You're wearing a gun," he stated, his eyes going dark with concern. "Has Fitzgerald been here?"

"No, it's just a precaution."

"Have there been signs of anyone around the camp?"

Juliana covered his hand with hers in an effort to reassure him. "No. Stop worrying. Henry and I both carry weapons. We're being careful."

His fingers gripped hers. "How experienced are you, though? Fitz is a professional."

She couldn't help but smile. "You're forgetting my cousins."

"Oh." His expression eased. "Right."

"Your only concern right now should be regaining your strength."

His gaze roamed her face. "I heard your prayers. That meant a lot. I said one of my own as well."

"Oh?" Her heartbeat quickened.

"There's so much I'd like to tell you." His lids grew heavy. "But I'm tired. Can't seem to keep my eyes open."

"There'll be plenty of time to talk later," she reassured. "Your body needs rest."

His fingers relaxed their hold on her hand. Within minutes, his breathing evened out. Juliana watched him sleep, her heart bursting with gratitude.

"Thank You, Jesus," she whispered.

God had heard their prayers, and in His infinite wisdom and kindness, healed Evan.

Knowing the others were expecting her, she went outside.

"Well?" Rose asked hesitantly.

Juliana's smile rivaled the sun. "He's fine. He's tired, of course. A little confused about what's been happening. But overall he's okay."

Henry put his arm around his wife and hugged her to him. "I do believe we've witnessed God's hand moving upon this man, just as we asked."

"Yes," Juliana agreed. "Words can't express how happy I am right now."

"Now that you know he's going to be okay, you need to rest. Henry and I will fix breakfast and wake you when it's ready, okay?"

"I can help—"

"No."

She *was* tired. No, exhausted. Not knowing whether Evan would live or die had taken a huge emotional toll on her. "You're right. I'm worn out. But be sure and wake me when breakfast is ready. I'll take cleanup duty."

As soon as she got comfortable on her pallet in the shade, she fell into a deep sleep. When she awoke, she had the feeling that she had slept a lot longer than an hour. Immediately she went to check on Evan. He was sleeping still, and she could tell by his breathing that he was resting soundly. She sat there watching him for a few minutes before hunger drove her outside.

Brilliant blue stretched across the wide expanse above her. The sweet-scented air was calm today, the sun heating the fertile earth. A hawk made lazy circles in the air before swooping down into the field to catch his lunch.

Like the graceful bird, her heart soared, free of its burden. Evan would recover, praise God. She refused to ponder the future with all its unknowns and what ifs. She would focus on his recovery and the blessings of today.

Her friends waved her over. There was a bounce in her step as she made her way to join them. The women spent the day catching up on laundry and entertaining Joy, while Henry and Matt fished for their supper.

Juliana checked on Evan throughout the day, at times hand-feeding him tea and broth. He was drowsy and not inclined to talk. She was a bit disappointed but realized his body needed time to mend.

The next morning, she was so eager to see Evan she tossed aside her blankets and rushed into the tent, heedless of her appearance. She was surprised to find him already awake, propped up into a sitting position and supported by a mountain of blankets. She hesitated just inside the opening.

"Good morning," she said with a tentative smile, "How long have you been up?"

"Long enough to wonder if you were ever coming to check on me," he drawled. The heavy growth of black stubble covering the lower half of his face made him look dangerous, at odds with his usually clean-shaven appearance. His eyes tracked her every movement, as if hungry for the sight of her. "You must've been exhausted to have slept so late."

"I was," she admitted. "I feel rested this morning, though."

He nodded. The silence stretched between them, thick with unvoiced emotions.

Juliana longed to feel his arms around her. She wanted his reassurance that everything would be all right.

"Juliana." He sighed heavily. "Don't look at me like that."

"Like what?" Her lower lip trembled, sudden tears burning her eyes.

"Come here," he said softly, his arms outstretched.

She hesitated a fraction of a second before vaulting into his arms and burying her face in his shoulder. He wrapped his arms around her in a comforting embrace, his fingers stroking her unbound hair, his low voice murmuring reassuring words as salty tears slipped from beneath her eyelashes.

Juliana was independent by nature, accustomed to being the one everyone else leaned on. How wonderful it was to be able to lean on someone else. To not have to be the strong one for once.

Once the tears had abated, she sighed contentedly and snuggled deeper into his embrace. He held her tight. Being close to Evan made her soul sing. Right now, in this moment, she refused to think about how wrong it was to love him.

Evan closed his eyes, buried his face in her hair, and inhaled deeply. Images of lush green meadows dotted with pale lavender blooms flooded his mind. He pictured Juliana in that meadow, dressed in purest white, her golden-red hair spilling over her shoulders, her green eyes brimming with laughter. He was there, too, in a three-piece suit fit for church. Or a wedding.

No, he cautioned, *don't think about forever. It's too dangerous. You'd never survive another loss. Especially not losing Juliana.*

Gradually, her trembling ceased. She sighed a small, contented sigh that told him she was comfortable in his arms. The need to tell her the truth gripped him. She deserved to know everything. He only hoped she could find it in her heart to forgive him. Again.

Chapter Fifteen

Juliana did not want to move from this spot. She felt safe. Protected. Cherished.

"Juliana."

His deep voice rumbled through his chest. She felt his hands come to rest lightly on her shoulders. With reluctance, she eased away from the haven of his embrace to stare up at him.

His gaze was a tender caress, filled with longing, affection and regret. With great care, he wiped away the wetness from her cheeks.

"I haven't been completely honest with you."

It took a moment for his words to register. She sat back, her thoughts bouncing off each other.

"About what?" She heard the tremor in her voice.

Oh, Lord, please don't let him have a wife. I'll die if he tells me he's married.

He hesitated, clearly uneasy, which caused her stomach to tighten with anxiety.

"I've kept certain things from you in order to protect you. At least, I *thought* I was doing it to protect you.

Maybe I was protecting myself. I don't know." He paused to draw in a lung full of air. "I'm not who you think I am."

What did that mean? He had an alias? "Your name isn't Evan Harrison?"

"No. I mean, yes. I am." He plowed his fingers through his hair, accidentally dislodging the bandage. "Can I take this thing off?"

"Maybe tomorrow," she said, distracted.

With his thumb and finger, he untwisted the strips and smoothed them against his forehead. "I'm not an outlaw. Despite evidence to the contrary, I am a law-abiding, God-fearing, honest-to-goodness farmer."

Juliana didn't move. She couldn't believe it! He was lying. Lying with a straight face. And oh, he was *good*. If she hadn't found that paper, his air of innocence would've fooled her. The knowledge stung. What else had he lied about? Her thoughts turned to the badge in his boot. No lawman in his right mind would give it up without a fight.

Evan paused, his head cocked to one side. "What is it?"

She forced the words out. "It's no use, Evan. I've seen the sign with your picture on it."

He was momentarily taken aback. "What are you talking about?"

Outrage and despair warred within her. She loved this man…a man who apparently had no qualms about lying to her. She'd never felt so low. How she wished she'd heeded her instincts!

"Your gun, remember?" she muttered. "I found the wanted notice with your name on it. Evan Trey Harrison."

His mouth quirked. "Ah. I see. You found that, did you?" A disbelieving laugh burst from him. "Why am I not surprised? After all, you found the badge I'd so carefully concealed. You are one surprising woman, Juliana O'Malley."

His reaction didn't make sense. Why wasn't he more concerned?

"Sheriff Tate and I had that drawn up just in case Roberts didn't trust me. You see, I had to make him believe I was an outlaw."

He was determined to conceal the truth. "Forget it." She moved to get up. "I'm done believing your lies."

His hand on her shoulder stopped her. "Juliana, please." His husky voice was pleading, bordering on desperate. "Hear me out. I'm telling the truth."

She stared into his molten blue eyes. There was no trace of deceit, only sincerity.

"What about the mercantile? I was there, remember?"

"And I ushered you inside, which landed you in a heap of trouble," he supplied, his gaze probing hers.

"Yes," she murmured, "we mustn't forget that."

His expression turned rueful. "I felt certain no one would come in until later. That's what I'd counted on, anyway. I figured we could get in and get out without being seen. Tell me, why were you there at that hour? You must've gotten an early start."

She recalled complaining to Megan about the early hour. "I needed supplies for my mother's birthday celebration. We had a lot to do to prepare, since we were expecting a lot of guests that night. Mr. Moore's a talker and, like you, I wanted to get in and get out as quickly as possible."

"Talk about bad timing."

"Why were you there in the first place, Evan?"

"Ten months ago, my brother James was gunned down in cold blood." Pain flashed across his face, stark emotion that couldn't be faked. "That day, I pledged to hunt down those responsible and bring them to justice."

Stunned into silence, Juliana couldn't breathe. His brother? *Murdered?*

"It is my mission," he continued. "That's why I was at the mercantile, and why I've been hanging around low-lifes like Fitzgerald and Roberts."

His jaw was set, his blue eyes hard and unyielding. His expression promised retribution.

Juliana's head spun. No wonder he hadn't acted like a criminal—he *wasn't.* She remembered all the things about him that just didn't add up. Her gut instincts had been on the mark. She hadn't lost her heart to an outlaw, but to a farmer-turned-undercover detective!

The implications were too huge for her to grasp at that moment.

"What happened?" she managed.

His hand covering his eyes, he massaged his temples with his fingers. His words were muffled when he spoke. "James was attacked by a band of thieves. He was traveling to Knoxville with a large sum of money. My guess is he resisted, and they killed him." When he lifted his head, Juliana sucked in a breath at the sorrow etched in his features. "James would've stood his ground even if he was outnumbered. He wasn't the type to give in without a fight."

Her heart ached for his loss. She tried to imagine what she would do in his situation and couldn't. The idea was too horrific to even comprehend. Reaching over, Juliana wrapped her hand around his. "I'm so sorry. I can't imagine how much it must've hurt to hear the news."

He flipped his hand over and held on tight. "I was ill." He spoke the words almost as an apology. "Pneumonia. I told him the trip could wait until I was well enough to go with him, but he wouldn't listen. If I had gone, I could've protected him. James would still be alive today." Regret rolled off him in waves.

"You can't know that for sure," she insisted, determined to make him see reason. He blamed himself for something he had no control over. "One extra gun wouldn't have made that much of a difference. If you had gone, in all likelihood you would've been killed, too."

"I could've tried to outrun them. I could've bargained for his life. Something, *anything* to change what happened."

Juliana searched for the right words. "I know this might be difficult for you to hear, but God alone controls our destinies. His Word says each person has a set number of days on this earth. Nothing we can do can change it."

A muscle in his jaw twitched. "Does that bring you comfort when you miss your father?"

"Knowing God is in control brings me comfort and peace," she answered, ignoring the sting of his words. He had responded out of hurt. "Of course I don't understand the reasons or the timing of my father's death, but I trust in God's goodness. When I was consumed with grief, He gave me the strength to go on."

He stared hard at her. "I've heard when tragedy strikes, a person either draws closer to God or falls away. Two guesses which category I'm in."

"It's okay to be angry with God. He already knows what's in your heart. The key is not to shut Him out. Talk to him. He'll help you work through your emotions."

He was quiet, staring straight ahead. "I've been angry with Him for a long time," he confessed, his shoulders slumping. "My parents' deaths didn't affect me the same way, maybe because of the way they died. No one was at fault. One day they got sick and died. I don't know why, but something inside me snapped when I heard what happened to James. Someone was to blame. Someone cut his life short."

He swung his attention back to her. "Before you came along, I was in pretty bad shape. Thoughts of revenge consumed my every waking moment. When I was with the gang, it was all I could do not to strangle each and every one of them while they slept. I was haunted by James's face. I studied each man, wondering which one of them had pulled the trigger. After a while, the only emotion in my heart was hatred. Then, suddenly, I had you to worry about, and everything changed. Avenging James's murder wasn't my sole focus anymore. Keeping you safe was my first priority.

"I believe God used this illness to get my attention. When I heard your prayers, I realized what a mess I'd made of things. I didn't want to die. I told Him I couldn't bear this burden any longer. And because He's a loving, patient God, He forgave me."

Her heart swelled with gratitude. God had worked a miracle in his heart. "I'm proud of you, Evan."

"Please don't say that. I'm not proud of the man I've become these last few months. And I have to be honest— it's gonna take some time for me to come to the place where I can forgive the men responsible. A big part of me still craves vengeance."

"It takes courage to own up to sin, even when we feel we're justified in our feelings. That's why I'm proud of you. Admitting when you're wrong is the first step toward change. Eventually, by God's grace, you will be able to forgive them."

She remembered the gold star. "Is the badge yours?"

"Temporarily. Sheriff Tate, whose office I'm working with, gave it to me. Just in case I got hauled into jail, I'd have proof to back up my claim."

Juliana was relieved he wouldn't be lumped in with the other outlaws, should they ever be caught. The authorities would only need to contact the Cades Cove Sheriff's Office to verify Evan's story.

"Are you positive you've got the right group of men?"

"Yeah, I'm sure." His mouth thinned. "But I don't have solid evidence. Before you came along, my next plan of action was to go back to the scene of the crime, to Knoxville. Visit the gang's hangouts and try to snuff out a witness. Those men like to brag about their crimes. I'm hoping they talked the night James was killed."

For his sake, she hoped he was able to find the answers he sought. As for his deception, Juliana needed time to sort out her feelings. If she were honest, his decision not to confide in her early on hurt. He hadn't trusted her.

"What are you thinking?" he asked.

"I'm wondering why you didn't tell me this in the beginning."

He closed his eyes. "I figured the less you knew, the better." Opening them, he looked at her with regret. "Now I know it would've made it easier for you, at least in the sense of knowing that I'm not dangerous."

Oh, how wrong he was, she thought. He *was* dangerous. In an ironic twist, he was even more of a threat now than before. There were no obstacles, no reasons for her to deny her feelings. And that was downright scary.

"I realize an apology can't make up for all the mistakes

I've made," he continued, "but I am sorry. If I could go back to that morning at the mercantile, I'd do it all differently, anything to have spared you and your family this grief. Do you think you can forgive me?"

Evan held his breath as he watched the emotions marching across Juliana's face.

"What happened wasn't entirely your fault. And you've worked hard at keeping me safe, even though it put your mission at risk. I wish you would've confided in me, however. You're right—knowing your identity would've saved me a lot of worry."

He could see the hurt reflected in her clear green eyes. His heart dipped. He didn't deserve her forgiveness, but he craved it. How could he live with himself if she couldn't move past this?

"I also understand that you felt you were making the right decision not to tell me."

He blew out the breath he'd been holding. The glow from the kerosene lamp highlighted the copper streaks in her thick tresses, tumbling down around her shoulders. How he longed to take her in his arms and hold her close. That was out of the question, of course.

"I never intended to hurt you, Juliana," he murmured.

Her lashes swept down to hide her eyes. "I know." Her voice lowered to match his.

"There are others my deception has hurt."

She lifted her head. "Henry and Rose?"

"Yes. I think it's best if I tell them the truth about us."

He paused to gauge her reaction. He sensed her apprehension. Would she agree or disagree?

"I definitely think it's the right thing to do."

He should've known she'd want to do the right thing.

He exhaled. "They won't be too happy with us," he warned. "Are you prepared for that?"

"They have every right to be upset. We tricked them. And they've been nothing but kind to both of us. They deserve the truth, even if it doesn't affect them directly."

"I agree." It wouldn't be pleasant, admitting his deception to his new friends, but he didn't want to put it off. "When do you want me to talk to them? Now?"

Juliana moved to her knees, lifted the flap and peered out. "Rose is busy. Henry is playing a game of chase with the kids. How about after lunch?" she suggested, peering over her shoulder at him. "We can talk over a cup of coffee."

"Coffee?" His black brows rose hopefully.

"You'll be having tea," she replied firmly, refusing to be swayed by his entreaty.

"Tea is for females," he grumbled. "I want coffee."

"I'm going to ignore that remark." She arched a brow at him. "Maybe tomorrow. For now, let's stick with the tea, okay?"

He scooted down until he was lying flat and stared up at the top of the tent. "Yes, ma'am," he sighed, amazed that a simple conversation could wear him out.

"Evan?"

She was crouched in the opening, looking like a vulnerable young girl with her earnest expression. "I'm glad you're better. There were times when I feared you wouldn't pull through. In fact, I—" Her breathing hitched, and her gaze skittered away. "Never mind. The important thing is that the worst is over, and you're on the mend."

He swallowed hard, with effort reining in his runaway emotions. "Any other woman would've bolted the moment I passed out," he declared. "You're a woman of great mercy and compassion, Juliana. I'll never forget your kindness toward me. I wish I could repay you somehow. Saying *thanks* doesn't seem to be enough."

"Your getting well is reward enough." Her tender smile warmed him deep inside. "Think you can get some rest?"

He didn't want to rest. He wanted to talk to her. "I'll try," he huffed, doing his best to sound pitiful.

Her eyes narrowed. "I'll be back soon."

She slipped out the opening, and Evan watched her boots, skimmed by the hem of her dress, until they disappeared from sight. His eyes remained on the spot she'd vacated, wishing for what he couldn't have. He closed his eyes and, although he wasn't sleepy, within minutes he drifted off to sleep.

Gnawing pains in his stomach woke him some time later. He was warm, so he tossed off the quilt and reached for his pants. It was a struggle to put them on while he was on his back, but finally he succeeded and had just finished buttoning them up when Juliana entered the tent. When her gaze fell on him, she almost dumped the soup on the ground.

"Oh! I'm sorry! I can come back—"

"It's okay, I'm decent. I hope it tastes as good as it smells." He had his long-sleeved undershirt on, so he didn't bother with finding his button-down.

"Be careful, it's hot."

Evan accepted the stoneware bowl and spoon from her. A quick glance at her face revealed two bright spots of color on her cheeks. He didn't comment. Instead, he focused on the steaming vegetables floating in rich broth.

Juliana had brought a bowl for herself, and she sat

down opposite him. He was pleased she had chosen to share her meal with him, even if they weren't inclined to speak. The silence was a comfortable one. At times, they commented on the weather or the Talbot children, but all in all it was a quiet affair.

When they had finished, Evan began tugging on his boots.

"What are you doing?" Juliana demanded, eyes wide.

"Four of us can't fit in here, can we?"

"I suppose not. Still, I'm not sure it's wise for you to be up and about so soon."

He heard the undertone of concern in her smooth-as-velvet voice, and it warmed him. "Juliana, I'm only walking to the nearest shade tree, no farther. I'll be just fine."

She bit her lip. "You might experience some dizziness. I'll walk beside you in case you do."

Evan didn't have any objections to that, of course. She went out first and waited for him. After being in the tent's dim interior for so long, it took a minute for his eyes to adjust to the bright sunshine. He would've liked to have his hat, but he hadn't seen it since before he got sick.

As Juliana predicted, weakness assailed him, and his knees threatened to buckle. Immediately, he curled his arm around her shoulders and leaned into her, allowing her to steady him as they slowly crossed the grass. Holding her close filled him with contentment.

His heart felt lighter than it had in a long time. As soon as he'd prayed to God and asked for forgiveness, peace had flooded his soul. Instead of being burdened by guilt, he now felt free to pray anytime he wished. The grief that had been his companion for nearly a year was still there, but now he didn't carry it alone. His Lord was there to help share the burden and make it bearable.

He was glad to be out in the fresh air. The sweet perfume of wildflowers teased his nose, and the whack of a woodpecker's beak filled his ears. Bees buzzed between blossoms, hovering for a time before darting off to the next one. As they passed beneath a leafy bower, he spotted a fuzzy-tailed squirrel above their heads. The little animal scurried away as soon as he saw them.

They settled in a shady area not far from the tent, but the short walk had left him feeling weak and out of sorts. That worried him. They needed to get on the trail as soon as possible.

Seeing Henry striding their way, Evan pushed his worries aside. First things first. He had some explaining to do. He didn't peg Henry Talbot as the type to hold a grudge, but he'd been wrong before.

Henry had two cups in his hand, one of which he passed to Evan. Seeing Henry's wink, Juliana protested.

"You know he's not supposed to have that." She eyed Henry sternly.

"He needs the energy." Henry smiled, not looking the least bit repentant.

Evan inhaled the aromatic steam rising from the dark liquid and sighed. The coffee smelled strong and bracing, just the way he liked it. Taking a long drink, he eyed Juliana over the rim of his cup. Then he held it aloft.

"I'm willing to share."

Her eyes widened and her lips parted. He didn't get to hear her response because Rose appeared at that moment with a cup for Juliana. Too bad. He rather liked sparring with her.

Evan didn't immediately bring up the issue of his

and Juliana's true relationship. He listened as the other couple spoke of their departure and their plans for the near future. Beside him, Juliana grew increasingly fidgety. Without looking at her, he snatched her hand up and, placing it on his knee, gave it a reassuring squeeze. She squeezed his hand in return.

He cleared his throat and threw a glance her way before addressing Henry and Rose.

"I, uh, have a confession to make," he began, feeling heat rush into his face. "There are some things I haven't told you about Juliana and myself, about how we met and the true nature of our relationship."

Henry looked bewildered. His wife's gaze searched Evan's face as if trying to guess the meaning behind his words.

Drawing in a deep breath, he said, "Juliana and I are not really husband and wife."

Henry stared hard at Evan, his dark gaze dropping to their clasped hands. With a light squeeze, Evan released her hand, which she quickly withdrew. He knew what the other man was thinking. Henry had witnessed that kiss and other displays of affection normally reserved for married couples. No doubt he thought they were living in sin.

"I want to assure you both that nothing improper has happened between the two of us. We met five days ago when our paths crossed unexpectedly, and we've been traveling together out of necessity. When you and your family showed up, I figured it was best to pretend to be married. Juliana didn't want to do it but I insisted, knowing how it would look if we didn't." He looked from husband to wife. "I'm sorry I lied to you both."

"I'm sorry, too," Juliana rushed to add, her expression

full of remorse. "I think of you as a dear friend, Rose, and I hope you can forgive me."

"Of course I forgive you," Rose said, her eyes full of questions. "I would just like to know what's going on. The man who's following you—the one who hurt you— is he the reason you are traveling together?"

"We know it isn't any of our business—" Henry began.

Evan interrupted. "No. You deserve an explanation. I'll have to start from the beginning, though."

Starting with the death of his parents, Evan told them everything leading up to that day in the mercantile. They listened with rapt attention, scarcely believing he'd actually kidnapped Juliana. When he'd finished, they sat in stunned silence.

Henry was the first to speak. "Juliana, you obviously have been through quite a lot this week. Are you sure you're all right? Would you like to add anything to Evan's account?"

"I'm fine—honest. God has carried me through these last few days. He's protected me, and I'm sure He's comforted my family as well. Evan has been a perfect gentleman. He's done nothing to make me feel afraid or uncomfortable."

Evan didn't know about the perfect part. He regretted the pain he'd caused her family, and realized he'd have to face them one day soon. That was one confrontation he wasn't eager to have.

"I see." Henry appeared thoughtful.

Rose Talbot's curiosity was not so easily satisfied. "I'm curious about something. Henry will likely say I'm being nosy, but I have to say what's on my mind. It seems to me the two of you have come to care for each other a great deal. The affection between you isn't pretend, is it?"

Evan feared they could hear his heart banging against his rib cage. How could he possibly answer this question? He wasn't ready to face the truth himself, much less admit to it in front of Juliana. She'd already said she didn't love him—the day he kissed her. And really, how could she? After everything he'd put her through...

His mouth dry, he took another swig of coffee. "Juliana is a remarkable woman, Mrs. Talbot. She's put up with a lot, and yet, she has found it in her heart to forgive me. I count myself lucky just to know her."

He hoped his answer would satisfy the other woman. He felt the weight of Juliana's stare, but he couldn't bring himself to meet it.

"I think I know the reason for my wife's questions." Henry leaned forward to address Evan. "You see, the two of you have spent days in each other's company without a chaperone. When Juliana's family finds out, they'll expect you to marry her. Have you thought about that?"

Evan bowed his head. It was true. A single man and woman traveling for days and nights on their own—no one would believe they were innocent of wrongdoing. Juliana's reputation was at stake.

"No," he heard Juliana say. When he lifted his head to look at her, he recognized the defiant tilt of her chin. She met his gaze, her eyes full of fire. "I won't be forced into marriage. It's not fair to Evan or myself."

Evan's gut twisted. He wanted to do what was best for her, but marriage wasn't in his plans. Marriage meant commitment and, eventually, attachment. He didn't want that. It hurt too much to lose someone you loved.

"Think what the townspeople will say, Juliana," Rose insisted, her face a mask of concern. "You'll be shunned by many."

"I don't care," she declared. "Those who know me know I'd never do anything to bring shame upon myself or my family."

Evan noticed her fisted hands in her lap and longed to soothe her, but he didn't think she'd welcome his touch right about now. He'd put her in this position. She had every right to be angry.

Rose's voice was gentle. "It's not fair, I agree, but it's the way of things. And it won't just affect you, my dear. Your mother and sisters will be treated the same as you."

Juliana shook her head. "I can't believe it of my friends. The people of Gatlinburg will understand. They have to."

Rose looked on her with kindness. "Perhaps you're right."

"What do you think, Evan?" Henry spoke up.

He caught Juliana's gaze and held it. Her inner turmoil was plain to see in her beautiful green eyes. It hurt to know he was the cause. "I want what's best for Juliana. If that means marriage, then so be it."

The second the words left his mouth, he knew he meant every one. He was willing to give her his name if it meant sparing her pain and humiliation. Somehow he'd find a way to protect his heart.

Her hand flew to her throat. "You can't mean that, Evan. It's not what you want, and you know it."

"What do *you* want, Juliana?" He searched her face for a clue. A myriad of emotions crossed her face—anger, fear, longing.

"I know what I *don't* want," she huffed, "and that's a sham marriage!"

Scrambling to her feet, she strode away.

"Wait—" He moved to rise, but Henry held up a staying hand.

"Maybe you should give her a few minutes alone. It's a lot to sort through."

Evan settled back down, his gaze following her to the lake. He doubted he could make it that far on his own strength, and it frustrated him. He didn't like feeling helpless.

He felt a hand on his arm. Rose said, "Don't worry, she'll come around. She just needs some time."

He summoned a small smile of thanks before excusing himself. Refusing Henry's offer of assistance, he made his way back to the tent and lay down to rest and think.

Chapter Sixteen

Juliana watched the swans glide gracefully across the sun-dappled water. How she envied their peace and tranquility! Her own soul was in turmoil. Like a tumbling house of cards, her thoughts heaped one upon another in quick succession until she couldn't make sense of a single one.

When she'd imagined how the conversation would go with the Talbots, talk of propriety and social expectations hadn't been on the list of topics for discussion. And certainly not marriage!

Remembering the expression on Evan's face when Henry brought it up, she dropped her head in her hands and groaned. The idea *terrified* him. Whether it was the prospect of marriage in general or marriage to her in particular she didn't know.

She had to admit—his reaction cut deep.

He didn't want a life with her.

Oh, she believed he liked her—perhaps even admired her—but he didn't love her.

Of course in the end he'd agreed to marry her—*if* she wanted him to. What girl wanted a husband on those terms? What kind of marriage could they have? Besides, she had a feeling he said it out of a sense of obligation.

Face it, you're just a liability to him, a little voice said, *an unwanted responsibility.*

As the truth sank in, the place around her heart ached with a dull pain. Tears traced uneven tracks down her cheeks. If she'd known how much it would hurt to love someone, she would've guarded her heart more closely.

But from the start, she'd been overwhelmed by her reaction to him. Evan was the first man to make her feel alive and very aware of her femininity. With a single touch of his hand, he could set her pulse racing and make her feel as if she'd just run a mile. Simply being near him thrilled her.

With each new glimpse of his soul, her compassion had taken root and developed into something more, something deeper. Their shared experiences had forged a unique bond between them. He'd seen her at her worst, and she him. They understood each other.

It had taken almost losing him to force her to face the fact that she loved him. And she hadn't cared that he was an outlaw. She was still adjusting to the fact that he wasn't a criminal at all, but a respectable man.

A life without Evan would be bleak. Miserable. Unbearable.

And yet that's the future she faced. In the coming days, she would be reunited with her family, and he would continue his quest for justice. She would go back to her mundane life while he spent his days and nights with criminals.

She wondered if he'd even miss her.

The sound of children playing reached her ears and, lifting her head, she swiped at the wetness on her cheeks.

The swelling was gone, and it hurt only if she touched it. She hoped the bruises disappeared before she returned home. She didn't want to go into the details of how and where she'd gotten them.

Tugging her snug bodice down, she went to find an empty pail. She wanted to be alone, and the best excuse was to go berry picking. Juliana found Rose tending to Joy. To her relief, the other woman didn't mention Evan or their earlier conversation, nor did she question Juliana's intention to go searching for berries. She did, however, insist that Juliana stay close by. With her bonnet and holster in place, she set off.

Juliana spent much of the afternoon meandering through the fields surrounding the lake, venturing as far as the tree line in the distance. She used the time to think and pray. While she didn't find a single berry bush, she did locate a cherry tree. With her pail swinging from her arm and brimming with plump, crimson fruit, she strolled back into camp.

She spotted Evan right away sitting in the shade, peeling potatoes. Matt was hunkered down next to him, chatting happily. The boy was clearly relieved to see Evan up and about. She'd seen how worried he'd been during Evan's illness.

As soon as Evan caught a glimpse of her, his hand stilled in midair and his back stiffened. Her steps slowed at his reaction. He didn't look at all pleased.

But she couldn't change course now. So she approached the twosome, unable to tear her gaze away from his. When she drew near, he rose to his feet and with a parting word to Matt, met her halfway.

He stopped a foot away and slipped his hands in his pockets. She was still trying to come to grips with the fact that he wasn't an outlaw. He was a law-abiding citizen and a believer.

Juliana swallowed hard, resisting the urge to throw herself in his arms. He was gorgeous, his pale blue shirt a complement to his tanned skin and dark hair, and so very dear. The only reminder of his illness was the pallor of his skin. She longed to caress his cheek as she'd done while he lay unconscious. Instead, she clasped her hands behind her back, the pail dangling from her fingers.

"You were gone a long time. I was worried."

His gaze roved over her from head to toe as if assuring himself she was unharmed.

"As you can see, I'm fine. I have protection." Her palm settled over the gun handle at her waist.

One black eyebrow quirked up. "I already know you're an adept hunter. But how much experience do you really have with a weapon?"

"Enough."

"Care to elaborate on that?"

His eyes held a hint of challenge, and she seized on it. "It'd be easier to show you than tell you. How about a demonstration after supper? We can even make it into a contest, if you want."

His expression turned disbelieving. "You against me? Are you sure you're up for the challenge?"

She flashed him a confident grin. "I'll do my best." Was he in for a big surprise!

"I'd expect nothing less." He grinned then, white teeth flashing. "I've got work to do." He hooked a thumb over his shoulder, indicating the pile of potatoes. "I'd better get back to it."

"It's nice of you to help Rose."

He lifted a shoulder. "I've been idle long enough. I needed something to occupy my hands."

"How are you feeling?"

"Normal, except for the fact I tire easily."

"That's to be expected. Are you sure you'll be ready to travel tomorrow? We could always wait an extra day."

With a look of determination, he said, "No, we can't. We need to get a message to your family as soon as possible. Besides, we'll be in the saddle most of the way. Lucky will be doing the exercising, not me."

Juliana had her doubts, but she could see that he wouldn't be swayed. She hoped he wouldn't overdo it and end up having a relapse.

She lifted the fruit for him to see. "Do you like cherries?"

"I do. Got anything special in mind for those?"

"Not exactly. I'm going to see if Rose has any suggestions."

"Ask her if she knows how to make a cherry crumble. If so, I've got plenty of cornmeal to spare. She's welcome to it."

"Is that a favorite of yours?"

"Not mine. My father's. I can still remember his excitement each time my mother made it. He was like a little kid in a candy store."

Hearing him laugh lightened her heart. After all the pain and suffering he'd endured, he deserved to be happy.

She realized that she didn't know much about his likes and dislikes. "If cherry crumble isn't your favorite, then what is?"

He thought for a moment. "I'm partial to apple pie. With lots of cinnamon."

For the first time in her life, Juliana wished she'd

learned how to cook. She would've liked to make something special for him.

"I guess it's been a while since you've had a home-made meal."

"Too long," he muttered. "Restaurant food is the closest I've had to Mom's cooking, and it still can't compare. I've enjoyed Rose's, though. She's done wonders, considering her limited supplies."

"Yes," she agreed, "maybe when I get home I'll ask Jessica or Jane to teach me a few things."

"That's a wise idea." His expression turned serious. "You'll have a husband and children to cook for someday."

"Yes, perhaps."

He took a step forward. "Juliana, we need to talk."

She stepped back, sensing he wanted to continue the marriage discussion. "Not now, Evan. Later. I—I have to go."

She made to move past him, but he caught her wrist. "You can't avoid the subject forever."

Juliana gazed at her boots. "We both have things to do."

He dropped his hand. "You're right. But we *will* talk about it. Soon."

She walked away without a word.

Arms folded across her chest, Juliana watched as Evan took aim at the target and fired off a shot. The ping of the bullet against tin reached her ears, and she knew he'd hit it dead on. As she'd suspected, he was a good aim. Now it was her turn.

They'd chosen this cool, quiet meadow because it was a good distance from camp and the noise wouldn't

bother the children or the horses. A tranquil place, Juliana would've liked to stretch out in the grass and relax
amid the lilacs and daisies. Instead, she stepped to the
spot he'd vacated and waited as he strung up a new target.

Juliana had managed to keep her distance from him
during supper and cleanup, but she knew better than to
expect him to drop the subject. He wasn't a man to let
an issue fester. Once a matter came to his attention, he
wanted it settled.

She checked her weapon. Everything was in order.

Evan came striding back, his long legs quickly eating up the distance. He stopped in front of her. "Are you
ready?"

"I am."

He moved to the side, putting enough space between
them so as not to crowd her. She felt his gaze on her, and
with difficulty she tamped down her sudden nervousness.
She was used to people watching, just not this particular
person. She realized his opinion mattered a great deal.

Raising the gun to eye level, she focused on the target
with one eye open and one closed. Then she squeezed
the trigger. Again the loud ping reached her ears, and
she let out a breath she hadn't realized she was holding.

Evan whistled as he approached, admiration in his
gaze. "I'm impressed, Irish."

The tension left her body and, confidence in its place,
she tossed out another challenge. "How about we do it
again from farther away?"

His eyebrows darted up. "Are you sure you wanna do
that? I've had lots of practice the last couple of months."

"Very funny," she retorted with a toss of her head. "I
wouldn't have suggested it if I didn't think I could pull
it off."

His hands braced on his hips, he leaned in close. His familiar clean scent wafted toward her. "Tell me something. If this is a competition, then what's the prize? What are you willing to give me if I win?"

Evan's nearness stirred her senses. She stood her ground, however. "Assuming you win, what is it that you want?"

His brilliant blue eyes dropped to her mouth, lingering there before ever so slowly lifting to meet her gaze once more. "One kiss."

Juliana felt as if she would melt into a puddle at his feet. Swallowing hard, she unconsciously licked her lips. "And if I win?" she croaked.

"Name your prize."

She couldn't think with him so close. "I don't know."

He flicked a gaze at her hair, still in a haphazard ponytail. "I could always braid your hair for you as I did the night of the rainstorm."

Juliana thought back to that night, recalling all too well the intimacy created by such an act. No matter who won, the outcome would be the same. Too much closeness for her peace of mind. It would be foolish to agree and, yet, she was tempted. She wanted nothing more than to be in his arms.

"If I win, you teach me to cook."

"You're on." A lazy grin curled his lips. "I'll be right back."

Her heart rate sped up as anticipation set in. He changed the target again and returned. "Are you sure you don't want to go first?"

"No, thanks. You go ahead."

Evan walked about fifteen paces past the first spot, turned on his heel and sought her approval. "Far enough?"

"Looks good to me."

He took his time, judging the distance with his eyes before lifting his arm to aim his weapon. Again, his aim was true. Juliana moved into position, wiping her damp palms down her skirt. When all was ready, she lifted her gun. At the same instant that her finger put pressure on the trigger, a bumblebee buzzed past her ear and she jerked. The bullet strayed a few inches to the left, missing the tin can altogether.

Disbelieving, she stood there, the gun still in her hand at her side. Evan rushed over. "What happened?"

"It was a bee." Feeling the heat rushing to her face, she couldn't meet his eyes. He probably thought she had lost on purpose. She sheathed the gun in its holster.

He chuckled. "A bee, huh?"

A thought struck her. She lifted her face to his. "How about giving me another chance? If it hadn't been for that bee, I could've made the shot."

He stroked his chin, as if considering her request. "Uh-uh. I don't think so."

"Why not?" she demanded.

Evan stared at her, all amusement fading. His voice dipped. "Because. Bee or no bee, I won, and I want the kiss you owe me."

Juliana's pulse accelerated and she struggled to breathe. She felt light-headed, and her knees threatened to buckle. "You're not playing fair," she accused in a whisper.

"*I* didn't send that bee."

He closed the distance between them and tugged her against his muscular body. His hands gripping her waist, he swooped down to cover her mouth with his own. He gave her no time to resist. Her hands splayed against his chest. Beneath her palm, his heart pounded fast and hard.

His soft lips moved over hers with insistence, coaxing and tasting until she couldn't think, only feel. Emotion left her weak, and she leaned against him for support. She slid her hands up and locked them around his neck.

He emitted a low, guttural moan. His hands moved up her back, and he pressed her even closer. He deepened the kiss, and trembling, she clung to him.

Evan became her anchor. In the haven of his embrace, she felt safe, cherished and more alive than she'd ever felt before. Pushing aside her reservations, Juliana kissed him with abandon, willing him to feel the depth of her love.

When he abruptly broke off the kiss and set her away from him, she nearly cried out in protest. His chest heaved as if he'd run a mile, and she could clearly see that he was fighting an inner battle. With a searing glance, he strode to where he'd left his hat. Retrieving it from the ground, he settled it smoothly on his head and walked back, stopping several feet away.

It was plain to see that he was upset and trying to conceal it. "When we get back to Gatlinburg, there are going to be a lot of questions. Your family will expect me to marry you and rightly so."

Juliana opened her mouth to speak, but he held up his hand to forestall her. "I don't want your reputation to suffer, Juliana. I don't want you to be treated like a social outcast just because you unwillingly spent a couple of days and nights in my company. You don't deserve that kind of treatment. You've done nothing wrong.

"I can shield you from all that by marrying you. I know it's not the best situation. I'm certain you pictured your life turning out a different way, but I'm willing if you are. The truth is I wouldn't mind being married to you."

Juliana couldn't speak. The man who had captured her heart was offering to marry her. That meant living together as husband and wife, day in and day out, sharing life's ups and downs, trials and blessings. Perhaps they'd even have children some day.

Oh, she was tempted. In time, she reasoned, he could grow to love her.

Or he could end up resenting her.

Did she dare take that risk?

Tears threatened, and she blinked them back. Squaring her shoulders, she dug down deep for the courage to say what was in her heart. "Thank you, Evan, for your kind offer. But you see, I don't want a man who simply doesn't *mind* marrying me. I want a man who *yearns* to be with me, whose utmost desire is to make me his bride. A man who believes life isn't worth living if he can't share it with me. Call me romantic or even foolish, but I'd rather face the disapproving stares and whispers of the townspeople than a loveless marriage."

Evan closed his eyes, as if her words caused him pain. "Love opens you up to a whole world of pain, my dear. I should know. I've lost every single person I've ever loved. Let me tell you, I wouldn't wish that kind of grief on anyone."

"It was good while it lasted, though, wasn't it?" she countered, desperate to make her point. "Isn't it better to experience love and joy for a little while than not at all? Yes, it hurt when I lost my father, but do I wish I'd never known him? Of course not." Juliana approached him and slipped her hand into his. "Evan. Do you honestly want to spend the rest of your life all alone? With no one to care for you?"

His eyes roamed her face, questions lurking in the dark depths. "I don't think I could endure another loss, Juliana." Lifting his hand, he gently cupped her cheek, his thumb stroking her skin. "A lot of marriages are built on friendship alone and are very successful. I may not be able to offer you my heart, but I can give you my friendship. Isn't that enough?"

His words stabbed at her. Pulling his hand away, she stepped back. "I'm afraid not."

His shoulders slumped in defeat, and she almost changed her mind. Instead, with a look at the setting sun, she muttered, "I think we'd best be getting back. There's a lot to do before we leave tomorrow."

Evan turned away, oddly defeated. He cared more for her than he knew was wise. Why else would he be pushing her to marry him? Of course he understood what she was up against if she didn't, and he didn't want to see her hurt. Especially because of something he'd done.

He fell into step beside her, his gaze on everything *but* her. He was afraid that if he chanced a glance at her now, he would kiss her again. And that would be a huge mistake.

Kissing Juliana was dangerous. It had taken every ounce of his willpower to stop. He'd wanted to go on holding her forever. If they were husband and wife, he reminded himself, he wouldn't have to stop. He could kiss her whenever he liked.

The thought kicked his heart into a wild gallop, and his stomach did a flip-flop.

Juliana was a beautiful, desirable young woman. He

couldn't deny that he was attracted to her. When she was near, he was lucky if he could put two words together. With those innocent green eyes and sweet mouth, she had the power to drive all rational thought from his mind.

He didn't necessarily enjoy not having control over his emotions like that.

Camp came into view then, and they parted ways without a word. It was just as well. He hadn't a clue what to say.

Chapter Seventeen

Breakfast was a solemn affair. After prolonged good-byes, they finally hit the trail. Juliana didn't seem inclined to talk, which suited him just fine.

He glanced upward, pleased to see not a single cloud in the vast blue sky. Anticipation bloomed in his chest. Soon he would be home. *Home.* It seemed like a lifetime had passed since he'd seen the place. He was eager to see for himself how the animals and crops were faring under his cousin's supervision.

In hindsight, Evan realized that he hadn't really handled the whole situation as well as he could have. His letters home had been few and far between. And he hadn't told Luke how much he appreciated everything he'd done since James's passing.

Well, he would have a chance to correct his wrongs that night. By suppertime, he fully intended to be sitting at his cousin's table.

"You weren't exaggerating, Evan. It's absolutely breathtaking."

Standing on the ridge overlooking his beloved valley, Juliana surveyed the scene.

Far below, encircled by majestic blue-green mountains, lay his home. Fields and fences, cabins and barns crisscrossed the verdant valley basin. Even the white clapboard church, with its white cross reaching toward the sky, was visible from the mountaintop. Shimmering ribbons of blue cut large swaths across the valley.

Evan appeared pleased by her declaration. He grinned at her, and she could see the excitement in his eyes. "Shall we go?"

Their descent took just under two hours. Evan halted Lucky near the first homestead.

At the mix of emotions crossing his face, Juliana asked, "Is that your cabin?"

"No, this is Luke's place. My land starts on the other side of that tree grove." He pointed to a spot about a mile distant. "We'll have supper with him first."

Apprehension warred with curiosity. She could only imagine the man's reaction when Evan showed up on his doorstep with a strange woman.

Juliana spotted a large dog on the front porch. He noticed them at the same time and let out a warning. The animal's noisy barking alerted Lucas Harrison, because almost immediately the front door swung open and a man appeared in the doorway.

Evan tipped his hat back and waved. "Hello, cuz," he called. "I sure do hope you've got supper on the table 'cause I've been dreaming of a home-cooked meal for days!"

A wide smile broke out on the stranger's face. With a word to the dog to stay put, he leapt off the porch and strode quickly across the grass to meet them. "My eyes must be deceiving me! I was beginning to wonder if you were ever coming home."

Evan held out his hand, which Lucas accepted only to tug Evan close for a quick but enthusiastic hug. Releasing him, Lucas turned his attention to Juliana.

Her cheeks burned beneath his scrutiny. He was obviously curious as to her identity but too polite to question her.

"Hello," he offered with a kind smile. "I'm Lucas Harrison. But my friends call me Luke."

Evan stepped closer to her, and she caught the warning glance he shot his cousin. "Luke, this is Juliana O'Malley."

He tipped his head. "It's nice to meet you, Miss O'Malley."

"It's a pleasure to meet you as well, Mr. Harrison." Evan's cousin was handsome and charming, although not quite as striking as Evan.

"Please, call me Luke. Whenever someone calls me *Mr. Harrison,* I automatically look around to see if my father's nearby. Can't seem to get used to it." His gaze volleyed between the two of them. "You both look parched. How does a glass of lemonade sound?"

"Wonderful," Evan huffed. "Juliana?"

"I'd love some."

"Evan, why don't you show Miss O'Malley to the house? I'll see that Lucky gets a drink, and then I'll be right in. We've got a lot of catching up to do." He clapped Evan on the shoulder. "Think you can remember where everything is?"

"I'll do my best." At Evan's dry response, Juliana hid a smile. She sensed the two cousins teased each other often.

Inside, the smell of meat roasting in the stove tantalized her nose. They'd had a light lunch of beef jerky and hard biscuits hours ago, and she was hungry.

A glance around revealed a home that was neat and tidy, if sparsely furnished. The windows were bare and the only touch of color in the room came from the blue settee sitting in front of the fireplace. Gauging from his home, Luke Harrison struck her as a man of simple tastes.

"Here you go." Evan appeared at her side with a tall glass of lemonade.

She sipped the cool, tart liquid and sighed. "That's delicious."

"We've been walking for hours. Why don't you have a seat? If you don't mind being on your own for a few minutes, I'd like to have a word with Luke before supper."

"I'll be fine." Placing her glass on the oval coffee table, she sank down onto the settee and untied the strings of her bonnet. "He must have a lot of questions."

He drained the remainder of his drink and set it on the table next to hers. "Juliana," he began, his eyes searching, "I plan on telling him the truth about our situation. Do you mind?"

"As I see it, we have no other choice."

He cocked his head to one side. "I could tell him it's none of his business."

Juliana could tell by his serious demeanor that the decision was indeed hers to make. Clearly, Evan wanted to tell his cousin everything, which meant he trusted him to keep it quiet.

"If you trust him, then so do I."

"I do."

"Who is she?"

Leaning against the stall door, Evan stroked the mare's nose and tried to formulate an answer. No matter how he said it, his cousin wasn't going to be pleased.

"I'm not going to like what you have to say, am I?" Luke said finally.

Evan decided to be blunt. "I kidnapped her."

"*What* did you say?"

"She walked in on a robbery. I tried to get her out of there, but my *colleague* had other plans."

Feet planted wide and arms folded across his chest, Luke leveled a steady glare in Evan's direction. "Do you realize how outrageous that sounds coming from *your* mouth? Those words don't even begin to match up with the man I know you to be. Explain yourself."

"I realize this is hard for you to swallow. Believe me." He thrust his fingers through his hair. "I'm having a hard time understanding it myself."

"Juliana didn't appear to be here against her will, however. In fact, the two of you seem to be on friendly terms."

"Yeah." Evan's mind drifted to the kiss he'd won and how it felt to hold her in his arms. Many times today he'd been tempted to do it again, but had resisted.

"Evan," Luke prompted sternly, "you look like a man in love. Tell me, how could that be?"

In love? With Juliana? He cared about her, of course. Surely he wouldn't have been foolish enough to let himself fall in love with her.

"I didn't come out here to talk about my feelings."

"So you admit to having feelings." He cocked an eyebrow. His lips tugged upward in a teasing grin.

Evan shot him a warning glance, but said nothing.

"Fine, I'll drop it. For now." Luke turned serious once more. "So why didn't you let her go? Why bring her here?"

He told him everything that had happened, including his belief that Fitzgerald had been trailing them.

"Oh, this is getting better by the minute," Luke groaned.

"I know I'm out of favors, but I need you to promise me that you'll keep an eye on her while I'm gone."

"You have my word," he agreed. "You look peaked. Have you been taking care of yourself?"

He really didn't want to go into his illness at that moment. He was bone-tired. Maybe he'd pushed himself too hard. He'd be hitting the hay early that night. Literally. "You know how life on the trail can be. Not the best of conditions."

"Let's go eat then, so you can go home and get some rest." He started for the barn door.

"Luke?"

He paused and looked back at Evan. "Yeah?"

"Thanks." Gratitude overwhelmed him, making it hard to speak. He'd missed him. "I owe you."

Understanding dawned, and Luke smiled. "Who knows? One day I may need a favor from you."

"All you need to do is ask."

As they waved goodbye to Luke Harrison, Juliana felt content. The meal, while nothing fancy, had been delicious—the tender beef roast dripping in rich gravy had melted in her mouth and the biscuits slathered with freshly churned butter and a touch of honey made her moan in delight. She grinned, remembering how surprised both men had been at the number of biscuits she'd consumed.

She'd enjoyed the lively conversation as well. Evan and Luke had entertained her with stories of their childhoods and teenage years. It was obvious the two men shared a close friendship, and she could tell both were pleased to be in each other's company once again.

As they left the front yard, Evan urged Lucky into a canter. His arm held her fast, securing her against his muscled body. She reveled in their closeness, knowing it would soon come to an end. He would take the next day to do errands in town and check on his animals and garden, then leave the following morning. How long it would be before he returned she hadn't a clue.

He slowed the big black when they emerged from the trees. They were on his land now. Crossing a shallow stream, they intersected a field with knee-high grass and entered another small cove before emerging beside long, even rows of plants. In the distance, a one-story cabin stood in the midst of several apple trees, the profusion of pink blossoms shining in the sun. Chestnut trees with spotted trunks lined the drive. A tall barn rimmed with animal pens stood just beyond the cabin.

Lush and green, with rounded blue mountain peaks in the near distance, his home took her breath away. With its tranquil scenery, she thought it even more beautiful than her beloved childhood home.

His cabin faced the mountains, with a wide porch on which to relax and enjoy the view. As they neared, she noted a glass-plated window on each side of the front door, as well as two rocking chairs. Stacked stone, likely from the nearby river, formed the foundation.

Halting Lucky directly in front, Evan jumped down and helped her out of the saddle. For the briefest of moments, he gazed down at her, his hands a warm weight on her waist. When he stepped back, she tried to hide her disappointment.

"Well, what do you think?" He swept his arm in a

wide arc, his excitement showing in his sparkling eyes and bright smile.

She quashed her sense of loss. "It's beautiful, Evan. You must be so proud. Did you and James help your father build it?"

"Yes, we did." He nodded slowly, his gaze moving along the roofline of the cabin, lost in memories. "Took us a month, only because we had a few locals helping. Otherwise, it would've taken longer."

"Where did you live during that time?"

"Live?" His black brows winged up. "Here. Under the stars."

"Your mother must've liked that," she responded in a dry tone. A few days sleeping outside was tolerable, but an entire month? Mrs. Harrison would've been itching for a stove to cook on and a nice soft bed.

"She didn't complain, but I'd catch her watching us at odd times during the day while we worked, as if she could somehow will the house to go up faster."

Juliana smiled at that but said nothing.

"Once the cabin was finished, we had a barn raising. That took three days because the entire community came out to help. Despite the hard work, it was fun. Everyone brought food and we ate under those trees yonder." He pointed to the sugar maples and oaks beside the barn. "When the sun went down, we had bonfires and music and dancing. Momma was thrilled to meet the other women."

"How long did your parents live here?" she asked gently.

He turned to her, a bittersweet expression stealing across his face. "Not nearly long enough. Four years."

"They were happy here? They didn't regret leaving North Carolina?"

"Very happy." Again, his gaze roamed the landscape. "We all fell in love with this place. About a year after we moved here, the tract next to ours came up for sale and, at my father's urging, my Uncle Clarence and Aunt Willa—Luke's parents—bought it sight unseen. The three of us grew up together."

In her mind's eye, she imagined the three boys racing across this land. "So when James died, in a way Luke lost a brother, too."

It was clear the notion hadn't occurred to Evan. He was quiet a long moment. "Yeah, I suppose you're right. I've never thought about it, but Luke was like a brother to us. I left immediately after the funeral. We never talked about our loss."

"It's never too late, you know."

"You're right. I might stop by his place before I head out in the morning."

Juliana gave him an encouraging smile. "I think that will help the both of you."

He held out his hand. "Come, let me show you inside."

Juliana took his hand and allowed him to lead her inside the cabin. Standing inside the front door, she scanned the spacious living area and kitchen. Considering the sparseness of Luke's cabin, she hadn't expected Evan's to be any different. But here there were cheerful yellow curtains adorning the windows, crocheted pillows piled on the sofa, and hand-stitched samplers hanging on the walls. Then she remembered that this had been his parents' home, and his mother had likely added the feminine touches.

"There are two bedrooms down here." He pointed to

a ladder lying against the wall. "And as you can see a loft up there. That used to be my room when my parents were alive."

"I see."

Still holding her hand, he urged her toward the largest bedroom. A pretty blue-and-white wedding-ring quilt covered the wide bed. She wondered if his mother made it. "This is mine now." He ran a finger along the dresser and scrunched up his nose. "Sorry about the dust. No one's been in here to clean while I've been away." He turned to face her. "You'll sleep in here tonight and the remainder of the time I'm gone."

She opened her mouth to protest, but he raised a hand. "No arguments. I'm sleeping in the barn tonight and tomorrow tonight, so you don't have to feel uncomfortable."

"The barn?" Her brows lifted. "There's plenty of space in here. Why not the loft? I don't mind."

Standing very close, he tilted her chin up with his finger. "I do."

Swallowing hard, she managed, "You've been ill. I'm not sure it's wise for you to sleep out there. If it's anything like our barn, there's no telling the measure of filth in the hay. And the varmints…"

"Juliana," his voice dipped to a husky rasp, "you don't realize the temptation you are to me, do you?"

At first the meaning behind his words didn't sink in. When she didn't speak, he gave a curt laugh and dropped her hand. "I didn't think so. I'm sleeping in the barn."

Evan awoke to the sounds of the cows shuffling down below and the hens clucking in their pen outside the barn. A glance outside the door told him it was after dawn, time to feed and water the animals before going inside to cook breakfast for himself and Juliana.

As he climbed down the ladder, he was met with the sound of an approaching rider. He strode outside, his hand on his gun. The tension left his body when he recognized Thomas Latham, the young man Luke had hired in Evan's absence to do chores around the farm. The two spreads were too much for one man to tend to, of course. The Latham family had moved to the cove a few years after Evan's, and he remembered Thomas as a shy sort.

He greeted the young man with enthusiasm and invited him to breakfast. Thomas refused with the excuse he'd already eaten. Evan explained he'd be leaving again the next day, and that Miss O'Malley was not to be bothered. Blushing, Thomas assured him profusely that he would not go near the lady. Satisfied with his response, Evan helped Thomas with the care of the animals before heading inside with a basket full of eggs.

The smell of coffee met him, but Juliana was nowhere to be seen. Then he noticed the closed bedroom door. He carried the eggs into the kitchen, and after washing his hands at the washstand, he prepared the cornmeal batter. He was in the midst of pouring it into the hot skillet when Juliana appeared with a soft greeting.

At the sight of her, Evan swallowed hard and willed himself not to drop the bowl on his toe. The white blouse she wore, with its fitted bodice, billowing sleeves and cuffed wrists, accompanied by a full skirt, lent her an air of elegance. Her hair, a deep, rich red with golden highlights, hung in a straight, silky curtain around her shoulders. She'd inserted a tiny silver clip just above her ear for decoration. Her porcelain skin was dewy fresh, her green eyes luminous in her oval-shaped face.

She fidgeted beneath his stare. "Are you regretting letting me borrow your mother's things?"

"What?" He shook his head to clear it. "Uh, no. Actually, I don't remember her wearing that at all. Probably reserved it for special outings, which back then were few and far between. You look beautiful."

Long, sooty lashes swept down to hide her eyes. A soft flush infused her skin. "Thank you." She touched her fingers to her hair. "I found this clip in the bottom of the trunk. I hope it's okay for me to use it."

"I told you, Juliana, help yourself to anything you need. Or want."

A line formed between her brows. "I waited for you last night."

He turned his attention back to the hoecakes, lest they burn. "I was worn out. After breakfast I have to head into town."

"I suppose I'll need to stay here," she said quietly, unable to mask her disappointment.

He held the spatula aloft. "I wish I could take you with me, but your showing up on my arm now would stir up a hornet's nest of questions. I don't have time for that."

"I understand. I'll use the time to explore your land, if you don't mind."

"I don't, but I want you to promise me that you won't wander too far." He told her about Thomas Latham and assured her that she wouldn't be bothered by him.

"I'll stay within sight of the house. Now, what can I do to help?"

Evan glanced around the kitchen. "You can pour the coffee and set the table. I keep a jar of molasses in the upper cupboard there."

Within twenty minutes, they had everything ready.

At the last minute, he remembered to pull out her chair for her and wait until she was seated to seat himself. He sat at the head of the table, with Juliana on his left. They simply stared at each other, silly smiles on their faces.

He could hardly believe that she was here—in *his* home—sitting at his table and sharing a meal with him.

With his palm outstretched, he waited for her to slip her slender hand in his and then bowed his head to say grace. It was with reluctance that he released it when the prayer was finished. As they ate, he answered her questions about the farm and the community, more than happy to talk about the home he loved. By the end of the meal, she was looking suitably impressed.

"I wish I could give you a tour of the place myself," he said over his shoulder as he carried empty plates to the kitchen. "I'll probably be gone a couple of hours, so I'll stop by Addie's eating establishment and bring us home some lunch. She makes the best fried chicken I've ever eaten."

"I'll clean this up while you haul in the bath water," she said, moving past him to grab a washcloth to clean the dishes. "Thank you for breakfast. I do feel bad that you have to cook every meal."

"Don't. I'd much rather cook than wash dishes."

"Ah, well, I'm a master dish cleaner because that's all I ever do in the kitchen." She smiled, a sparkle in her eye. "Jessica, Jane and sometimes Megan are in charge of the cooking and Nicole and I handle the clean up."

Evan moved to the door, his hand on the handle. "Speaking of that, the first thing I'm going to do when I get to town is send that telegram to Gatlinburg. Your family will finally get the news they've been waiting for."

Her smile widened and her expression was one of true happiness. "They will be so relieved."

Eager to get ready and be on his way, he hooked a thumb over his shoulder. "Well, I'd better get a move on if I'm going to get everything done before lunch."

"Go." She shooed him out. "Do whatever you have to do."

"Remember what I said," he reminded her an hour later from his perch on the wagon seat.

"Yes, of course." She stood on the front porch, one hand shading her eyes from the bright sun. "Be careful."

Evan stared down at her, wondering if it had been a mistake to bring her here. Forever stored in his memory would be Juliana in his home—standing on his porch, sitting on his sofa, eating at his table. He wouldn't have to imagine her presence here, which meant her absence would be all the more noticeable.

Not for the first time, his thoughts returned to their conversation of the evening before when she'd rejected his offer of a marriage based on friendship. He knew that he was fast approaching the point of offering her his heart merely to keep her near. When he was with Juliana, the grief and loneliness faded away and he felt content to simply be in her presence.

The truth was that Evan didn't want to be alone anymore. Why not share his life with her? Everyone would expect them to marry anyway for propriety's sake. If they married, he would have a companion and her reputation would be protected. Problem solved.

Now all he had to do was convince Juliana.

He tipped his hat. "I'll be back as soon as I can."

Chapter Eighteen

Juliana watched his wagon disappear around the curve before going back inside. As she walked past the fireplace, her glance fell on a small daguerreotype lying flat on the mantel. Picking it up with the tips of her fingers, she stared at the image of a handsome couple and two teenage boys. She recognized the taller boy right away. If her guess was correct, Evan looked to be around the age of fourteen or fifteen. Although thinner, his features less defined, he was handsome even then.

Next to him stood his younger brother, James.

After studying the image, Juliana decided that both boys took after their father in height and coloring, but their noses and mouths resembled their mother's. She placed it back upon the mantel, propping it up against the wall.

Juliana wondered what it would feel like to be the last one left of her entire family. To have nothing left but bittersweet memories. The mere idea made her unbearably sad.

Moving past the mantel, she retrieved her bonnet from the bedroom and walked back outside into the golden sunshine. The air was heavy with moisture, the sun's rays already uncomfortably hot.

Turning in the direction of the barn, she passed beneath the branches of several apple trees, inhaling the pleasant scent of apple blossoms. The shade was pleasant. Beyond the trees, she encountered a chicken coop and a small shed that she didn't explore.

Inside the darkened interior of the barn, she made friends with a calico cat and a sweet gray mare who appeared to be the sole occupants. Everything was neat and tidy—not unlike Evan himself—until she stumbled upon the tool area he'd mentioned before, the place where he liked to invent things. In the far corner of the barn stood a rough wooden table piled high with tools and gadgets of all shapes and sizes. She didn't dare touch a thing lest the whole pile tumble to the dirt floor. If there was enough time, perhaps he would agree to give her a demonstration of one of his devices.

The moment she stepped outside, a warning bell went off inside her head. Something was different. Wrong. The cheerful day had taken on a menacing edge.

Her wide eyes cast about for a clue as to what had sparked her alarm and came up empty. Nothing was out of place. No wild animals. No revenge-seeking outlaws.

Then, a flash of color in the woods. Adrenaline surged through her veins, and she automatically reached for her gun. When her fingers found the empty holster, her heart sank. A lot of good it would do her back in the cabin!

Crouching down, she used the barn door as a shield. Her stomach clenched into a hard knot. She scanned the woods again. Nothing.

She stayed in that position until her legs ached with fatigue. Maybe she'd imagined the whole thing.

Another fifteen minutes dragged by. Finally, she bolted for the cabin. Slamming the door closed and sliding the lock in place, she rested against it trying to catch her breath.

Her gun. She needed her gun. Now.

She found it where she'd left it, checked the chamber and placed it in her holster.

Filled with unease, she peered out the window for what seemed like an hour. When Evan's hired help strode into view, she gasped. Unaware that he was being watched, he strolled casually toward the animal pens.

Irritated with herself, she dropped the curtain. *Silly, Juliana. That's what you are.*

She decided then and there *not* to tell Evan. She wouldn't bother him with what was probably a result of her overactive imagination. He had enough worries. No need adding to them.

He would be leaving in the morning, and she would stay here. Alone.

The more she thought about it, the less she wanted to be left behind. Although she knew he wasn't likely to agree, she would at least try to change his mind.

"I need to talk—"

"There's something I want—"

Speaking at the same time, they both stopped and smiled.

"You first." Evan gestured from his spot on the blanket. They had polished off a delicious lunch of crispy fried chicken, boiled new potatoes, coleslaw and yeast rolls. There were two slices of peach pie, but dessert would have to wait. They were stuffed.

Juliana sat with her legs curled to the side, her pale

skirt billowing around her. She watched the river water meander past, the grayish-brown stones glistening in the sun.

"I want to go with you tomorrow." There, she'd said it.

His brow wrinkled in confusion. "We agreed this was the safest place for you. I know you're eager to see your family, but you won't have to wait long. Alone, I can ride hard and fast and be there in two days. I'll be back for you in no time."

"Don't leave me behind. If I rode one of your other horses, I wouldn't have any trouble keeping up with you. You won't have to worry about me slowing you down, I promise."

"What is it, Juliana?" He gave her a measuring look. "Does the thought of being here alone make you uneasy? If you want, I can arrange for you to stay in town with one of the families there. There will be questions, of course, but we can handle it, if we must."

She thought back to her scare earlier in the day, but brushed it aside. "No, it's not that. I feel safe enough, especially knowing your cousin is nearby. To be honest, I'm worried about your traveling alone." A grasshopper landed on the sole of her boot, and she flicked it off with her finger. "What if you get sick again? Who would take care of you? Or what if something happened to Lucky? What then?" The idea of him stranded in the mountains, perhaps sick or hurt, worried her to no end.

His voice firm but kind, he said, "I appreciate your concern, but you're borrowing trouble. I feel fine. My strength has returned, and I haven't had a weak spell in two days. We'll just have to trust the good Lord to keep me safe. Wasn't it you who reminded me the other day that God is in control?"

His admonition shamed her. She knew better than to give in to worry. Rose's words came back to her—what ifs opened the door to fear. Juliana needed to place Evan's safety in God's hands and trust in His protection.

Her head dipped. "You're right, of course."

With his finger beneath her chin, Evan lifted her face. "I'll be fine, you know."

A sigh escaped her lips. "With God's help, I'll try not to worry while you're gone."

"Good girl."

His affectionate smile eased her tension, making her want to reach over and hug him close. She wanted to feel his strong arms around her, sheltering her.

"Your turn," she announced, shifting position to ease the stiffness in her legs. "What were you about to say before?"

Hooking a hand behind his neck, he hung his head. Whatever it was, he didn't appear eager to discuss it. When she'd decided she couldn't handle the suspense any longer, he lifted his head and looked her square in the eye.

"Look—I like you, Irish. I like being around you. I'm comfortable with you, and I think you feel the same way. This is hard to admit, but I-I'll miss you when you're not around. I think we make a good team, don't you?"

He stared at her, waiting for her to answer. She couldn't. It was as if her brain had suddenly stopped working. When she didn't respond, he plunged on ahead, his words jumbling together in his haste. "You made it plain what you want in a marriage. What if I said I'm open to more than a friendship marriage? Maybe you thought I meant that I didn't want children, but I do. You and I...well, there's something between us. Call it what you want, but I've no doubt we'd be good together."

Juliana sat there, dumbfounded. Was he talking about the marriage bed? A dozen butterflies danced in her stomach as her skin heated beneath his gaze. Evan apparently felt no embarrassment discussing such an intimate subject.

"Exactly what is your point, Evan?" she managed to get out.

"While I can't offer you my heart, I can offer you a normal husband-and-wife relationship. With God's blessing, of course, you'd be able to bear children and be a wife and mother and perhaps even someday a grandmother. What do you say?"

Juliana felt her cheeks burn with humiliation. With hurried movements, she began to stuff the food back into the basket. "I don't think this is a subject I'd like to discuss."

"I didn't intend to offend you, Juliana. I apologize."

She couldn't look at him. "It's too hot out here. I'm going in."

He placed a staying hand on her forearm. "Please, stay. I promise not to bring it up again."

"I can't," she murmured, pulling her arm from his grasp. Forgetting all about the food, she hurried back to the cabin. Mortified both by his words and by her reaction, Juliana fled to the bedroom and bolted the door.

Juliana dashed away the tears leaking from her eyes. So Evan *liked* her. He thought they made a great *team*.

With a soft moan, she sank down on the bed and buried her face in her hands.

So this is what misery feels like.

That day in the mercantile had turned her life topsy-turvy. It was as if that one event bisected her existence— pre-Evan, a time of stability and simple pleasures, and post-Evan, a time of unpredictability and upheaval. Her emotions were not in the least reliable anymore. Her heart had been ensnared by a man who didn't return her love, and she feared that she was destined to mourn for him for the rest of her days.

A fresh wave of tears threatened and, sinking back down on the mattress, she curled into a ball on her side and fell into a troubled sleep.

Juliana awoke to the sounds of Evan knocking around in the kitchen. A glance at the window told her that she'd slept through the evening hours and all night. No doubt her mental anguish had played a part in that. She lay there staring up at the wooden beams, praying for enough strength to make it through the next hour or so until he left.

After yesterday's conversation, she had mixed feelings about his leaving. A part of her was relieved he was going so she wouldn't have to be constantly reminded of what she couldn't have. The other part wanted to fall down at his knees and beg him to take her with him.

A knock on the door startled her out of her reflections.

"Juliana." Evan's voice was muffled. "Are you awake? Breakfast is ready." A pause. "I'd like to see you before I leave."

Exhaling, she sat up. "I'll be out in a few minutes."

"All right." Was it her imagination, or was there relief in his voice?

From among his mother's things, she chose to wear a buttercup-yellow dress with simple lines—a scooped neck, flowing sleeves, a fitted waist and a fluttering skirt. Using the same silver clip, she gathered the hair above her ears and clipped the mass in the back, allowing the rest of her hair to flow around her shoulders.

Stiffening her spine, she sailed with determination toward the dining area.

You can do this, she assured herself. There was no need for tears. Throughout the entire meal, she would remain calm. She could collapse into a worthless heap after he'd gone.

"Is there anything I can do?" There, her voice sounded almost normal.

When his bright blue eyes collided with hers, her lungs struggled to draw in air. The force of his gaze threatened to turn her knees to jelly, and she reached out for something to hold on to. Fortunately, she was standing behind the table and her hands encountered the chair back.

"Have a seat." He indicated with a dip of his head. "Coffee's hot, but I can make tea if you prefer."

She slid out the chair and sank into it gratefully. "Coffee's fine."

He placed a steaming mug in front of her, along with a small jug of cream and a bowl of sugar. That he'd remembered touched her. As if reading her mind, he smiled knowingly. He placed a plate heaping with bacon, eggs, grits swimming in butter and two biscuits in front of her. She waited with her hands in her lap as he readied food for himself. When he sat down beside her, his clean scent wafted in her direction. She breathed it in without being too obvious about it.

"Juliana?"

Her eyes flew open, heat rushing to her cheeks. She hadn't even realized her lids had drifted closed! "Yes?"

"I'm going to pray now," he said, his open palm sliding toward hers.

She placed her hand on top of his and bowed her head. As he prayed, his thumb lazily grazed her skin, making the nerve endings along her arm tingle with awareness. At his *amen,* she snatched back her hand and, ignoring his questioning expression, began to eat without really tasting anything.

Neither one spoke. The silence was almost unbearable for her, not because she knew what to say but because she felt as if they should be taking advantage of this last time together instead of being awkward. When at last he set down his fork and leaned back in his chair, she followed suit even though there was still quite a bit of food left on her plate.

"You're not hungry this morning?" he asked, concerned.

"Not really."

"There's food in the larder for sandwiches and soup. Do you know how to make soup?"

"I won't starve, if that's what you're worried about." She flipped her hair behind her shoulder, irritated at herself. He was worried about her having enough to eat because he knew she had no culinary skills.

"I didn't mean to make you mad," he began, his mouth pensive. "That applies to yesterday, too."

No, she would not rehash *that* conversation, not in her present state. Standing abruptly, she began cleaning the table. He joined in the cleanup without a word, and in minutes the table was wiped clean.

Evan stood near the door. He cleared his throat. "Lucky's outside. My bags are packed and loaded." Lifting the curtain, he glanced out the window. "Dawn's approaching. Guess it's time to hit the trail."

Juliana was so nervous her palms were sweating. Her

emotions were in a jumble. She didn't know what to say or do. So she said nothing.

Their gazes locked, they stared at each other from opposite sides of the room.

"Juliana," he bit out, his voice strained, "aren't you going to say anything?"

Swallowing past a lump, she managed, "Take care of yourself."

"That's it?"

"What else do you want me to say?" She splayed her hands wide.

A muscle jumped in his jaw. He shifted from one foot to the other, an expression of indecision on his handsome face. How she wished she could read his thoughts at that moment.

Especially when he flung his gloves on the table and strode across the room. Juliana was too shocked to move or speak. What was he doing?

He stopped directly before her, his body crowding her back against the cupboard. Not daring to meet his gaze, she allowed hers to roam over his neck and shoulders. The top two buttons of his shirt gaped open, revealing the smooth hollows of his throat and the rapid beat of his pulse.

With deliberate movements, he cupped her neck and eased her face up with slight pressure from his thumbs. As if in slow motion, he lowered his mouth inch by excruciating inch. Perhaps he was giving her a chance to protest. She couldn't. She craved his kiss.

When at last his lips brushed against hers, a sigh of contentment escaped her. He eased back and his blue eyes, hazy with need, sought permission to continue. In answer, Juliana lifted her mouth, and he met hers once again in an unbearably tender kiss.

Overwhelmed by his need for her, Evan forced himself to go slow. Her lips clung to his in sweet innocence as he explored her generous mouth.

Holding her in his arms, Evan entertained thoughts of forever. The thought of leaving her weighed heavy on his heart. If he were completely honest with himself, he'd own up to the fact he didn't want to ever let her go.

When he abandoned her lips to rain kisses along her jawline and the sensitive spot beneath her ear, her swift intake of breath stopped him in his tracks. Lifting his head, he gazed into her green eyes. That one look was all it took. With an abruptness that startled her, he set her away from him and strode across the room. If he didn't put some space between them, he wasn't sure what he might say or do.

"Goodbye, Juliana."

Slamming the front door, he bounded off the porch and hurled himself into the saddle, burying his heel in Lucky's flank.

Chapter Nineteen

Juliana stared at the door. He was gone. Without a single word. How could he kiss her as if she were the most precious thing in the world and then turn around and leave like that?

She rushed to the window and pulled the curtain aside. There was a cloud of dust in the distance, but she couldn't make out his form or that of his horse. She lingered there until the dust settled and the spark of hope that he'd turn around and come back flickered out. He wasn't coming back. Not today, anyway.

Emotions running high, she turned back to the kitchen and attacked the pile of dirty dishes. She was shaky and weak, her lips still tingling from his kiss. His scent lingered in the air, which only intensified her misery. She tried to pray, but the words simply wouldn't come. So she said the only thing she could manage. *Jesus, I need You.*

When she finished cleaning the kitchen, she went to the bedroom to retrieve Evan's Bible. She needed to read those reassuring words and hear her Savior's quiet voice. Nearing the bed, she spotted a small brown package tied up with white twine. There was a note attached with her name printed neatly across it.

Juliana stared at it for the longest time. What had Evan left for her?

With trembling fingers, she picked up the white paper. It fluttered open in her hands. She stared at the tidy black script and imagined him seated at his desk composing the letter.

Dear Irish,
I noticed that day in the mercantile your dress appeared quite new. It didn't take long for it to succumb to the rigors of the trail, however. I've taken the liberty of purchasing you a new one, although it isn't an exact copy. If it doesn't fit correctly, there is a seamstress in town we can visit as soon as I get home. Please don't think me forward. I know it isn't the proper thing for a single man to purchase personal garments for a lady, but I owe you. And you did say it was a favorite of yours.
Sincerely,
Evan

Laying aside the note, Juliana slid the bundle close to the edge of the bed and untied the string. She lifted the brown paper, a tiny sigh escaping her lips at the sight of the luxurious fabric. The dress wasn't blue at all. Instead, it was the same lush, vivid green as the forest. The same hue as her eyes. Which was the reason he'd chosen it, she supposed.

Holding up the dress, she saw that it was very similar in style to her other one, with a fitted bodice, full sleeves

and pleated skirt. Eager to see how it fit, she quickly un-
dressed and slipped it over her head. The smooth material felt wonderful against her skin. Twirling in a circle,
the skirt billowed around her legs before swishing back
into place. Perfect.

If only Evan were here to see her in it. With a sigh,
she sank down on the bed and picked up the note, reading his words until she had them memorized. She missed
him so much it hurt.

How would she ever get through the days ahead?

Evan was so lost in thought that he nearly rode straight
past Luke's place.

Slowing the big black to a walk, he approached the
cabin and dismounted.

He didn't bother knocking. Luke looked up from his
place at the table, surprise registering on his face.

"Morning." He wiped his mouth with a napkin. "Want
something to eat before you head out?"

"No, thanks." He went over to the table and sat down
opposite Luke. "I came to remind you to keep an eye on
Juliana."

"Do you want me to go over there at lunchtime or wait
until the afternoon?"

"Thomas will be around during the day, so why don't
you go around suppertime? She doesn't know how to
cook. Could you rustle up something simple?"

Luke's brows shot up. "I thought every woman knew
how to cook."

For some reason, Luke's reaction set his teeth on edge.
He was immediately defensive. "Apparently not. Don't
mention it to her, okay? She's touchy about it."

He held up his hands. "My lips are sealed. I'll make

it appear as if I'm just being neighborly." A speculative gleam entered his eyes. "We've known each other a long time, Evan. I've never seen you act this way, which tells me this girl is special. Tell me the truth. Are you in love with her?"

Evan's gaze fell away. "Don't be ridiculous."

Luke fingered his chin. "Oh. Then you won't mind if I court her? In case you've forgotten, I've always been partial to redheads."

He *had* forgotten. The thought of any man—family or no—looking at Juliana with romance on his mind set his blood boiling. "Don't even think about it," he said through gritted teeth. "She's off-limits."

Luke drew his head back. "Well, if you don't want to pursue her, why can't I?"

Evan glared at Luke. He got the feeling his cousin wasn't truly interested, but was testing him. Standing abruptly, Evan rocked the chair back; it would've crashed to the floor if he hadn't caught it. He strode to the window and looked out. Streaks of pink and orange brightened the horizon. He didn't need this right now. Time was slipping away. Still, something held him back.

"Or do you really want her for yourself?" Luke moved up beside him. "That's it, isn't it? You love her, but you don't want to admit it. To yourself or anyone else."

He shook his head, irritated with himself, his cousin and the conversation. "You wouldn't understand." He ignored the little voice inside that said it was too late.

Luke's hand settled on his shoulder. "Don't let fear ruin your chance at happiness."

Unwilling to listen to reason, Evan pushed past him. "I have to go."

"Still running, I see."

Evan stopped in his tracks. He slowly turned around. "I've got a job to do."

"Why don't you let the law handle it?"

"This is personal, and you know it."

Sorrow etched his features. "I lost James, too. I grieve for him just as you do. Every day. You two were the brothers I never had. And I've been mighty worried about you, Evan. I've spent many nights by my bedside asking God to keep you safe and bring you home where you belong."

"You're right." Shame and guilt coursed through him. "I was so caught up in my own grief that I didn't stop to think how James's death had affected you. I'm sorry. Will you forgive me?"

"There's nothing to forgive. I know you didn't do it intentionally."

"Thanks, Luke." Evan made to leave. "Would you mind continuing those prayers? I have a feeling I'm gonna need them."

Evan had been on the trail about an hour when he suddenly changed direction. As much as he hated to prolong his absence, he couldn't shake the feeling something or someone awaited him in Knoxville. It wasn't that far out of his way, and he would stay just one night.

James's murder had happened in the outskirts of the sprawling city, and if there were any witnesses to be found, they'd most likely be there. Shortly after his brother's death, Evan had spent two weeks frequenting saloons and gentlemen's clubs, searching for information. It was in one of these saloons that he'd overheard Cliff Roberts and his men boasting about a large amount of cash they'd lifted from an unsuspecting traveler.

But in the eleven months he'd spent with them, he

hadn't been able to get his hands on a single piece of evidence. Nor had he gotten any of them to talk. Sometimes he had the scary thought he had the wrong group of outlaws. That another gang was responsible for James's murder, and he'd wasted nearly a year of his life.

No, his mind rebelled. He had the right gang. He could feel it in his gut. But how long could he live like this? How could he ever leave Juliana and go back to living a lie?

He prayed for guidance. He also asked God to lead him to the right place, to help him find evidence so that he could finally bring those responsible to justice.

The sun was setting when he entered the city, down near the waterfront. Mostly men loitered on the street, some searching for entertainment, some for trouble. Normally, Evan wouldn't frequent this part of town, but he wasn't going to find what he was looking for among the upstanding citizens of society.

He dismounted near Lucy's Café, unhappy about the prospect of eating in the greasy establishment. But he didn't want to waste time searching for a reputable eatery. He just needed something to fill his stomach so he could get on with his search.

A half hour later, he exited the place with a bad case of heartburn. With a sigh, he headed down the street toward his first stop for the night—the Red Rose Saloon. The moment he stepped inside the dark, smoky room reeking of unwashed bodies and stale liquor, he knew it was going to be a long night.

Juliana stood with Lucas Harrison on the front porch of Evan's cabin. He was eyeing the darkening clouds with some concern.

"Looks like we're in for a storm. I'd better head home before it lets loose."

"Thank you for the lovely meal." She smiled over at him. "You're a wonderful cook."

Evan's cousin had arrived a few hours earlier with a whole chicken for them to share. He'd also brought green beans with bacon, corn on the cob, and those light-and-fluffy biscuits she liked so much. There were enough leftovers to feed her for a week.

At first she'd been self-conscious in his company, but he'd quickly lightened her mood with silly jokes and more stories of his and Evan's childhood pranks. Luke was a kind man with a good sense of humor. He was also handsome. She'd found herself wondering which of her sisters would be a good match for him.

"Glad you enjoyed it," he interrupted her musings, his eyes twinkling. "My mom taught me everything I know about cookin'. I'm real glad she did, too, since I don't have a wife to cook for me. I'd hate to eat beans and corn bread every night like some bachelors I know."

Juliana merely smiled and dipped her head. She wouldn't pry.

He dropped his hat on his head. "You know where to find me if you need anything. You can trust Thomas, too. He's a good kid."

As he descended the stairs, she walked to the edge of the porch. "I'm glad you stopped by, Luke. You helped get my mind off things."

He stood next to his horse, his expression serious for the first time that night. "Don't worry. Evan will be back as soon as he can manage it."

She hoped he was right. Thunder sounded in the distance, and she felt a spatter of rain. "You'd better hurry."

He climbed into the saddle. "Remember, keep your eyes and ears open. And don't go anywhere without your weapon."

Juliana nodded, thinking he sounded a lot like Evan at that moment. "I'll be careful. Good night."

He lifted his hand in farewell. She waited until he disappeared from sight to go inside.

She slid the lock in place and walked to each of the windows, pulling the curtains closed. Lightning flashed in the distance. Suddenly, the rain pounded on the rooftop and battered the windows. The dirt turned to mud within seconds.

She doubted Luke made it home in time to stay dry.

Once she had lit the kerosene lamps, she retrieved her coffee and got comfortable on the sofa, her thoughts consumed by Evan. Where was he? Was he safe? Well or ill? Was he thinking of her and, if so, what were his thoughts?

A loud crash near the back of the house brought her to her feet. Heart hammering, she hastily set down her coffee mug and reached for her weapon on the side table. Nerves on high alert, she gripped the gun handle and forced her feet to move toward the bedroom door.

Her mind raced with possibilities. A fallen tree limb? A lightning strike? Or something more sinister... She couldn't be sure if the sound had come from outside the house or inside.

When she reached the doorway to Evan's bedroom, she regretted not grabbing a lamp. Shadows lurked in the corners. Squinting, she was barely able to make out the outlines of the heavy furniture.

Her blood roaring in her ears, she stood stock-still, half expecting someone to jump out at her. Nothing happened. Exhaling, she crept toward the windows she'd forgotten to cover.

When she reached the first window, she peered out into the inky darkness. Flashes of light illuminated the yard. She couldn't see any fallen limbs or overturned barrels. She slid the curtain in place.

As she rounded the bed and neared the second window, she noticed a hairline crack in the glass, so tiny it was barely visible. Bending over to get a closer look, she touched the tip of her finger to the cold pane. Strange. She hadn't noticed that before.

In that moment, lightning split the sky just as thunder cracked directly above her head. She screamed and jumped back, her hand pressing against her heart.

The sky went dark again. She blew out a breath. *You're being silly, Juliana. There's nothing out there. You're letting your imagination run wild.*

Setting the gun on the side table, she reached for the curtain. As her fingers closed over the material, the sky brightened once more. There, near the barn door, stood a man.

Juliana froze. No. Couldn't be. Was she seeing things? She closed her eyes. When she opened them, darkness once again shrouded the outbuildings.

Feeling ill, she wrenched the curtain closed, grabbed her gun and ran back into the living room. She extinguished all the lamps except one.

Adrenaline pumping through her body, she hurried up the ladder to the loft. She crouched with her back against the wall. Up here, she would have a clear view of the front door. She extinguished the light, plunging the cabin into utter darkness.

If and when Lenny Fitzgerald walked through that door, she would be ready. Waiting.

At two in the morning, Evan left the saloon on Collier Street, his eyes gritty from cigar smoke and a bad taste in his mouth. Sharp disappointment settled on his shoulders. He'd struck out. A dozen saloons. Countless questions. No answers.

Lord, I know You want justice for James as much or more than I do. I don't know where to turn. I could use some help here.

He was beyond tired. Weariness seeped into his bones. And he missed Juliana. He was lonely without her.

Despite the late hour, men—most of them drunk—still milled about the street. Evan mounted Lucky and pointed him toward the hotel where he would sleep a few hours before making his way to Gatlinburg.

He had almost reached his destination when he noticed a pair of men engaged in a heated argument. He urged Lucky to the opposite side of the street. This late at night, the men were likely to be drunk. And whenever alcohol was involved, an argument could quickly turn deadly. The last thing Evan needed was to get caught in the crossfire.

Wary, he watched them carefully. Light from the lamppost illuminated their faces. There was something oddly familiar about the shorter man. Evan racked his brain. Who was he and where had he seen him before?

He was young, possibly early twenties. Light hair. Angular jaw. Ears that stuck out a bit too far…

Evan straightened in the saddle. Randy Roberts. Cliff Roberts's son.

Something told him he needed to stop and talk to Randy. With a silent petition for wisdom, Evan halted Lucky and dismounted. The other men paid him no mind, so intent were they on each other. He approached them with caution.

"Randy Roberts? Is that you?" he called out in a friendly voice.

The blond man turned startled eyes on Evan, while the other man scowled. Evan's gaze noted that the man's hand moved to his weapon. To Evan's surprise, neither man appeared to be under the influence.

"I haven't seen you in months!" Evan walked closer. "How've ya been?"

Randy's brow furrowed. "Do I know you, mister?"

"Not exactly." He nodded to the other man before turning his full attention to Randy. "But I know you. I work for your father."

A curtain fell over his features. "My father and I haven't spoken in nearly a year."

"What do ya want, stranger?" the other man growled. "We've got business here."

"Cliff is in a heap of trouble, Randy," Evan tried to appeal to the young man's sense of duty, if he had any. "He needs your help."

A worry line appeared between his brows. "What kind of trouble?"

"Forget it, kid," the man said. "Like you said, you haven't seen your old man in months. Why should you care?"

Evan watched as various emotions danced across Randy Roberts's face. Somehow, he had to get Randy alone.

"Look, I just want to talk to you for a little while about your dad." He shot a glance at the other man. "Alone."

Randy hesitated. Then he looked at his partner. "If my father is in trouble, I need to know about it. We can talk tomorrow."

"This won't wait," the other man bit out.

"Look, if the law comes down on my father, it could affect what we've got going here. And I don't think you want that."

He shot Evan an irate glance. "I'll be around tomorrow afternoon. You'd better be where I can find you."

Randy watched without a word as the other man walked away. Then he turned to Evan. "Silver Creek Café is around the corner. We can talk there."

The café was practically empty, not surprising considering the late hour. Evan led the way to a table in the far corner, ordering two coffees when the waitress stopped for their order.

Across from him, Randy sat on the edge of his seat, his expression a mix of concern and resignation. "So what's the charge against my father?"

For a brief moment, Evan considered lying in order to get his information. But he'd had enough of deceit. He would be honest and hope the young man would co-operate.

Leaning back, his arms crossed, Evan shrugged. "There isn't any. Yet. Truth is, I'm not here to talk about Cliff. I need information, and I figure you might be able to help me get it."

Randy stiffened in anger. "Has the law caught my father or not?"

"Nope. He's still a free man."

"Then I'm out of here."

When he made to rise, Evan spoke. "Don't you want to hear what Fitzgerald's up to these days?"

At that name, Randy froze halfway out of the seat. The waitress appeared then with two steaming cups of coffee, her gaze curious. Evan passed her enough money to pay the bill plus a little extra.

"At least stay and drink the coffee," he suggested after she'd walked back to the kitchen. "I can fill you in on what's been going on since you left."

Randy sat with a huff. He was holding the warm mug between his palms but not moving to take a drink. "I disliked that no-account on sight. Never did understand why my father took up with him. Before that, we stuck to stealin' money. Maybe a horse here and there. The first time I watched Fitzgerald shoot a man, my gut told me it wouldn't be the last." Bitter regret hardened his young features. "Tried to reason with my father, but he wouldn't budge. So I left."

"Why didn't you take Art with you?"

"Art?" His brows drew together. "He's still with you? He told me he was leaving after the next robbery. Needed money to get home."

Evan wondered what had happened to those plans. The next time he saw the young man, he'd be sure to ask. He didn't like to think he'd been intimidated into staying, but that could've happened.

"If you see Art again, tell him to come and find me," Randy said.

Evan agreed that he would, then gave him the short version of the events of the last eleven months. "He's trailing me now. Wants revenge for what my friend Juliana did to him." He told Randy how she threw hot grease in Fitz's face in order to escape.

A glimmer of amusement entered his hard eyes. "I like the way she thinks."

"Yeah, well, she's alone right now. And Fitz is still out there."

"Which begs the question, why are you here and not with her?"

Evan inhaled sharply. "My brother was shot and robbed not far from here. I have reason to believe someone in Cliff's gang is the shooter. I think you might know who that man is."

"No." He shook his head vigorously. "I'm not a squealer."

"Randy." Evan leaned over the table, crowding the younger man as anger surged. "I don't think you understand the seriousness of this situation. An innocent man was gunned down in cold blood. Someone must pay."

"Look. I'm sorry about your brother, but I won't talk." He clamped his lips shut in defiance.

Trying to rein in his emotions, Evan leaned back against the hard wooden chair and glared at him. "Fine. But when I go to the authorities about Cliff and his gang, I'll conveniently remember you as one of the former members."

He barked a laugh. "Right. *You're* gonna go to the law. And what about the bounty on your head? Think they're gonna overlook your crimes just for information? Information you can't prove?"

Slipping his hand in his pants pocket, he held up the sheriff's badge. The color drained from Randy Roberts's face and he slumped in his chair.

Evan smirked. "Still don't feel like talkin'?"

* * *

Juliana ached all over. Weak sunlight filtered through the curtains down below, which meant the storm was long gone. And so was the mysterious intruder, if, in fact, there had ever been one. She struggled to her feet, every muscle in her body protesting the movement.

Down in the kitchen, she started a fire in the stove and put on a pot of water for coffee. While waiting for that to boil, she went to the windows and peeked out. Looked the same as it had the day before. Nothing out of the ordinary.

What she saw had probably been a shadow. A trick of light. Perhaps she needed spectacles.

Sitting at the table with her coffee and a biscuit left over from the night before, her thoughts strayed to Evan. She prayed for his safety and swift return.

The ache in her heart was so great that she was seriously considering marrying him, despite everything. At this point, she couldn't imagine life without him. The mere thought of him dropping her off at her mother's and leaving her behind filled her with sorrow.

The biscuit, which had tasted so delicious the night before, now felt like sawdust in her mouth. Her appetite had fled. Resigned to the long day ahead, she gathered her dirty dishes.

She was elbow deep in dishwater when she heard heavy footfalls on the front porch. She stilled. Had Evan changed his mind and come back for her? Hope surged within her breast.

The door burst open with such force it banged against the inside wall. The man in the doorway was not Evan. Lenny Fitzgerald's evil presence filled the doorway, his soulless eyes boring into her.

Her heart sank. Her gun was six feet away. On the table.

He spotted it and grinned. Then he slammed the door behind him and advanced toward her.

Her last thought before her piercing scream rent the air was that Evan would never know how much she loved him.

Chapter Twenty

Peace. Sweet, glorious peace. The need for justice no longer smoldered like a cantankerous ulcer in his gut.

Evan stood on the boardwalk in front of the sheriff's office and watched Randy Roberts melt into the bustling morning crowd. He took a deep breath.

James, he thought, *you're finally going to get the justice you deserve.*

Thank You, Father, he humbly prayed. If it hadn't been for Randy's testimony, Evan would still be on the hunt for evidence. Still living a lie. He'd be headed for Gatlinburg right now.

Instead, a dozen or so sheriff's deputies, armed and carrying arrest warrants, were on their way to the little cabin outside Juliana's hometown. They would also be hunting Fitzgerald.

He flashed back to Randy's statement. Seemed his instincts had been right all along. Fitzgerald and another man Evan had never met, Harold Greene, were there the night of James's murder. Both men had fired their pistols. Both were guilty of murder.

It had been tough, sitting there in that stale, dusty office and listening to Randy recount the events of that night. He relived every emotion his brother must've experienced. Shock. Anger. Disbelief. The need to fight back.

But he'd sensed God's presence, helping him work through the fresh wave of grief and pain. Again, he reminded himself that God would handle the wicked. Evan's job was done.

Approaching his mount, he swung up in the saddle and pointed Lucky toward home.

Once on the open trail, he lifted his face to the cheerful morning sun and tried to imagine Juliana's surprise when he arrived home unexpectedly. Lord willing he'd get home by late afternoon. He wondered if she'd still be angry or if she'd be pleased to see him.

One thing was for sure—he had to convince her to marry him. He wanted to share his life with her. While he wasn't ready to admit that he loved her, he had his doubts about whether he'd ever be able to ride away from her.

Because he was eager to get home, time dragged. Seemed he was checking the position of the sun every twenty minutes. He stopped only a handful of times, when he felt Lucky needed a rest and a drink.

Finally, at about four o'clock, he rode onto his cousin's land. As he neared Luke's house, he decided he'd forgo a visit. Time enough tomorrow to let Luke know about his return. He was impatient to see Juliana.

But then he spotted Thomas barreling into the yard on his chestnut. Evan was suspicious at once. The young man wouldn't be here unless there was a problem.

Yanking on the reins, he turned his horse around. By the time he'd reached the cabin, Thomas and Luke were waiting for him.

"Evan!" Luke shouted. "What are you doing back here?"

Evan ignored the question, his gaze focused on Thomas, who was red-faced and winded. Evan steeled himself for bad news. "What's wrong?"

"Mr. Harrison," he panted, "I can't find Miss O'Malley anywhere."

"Why were you looking for her in the first place?" he demanded.

The young man's eyes widened. "I wasn't. I walked past the cabin on my way to the barn and noticed the door ajar. I thought that was unusual, so I called for her. I called and called and she didn't answer."

"Did you go inside?" Evan said, trying to keep a firm rein on his emotions. There had to be a logical explanation. "Maybe she was taking a nap."

"I didn't want to, it being your home and all—"

"Just get to the point," Evan interrupted.

"Yes. And she wasn't there."

"What about the loft? Did you check up there?"

"Well, no, I didn't."

Evan had heard enough. While it was entirely possible she could've gone up to the loft to lie down, he didn't think that was likely. And she would've heard Thomas calling her. Something was very wrong.

"Let's hope she decided to go swimming." He strode past Thomas toward Lucky.

"I checked the water. She wasn't there, either."

"I'm coming with you," Luke called out, already on his way to the barn to saddle his horse. "Go on ahead, I'll catch up."

When Evan rode into the yard and saw the door standing wide open, an odd feeling washed over him. This couldn't be good.

"Juliana? Are you in here?"

He stormed into the cabin. The air was still and silent. "Juliana?"

As he turned to go back out the door, his gaze fell on a smattering of dark spots on the floorboards near the base of the washstand. Strange. He rounded the ceiling-high cupboard and stopped, his mouth falling open when he spied the mess.

Dishes lay in a heap on the floor. Everything else in the room was in order except for this one spot. He snapped his mouth shut. Dread flooded his soul. It was as if she'd dropped the pile of them and had left in a hurry.

One question burned in his mind. Had she left of her own free will or had she been forced?

Evan searched the entire cabin with an urgency born of desperation. Nothing was out of place, not a pillow or quilt disturbed. He ran out into the front yard, yelling her name in hopes that she had merely to run to the outhouse. Or perhaps she'd heard an animal in distress and had gone to check it out.

A shiny object on the bottom step caught his eye, and he lunged for it. Holding it in the palm of his hand, his stomach did a nosedive. It was his mother's silver clip, the one Juliana often wore in her hair. Surely it wouldn't have come undone by itself!

Had she dropped it there intentionally for him to find? Or had it fallen out during a struggle?

Panic was quickly setting in. The one suspicion he couldn't ignore was that Fitzgerald had followed them here and bided his time until Juliana was alone and unprotected to make his move.

She wasn't in the barn. Or the shed. Nor was she anywhere near the animal pens.

Dear God, no. Please. I can't lose her. I can't face— He broke off midprayer, incapable of finishing the thought.

He squeezed his eyes shut. If he lost her now, he would never recover.

Unbidden, a verse he'd learned long ago came to mind. *For God has not given us a spirit of fear, but of power, of love and of a sound mind.*

Help me, Father. Lead me to her. Keep her safe.

Feeling slightly more in control of his emotions, Evan tried to think rationally. If Fitzgerald had indeed taken her, where would he go? What would he do?

He knew Fitzgerald well enough to figure he'd want to see Evan suffer. If Fitz thought he could get to Evan by hurting Juliana, he'd do it in a heartbeat. Which meant he wouldn't go far. He'd wait until an opportune time to show himself. After that, it was anybody's guess what he'd do.

Luke and Thomas rode up in a hurry.

"Anything?" Luke asked, his horse prancing from side to side.

"No." Evan scanned the grounds, on the look out for anything out of the ordinary. "I think I know what happened. And this is what we're gonna do about it…"

Juliana was living her worst nightmare. Slumped against a tree, she strained at the tight ropes binding her wrists. The gag in her mouth smelled of stale sweat and alcohol, making her stomach roil with nausea.

She kept a wary eye on her captor. Crouched down behind a bush, gun drawn, he kept watch on the cabin. So far he hadn't hurt her. But what would he do when he realized Evan wasn't coming back any time soon? Shuddering with the possibilities, she pleaded to God for mercy.

Lenny Fitzgerald hated Evan and wanted to make him suffer. And he wanted revenge for what she'd done to him.

Evan, my love. Why didn't I tell you how I felt?

The realization he might never know made her want to weep. Filled with profound sadness, she ducked her head and blinked back a rush of tears. She couldn't let Fitzgerald see her weakness. It would only make things harder for her.

Too bad she couldn't change the past. If only she'd thought to put the gun belt on that morning. If only she'd told Evan about her strange experience yesterday afternoon. If only—

A voice calling in the distance split the silence. She whipped up her head. *Thomas,* she thought, *the hired man.* He'd no doubt come to the cabin for something and found the mess in the kitchen. What would he do when he couldn't find her? Would he go to Luke Harrison's place or wait around for her to come back?

Her captor glared at her over his shoulder. Angry red welts marked his face where she'd burned him. "Looks like loverboy came back. Good. I didn't want to wait around here much longer."

Juliana gave a quick prayer, asking God to protect the unsuspecting Thomas.

The voice grew closer. He was calling her name over and over again. Odd. She wouldn't have thought he'd be all that frantic. After all, he didn't know her. Maybe he was afraid Evan or Luke would blame him if something happened to her. She hoped that wouldn't be the case.

"There he is!" he growled.

Her captor leapt up, startling her. Before she could react, he seized her arm in a bruising grip and, hauling her up, began dragging her away from the dense stand of trees. Without her bonnet to shade her eyes, the sun's rays temporarily blinded her.

Ignoring her whimpers of protest, he forced her to stand in front of him. Repulsed at being held against his foul body, she tried to inch away. He bit out a curse and wrapped his beefy arm around her neck, nearly cutting off her air supply. She started to struggle once more, but instantly stilled when she felt the tip of a gun barrel pressed against her temple.

Icy shards of fear skittered down her back. *Oh, God, no! Not like this!*

"Harrison!" he bellowed, jarring her eardrum. "Is this what you're looking for?"

Was Fitzgerald blind? Thomas Latham was shorter than Evan, not to mention a whole lot leaner. He didn't have the muscular frame Evan did. Juliana squinted, trying to get a better view.

"Let her go, Fitz," an achingly familiar voice carried across the field. "This is between you and me."

Juliana stiffened in alarm. It couldn't be. Evan was long gone by now! Wasn't he?

Gun aimed in their direction, his long, confident strides ate up the distance. The clothing told her that it was indeed Evan—he'd been dressed all in black. But what was he doing here? Hope and fear warred with one another. What if Fitzgerald shot and killed him before her very eyes?

Fitzgerald snorted. "Nope. I've been watching the two of you long enough. This girl's caught your fancy, and I'm gonna enjoy watching your face as I put a bullet through her skull."

His words chilled her to the bone. This was a man

who'd killed before and wouldn't hesitate to do it again. She meant less than nothing to him.

"Besides," he growled in a voice filled with hatred, "she scarred me for life. I owe her."

He jammed the barrel hard against her temple and spots danced before her eyes. She blinked hard, trying to clear her vision. Her heart was racing like a runaway wagon.

There was no doubt in her mind her very life was on the line. There was a gun pointed to her head, and the man with the finger on the trigger was not in possession of a conscience.

"You have to admit you weren't that good-looking to begin with," Evan drawled, goading him. "I doubt a few scars are gonna make that much difference."

"You always were so sure of yourself, Harrison. But I told Cliff I didn't trust you. Something was off from the beginning. Looks like I was right." He slid the hammer back with a click.

Juliana moaned through the gag in her mouth. Evan's hard gaze flew to her, and he faltered. Alarm flashed across his face.

Fitzgerald caught the look. He let out a cruel laugh. "Not so sure of yourself now, huh? How does it feel now that I've got the upper hand?" He jerked her roughly to one side. "Throw down your weapon."

Evan fought for control. Loathing and rage churned in his gut. His sole desire in that instant was to blow a hole through Fitzgerald's chest.

This man had already stolen his brother away from him. And now Juliana was a hairsbreadth away from death. One false move could prove disastrous.

Her eyes begged him not to do it. He had no choice. Every muscle in his body tense and ready to spring into action, he warily tossed the gun on the ground.

Please, God. Help us save her. I wasn't there to save James. But there's still a chance here. Were Luke and Thomas in position? He couldn't make his move until they were. He'd have to keep him talking.

"Kick it over here," Fitz commanded.

Again, Evan did as he was told.

"Get down on your knees."

A muscle twitched in his jaw, and his mouth hardened to a grim line. His movements slow and calculated, he eased down onto his knees, palms up. "Okay, you have me where you want me. Let her go."

His mouth contorted into a sneer. "Why would I do that? She's my ace."

"What are you going to do?" Evan said, his eyes cold as a winter snow. "Kill us both? What will that get you besides more time in a jail cell?"

"If I'm going down, I'm bringin' you with me," he spat. "You and me are on the same side of the law."

"Yeah, about that…" He cocked his head to one side, his eyes narrowing.

"Stop!"

Evan jerked his head to the left and spotted Art jogging across the field, his gun aimed at Fitzgerald. Dread curled through his bones. The boy was likely to get himself killed.

"Don't do this, Fitz!" Art pleaded. "Miss O'Malley doesn't deserve this! And Roberts will kill you if you shoot Harrison!"

"Go back to your post, you idiot." Fitzgerald dismissed him. "This is my business, not yours."

Art stiffened. "I may be young, but I'm not an idiot. And, unlike you, I have a heart. Now let her go."

"I don't think so." Fitz trained his gun on Art.

Juliana cried out. Evan's gaze flew to her. She struggled against Fitz's tight hold, her fingers clawing the arm he held around her neck. *What was she doing?* He stiffened, ready to hurl himself at the other man.

Chapter Twenty-One

Juliana couldn't breathe. His arm tightened around her throat, choking her. She fought against him, unmindful of the gun. She needed air!

"Juliana, don't!"

Evan's plea reached her ears seconds before the loud crack of a weapon. Eyes squeezed tight, she hunched down and braced against the explosion of pain that never came.

Someone shoved her to the side. She landed hard. Gritting her teeth at the jarring discomfort, Juliana scrambled to get out of the way. The ropes dug painfully into her wrists. Her heel caught the edge of her dress, ripping it.

Voices volleyed all around her, as did the sounds of scuffling and muttered oaths.

Frenzied thoughts bounced around in her mind. Had Evan been shot? Was Art okay?

When she felt she was at a safe distance, she craned her neck, searching for Evan. Her hair fell in her eyes, and she shook her head to dislodge it. She recognized Luke. He was scrambling to hold down Fitzgerald. Thomas was there, too, doing his best to pull Evan off the outlaw.

Tears of relief clogged her throat at the sight of Evan unharmed. He was safe, thank God!

She wanted to scream at Evan to stop, to let the authorities mete out Fitzgerald's punishment, but the gag silenced her. Gone was the control of a few minutes ago. Fury marked his features. She'd never seen that expression on his face. Anxious over what he might do, she prayed Thomas would be able to hold him.

A movement to the side of her vision caught her attention. It was Art, and he was lying on his side cradling his shoulder. Blood trickled onto the ground from the gaping wound in his arm. No! The gag muffled her cry of distress.

Slowly, Luke's voice penetrated the haze of fury clouding Evan's brain. Staring down into his enemy's unrepentant face, he slackened his grip on his neck. He wouldn't lower himself to the other man's level.

Twisting out of Thomas's hold, Evan stumbled back, chest heaving with exertion. Sweat poured off his face. He watched as the two men tied Fitzgerald's hands and feet. Foul language spewed from the outlaw's mouth.

Satisfied Fitz was no longer a threat, Evan sprinted to Juliana's side. He dropped to his knees and eased her up into a sitting position. "Are you hurt?" He made quick work of the knot at the back of her head and removed the gag.

"Evan," she gasped. She fell against him, her head heavy on his chest.

"Everything's all right now, my darling." He lightly stroked her hair, smoothing the damp tendrils from her face. Tears burned his eyes. Overwhelming gratitude made him want to shout for joy. He held her close, hardly daring to believe she was safe in his arms. For a few minutes back there, he'd feared the worst. "You're safe. I promise that as long as I'm around to protect you, nothing like this will ever happen again."

"Evan, please." She sucked in air, her eyes pleading, "Art's been shot."

"What?" He glanced over his shoulder. "I'll see to him." He sliced through the thick rope binding her hands and helped her up. "Are you all right to walk?"

"I'm fine."

When they reached Art, Evan noticed the young man's pallor. "Art, I'm gonna check the wound. I'll be as easy as I can, buddy."

With a curt nod and a grimace, Art braced himself. Juliana moved to sit on his other side and took his hand in hers. "I'm praying for you."

He eased his eyes opened. "If it eases your mind any, ma'am, I asked Jesus to be Lord of my life. To forgive me for my sins."

The emotion on Juliana's face mirrored the feelings in Evan's heart. This was amazing news!

"Oh, Art, I'm so happy for you."

"I'm proud of you," Evan added. He squeezed Art's good shoulder before turning to tend to his injury. Luke walked up and assisted him. They were able to stop the flow of blood. It appeared that the bullet had gone straight through. There'd be no need for surgery, other than stitching up the opening.

Luke helped Evan load Art into the back of the wagon where a bound-and-gagged Fitzgerald awaited his trip to jail. Ignoring the outlaw, Evan patted Art's leg. "Juliana and I will stop by the doc's office shortly to check on you."

Humble gratitude shone in his eyes. "I'd be mighty grateful if you'd send my ma a telegram for me. Tell her where I am."

"I'll get the information from you and send it today. How's that?"

"Thanks, Harrison. For everything."

"Watch that shoulder."

Evan turned to his cousin and Thomas and shook both their hands. "I owe you both."

"You go take care of that young lady," Luke advised. "Remember, no fear."

Evan smiled. "I remember."

He waited until the wagon started rolling down the drive to turn his attention to Juliana. She was sitting on the porch steps, watching him. He eased down beside her, his hungry gaze freely roaming her uplifted face. "Are you all right?"

Her luminous green eyes seemed just as eager to drink him in. "I'm fine. The Lord kept me safe, and He sent you to rescue me." As if a thought struck her, she tilted her head to one side. "Why did you come back?"

"I'll explain later. Right now, all I want is to look at you. Maybe the fact that you're safe and sound will start to sink in."

Summoning courage, Juliana lifted a trembling hand to caress his face. "I love you, Evan." Ignoring his sharp intake of breath, she rushed on. "And if your offer of marriage still stands, I—I accept. I understand it will be a union based on friendship alone. I know you don't return my feelings—"

"You're wrong." He suddenly gripped her shoulders. "I *do* love you, Juliana. My heart belongs to you. Has for a long time."

Juliana stared at him in disbelief. Had she heard right?

His eyes were soft with emotion. "I don't blame you for not believing me. I've been an utter fool. I thought if I ignored my feelings long enough they would go away. I was wrong." He stroked her cheek with the back of his hand. "I realized that I've been letting fear rule my life. I don't want to worry anymore about what ifs. I want to focus on the here and now."

"Oh, Evan," she breathed, her heart bursting with joy, "I think I've loved you since that first day. You were so furious when Fitzgerald hurt me, you took it personally even though you didn't know me. And you were protective, so careful in your treatment of me. Deep down, I knew you were a good man."

His mouth parted in surprise. "Are you saying you cared for me all along? Before you knew the truth?"

She laughed softly. "I kept telling myself all the reasons I shouldn't fall in love with an outlaw, but my heart wouldn't listen."

"Juliana," he breathed her name with awe, lowering his head to kiss her. He held her as if she were a rare treasure, the movement of his lips against hers achingly tender. Easing away, he sent her an earnest smile. "Remember you said you wanted a man who was desperate to marry you?"

Her heart skipped a beat. The love shining in his eyes made her feel so special. "Yes, I remember."

"You're lookin' at him," he claimed softly, his hands framing her face. "You bring me such joy, Juliana. I don't want to imagine my life without you in it. Please say you'll marry me."

"I want nothing more than to be your wife. To share

the rest of my days with you." She beamed, blinking back tears of joy.

"Let's start with today." He grinned, his expression more serene than she'd ever seen it.

"What do you mean?"

"I want to marry you today. We can have the pastor here perform a simple ceremony with Luke as our witness. Then we could have a fancy one in Gatlinburg for all your friends and family. What do you think of that idea?"

The dress and cake and decorations didn't matter to her. The most important thing was the joining of their lives.

Juliana wrapped her arms around his neck and lifted her face for a kiss. "Brilliant. How soon can you be ready?"

Evan held her tight against him and kissed her thoroughly. "One hour?" he whispered, his forehead resting against hers.

At this point, she would agree to anything he suggested. He *loved* her. She was still working to understand that fact. "You've got yourself a deal."

"I love you, Juliana. I always will."

His tender vow touched her deep inside. "And I you."

Epilogue

Flanked on either side by her twin sisters, Juliana waited near the cake table for her husband to join her. Dusk was fast approaching. Already lanterns were being lit and placed on the tables. Lightning bugs flitted about, their flashes of light illuminating the darkening sky. Their guests, dressed in all their finery, mixed and mingled under the trees in her mother's front yard. A month had passed since their wedding in Cades Cove. Tonight was all about celebrating their union, a way for family and friends to share in their happiness.

"You are so lucky, Juliana," Jessica gushed, her youthful face alight with happiness.

Jane, older by three minutes, declared, "It's all so romantic! And Evan is the most handsome man I've ever seen." She sighed, a dreamy look in her eyes.

Evan stood talking with his cousin Luke across the yard, and when she caught his gaze he held up a finger to indicate one more minute. Grinning, he winked at her. Her heart skipped a beat, and she grinned back.

Seeing her husband relaxed and happy thrilled her. He'd endured much loss in his life. During the last two weeks, she'd witnessed her family slowly filling the void left by the loss of his loved ones.

"What do you think, Megan?" Dark-haired Nicole, wearing an elaborate robin's-egg blue creation in the latest style and shipped straight from New York City, addressed their book-loving sister. "Would their story be a best seller?"

Juliana locked gazes with Megan and waited for her answer. "I'm not sure. All I can say is that I'm thankful this one has a happy ending." With a sweet smile and moisture in her eyes, Megan hugged her close. "I'm happy for you, sis. You finally have your very own hero."

Juliana whispered, "One day your hero will come."

Laughing softly, Megan shot back, "I hope his arrival is not quite as dramatic as Evan's."

"Juliana, my dear."

Releasing Megan, Juliana turned to her mother, radiant in her lavender brocade jacket and full skirt and looking much younger than her fifty years. Of all her family members, Alice O'Malley had handled the news of Juliana's marriage with the most grace and restraint.

"Do you have a moment? Joshua would like a word with you."

Glancing beyond Alice, Juliana spotted her cousin standing apart from the guests. He gave her a brief wave. "Of course." To her sisters, she teased, "No one lay a finger on that cake! I'll be right back."

As she approached, she noted his slumped shoulders and pursed lips. He appeared deep in thought. "Hey you." She tugged on his jacket sleeve. "Penny for your thoughts."

Joshua's smile couldn't mask the sadness in his blue eyes. "I got you something."

She looked down at the neatly wrapped package he placed in her hands. "What's this?"

"Open it."

Carefully untying the pink ribbon and peeling back the material, she admired the elegant stationery and small book with blank pages—a journal to record her experiences in her new home. "Thanks, Josh." She smiled up at him, tears springing to her eyes. She would miss his good-natured teasing and ready smile. "I can't think of a better gift."

Slipping his hands in his pockets, his expression turned solemn. "I'm gonna miss you, Jules. Who am I supposed to go fishing with once you're gone? And what about our shooting contests? It won't be the same without you here to make Caleb hoppin' mad."

She gave him a lop-sided smile. "Soon your fiancée will arrive. You can teach her all the things you taught me."

"Francesca is a city girl," he protested, "more suited to fine drawing rooms and needlework than outdoor pursuits. I doubt she'd be interested."

Juliana had never met the oil heiress, but she couldn't help but wonder if Francesca was a good fit for Joshua. "I don't mean to question your judgment, but are you certain she's the one for you?"

"I could ask the same of you," he responded.

At first, Joshua hadn't been at all happy about her decision to marry Evan. The initial confrontation between the two men had nearly ended in blows. Joshua was only being protective, of course. He wanted the best for her, just as she wanted the best for him.

"Evan is a good man."

Joshua nodded. "I have to admit he's growing on me."

To her relief, the men had formed a tenuous friendship over the last few weeks.

"Ah, here comes your husband now."

Juliana turned to see Evan, darkly handsome in his black suit, crossing the lawn with determined strides. Reaching her side, he slipped his arm around her waist and tugged her close. "Sorry to keep you waiting, sweetheart." He nodded to Joshua. "Josh. Everything all right?" His gaze drifted from one to the other.

"Fine," Joshua said. "I'm thirsty. Think I'll go grab a glass of punch."

"Josh, wait."

Stepping in front of him, she placed her hand over his heart. He'd been her dearest confidant all through childhood. They shared a lifetime of memories. "I love you, my friend. Remember we're just a few days' ride over the mountains. You're welcome anytime."

His eyes brimming with affection, he covered her hand. "I love you, too, Jules. We'll visit often. And I may even write from time to time."

"I'll hold you to that."

His voice gruff, he said to Evan, "Take care of her, Harrison."

"I love her, too," Evan said gently. "You don't have to worry."

With a curt nod, he walked away.

Evan stepped up behind her. "Are you okay?"

"I'm fine."

"Did I mention how stunning you look today, Mrs. Harrison?" he whispered near her ear, his warm breath scattering goose bumps along her neck and shoulders. Juliana relaxed back against him and gazed contentedly at the festive scene before her.

Juliana smiled. "I'm glad you approve of my dress."

"It's not the dress. It's you *in* the dress." His deep voice was a caress. "And I like all the sparkly things in your hair. You look like a fairy princess."

Her hands tightened on his.

Evan had meant it when he'd said he didn't want to wait to make her his bride. Within hours of his proposal, they'd stood before the minister in the valley's quaint white church and said their vows, their only witness Luke Harrison. The ceremony's beauty was in its simplicity, the focus solely on their love for each other. Juliana was grateful for that intimate, private ceremony and the wonderful days that had followed.

Evan had only one meeting with Sheriff Tate to discuss the case. After that, the sheriff had arranged for the transportation of Lenny Fitzgerald to Knoxville where James's murder trial would eventually be held. Thanks to Evan's tip, Cliff Roberts and his gang had been captured during their attempt to rob the Gatlinburg Bank. They were already in Knoxville awaiting trial.

As soon as a court date was set, Evan and Juliana would travel there as well. He was eager for justice. And at long last, he was allowing himself to grieve for his brother. The process was slow and at times painful, but he was relying on the Lord to help him through.

Gazing at the guests, she spotted Art and his mother talking quietly. The experiences of the last few weeks had changed him. He was more mature. There was a confidence about him now that hadn't been there before.

Sheriff Tate had agreed to let Art go free in exchange for his testimony. Juliana would forever be grateful for the sheriff's leniency.

Evan pressed a kiss on her cheek. "As long as I live, I don't want to ever spend another night without you."

She turned in his embrace and slid her arms up and around his neck. "I missed you last night, too."

His hold tightened. "Whose idea was it to consign me to your cousins' house, anyway?"

Juliana smiled. "I don't remember. Megan, perhaps. She'd think it was romantic. Was it that bad?"

"So bad I was tempted to sneak over here and kidnap you a second time."

"I'm disappointed that you didn't."

His blue eyes heated. "I love you, Juliana Harrison."

Looking over at her husband, the man she adored, she was overcome with emotion. Juliana was in awe of God's mercy and grace. His ways were indeed above her ways, His thoughts above her thoughts. On that morning in the mercantile, she never could've imagined what lay in store for her. He had taken a seemingly impossible situation and turned it around for good. God had blessed her beyond measure.

* * * * *

THE BRIDAL SWAP

I have swept away your offenses like a cloud,
your sins like the morning mist.
Return to me, for I have redeemed you.
—*Isaiah* 44:22

For Jacob.

Your dad and I are so proud of the thoughtful, caring young man you've become.

Just remember to keep God first in your life. I love you!

Chapter One

Gatlinburg, Tennessee
September 1880

Josh O'Malley's life was about to change. Standing on the boardwalk in front of Clawson's Mercantile, a bouquet of wildflowers in his hand, he watched intently as the carriage rolled to a stop. The team of midnight-black horses snuffed and tossed their heads, their massive chests quivering with exertion. The driver, dripping sweat and wearing an inch-thick coating of dust, remained seated while a second, well-dressed man climbed down with haste and swept open the door as if royalty waited inside.

Time stood still. The sounds of the town—snatches of conversations, the bell above the mercantile's entrance, wagons lumbering past—all faded as he waited for a glimpse of his fiancée, Francesca Morgan. Six long months had passed since he'd last seen her.

Anticipation swelled within him like the Little Pigeon River after a heavy downpour. His fingers tightened on the stems. Would she like it here? Not for the first time, doubts flickered in his mind. How would this oil heiress from New York City adjust to his small town, tucked deep in the Smoky Mountains?

He shoved such thoughts aside. Together they would deal with any hurdles.

Then she was there, in the doorway, placing her gloved hand in the man's and floating down the steps in a cloud of seafoam green. All he could see was the top of her fancy hat. This was the first day of their lives together.

"Hello, Francesca."

Her head whipped up, and he found himself staring into a stranger's face.

"Pardon me, Miss." Josh retreated a step. He glanced around her to find the carriage interior empty. Confused, he looked at her once more. "Excuse me, I was under the impression this was the Morgan carriage."

The young lady's eyes flared wide as if she recognized him. But that was impossible.

With a slight incline of her head, she dismissed the man at her side. "Thank you, Mr. Crandall." Her eyes held a mix of compassion and apprehension.

"Mr. Joshua O'Malley?"

His gut clenched. She couldn't know his name unless… "Yes, that's me."

"My name is Katerina Morgan. I'm Francesca's younger sister."

Sister? Surely not. This lady and his fiancée looked nothing alike.

Francesca was tall, lithe and graceful, her peaches-and-cream complexion the perfect foil for her corn-silk hair and baby-blue eyes. The young lady standing before him was altogether different. Petite and fine-boned, yet in possession of captivating curves, the top of her head barely grazed his chin.

Katerina was a delicate lady…like a doll come to life. Her face was a perfect oval, with rounded cheekbones and dainty chin. Her almond-shaped eyes shone the same hue as her pale green dress, and her pouty, pink lips could've been sculpted by an artist. Her hair was the color of decadent chocolate and arranged in elaborate twists and curls.

"Where is Francesca? Has something happened?"

"Please—is there somewhere we can speak in private?"

Curious townsfolk had stopped to watch their exchange. Gatlinburg was a small town, and most knew his fiancée was arriving today.

"Over here."

They would be out of sight behind the mercantile. Taking gentle hold of her arm, he helped her across the grass and caught a whiff of her perfume, a subtle scent with notes of citrus. Like her elegant outfit, it was most likely the latest fashion from Paris. And worth more money than he'd see in a lifetime.

"What lush beauty." Her steps faltered. "Why, I doubt I've ever seen its equal. You are fortunate, Mr. O'Malley, to wake up to this day after day."

He followed her uplifted gaze to the rounded mountain peaks on all sides, the clear blue sky a perfect backdrop against the autumn foliage visible even at the higher elevations. He understood her reaction. Most newcomers agreed this part of East Tennessee was a tiny slice of paradise.

"I can't imagine living anywhere else," he murmured.

The hushed hum of rushing water met his ears as they neared the bank's edge. Releasing her arm, he warned, "Mind your step. There's a steep drop-off." About ten feet below, the water's surface reflected the trees' changing colors—dusky green with patches of red and orange.

"It's lovely," she breathed.

Enough small talk. "Why isn't Francesca here?" *Instead of you?*

She faced him, shoulders squared and hands clasped at her slim waist. "I'm afraid I have unse°ttling news." She paused, clearly uneasy. "Francesca has married another man."

Married? "That's impossible." Josh struggled to make sense of her words. "She promised to marry me." The date was set. Saturday next, they were to stand before Pastor Monroe and exchange vows. Friends and family had already been invited.

Her lips compressed in lines of regret. "I am truly sorry."

"I don't understand."

What about all those letters? Had she only pretended to be excited about starting a new life with him?

"Who is he?" he ground out.

"Someone she knew before she met you," she said gently. "They had a falling-out a few days before she left for her visit with the Meades."

He'd met the lovely heiress at the Meades' home in Sevierville, had gone to deliver a pair of rocking chairs and nearly run her over in the doorway of the grand mansion. Nothing in her behavior had hinted of another attachment. Surely he would've seen the signs!

"I realize this is difficult news—"

"How long ago did she go back to him?" he demanded. "And why did she send you to do her dirty work?"

She blanched. "They were married two weeks ago. And she did not send me. Despite my insistence that you should be told in person, she refused to come."

Whirling away from her, Josh battled conflicting

emotions. Anger. Outrage. Disbelief. If the marriage had taken place two weeks ago, then they'd reconciled some time before.

He'd been duped.

His head pounding by this time, he strode to the edge of the embankment and hurled the bouquet, the kaleidoscope of colors cascading to the water's surface and swirling downstream. He needed to be alone, needed to think through this upheaval in his plans.

"I appreciate your coming here, Miss Morgan. Now I must go." He gave her a half bow. "Good day."

Kate's gaze lingered on the tender petals being crushed by the current before skittering to his retreating back. Collecting her skirts, she hurried after him. "Mr. O'Malley?"

When he stopped and glanced back, the tortured look in his eyes nearly took her breath away. "Yes?"

Kate stared at the man Francesca was to have married, unable to utter a word.

She'd looked at his picture when no one else was around, memorizing each feature. Intelligent brows, patrician nose, square jaw. His was a photogenic face.

On paper, he was merely a handsome stranger. The flesh-and-bone man was another matter entirely. In a word, he was intoxicating.

His dusky-gray, pin-striped suit, with its simple lines and understated elegance, molded to his broad shoulders and lean torso. His tan skin glowed with health and vibrancy, and his honey-brown hair was short, the ends bleached blond by the sun.

The neatly trimmed mustache and goatee covering his chin were new. Not usually taken by facial hair, Kate found his fascinating. He looked…mysterious. A bit untamed.

"Did you need something?" he prompted.

He dwarfed her by at least a foot. That wasn't unusual. Most men did. "Can you direct me to Charlotte Matthews's house?"

A muscle in his jaw jumped. "You know Mrs. Matthews and her son?"

"She was my governess for many years. I haven't met Tyler, but she mentions him quite often in her letters."

"I see." His eyes were an intriguing color, the shimmering, metallic blue of a blue morpho butterfly's wings, pale around the pupil with a deeper ring of blue around the edges. So beautiful it made her wish for color photographs.

"Their farm is a mile or so outside of town. What time is your driver planning to leave?"

"As soon as I get settled at Charlotte's."

"You're staying here tonight?"

"Actually, I'm planning to be here for at least a month, perhaps longer."

His brows slashed down. "That long? May I ask why?"

"I'm here to take photographs of the mountains. I'm considering publishing a book about this area."

"A book," he repeated, clearly displeased. "You're a photographer?"

Was he one of those men who disapproved of female professionals? "I am."

His brilliant blue gaze assessed her. No doubt he was comparing her to her sister. She inwardly winced. She'd learned long ago that she didn't measure up, would forever be in Fran's shadow.

Men adored Fran. Women wanted to *be* her. Even their parents favored her—their mother especially.

Patrick and Georgia Morgan had wanted only one child. Francesca—the epitome of grace and loveliness—fulfilled their every dream of what a proper daughter should be. So when dark-haired, demanding Katerina arrived unexpectedly, Georgia had been less than thrilled.

A lengthy bout of colic made matters worse. For months, Georgia refused to visit the nursery, leaving Kate in the care of nannies. Perhaps that rough beginning had cast a pall over their relationship. Whatever the case, the distance between them seemed to grow wider with time.

Kate had given up trying to earn her mother's love.

"If you'd rather not help me," she said after a lengthy silence, "I'm sure I can find someone else."

He blew out a breath. "It's too far to walk. Mind if we take your rig?"

"Not at all." They fell into step, as he matched his stride to hers. "I appreciate this."

He merely nodded, his mouth set in grim lines. Once he'd given directions to her driver and tethered his horse to the rear of the carriage, he settled his tall frame in the seat across from her. Holding his hat in his hands, he took in the sumptuous mahogany fabric that covered every square inch of the carriage interior. What was he thinking?

His letters, which Fran had read aloud in the drawing room during afternoon tea, had been filled with descriptions of his family's home and the town of Gatlinburg. Fran had laughed, calling him provincial. Kate disagreed. Josh's letters had revealed a charming, thoughtful man who dearly loved his family and hometown.

Glancing out the window, she caught sight of Clawson's Mercantile, the post office and a quaint white church framed by the mountains.

"Everything looks just as I'd imagined it," she said without thinking. "Your description of Main Street makes me feel as though I've been here before."

His voice dripped icicles. "You read my letters?"

"I… We…" she sputtered. "Well, y-yes. Fran read them aloud." Mortified at her slip, Kate pretended an exaggerated interest in the tips of her tan leather ankle boots.

"Those were my private thoughts, intended for no one but Francesca."

Silence settled heavy and oppressive between them.

"I am truly sorry," she murmured. "I've hurt you—"

"No. Your sister did that all on her own." He turned his head to glare out the window. "It's becoming quite clear she did not hold me in the same regard as I did her."

What could she say? That Fran was interested only in social standing and wealth? Why she'd ever accepted Josh O'Malley's proposal was beyond Kate. Perhaps to make Percy jealous, so he'd come crawling back to her? If that was the case, the ploy had worked.

The man across from her looked lost. Adrift in a vast ocean with no rescue in sight. Fran had done this to him, but Kate had delivered the news. Did he despise her for listening to his letters? Did he consider her the enemy— guilty by association?

The carriage soon slowed and turned onto a rutted lane. The vegetation was thick on either side, and tree branches scraped along the sides of their rig, slapping against the half-open glass. Pine needles littered the bench seats and carpeted floor. Mr. Crandall, her fastidious footman, would be none too pleased.

Anticipation curled through her at the prospect of seeing her former governess again. For a time, kindhearted Charlotte Matthews had been the one bright spot in her otherwise lonely existence. They'd reconnected through correspondence, and the older lady had made it plain that Kate was welcome to visit anytime.

They rolled to a stop before a squat, haphazard dwelling nearly engulfed with ivy. Only the window and the door had not succumbed to the ivy's onslaught. She frowned. Would there be room for her here?

The door swung open, and Mr. Crandall stood ready to assist her. Joshua O'Malley descended the steps after her, his expression an inscrutable mask.

Hands clasped at her waist, she turned to thank him, but he was already headed for his horse. It appeared he'd had all of her company he could stand. With a mental shrug, she approached the cabin and knocked twice.

A chair scraped against the floor and the vibrations of heavy footsteps could be felt on the porch. That didn't sound like a lady. Instead, a disheveled, dark-haired man about her age appeared in the doorway. "What do ya want?"

"Hello, I'm looking for Charlotte Matthews—"

She wasn't prepared for the hand that shot out and gripped her wrist in a painful hold. The stranger yanked her forward, and her free hand flew up to stop her fall, only to encounter an unyielding wall of muscle. Gasping in fright, she stared into his shocked brown eyes.

"Lily?" he ground out.

"N-no, it's Kate."

He tugged her against his long length. "I can't believe you've come back to me." His stale breath, reeking of whiskey and tobacco, washed over her.

She recoiled. "You're mistaken! I don't know you."

His dark brows lowered, and anger flashed in his eyes. "Don't play me for a fool, Lily."

His fingers dug into her flesh, and she flinched. "Please," she whimpered, "let me go."

Somewhere behind her, she heard the click of a gun hammer. "I'd advise you to get your hands off the lady."

She couldn't see Mr. O'Malley, but his voice rang with deadly promise.

Uncertainty flickered in the glazed eyes. "My wife is my business."

"The booze has scrambled your senses, Matthews." He came closer. "Kate Morgan just arrived today. Look at her fancy clothes. She's from New York City. A Yankee."

This man was Tyler Matthews? Charlotte's son was a dangerous drunk?

"I don't understand." His grip loosened, but he didn't release her. His bloodshot gaze roamed her features. "You aren't Lily?"

Her mouth suddenly dry, she croaked out a response. "No."

His hands dropped abruptly to his sides. Immediately, Mr. O'Malley took her elbow and eased her to his side so as not to draw the other man's attention. Her knees felt like gelatin. Unsteady, she held on to his arm as if it were a lifeline.

He appeared calm, but Kate sensed the tension humming through his body. His jaw was set in rigid lines. "Why don't you go back inside and sleep it off?"

Head bent, Matthews rubbed the back of his neck. "I, uh, haven't been sleepin' too good lately."

"Then maybe you should lay off the drink."

Mr. O'Malley obviously knew this man and his history. What had happened to his wife? And why had he mistaken Kate for her?

"Yeah." Turning, he went inside without another word.

Her rescuer angled his face down toward hers. "Are you all right?"

His low, easy drawl flowed over her like decadent, sugary caramel.

Kate gulped. She avoided all sweets, in particular caramel. One taste was never enough.

Suddenly conscious of her viselike grip on his arm, she let go and took a quick step back.

"I'm fine," she said, tugging her snug-fitting jacket down. Her arms smarted from where Matthews had held her prisoner, but she wouldn't mention that to him. "Thank you for intervening."

Mr. Crandall rushed forward. "I second that sentiment, Mr. O'Malley. Are you quite certain you're unharmed, Miss Morgan?"

"Yes."

The brim of his black hat shading his eyes, Mr. O'Malley slid his weapon back in its holster and nodded to the carriage. "Let's go before he has a change of heart."

"Go where?" It suddenly dawned on Kate that she had no place to stay.

"My house."

Chapter Two

This was not the day he'd had planned.

He should've been acquainting his intended with her new home. Instead, he was saddled with her sister. Troubled and pale after her ordeal, Kate stared out the carriage window, seemingly a million miles away.

"Where do you suppose Charlotte is?" Her gaze settled on him, seeking answers.

He hitched a shoulder. "I don't know."

"I thought everyone knew everyone else's business in small towns."

"That's true to a point. However, I personally don't keep track of everyone's comings and goings." He shifted on the swaying seat. When a worried crease appeared between her brows, he added, "We'll ask my mother. She's friendly with Mrs. Matthews, so there's a good chance she'll have an idea where she's gone, if anywhere. For all we know, she could've been visiting a friend or picking up necessities."

Her expression brightened, then dimmed an instant later. "Even if she is nearby, I can't possibly stay there.

Not with her son." The fingers plucking at the lace edging her sleeves stilled. "Where is Lily Matthews?"

"Dead."

Her lips parted. "I don't understand. Then why—"

"You resemble her." He shoved a hand through his hair. "Matthews used to be a productive member of this town, but he hasn't been the same since the accident." He'd heard of the man's tendency to drink, but he hadn't realized the severity of the problem. If he had, he wouldn't have taken Kate out there.

"Does Gatlinburg have a hotel? Or a boardinghouse?"

"No hotel. No boardinghouse. The Copelands occasionally have rooms to let, but their son and his family are visiting from out of town."

Again, she got that worried look.

"My parents may know of somewhere you can stay," he tacked on. "Or you could go back to New York."

She stiffened. "That's not an option."

"Why not?"

"I came here to do a job." At his puzzled expression, she sighed. "The book, remember?"

"Ah, yes. I remember. You're a photographer." While he had no issue with working women, he couldn't picture this elegant, delicate young lady as anything other than a privileged socialite. "Your coming here proved to be very convenient for Francesca, didn't it? Why not let you deal with the unnecessary groom?"

"Mr. O'Malley, I'm sorry—"

He held up a staying hand as the driver halted the team outside of the livery. "It's not your place to apologize. Forget I said anything."

Kate didn't speak as they exited the carriage. Replacing his hat on his head, he gave instructions to the driver and footman.

"We'll leave your trunks here until we figure out where you'll be staying."

She glanced up and down the busy street. "I thought we were going to your house."

"We are. It's not far. I thought you might like to stretch your legs after being cooped up much of the day."

Surprised that he cared one whit for her comfort, she fell into step beside him.

Passing the last business on the right, Leighton Barbershop, he led her across a quaint, wooden bridge overlooking the river.

The shaded lane enveloped them in a vibrant cocoon, leaves hanging mere inches from their heads. To the right and left stood an endless parade of stately trees reaching for the Heavens, the thick, dark trunks anchored in a sea of gold created by the shorter tulip trees' golden leaves.

What beauty! *How many are your works, O Lord! In wisdom You made them all; the earth is full of Your creatures.*

She wished suddenly for a cushioned chair, a steaming cup of Earl Grey and a copy of *Scientific American*. She'd stay here in this lane for hours if he'd allow it.

Around the bend, the trees opened up to an expansive clearing, the green grass a lush carpet leading to a two-story cabin with a long, narrow front porch and beyond, a weathered barn and several outbuildings. It was just as he'd described, but of course the reality far surpassed her imaginings.

Pigs squealed in the distance. The sizable garden was bursting with jewel-toned vegetables—plump orange pumpkins, glossy eggplant, striped squash of different sizes and shapes, and green peppers.

Temporarily forgetting her dilemma, Kate grinned, ecstatic to see a real farm up close for the first time.

Pointing to impressive rows of trees, she asked, "Are those apple trees?"

He nodded. "McIntosh apples. They'll be ripe in about a week."

"That's a lot of apples."

"We won't eat them all fresh. They'll be used to make cider, vinegar, applesauce and apple butter, not to mention pies and other desserts."

"You have a beautiful home," she breathed, a note of wistfulness in her voice.

He glanced over at her. "The good Lord has blessed us."

As they drew nearer to the house, Kate's nerves assailed her. How would his parents react to her presence once they learned her awful news? Mouth dry and palms damp inside her buff-colored lace gloves, she slowed her steps.

The front door opened. A man and woman emerged, their faces alight with anticipation. "It's about time, Joshua!" the woman exclaimed. "We were beginning to think something had happened." Advancing down the steps, she crossed to meet them, her husband not far behind.

"Sorry to worry you, Ma," Josh said. "This is—"

"Francesca!" To Kate's surprise, Mrs. O'Malley clasped her hands in hers. "I'm so pleased to meet you!"

Oh, no. This was not good.

"I—"

"This isn't Francesca." Josh ran a finger beneath his

shirt collar as if to loosen it. "May I present Kate Morgan? My ex-fiancée's little sister."

"Ex-fiancée?" his mother repeated, brow wrinkling in disbelief. "What's happened, Joshua? Isn't Francesca coming?"

More than once during her long journey to Tennessee, she'd faced Josh in her imagination. Rehearsing what she'd say. Envisioning what he might say. She hadn't considered his family's reaction. Standing here with Mr. and Mrs. O'Malley regarding her as if she were a creature from another planet, she regretted the omission. Not a word came to mind.

Josh's level gaze was on her as he spoke. "Francesca changed her mind about the marriage. Kate thought it best to bring the news in person."

"I'm sorry, son," said Mr. O'Malley, as he placed a comforting hand on Josh's shoulder.

His mother approached, questions lingering in her eyes. Her tremulous smile lessened Kate's apprehension a notch. "Kate, I'm Mary. And that's my Samuel. It's a brave thing you did, coming here in your sister's place. Thank you."

Kate released the breath she'd been holding. She wasn't going to be berated, after all. "I regret to have to deliver such dreadful news."

Unlike Georgia Morgan's cool, aloof beauty, Mary O'Malley's appearance was one of sweet femininity, her wavy brown hair styled in a casual upsweep and a simple gold chain with a cross to complement her blue calico dress. And tall, lean Samuel O'Malley, with brown hair much like Josh's, had a pleasant face.

"We appreciate your consideration of Josh's feelings," Samuel added.

The tips of Josh's ears reddened. "I'm sure Kate would appreciate something to drink after her long trip."

"Where are my manners?" Mary gasped. "Come on in! I've a fresh batch of crybabies already cooling on the table."

Crybabies? What on earth?

Josh's parents went inside first, and he gestured for her to go ahead of him. She felt the weight of his gaze on her back as they passed through the doorway.

Her first impression of the O'Malley home was that it could've fit inside the dining hall of her parents' estate. Instead of silk damask wall panels, these walls were bare wooden planks. There were no ornate candelabras or wall sconces, only kerosene lamps placed in key areas about the room. Compared to her estate's marble hallways, plush Oriental rugs and the finest furnishings money can buy, this home was indeed humble.

However, there was no denying it was an inviting space, cozy and cheerful and decorated with care. Blue-and-white gingham curtains hung at every window, and landscape scenes of mountains and meadows hung on the walls. A serpentine sofa with blue brocade cushions and walnut trim, along with two matching chairs, were situated around a charming stone fireplace.

"Not exactly what you're used to, is it?" Josh stopped at her side.

"It's lovely."

He studied her, weighing her words and expression as if trying to gauge her sincerity.

"Please, make yourself comfortable." Mary gestured to the sofa. "I'll get the refreshments. Samuel, can you give me a hand?"

The couple passed through the dining area and rounded

the corner into what she assumed was the kitchen. She couldn't make out the words of their quiet conversation, but no doubt they were discussing her sister's cowardice and lack of decency.

"Would you like to have a seat?"

Kate swallowed hard. Josh's steady assessment set her nerves on edge.

"Yes, thank you."

Moving to the nearest wingback chair, she sank gracefully onto the cushion and arranged her skirts with care. He didn't join her. Instead he began to pace the length of the couch, hands in his pockets. Every now and then a muscle in his cheek twitched.

She could just imagine his thoughts. Wringing Fran's neck, perhaps?

His parents returned at last with a tray of glasses filled with ginger water and a plate piled high with cookies, which they placed on the low coffee table in front of her. The sweet aroma of molasses teased her nose. Were these the crybabies, perhaps?

Mary handed her a glass. "Here you are."

"Thank you." The tart liquid washed the dust from her throat.

When they were settled in the sofa across from her, Mary said, "You've traveled a great distance, haven't you, Kate? What are your plans now that you're here?"

"I'm actually here to take photographs. And to visit my former governess, Charlotte Matthews." Her gaze shot to Josh, who was still pacing. "Everything was arranged and she knew to expect me. She wasn't at home, however."

Absently, she rubbed the tender spot on her wrist where Tyler had held her.

"We thought you might know her whereabouts." Josh

had stopped pacing. Resting his weight against the sofa, his hands gripped the wooden trim. His gaze caught her movement and narrowed. Kate covered the spot with her hand.

"You know Charlotte? She's a dear lady." Mary frowned. "She's been facing some hard times lately. Tyler isn't coping well with the death of his wife. And now his sister, Carrie, is expecting and has been terribly ill. Charlotte left last week to be with her until the baby comes. I'm afraid she won't be back for quite some time."

Kate lowered her gaze to her lap. This wasn't welcome news. Charlotte must've been too preoccupied to send her a letter explaining the situation.

"Miss Morgan needs a place to stay," Josh spoke into the silence. "Do you know of anywhere?"

"You can stay here, of course." Mary beamed. "With four males stomping around this house, I get lonesome for female company."

"Mary, I'm not sure…" Samuel shot a meaningful glance at Josh.

Her smile faltered. "Oh, yes, I didn't think—"

"She can sleep in my cabin," Josh announced bitterly. "I won't be needing it after all."

"Are you sure?" Mary peered up at him, her eyes full of concern.

"Positive. It won't take all that long to move my things back into my old bedroom."

"Wait." Kate hastily replaced her drink and came around the sofa to face him. "The last thing I want to do is push you out of your home."

"A home I built for my future wife." The pain of betrayal flashed hot in his eyes. "But she's not here, is she?" Turning his back, he strode for the door. "You're welcome to it."

* * *

His boot had connected with the bottom step when he heard the door open and close and Kate call his name. What now? Couldn't she see he wasn't in the mood for company?

With great reluctance he pivoted back, squinting in the afternoon sunshine. She edged forward, her face shadowed by the hat's brim. Loosening the ribbons of her reticule, she withdrew a long parchment envelope and held it out to him.

"I have a letter for you. From Francesca."

He stared at the letter, not sure he wanted to read it. "What does it say?"

Her lips parted, and dark lashes swept down to hide her eyes. Pink washed her cheeks. "I don't know. She didn't share the contents with me and, to be honest, I'm glad she didn't."

Tucking the letter in the inside pocket of his suit jacket, Josh nodded in silent farewell and left her standing on the porch. If he didn't get alone soon, he was going to come undone. What he wanted to do was hunt down the man who'd stolen his future and plant a facer on him. Then he'd confront Francesca and force her to confess her perfidy to his face.

But that wasn't an option. Not today, anyway.

With effort, he ruthlessly tamped down the emotions clawing at his insides.

Ignoring the letter burning the lining of his suit, he gathered his clothes and books from his home, not stopping to linger and mourn his loss. To his relief, his mom was showing Kate the kitchen when he went inside the main house, so he was able to put his things away, change clothes and duck back outside without being seen.

During the entire trip to town and back to retrieve her luggage, the letter and what it might say dominated his thoughts. Why hadn't Francesca had the decency to face him herself? Why put it off on her little sister?

Finally, when the wondering became too great, he pulled the envelope from his pocket and sank onto the top step of his porch.

Heart thumping against his rib cage so hard it hurt, he unfolded the paper and, holding it to his nose, inhaled her flowery scent. He felt achy all over.

Dearest Josh,
I am not sure what to write, for I know nothing I say will change your low opinion of me. Katerina was adamant that I give you some explanation, and I admit she was right. You must know that I care for you, but you and I together for a lifetime never would have worked. Percy can provide the type of life I need to be happy.
Sincerely,
Francesca Morgan

Stunned, Josh flipped the paper over and found the other side blank.

There was no apology. She'd basically admitted to wedding this man for material gain.

Francesca's nonchalant attitude, her utter lack of remorse, stung. Anger boiled up once again, threatening to overwhelm him.

Once again, he was facing a lonely future.

In the shade of the back porch, Kate leaned against the wooden railing and stared out at the idyllic scene.

Gently rolling fields of green, knee-high stalks waving in the breeze, gave way to rounded mountain peaks rising in all directions in a patchwork display of burnished reds, golds and greens. God's magnificent handiwork for all to see and savor.

She was eager to explore, to seek out potential images for her book.

But first she had to find Josh, as Mary requested. Supper awaited.

Above the lowing of cattle, she heard the insistent pounding of an ax.

Following the sound, she strolled across the yard toward the barn, casting a glance inside the shady interior as she passed by the open doors. Dust motes hung suspended in the dim light, the smell of hay and animals reminding her of the stables back home.

Rounding the corner, she came to an abrupt stop.

A flash of sunlight on glistening skin, sculpted muscles straining, stretching, Josh handled the ax with ease, slicing through the wood like butter. He'd exchanged his neat suit for a pair of dark denim trousers and sturdy brown work boots. His sleeveless undershirt gave her a clear view of molded shoulders, thick biceps and corded forearms.

She gulped. Oh, dear.

Glancing away, she saw the high stacks of kindling by the barn wall. Surely they didn't need more. Then it struck her. He wasn't doing this out of necessity. He was venting.

Compassion for his plight brought moisture to her eyes. She blinked hard. She couldn't let him see her tears. He'd assume she was feeling pity for him, and she had a feeling he wouldn't like that.

When she moved into his line of vision, he wedged the ax into the stump, turned his back and, retrieving his white shirt, shrugged into it. Still working the buttons, he faced her, brows raised in question.

"Sorry to interrupt," she ventured. "Your mother sent me to tell you the meal is ready."

"Just a minute."

She stood by quietly, fingers toying with the lace peeking out of her sleeves as he quickly stacked the wood before joining her. He was a rumpled mess, his short hair mussed and shirt untucked, the sweat-dampened material sticking to his frame. It only added to his appeal.

"Have my parents kept you entertained this afternoon?"

"Your parents have been welcoming and friendly."

Strangers who were more attentive than her own parents.

Walking beside him, she sensed the coiled tension in him. Had he read the letter? She wondered what it had said, feared Fran's words had inflicted further pain. Her sister wasn't known for her tact.

He stopped at the pump to clean his hands and douse his face. When he'd wiped off the excess moisture and tucked the cloth into his back pocket, he startled her by taking hold of her hand.

"What are you—"

Carefully, he slid her sleeve back, revealing the purple marks marring her pale skin. His eyes darkened. "Matthews did this?"

The scent of pine clung to him. Kate couldn't think with him standing so near, his strong, warm hands cradling hers with such tenderness. Back home in Francesca's room, gazing at his portrait and committing his face to memory, she couldn't have guessed the impact of his physical presence.

She dragged in a breath. "I'm fine, really."

"Steer clear of him, Kate. He's unpredictable."

It was his first use of her name. She had to admit it sounded good on his lips.

"Kate?" he prompted impatiently.

"You don't have to worry. I won't go near the man."

"Hey, Josh!"

Two men were headed in their direction. Josh's brothers?

Releasing her, he crossed his arms and waited. Their attention didn't waver from her as they approached. Feeling like a specimen underneath a microscope, she fought the urge to squirm.

"Kate Morgan, these are my brothers, Nathan and Caleb."

Nathan shot a startled glance at Josh, but he quickly masked his confusion. His eyes were kind as he welcomed her. "It's nice to meet you." Two years younger than Josh, he was twenty-two.

Twenty-year-old Caleb scowled and said nothing. Josh had mentioned in his letters that his youngest brother didn't like to be around people, something to do with a scar he'd gotten from a recent accident. She didn't see evidence of one, but she noticed he kept his face turned to one side.

"Where's Francesca?" Nathan asked.

Josh stiffened, his voice flat. "She isn't coming, after all."

"Did something happen?" Nathan asked quietly.

"Yes." Josh's voice held an edge. "She decided to marry someone else." At Caleb's intake of breath, Josh held up a staying hand. "Kate is her sister. She's staying with us for the time being."

He didn't seem pleased with the turn of events. And why should he be? Her sister should've been standing here meeting his family, not her.

Mary pushed open the door. "Supper's ready."

She didn't miss the flash of relief on Josh's face. No doubt he was growing weary of explaining her presence to everyone.

Sitting at the far end of the table, Josh listened to the ebb and flow of conversation without contributing to it. This was the last place he wanted to be, surrounded by people pretending nothing was wrong. Pretending he hadn't just been cast off.

Suppertime in the O'Malley household was typically loud and lively, and tonight was no exception. His father and brothers made sure of that. One glance at Kate Morgan's mystified expression suggested family dinners at the Morgan estate were a much more sedate affair.

Her regal bearing and expensive clothing set her apart from everyone else at the table. She'd removed her hat, gloves and jacket. Beneath her brocade vest of matching material, she wore a filmy cream-colored blouse with lace at her neck. The color of her eyes matched the peridot earrings dangling from her ears, the vivid green gems flashing with every turn of her head.

Watching her, Josh realized he'd been a fool to think Francesca could ever be satisfied with his way of life. The Morgans lived a life of luxury. Nothing was out of their reach.

He lived simply. He worked hard to carve out a life for himself, yet he had no complaints. He loved these mountains, this land. And he wanted someone to share his life with.

God, I don't understand Your ways. Nothing is turning out the way I thought, and it's hard. So hard.

"Time for dessert." His mother placed a warm pecan pie in the middle of the table.

Standing, Josh brought his empty plate to the counter. "I'll pass tonight."

"But it's your favorite," Mary protested, carrying dishes into the kitchen.

He squeezed her shoulder. "Save me a piece for tomorrow?"

Kate approached, her plate still half full. "You are a marvelous cook, Mary. However, I'm afraid I couldn't finish it all." She smothered a yawn.

"Oh, my. You've had a long day, haven't you, dear?" Mary said. "Joshua, will you walk Kate out to the cabin?"

His and Kate's gazes clashed. Then her lashes swept downward, her expression neutral.

What could he say? *No, I don't want to spend even a second alone with her? This woman reminds me of Francesca's treachery and my glaring failure.*

He swept out his arm. "After you."

Chapter Three

With her hat in one hand and her skirts in the other, Kate swept past him onto the narrow porch, her shoulder brushing against his chest and a stray chocolate curl caressing her cheek. The creamy skin of her nape glowed alabaster in the moonlight. Her fresh, citrusy scent, carried on the gentle breeze, filled his nostrils and stirred his blood.

Closing the door behind him, Josh inhaled the cool, pine-scented air in an effort to displace her scent. Kate was a lovely woman, and he was a man craving comfort. Disgusted with himself for even noticing, he gave her a wide berth and started across the lawn.

"Mr. O'Malley?"

She hadn't moved an inch. From the soft golden glow spilling through the windows, he saw her hesitation and retraced his steps.

"It's Josh. What's wrong? Did you forget something inside?"

"No. I, um— It's pitch-black out there." Her voice faltered. "Back home, gas streetlamps line the streets and give off quite a bit of light."

He held the kerosene lamp aloft. "This will light our way."

An owl hooted. Kate's gaze darted to the dense woods. "What about wild beasts? I've read a few books about this area. There were accounts of black bears attacking people."

He suppressed a smile. "While it's true there are bears in these parts, they normally stay in higher elevations. Bear attacks are rare and most likely the result of some-one coming too close to a momma bear and her cubs."

He approached and held out his arm, but she didn't immediately take it.

"So you've never seen a bear anywhere near here?"

"I didn't say that. But mostly they keep to themselves."

Her slender hand curled around his biceps, the warmth of her light touch seeping through his shirt. "I'm safe out here then?"

He guided her across the yard. "I can pretty much guarantee a bear isn't going to break into the cabin while you sleep. You should watch out for snakes, though, es-pecially rattlers and copperheads."

Her nails dug into his skin. "Snakes?"

"And spiders," he added, disregarding the twinge of his conscience. He was only telling her the truth. "Black widows and brown recluses are the ones to watch out for. Nasty bites. You could lose a limb."

"Oh, dear." She shuddered. "My books didn't men-tion any of that."

"Just be careful around tall grass. And don't reach into dark corners and crevices where crawling insects like to hide." He pulled away from her. "Here we are."

Opening the door for her, his gaze fell on the burst of color in the corner of the room. More wildflowers. He'd borrowed his mother's only crystal vase and placed the arrangement on the dining table as a small token for his wife-to-be.

He frowned. This night was supposed to have played out much differently. He'd imagined Francesca's reaction to the home he'd built for her, had hoped she'd be pleased.

Instead, a stranger stood beside him.

Moving forward, her skirts whispering in the silence, Kate's gaze assessed the airy, open space that made up the seating area and kitchen.

"You built this yourself?"

He nodded. "With help from my father and brothers."

"You did a great job." The admiration shining in her eyes was a soothing balm to his battered soul.

"Thanks."

In the kitchen, she trailed her fingers along the gleaming walnut tabletop. Her gaze shot to his, a small wrinkle between her brows.

"This is similar to the one at your parents', only smaller."

It was one of his most recent pieces, carved with his own hands. For some reason he couldn't identify, he was reluctant to tell her about his furniture business. Not even Francesca knew.

Slipping his hands into his pockets, he asked casually, "Do you like it?"

She stepped back to study it. "It's sturdy, solid. Simple lines. But here—" she traced a fingertip along the carved edge "—this is truly magnificent. The detail of the leaves and flowers is amazing. Was it done by a local craftsman?"

He hesitated. "Yes."

"Does he live nearby?"

Closer than you think. "Yes. Very near."

"You should tell him his furniture would sell extremely well back East." Her praise brought a rush of pleasure, especially considering her family's estate was most likely furnished with the finest money could buy.

"I'll do that."

She smothered another yawn. Time to go. He wasn't sure why he'd lingered anyway.

"Good night, Kate." He paused. "Lock the door. You'll feel safer."

Kate stared at the closed door a full minute before crossing the room to slide the wooden bar in place. His woodsy scent lingered in the silent room. He'd been stiff, watchful, his blue eyes revealing his misery. *Oh, Fran. How could you?*

Her heart ached for the pain he was enduring.

Turning, she relaxed against the rough wood and stared at the home intended for her sister. Prestige and money were everything to Fran. If she were here, she would scorn this rough-hewn dwelling, no larger than her private bathroom. She would not appreciate its charm, the love and care poured into it. Everywhere she looked, Kate saw little touches meant to cheer.

The bouquet on the table. The floral-print high-backed chair beneath the curtained window. A rainbow-striped rug in front of the stone fireplace. A painting of a waterfall on the wall behind the sofa.

Josh obviously loved her sister. What would it feel like, she wondered, to be loved like that? Sadness pressed in on her. She couldn't recall hearing the words *I love you* a single time.

Her parents weren't given to displays of affection. That

was for the lower classes, her mother had said when Kate questioned her.

She recalled walking through the park with her nanny, envious of the children holding hands with their mothers, the little boys balanced on their father's shoulders looking happy as could be. The longing for love and affection had only grown with time.

God loves you, a small, still voice told Kate. Her eyes smarted with unshed tears. *Help me remember, Father, that You love me even when I'm unlovable.*

The stillness reminded her that she was alone. For the first time in her life, there were no ladies' maids waiting behind the scenes to help her undress or fetch her a soothing cup of tea. The realization was both heady and daunting. What would it be like to be an independent woman?

Exhausted from days of travel, not to mention emotionally drained, Kate decided to deal with unpacking later. Instead, she began the tedious process of undressing. First the skirt, then the underskirt. Bustle. Corset cover. Petticoat.

The ivory satin corset presented a problem. Without assistance, it was next to impossible to undo the tight stays. Huffing and grunting, arms twisting every which way, she was at last able to free herself from the rigid contraption. She resisted the unladylike urge to toss it across the room.

Tucking the despised article beneath her arm, she went to investigate the bedroom. Covering the wide bed was a handmade quilt similar to the one on the sofa, this one in pale blues and pinks done in the pattern of interlocking rings. She thought of the thick, luxurious silk coverlet on her own bed. Beautiful, yes, and expensive, but not unique. Before she left, she would ask Mary if she'd be willing to sell her one of hers.

Locating her satchel, she changed into her night rail. Next to the bed was a waist-high table where the oil lamp stood. Extinguishing the flame, the room was plunged into inky darkness.

Kate froze. The blackness closed in on her. Images from her childhood flashed through her mind. Her nanny's contorted, angry face. The dark closet. Musty-smelling coats, piles of boxes and broken, discarded toys distorted by the shadows. Her lungs struggled to draw in air.

How she hated the dark!

This room was small, the ceiling low. And there were no windows to open, as in her spacious, airy bedroom at the estate. No gentle light from the row of streetlamps to ease her fear, or the occasional sound of horses clomping down the lane to comfort her.

No. I mustn't give in to the memories.

But they came anyway…of another time, another place. The wine cellar. A man she'd adored. The extinguished candle. Her panic. His calm reassurances and mesmerizing touch. She'd felt so loved…

No! Reining in her thoughts before the shame consumed her, she scrambled beneath the covers and tugged them up to her chin.

Father God, I need You. I don't want to remember.

He will keep him in perfect peace, whose mind is stayed on Thee. She repeated the verse until her muscles relaxed and she drifted off to sleep.

Dressed to go visiting Saturday morning, Mary placed fresh-baked loaves of sourdough bread into the basket on the counter. "How are you holding up? I know it must be difficult having Kate around. I could ask Betty if she'd mind her staying over there."

Leaning back in his chair, Josh toyed with the handle of his coffee mug. A dear friend of his mother's, Betty Stanley would welcome Kate into her home. He didn't doubt she'd treat her with kindness. On the downside, she had five sons. All single. And a touch wild. Sending a delicate beauty like Kate over there would be like throwing a rabbit to a pack of hungry wolves. He couldn't do it.

Besides, he wasn't sure he wanted to sleep out in the cabin. All alone. With nothing but his thoughts to keep him company.

"No. I'm fine, Ma." At the questioning arch of her brow, he added, "Honest."

"If you change your mind, let me know. I'm sure Kate would understand."

"I'll do that."

"What are your plans for the day?"

"I'm working on Mr. Wilcox's dining table. He's anxious to have it before his in-laws arrive next weekend."

She paused in her preparations. "Could you put it off for a couple of hours? I need someone to keep Kate company while I deliver this." When he opened his mouth to speak, she tacked on, "I wouldn't ask, except Nathan has been up all night with Bess. I took his breakfast out to the barn about an hour ago, and the calf still hasn't made an appearance. And your father and Caleb are milking the cows."

He didn't want to play babysitter for Francesca's little sister, but what choice did he have? His mother went out of her way to make life comfortable for him and his brothers, so whenever she asked a favor, he did his best to comply.

"Fine. I'll do it."

"You're a sweetheart, you know that?"

"Don't tell anybody."

Amid her soft laughter, there came a light knock on the front door.

"That's probably her. Do you mind, dear?"

Swallowing a sigh, he went to greet their guest. At the sight of her, the greeting on his lips fell flat. Her clothing, fancier even than the previous day's, was utterly out of place here.

Her silk brocade ensemble put him in mind of the eggplant growing in his ma's garden—deep, luxurious purple. The slim jacket had sleeves that bloomed out at the shoulders and tightened at the elbow on down to the wrists. A beribboned V emphasized her trim waist, erupting into a six-inch ruffle. The straight skirt below had slits revealing pleated skirts underneath. Corded rosettes adorned both the jacket and skirt, and frothy white fringe peeked out of the wrists.

Her elegant look was spoiled by the mass of chocolate waves tumbling past her shoulders. My goodness, she looked all of sixteen with her hair down. Young and vulnerable. Sweet.

Nope. He took a step back. *He refused to be drawn in by her beauty.* If anything, Francesca had taught him outward beauty, no matter how innocent-looking, didn't guarantee a beautiful heart.

"Good morning, Josh." Her cheeks were a becoming pink. "Might I speak with your mother, please?"

"She's in the kitchen."

With a stately nod, she walked past him. He remained

where he was, unable to pull his gaze from her retreating form. She moved with grace and poise, head high and spine straight as an arrow, like a queen before her royal subjects.

Frowning, he shook his head. How many hours of practice had it taken to perfect such posture? Time better suited to more productive pursuits.

Bits and pieces of their conversation drifted out to the living room.

He heard the self-deprecating humor in Kate's voice as she asked for help with her hair. "It appears I'm helpless without my staff."

"Don't worry, dear. Let's go up to my room and see what we can do."

"Since I'll be on my own for a while, maybe you can give me some pointers."

Josh stuffed his hands in his pockets, finding it odd that a young lady would need help fixing her hair.

As the pair ascended the stairs, he wondered how Francesca would've coped without servants to do her bidding. He hadn't given it a thought before this moment, all the changes he'd expected her to make. Instead of being waited on hand and foot, she would've had to do everything herself. While he'd been blinded by love, she'd obviously been thinking of more practical things.

In less than ten minutes, Kate and his mother were making their way back downstairs. His mother reached the bottom steps first. "Will you make Kate a cup of hot tea? Her breakfast is on the stove."

To Kate, she said, "I'm sorry to run off, but Laney Hedrick has been ill. The ladies in our sewing circle are taking turns delivering meals, and today happens to be mine. Would you mind spending the morning with Joshua? He's agreed to show you around."

Pausing on the last step, Kate's fingers tightened on the banister. Her gaze shot to his face, then away.

"I'd like that."

His gaze narrowed. Kate Morgan's perfect manners couldn't conceal her wariness. Was it him? Did he make her uncomfortable? Did she think he'd lash out in anger at her because of what Francesca had done? Or was she simply a timid young lady?

Their temporary guest was a stranger to him. Francesca had spoken at length of her parents but when it came to her sister, she'd been strangely reticent. He wondered why that was. Was theirs a strained relationship?

"I'll be back in time to fix supper, I hope. If not, there's smoked ham and bread for sandwiches."

"Don't rush, Ma. We'll rustle up something if you're late."

The back door clicked shut. Silence hung thick in the air. Kate avoided his gaze, staring with great interest at the white pine floorboards.

Clearing his throat, he headed for the kitchen. "I'll get your breakfast."

While he set the water to boiling and retrieved a teacup and saucer from the cabinet, she stood gazing out the windows overlooking the front yard. He wondered what she was thinking. Why the forlorn expression? Did she miss the big city already?

At the sight of the heaping portion of eggs, bacon and biscuits, her eyes widened and she pressed a hand against her midsection. "I can't possibly eat all that."

Swallowing his irritation, he gripped the top rung of

the chair in front of him. "You want me to make something else?" *Your Royal Highness?*

She looked doubtful. "I normally have a bowl of oatmeal or a slice of toast with marmalade."

He thought back to the few weeks in March he'd spent with Francesca. "Your sister has quite the appetite."

Hurt flashed across her face, which she quickly masked. "My sister can eat anything she likes and it doesn't affect her figure."

Josh stood mute. What had he said to cause her pain? His heart beat out a warning. He'd known Kate Morgan less than twenty-four hours, and already she was getting under his skin.

"Well, you certainly don't look as if you need to worry about that," he said brusquely. "I'll check if we have oatmeal."

Her eyes flared with surprise. "Wait. Please don't go to the trouble." Lowering herself into the chair, she indicated the plate. "This smells delicious."

At least she wasn't sulking. Francesca would have.

He retrieved her tea from the kitchen and set it on the table, along with a crock of honey, then sank into the chair across the table. He watched her eat, thinking he'd never seen such refined manners. She ate carefully, her jaw barely moving as she chewed, dabbing her mouth with her crisp napkin.

"What would you like to do today?"

"I'd like to scout out some possible sites for photographs. Can you suggest any particularly interesting spots?"

"First I need to know what you're interested in photographing. What kind of book is this going to be?"

"A sort of travel guide. I'd like pictures of the mountains, of course." Her eyes sparkled as she warmed to her topic. "Churches make interesting photos. Barns. Wagons. Everyday scenes of life on a farm. Would you show me your farm?"

"Sure."

"I also like to take portraits of people. I noticed the one of your family on the fireplace mantel. Perhaps I can take another one and give your mother a print."

"She'd like that, I'm sure. That was taken many years ago." He sipped the stout, black brew. "As to possible sites, I'll have to give it some thought."

"Thank you."

"How long will it take you to gather all the photographs you need?" *In other words, how long before you leave?*

"I'm not certain. But I'm not in any hurry to go back. My parents are touring Europe for the next two months. Francesca is on her honeymoon—" She broke off, her gaze shooting to his. Flustered, she rushed ahead. "Anyway, I didn't like the idea of rattling around the estate with only staff for company."

"I'm curious why you didn't go with your parents. Surely Europe is a more interesting subject than our mountains."

"Simple. They didn't ask. My parents prefer to take their vacations alone."

"I see." Taken aback by her candid response, he said, "Well, I imagine you'll soon be bored here."

"If that happens, then I will know it's time to go home."

"Don't you have fancy parties to attend? Shopping to do? I'm sure you noticed our one and only general store."

Her eyes dulled. "If my presence here is inconvenient, I will leave immediately."

Now he felt like a heel. He'd been insensitive. "Forgive me. I didn't mean to make you feel unwelcome."

Lashes lowered, she sipped her tea. Her fingers were elegant, nails trim and shiny, skin like satin. One gold filigree ring adorned the fourth finger of her right hand. They were the hands of a privileged lady, unblemished by hard work.

How would he handle the strain of seeing Francesca's sister every day? Reminding him of all he'd lost. And the gossip her presence would stir up...

Undoubtedly, he was going to be the subject of a lot of talk. That's simply the way things worked in small towns. Wasn't every day a man's fiancée up and married someone else.

"Are you ready for that tour?" He pushed back his chair.

She hesitated. "If you have something you'd rather do, I can entertain myself. I brought quite a collection of books with me, as well as my harp. I'll be fine on my own."

"You brought your harp?" Who traveled with musical instruments? He'd never understand the whims of the wealthy.

"It's a Celtic harp, small enough to hold on my lap. I've played for many years. The music soothes me."

"I know what you mean," he said, surprised they had something in common. "About the soothing part. I play the fiddle."

"Oh?" Interest stirred in her expression. "I would like to hear you play sometime. Fran didn't mention that you played an instrument."

"That's because I didn't tell her."

One pitfall of relationships conducted at a distance was that important details were often overlooked or left out entirely. In Francesca's case, details like another suitor. Thoughts of her with another man churned up unpleasant emotions. The betrayal affected him deeply. If and when he ever decided to court another lady, he'd be certain to keep things simple.

And the lady sitting across from him was anything but.

Chapter Four

Strolling about the O'Malley farm, Kate's gaze was drawn repeatedly to her handsome guide. Sunlight filtered through the leaves overhead, showering patches of light on the navy cotton shirt stretched taut across his back and shoulders. Josh's rich drawl made each word sound like a caress. Listening to him explain the names and uses of each structure lulled her into a state of contentment.

He'd spoken hesitantly at first, his expression guarded, as if he expected her to be bored. Her many questions had brought about a change in his tone and manner, however. He was clearly proud of his family's farm. And from what she'd seen, he had reason to be.

She surveyed her surroundings with a practiced eye. People back home would enjoy seeing these rural images. The wealthy would use them as a guide to plan sojourns to the mountains. Those who couldn't afford to visit would at least be able to glimpse the beauty of East Tennessee. She could hardly wait to get started!

Kate found the workings of a farm fascinating. Here

people had to be self-sufficient, working with the land and its offerings to provide for their needs.

She would never tell him Francesca would've been less than thrilled with her new home. No doubt, she would've taken one look and hightailed it back to the city.

Pushing away from the corn crib, he jerked a thumb over his shoulder. "All that's left to show you is the apple house."

"Apple house?" Five rows deep, the orchard fanned out in both directions behind him. There wasn't a building in sight.

"It's where we store the apples we don't immediately use." He extended his arm. "The ground is uneven in places. I wouldn't want you to stumble and fall."

She slipped her hand into the crook of his arm, his muscled forearm bunching beneath her fingers. They strolled at an even pace to the orchard. A gentle breeze stirred the trees, carrying with it the fragrant, tangy scent of the fruit hanging from the branches.

"I don't see a house."

He pointed to the steep hillside beyond the trees. "Look there. See the door?"

Squinting, she could just make out a low roofline and a child-size door. "It looks like a child's playhouse."

He laughed. "Come, I'll show you."

As they drew closer, she saw that it had been built into the hillside and only the front facade of stone and timber was visible. When she questioned him, he said it was to maintain the temperature inside at an even level and thus keep the apples from spoiling. Again, she was impressed by the family's ingenuity.

Using his shoulder, he edged open the door. With a flourish of his hand, he said, "Ladies first."

She bit her lip. From where she was standing, the interior looked awfully dark and cavelike. But he was waiting patiently, assessing her with those intense blue eyes.

She didn't have to stay inside, she reasoned. What could a quick peek hurt?

Drawing a deep breath, Kate stepped through the doorway, bowing her head to avoid the low crossbeam. Cool, musky air filled her nostrils. Stacks of empty baskets filled the long, narrow space.

It wasn't so bad.

Then Josh came in behind her, his body blocking out the light.

Her heart tripped inside her chest. Nausea threatened, and she felt strangely light-headed.

Memories from the past swept over her, and spinning on her heel, she collided with his solid chest. "Please, I need to get out."

His hands came up to steady her. "What's wrong?"

Without answering, she ducked beneath his arm and shot out the door. Once again in the open field, she sucked in a lungful of air. *Please don't pass out.* Pressing a palm against her clammy forehead, she willed herself to remain calm.

"Hey." He came abreast of her, his hand cupping her upper arm. "You're as white as a sheet. Let's go over here and sit for a spell."

Kate leaned on his strength as he guided her to a fallen log beneath a nearby apple tree. He helped her settle, then sat close beside her. She couldn't dwell on his nearness, only her acute embarrassment.

What must he think of her?

"I—I'm all right now."

"What happened back there?" he prompted, his voice

thick with concern. "Did I do something to make you uneasy?"

"No, it wasn't you." Eyes downcast, she plucked at the ruffles on her sleeve. "I don't like small, confined spaces. I tend to panic, as you've just witnessed." Her heart rate was slowing to normal, the nausea fading.

"I wouldn't have insisted on your going inside had I known. I'm sorry."

She shifted her gaze to his hands, resting on his knees. Tanned and smooth, they were strong, capable hands.

"It wasn't your fault. I knew better."

"Have you always felt this way?"

No, not always. "For a long time, yes." *Please just leave it at that.*

He was quiet. Then, reaching up to the limb suspended above their heads, he plucked two apples and offered her one. "Feel like eating something? The natural sugar might put some color back into your cheeks."

She met his assessing gaze and got lost in the blue depths. The quirk of his lips in a friendly smile broke the spell.

Accepting the fruit, she balanced it in the palms of her hands, wondering how she'd be able to eat it without making a mess of herself and her outfit. Come to think of it, she hadn't eaten an uncut apple since she was a little girl. It was one of those simple acts classified as unlady-like. A young lady of her social standing should never appear less than picture-perfect.

Beside her, Josh was already enjoying his.

A tiny seed of rebellion sprouted in her mind. She wasn't in New York. This wasn't the estate. She was on a farm in the Tennessee mountains. Surely the rules of what her mother considered proper conduct could be bent a little.

Sinking her teeth into the firm flesh, Kate relished the sweet-tart explosion on her tongue. Maybe it was the combination of warm sunshine and fresh air or Josh's presence beside her, but she was certain this was the most delicious apple she'd ever tasted.

When the core was all that was left, she glanced over to find him grinning at her.

"What?"

"You, ah, have juice dribbling down your chin."

"I do?"

He caught her wrist. "Wait. Use my handkerchief."

Pulling a clean white square of cloth from his pants pocket, he reached over and wiped her chin. His other hand still held her wrist, the pads of his fingers pressed against her skin so that surely he could detect the spike in her pulse.

He lowered his hand. "There," he murmured with a distracted air, "good as new."

"Thanks," she managed in a weak voice.

Then, as if just noticing he still held her, he dropped her wrist like a hot coal.

Surging to his feet, he put distance between them, stroking his goatee in a nervous gesture. "Well, that's all there is to show you. Tour's over." He jerked a thumb over his shoulder. "Guess we should head back to the house so that I can warm up the soup Ma made for lunch."

What had just happened? Whatever it was, he'd been affected the same way she had. And he didn't seem at all pleased.

What was he thinking? Allowing himself to be affected by Kate Morgan. Of all the foolish, irresponsible… Hadn't he learned a thing from his tangle with one spoiled heiress?

Annoyed, he was quiet on the walk back and throughout the meal. Kate, perhaps sensing his mood, was quiet as well, seemingly content to listen to his father, brothers and himself discuss farm business.

With the afternoon stretching before them, he'd decided to show her around town. Strolling beside her, he glanced at her profile.

She was soaking in their surroundings as if imprinting the scene upon her memory. Was this city girl a nature lover or was this intense observation a result of her profession?

Her expression brightened. "Look!"

He followed her gaze to a hollowed-out tree trunk where a momma raccoon and four kits lay curled up in their nest, a tangle of gray-and-white fur.

"What an adorable sight!" she whispered, her smile full of girlish excitement. "How old do you think they are?"

"I'd say four or five months." He matched his voice to hers so as not to disturb the sleeping family.

"To see them in real life is such a treat!"

"What? You don't have raccoons in the big city?"

She appeared thoughtful. "Perhaps in Central Park. The deer are plentiful there, I'm told, as are foxes."

The largest city he'd visited was Knoxville. Amid the noise, crowded streets and hectic pace, he'd quickly discovered he preferred country life.

"You've never been there?" he asked, wondering for the first time what she did to pass the time.

"A handful of times. I wasn't fortunate enough to see any wildlife."

"Well, there's plenty of it here."

Her gaze was drawn once again to the sleeping raccoons. "I'm continually struck by God's handiwork. His imagination and creativity. Nature reflects His majesty, wouldn't you agree?"

Josh was surprised to hear her speak about God. He'd tried on several occasions to engage Francesca in a conversation about faith, but she'd skirted the issue, saying only that she was a frequent church attendee. Was this another area of difference between the sisters?

"I agree wholeheartedly."

Something in his voice must've snagged her attention, for she turned and thoughtfully regarded him. They shared smiles of understanding, an acknowledgment that on this important subject they were in agreement.

Then, before he could get too accustomed to her heart-melting smiles, he resumed walking. She fell into step beside him.

Crossing the bridge into town, the first business they passed was his friend Tom's barbershop. Since it was midafternoon, the shop was empty of customers. Tom stood in back, polishing his tools.

Glancing out the window, he spotted Josh and waved, his brows hiking up when his gaze lit on Kate. He flashed Josh a wolfish grin and a thumbs-up. He must not have heard of Francesca's defection.

The tips of his ears burning, Josh slid his gaze to Kate, who appeared unaware of the exchange. Her stiff black bonnet shielded the sides of her face, so it was unlikely she'd seen anything.

Great. Everyone was going to assume she was his bride-to-be. He'd forever be explaining himself. It'd be easier to call a town meeting and set the record straight once and for all.

They walked in the direction of the mercantile. Out of habit, his gaze homed in on the empty store for sale across the street, the one he'd been saving up to buy. When he saw the owner, Chadwick Fulton, ducking inside, he stopped abruptly.

"I see someone I need to talk to. Would you mind if I met you at the mercantile in about fifteen or twenty minutes?"

"No, not at all." Curiosity marked her expression.

He hesitated, suddenly remembering his and Francesca's outings in Sevierville and her insistence that he stay by her side. "Are you sure? I wouldn't want you to feel ill at ease, you being new in town. I can put it off until another time."

"Don't worry," she surveyed the single road of businesses and smiled, dimples flashing. "I'm fairly certain I won't get lost."

Pleased by her response, Josh smiled back. Apparently, Kate Morgan could take care of herself. "Clawson's is the last business on this side of the street. You can't miss it. I'll catch up with you."

He waited until she'd gone inside to cross the street and study the storefront. He imagined the words *J. D. O'Malley Furniture Company* scrolled in large letters across the plate-glass windows. His dream of opening his own furniture store was so close to reality.

"Good morning, Mr. Fulton," he greeted as he entered, closing the door behind him.

Seated behind the only piece of furniture left behind, a scuffed hunk of wood masquerading as a desk, the old man looked up and grunted. "O'Malley."

"How are you today?"

"What do ya want?"

Fulton's grumpy response wasn't unusual. He was an unhappy, crotchety old man.

"Sir, I came by to let you know that I've almost got the money to buy this place. I'll be paying you a visit as soon as I finish a few more orders."

"The sooner I sell it, the better," he groused, then shook a gnarled finger at Josh. "Remember, I ain't holdin' this place for you. Cash talks, and so far you ain't shown me any."

Josh understood it was the way of business, but he didn't have to like it. Mr. Fulton wouldn't agree to accept a deposit. "Yes, sir. I understand." He tugged on the brim of his hat. "Good day."

"Yeah, yeah." He waved him out. "G'day."

After taking one last look around the space and mentally calculating how many pieces he'd need to fill it, he left. He eyed the mercantile across the street, deciding he had time to stop by the post office and see if he had any letters from his cousin Juliana. He wasn't consistent in his replies, but so far she'd overlooked that fact and kept the letters coming. They never failed to lift his spirits.

She'd only been gone a month, but it felt like a lifetime. He took comfort in the fact that her new husband was making her happy.

Inside the post office, he was surprised to see a line of people. He had time, though. Kate didn't seem to be the type to fuss if a man was a few minutes late.

* * *

Kate strolled along the boardwalk carrying the small brown sack of hairpins and hand mirror she'd just purchased. Though not a large store, she'd been pleasantly surprised by the variety and quality of goods. The proprietor and his wife had been friendly and helpful without being overbearing. And customers greeted her with either a nod or a smile.

The overall atmosphere of the town was one of easygoing charm. People back home seemed to be more formal, keeping to themselves as they went about their business.

Glancing up and down the street, she searched for Josh. She wondered what could be keeping him. He'd certainly been intent on some task. Perhaps it had taken longer than expected.

She decided to head in the direction of the shop he'd disappeared into. Waiting for a wagon to pass, she lifted her skirts off the dusty ground and hurried to the other side. She didn't notice the two men standing outside the post office until she was almost upon them.

The shorter of the two elbowed his companion in the ribs and muttered words too low for her to hear. That man, whose face had been obscured by his hat's wide brim, lifted his head and stared hard at her. She recognized him at once. Tyler Matthews.

Her feet slowed as his hungry gaze devoured her, looking her up and down as if she were a slice of pie to be savored. Feeling violated, she stopped, unwilling to go any nearer. When he advanced a step toward her, Kate whirled and walked as quickly as she could in the opposite direction while trying not to attract attention.

Glancing back to see if he still followed her, she collided with a muscled chest and her sack slipped out of her hands. It hit the weathered boards with a thunk. Hands came up to steady her.

"Kate?"

Josh. "I'm sorry," she panted, "I didn't see you."

"What has you upset?" Holding her steady with a gentle grip, he gazed down at her with concern.

"I saw Tyler. He started to follow me."

Lips compressing in irritation, he scanned the boardwalk behind her. "I don't see him. He must've ducked in between the buildings. Where did you first spot him?"

"Outside the post office."

Slowly she became aware of his thumb lazily stroking her arm, an unconscious gesture meant to soothe.

His brows came together. "You okay?"

"Yes, just a bit unnerved. This is something I've never experienced before, having someone fixated on me." She shuddered. His fingers flexed in response.

Josh was near enough for her to feel his body heat, to see the leap of his pulse in the hollow of his neck. The dark shirt complemented his tanned skin and brilliant eyes. Her gaze fell to his mouth, noting that his lips looked warm and generous. What would it be like to be kissed by Josh? she wondered suddenly.

Had he ever kissed Fran? Her sister had been surprisingly coy on the subject, never hinting either way. Jealousy gripped Kate's heart, startling her. She had no business entertaining such thoughts!

Tearing her gaze up to his, she sucked in a breath at the confused interest in his eyes. With an almost imperceptible shake of his head, as if to clear his thoughts, he swallowed hard.

"I want you to be careful." He bent and picked up her

sack. "Stay alert to your surroundings, especially when you're alone."

"Of course, I—"

"Josh!" a female voice trilled. "Aren't you gonna introduce us to your fiancée?"

Chapter Five

Two young ladies stood watching them, eyes wide with curiosity.

Kate flushed with embarrassment. No doubt they were drawing their own conclusions to what appeared to be an intimate moment. What would they think when they realized she wasn't Francesca?

"Girls, I'd like you to meet Miss Kate Morgan." Josh put distance between them. "Kate, these are my cousins. Megan and Nicole O'Malley."

Like Kate and Francesca, the O'Malley sisters did not resemble each other in the slightest. With her dusky-blond curls and angelic countenance, Megan radiated a sweetness not present in Nicole, who was a striking beauty with raven hair and china-blue eyes.

Megan's friendly smile put Kate instantly at ease. Nicole stared at her with undisguised awe, her gaze taking in every inch of Kate's attire. Compared to their comparatively simple dresses, she supposed her ensemble was a bit much.

"It's a pleasure to meet you."

"Welcome to Gatlinburg, Kate," Megan said.

"Kate? But I thought—" Nicole began, only to stop when Megan nudged her shoulder. "Uh, it's nice to meet you."

Hating that Josh had been put in the position yet again of having to explain this horrible situation, she saved him the trouble. "My sister, Francesca, isn't coming, I'm afraid."

"We'll discuss it later," he said firmly, searching the street for onlookers.

That was one advantage of living in a large city, she thought—a person could blend in with the crowd. No one knew your business, and no one cared.

It was obvious the girls respected Josh, for they dropped the subject like a hot potato.

"We were on our way to Plum's for tea. Would you like to join us?" Megan asked, her eyes hopeful.

"It's our town's very first café," Nicole gushed. "Mrs. Greene, the proprietress, says one day soon we'll have loads of people coming through here looking at our mountains and that they'll all need a place to eat. Ma thinks she's lost her mind—"

"Nicole, please." Megan shot her an exasperated glance.

She waited for Josh to reply, who deferred to Kate. "It's up to you."

After the near run-in with Tyler and her disturbing awareness of Josh, a cup of hot tea might help her to relax. "That sounds like a splendid idea."

"Wonderful." Megan beamed her pleasure.

Kate hadn't always been the best judge of character, but she got the feeling Megan O'Malley would make a good friend. And she didn't have many of those. Most of the young socialites of her acquaintance were like Fran, interested only in the latest fashions, the finest parties and, most importantly, finding a rich, suitable husband.

While she liked nice clothes, she would much rather take photographs than spend hours poring through *Harper's Bazaar* or standing for fittings. Parties among her set were overrated. Same food, same music, same people. Different setting.

As for a husband, she did want one of those. Longed, actually, for someone to love who loved her heart, mind and soul. But after what had happened with Wesley, well, she worried no man would want her—a used woman.

He certainly hadn't wanted her. Once had been enough for him.

While she'd been sure he would show up the next day with a ring and a proposal, he'd boarded a ship for England instead.

Shoving the remembered pain and humiliation aside, she crossed the dusty street with Josh, the sisters walking ahead of them. They were chattering and laughing, seeming as close as sisters could be, and Kate experienced a familiar twinge of regret. She and Fran had never shared such a close bond, not even as children. Now that her sister had a new husband and a home of her own, Kate doubted they ever would.

Plum Café was an unexpectedly charming establishment. Mauve tablecloths covered the round tables, and matching curtains edged with gold ribbon adorned the windows overlooking the street, softening the harsh glare of sunlight.

An assortment of tantalizing aromas hung in the air. Voices and the clatter of dishes could be heard coming from the kitchen in back. Only one of the tables was occupied—an elderly couple who smiled and nodded but otherwise minded their own business.

Josh pulled a chair out for each of them and once they were seated, lowered his tall form into the one beside her. He took off his hat and hooked it on the back of his chair, then ran a hand through his hair. It was impossible to judge his mood by his closed expression. Was he thinking of his canceled wedding?

The proprietress, a meticulously dressed, middle-age lady, appeared and took their orders.

Nicole leaned eagerly forward. "Kate, you must tell us about New York. Have you been to Macy's? What's it like?"

Kate smiled. "Macy's has the most amazing window displays. The staff is attentive and knowledgeable. There is so much to see, you could spend days browsing the aisles."

"Is there a library in the city?" Megan looked hopeful.

"There are two—the Astor Library, used primarily for research, and the Lenox Library, which has mainly rare, religious books. I don't visit either one, since our estate houses a grand library with both classics and recent works."

"What a treat to have all those books at your disposal. Why, I doubt I'd get much else done if I lived there!"

"What type of books do you like to read?" Kate asked. "I brought a crate full with me. You're welcome to borrow as many as you'd like."

"Honest?" Megan seemed pleased with the offer.

"All she reads are love stories." Nicole rolled her eyes. "Nothing else."

"That's not true," the other girl protested. "I like adventure stories, too."

"If I have to hear about Mr. Darcy and Miss Bennet one more time," she exclaimed, "I think I'll be sick."

"Nicole!"

Kate dipped her head to hide a smile. Their drinks arrived then, along with a plate of gooey, pecan-sprinkled cinnamon rolls.

Josh held up a hand. "We didn't order these, Mrs. Greene."

"Consider it an engagement gift." The lady's smile encompassed Kate and Josh. "Congratulations."

Before they could correct her, she disappeared into the kitchen.

"Oh, dear." Cheeks burning, Kate lowered her gaze to her lap.

When she felt his touch on her shoulder, she looked up and got lost in his impossibly blue eyes. "Forget about it," he said quietly. "It'd be a shame to let these go to waste. I'll clear things up with Mrs. Greene later."

"Here you are." Megan set a roll in front of her. "That woman is an amazing cook. You have to try one."

Nicole was already biting into the pastry, an expression of rapture on her youthful face. "Mmm."

She supposed she could set aside her self-imposed aversion to sugar-laden treats just this once. "Fine. But just so you know, I don't normally do this."

All eyes were on her as she lifted the first bite into her mouth. The rich, cinnamon pastry melted on her tongue. She stifled a moan of appreciation.

She attempted a stern expression. "Now I'm in trouble. I will have to make a point of avoiding the Plum Café from now on and maybe even this entire side of the street."

The sisters chuckled. Even Josh managed a smile.

"Want to know what I think?" He set down his coffee mug. The teasing light in his eyes was unexpected, stealing her breath. "Now that you've tasted them, you won't be able to resist."

"I disagree," she challenged with a lift of her chin. "When it comes to sweets, I happen to have unwavering willpower."

His gaze dropped to her mouth. His eyes darkened, all emotion hidden. "You, um, have a spot of cinnamon." He indicated the corner of her lips.

Self-conscious, Kate used her napkin. "Better?"

"Yes." Shifting in the chair, he addressed Megan. "I was at the post office just now and picked up a letter from Juliana."

"Oh?" She exchanged a pointed glance with Nicole. "What did she say?"

Nicole giggled.

"I haven't read it." He stared hard at them. "What's up?"

"Juliana's expecting!" Nicole blurted.

"You weren't supposed to tell," Megan admonished in a hushed whisper.

Beside her, Josh went very still. "Why keep it a secret?"

Eyes averted, Nicole toyed with her teacup. Megan met his gaze head-on.

"It's not a secret, of course. It's just that, well, Juliana wanted to tell you herself. No doubt it's in your letter." To Kate, she explained, "Juliana is our eldest sister. She was married last month and now lives with her husband, Evan Harrison, in Cades Cove. She and Josh were best friends."

Gulping the last of his coffee, Josh set the cup down with a thud. "Are you two going straight home after this?"

"Yes."

"Would you mind walking Kate home?"

"Not at all."

Grabbing his hat, he looked at her. "Is that okay with you?"

"Certainly."

Standing, he slipped Megan a banknote. "This will take care of the bill and tip."

"Josh—"

He silenced his cousin with a look.

The three sat without speaking as they watched him leave. As her seat was facing the window, she could see him striding purposefully down the street. He was obviously distraught by this sudden news. Her heart went out to him.

"Kate, did your sister call off the wedding?" Megan's troubled countenance revealed how deeply she cared about her cousin.

"Yes. In fact, she has already married someone else."

Kate cringed at Nicole's shocked gasp. Megan's eyes glistened with unshed tears.

"He must be heartbroken," she whispered. "He was already sad about Juliana's leaving."

"She and Josh were practically joined at the hip."

"He lost his best friend," Megan confirmed. "And now his bride…"

Lounging on a sun-warmed rock, Josh stared unseeing at the water coursing past. The fish weren't biting today.

He'd been in his workshop since leaving the café, working most of the day to finish Mr. Wilcox's dining table. His hands ached from the amount of sanding and polishing he'd done, but it was a small inconvenience. The table was finished. The money he'd get from it would bring him one step closer to his dream.

If someone else didn't beat him to the punch, that is.

A twig snapped. Josh whipped around, his hand going to the pistol in his holster. Spying Kate, he relaxed.

She'd abandoned her stiff jacket and wore only a long-sleeved, ruffled black blouse with her deep purple skirts. Slung over her shoulder were an odd-shaped bag and a leather strap attached to a square box. With the other hand, she carried a tripod stand.

Her porcelain skin was flushed pink. Chocolate curls had escaped confinement to brush against her cheeks. It was obvious she hadn't seen him. Her gaze scanned the woods, occasionally dropping to the ground as she maneuvered fallen logs and uneven terrain.

"Kate."

Her hand went to her throat. "You startled me!"

"Sorry." Standing, he removed his hat. "Do you need help?"

"I can manage." Changing direction, she headed his way.

He met her halfway and took the tripod.

With careful movements, she set the box and bag on the leaf-strewn ground.

She held out her hands for the tripod.

"I'm sorry about earlier," he said. "I shouldn't have left."

"I survived," she huffed. "Although you could've warned me about Nicole's propensity to talk endlessly of fashion." If it weren't for the teasing light dancing in her eyes, he would've thought she was serious.

Again, her reaction was unexpected. Francesca would've pouted over such carelessness on his part, no matter that he was upset, trying to absorb one change after another.

"It's a topic of great interest to her, I'm afraid." He sighed, a hint of answering humor in his voice. "She drove you to distraction, I take it?"

"Not at all! I like Megan and Nicole very much. They are nicely mannered young ladies."

"Glad to hear it. I'm rather fond of them myself."

"The sisters you never had?"

"Living next door to each other, we were practically raised as one big family. They do like to accuse me of assuming the role of protective older brother."

"You were upset earlier. Is everything okay with the one who moved away?"

"Juliana's fine." He slipped his hands into his pockets. "Better than fine, actually. Ecstatic. I'm thrilled for her. It's just that so much has changed the past few weeks."

Her expression turned pensive. "Yes, I can imagine it's a lot to take in."

Certain she was thinking of his canceled wedding and not at all interested in going down that path, he resumed his post and picked up his rod.

Indicating his empty pail, he said, "I was hoping to have trout for supper, but so far the fish aren't obliging."

A ghost of a smile gracing her mouth, she surveyed the pebble-strewn stream and dense forest spreading out around them. It was quiet here. Restful. Nothing but the trickle of water and the rustle of leaves overhead.

"There's something magical about this place," she said, her voice hushed. "It's so beautiful it almost defies description."

With the onset of fall, the leaves were already beginning to thin out. "You should see it in spring and summer. The greenery is so thick you feel like you're the only creature for miles around, save the birds and squirrels."

Her gaze settled on his. "I'd like that."

He hadn't meant it as an invitation. It wasn't that he didn't like her. Kate seemed nice enough. But she didn't fit in here. And although the physical similarity wasn't there, in his mind he'd never be able to separate her from Francesca and her heartless betrayal.

He pointed to the box. "What do you have there?"

"My camera."

Crouching down, she flipped open the lid and lifted it out. Made of polished cherrywood with brass fittings, black accordion-like material in between the two ends, it appeared to be an expensive piece of equipment. "Would you mind if I took a photograph of you?"

"What? Now?" He wasn't primped and primed for a portrait. Far from it.

"Yes, now." She stood. "Not every photo has to be staged in a studio."

"But I'm not dressed—"

"You look fine." Her gaze flicked over his shirt and trousers. "Natural. I wouldn't expect you to be fishing in a three-piece suit, and neither would anyone else." She paused in sliding a piece of square coated glass into the camera. "If you'd rather not, I understand. I don't want to make you uneasy."

"No, it's fine."

"Great." Her wide smile elicited one of his own. "I'm going across."

There was a natural bridge to the other side, a mound of earth and rocks she crossed without incident. When she was directly across from him, he said, "I thought photographers had to travel with portable darkrooms." The stream wasn't all that wide, so he didn't have to raise his voice.

"Not with the invention of the dry plate." She steadied the stand before placing the camera on top. "The image is fixed and doesn't have to be processed right away."

"I haven't heard anything about it."

"That's because they've only recently been manufactured for widespread sale. Okay, look directly at me. And sit as still as possible." Peering into the camera, she removed the cover and waited for a full minute before replacing it. Straightening, she seemed pleased. "That's going to be a good one, I think."

Crossing back over, she was replacing the camera in its box when he spoke.

"Tell me about Francesca's husband."

Her hands stilled. She looked uncertain.

"I don't even know her married name," he persisted.

"His name is Percy Johnson."

"Francesca Johnson. I think Francesca O'Malley has a nicer ring to it, but that's just my opinion."

Her mouth flattened. "I'm sorry."

"I know he's not a common laborer, like me. What does he do? Or rather, what does his family do? He probably hasn't worked a day in his life." He couldn't disguise the bitterness in his voice.

I'm sorry, God. I can't help envying the guy. He got the girl, and I'm left here to pick up the pieces.

Indignation flashed in her eyes. "There's nothing common about you. My sister chose flash and glamour over depth and substance. She made a foolish decision."

Her words sparked an odd pang in his chest. He couldn't figure out why she was defending him. She didn't know him. Not really. Except, she *had* listened to his letters and glimpsed into his soul without his consent.

"Don't get me wrong," she hastened to add, "I love my sister. It's just that we each have our own opinions of what's important in life."

He found that difficult to believe. They might disagree on specifics, but their outlook couldn't be all that different. They shared the same upbringing, the same advantages.

Proposing marriage to a woman so far above his station had been a colossal mistake. He should've realized from the beginning that their worlds were too far apart.

"I just don't get it," he wondered aloud. "Why not break off the engagement the moment she decided to patch things up with him?"

She edged closer to the water, stepping on a smooth, slanted rock scattered with orange leaves. "I wish I had an answer for you. Her behavior is as much a mystery to me as it is to you."

"The two of you aren't close?"

She frowned. "No."

He wanted to question her further, to ask why her parents hadn't invited her to join them in Europe, but it was none of his business. Soon she'd be gone and he wouldn't have to spare another thought on the Morgan family.

She pointed to a rounded shell bobbing above the surface. "Do you know what kind of turtle that is?"

"Can't rightly say, but there are a number of painted box turtles hereabouts."

"A pity it moves too quickly for my camera."

His eyes on the turtle, he hadn't noticed her getting closer to the rock's edge.

"Be careful," he warned, holding out a hand. "Those rocks can be slippery—"

"All I want is a closer look."

One moment she was standing, bent at the hip with hands braced against her knees. An instant later, she was facedown in the stream.

Dropping his pole, Josh strode through the thigh-deep water. Wrapping his arm around her, his hand curled around her waist, he helped her stand. "Are you hurt?"

A bubble of laughter escaped as she wiped the moisture from her eyes. Her mouth a breath away from his ear, the soft, husky sound shot liquid fire through his veins.

"I'm fine." Taking stock of her sodden clothing, she grimaced. "My pride is a bit bruised, however. You did warn me, didn't you?"

Josh couldn't stop his smile. "Did you get that closer look you wanted?"

"No. I guess he didn't want to stick around for all the excitement."

A shiver coursed through her body. Though it was a warm September day, the water was cool. And she was wet from head to toe, the layers of clothing clinging to her petite yet womanly frame. Water dripped from her hair onto his shirt.

His gaze dropped to her mouth. What would it feel like—

Stiffening, he dropped his arm and stepped back, the water swirling around his legs.

Have you lost your mind? This is Francesca's sister, remember?

"Let's get you back to the cabin," he muttered, avoiding her curious gaze.

Once he'd helped her to the bank, he was careful to

keep his distance the entire walk home. Nor did he attempt conversation. If Kate wondered about his mood, she didn't comment.

Leaning the tripod stand against the porch railing, he directed his gaze to the blue mountain ridges framed by the sky. Anything to keep from looking at her. "I'll ask Ma to bring you a cup of tea."

"That's not necessary," she countered in a subdued voice. "I'm certain she has more important things to do than wait on me."

He clenched his fists. Of course she would be gracious. He couldn't imagine that ever coming out of his ex's mouth. From what he'd seen, Francesca had relished being waited on.

Again, his mind discharged a warning signal. This woman was dangerous.

"You're our guest. She wants you to be comfortable here."

"Yet I don't make you comfortable, do I?"

He did look at her then. Even with her wet hair plastered to her face and head and her clothes disheveled, she was beautiful. The vulnerability he sensed in her touched a chord deep inside.

Setting his jaw, he hardened his heart. "You don't affect me at all, Miss Morgan. Evenin'." He tugged on his hat's brim and, pivoting on his heel, left her staring after him.

Chapter Six

Stung by his cool dismissal, Kate watched him stride away. He held himself stiffly erect, his broad shoulders taut with tension. Well, he'd certainly told her, hadn't he? She'd been forward and assuming. What did she expect?

Josh was merely tolerating her presence. She was an interloper, a painful reminder of loss and betrayal.

She didn't fit in at home, and she certainly didn't fit here.

Shivering in the late-afternoon sunlight, she went inside to change. The quiet that greeted her inside the quaint space compounded her loneliness. At the estate, she was never completely alone. Butlers, footmen, housekeepers, ladies' maids and manservants moved discreetly about, attending to their business, seeing to the day-to-day running of the expansive mansion and tending to the needs of its occupants.

Though New York was her home, she wasn't happy there. And while she gained immense satisfaction from her photography work and her gardening, she lived with the knowledge that her presence wasn't wanted or needed by anyone. She didn't brighten anyone's day or bring a smile to a loved one's face. No one was eager to share secrets with her or give her a hug.

From the time she was a little girl, she'd known something was wrong with her. Her mother had never looked at her with pride and pleasure, as she had Francesca. Instead, whenever her gaze lit on Kate, her mouth would tighten and a wrinkle would form between her brows, as if puzzling out an impossible riddle.

The nightmare with Nanny Marie underscored her feelings of inadequacy.

By the time Wesley Farrington IV entered her life when she was seventeen, she'd been desperate to forge a connection with someone, anyone.

Seated on the edge of the bed combing out the tangles in her hair, her eyes drifted shut as she recalled their first meeting. Her parents were hosting an elaborate party, and everyone who was anyone in New York society had made an appearance. The ballroom glittered and sparkled like the contents of a jewelry box with its crystal and gold chandeliers, gilt-edged mirrors and jewel-toned carpets. The air was sweet with the fragrance of fresh flowers spilling from vases placed about the room, the sets of French doors thrown open to the balmy night.

While Kate had watched from the sidelines as gaily dressed couples swirled and dipped across the marble floors, Francesca had been surrounded by a bevy of admirers.

She'd noticed Wesley the instant he entered the room. Darkly handsome, with a smile that hinted of secrets and promises, the Oxford graduate had captured the attention of nearly every female under the age of sixty. Kate watched him charm each one, in turn, never dreaming he'd spare a word for her.

So when he'd appeared at her side not an hour later and requested a dance, she'd gaped at him. He laughed and repeated the request. They danced the next two dances, then escaped outside to stroll through the gardens. By the end of the night, she was certain she was in love.

Over the course of two months, he took her on carriage rides in Central Park and showered her with trinkets and roses and boxes of chocolates from Paris.

Kate had never been happier. Wesley treated her as if she were the most special girl in the world. He loved her. He hadn't voiced the words, but she could see it in his eyes.

It was that assumption that had ultimately led her to make the worst decision of her life. One night of pleasure had cost her not only her virtue, but a future with him.

Wesley never explained why he left. For months afterward, she'd waited impatiently for correspondence from him. Surely he would apologize for leaving so abruptly, reveal his reasons for abandoning her. She waited in vain.

She concluded that she must've done something wrong. Or disappointed him somehow.

When her mother questioned her, Kate made the mistake of confiding in her.

Georgia had railed at her. She had risked the family's reputation and ruined forever her chances of marrying a decent man. She was damaged goods.

A sharp rap on the door startled her, and the brush slipped out of her hand and clattered to the floor.

Her stomach flip-flopped. Was it him? Had he come back to apologize?

"J-just a minute," she called, her fingers going to her neck to make sure the buttons of her china-red housecoat were buttoned. She wasn't dressed to receive visitors, but this wasn't the estate. There was no one else to open the door.

Pulling it open, she found Nathan standing on the other side with a tray in his hands.

"Hi. Josh told me about your dunking." His smile was gentle. "He fixed a pot of tea and asked me to deliver it."

With a grateful smile, she gave him room to enter. Josh had ignored her refusal and sent the tea anyway.

Nathan set the tray on the table, and the tangy scent of ginger filled the cabin. There was a rose-emblazoned teapot, a matching cup and saucer, honey and a dessert plate bearing four pillowlike cookies. Her mouth watered. What was he doing, sending her sweets?

"Is there anything else you need?"

"No." Kate rested her hands on the top of the chair. "Thanks for bringing this over. Would you like to join me?"

"I wish I could, but I gotta check on the new calf."

She lifted the dessert plate. "Take at least one of these with you."

Grinning, he held up his hands. "There's a dozen or more of those in the kitchen. I've already had my fair share." He started for the door. "See you at supper."

When he'd gone, she stared at the table, her gaze caught by the lone cup and saucer. Tears sprang up. It seemed she was destined to always be alone.

Seated at the end of the pew with Mary on her left, Kate admired the church's stained-glass windows and ornately carved wooden podium. It was not a large building, by any means, but it was well-maintained and the pews gleamed in the muted, rainbow-colored light.

"What a lovely church," Kate murmured.

Mary sat with her gloved hands folded primly in her lap. "Do you attend services back home?"

"Yes." Kate pictured the grand, overstated auditorium and the fashionably dressed men and women who attended the services. The preacher there was nice enough, though she often left feeling dissatisfied. "I'm eager to hear Reverend Monroe."

"He's a good speaker." She nodded. "I like his practical style. He's humorous, too."

"It was good of him and his wife to take in my driver and Mr. Crandall the other night. I'll have to personally thank them."

"I'll introduce you after the service."

"Thank you."

Mary leaned close, her voice hushed. "You didn't happen to see Joshua this morning, did you? He's never late."

"No, I didn't."

He wasn't at supper last night. When no one remarked at his absence, she'd assumed he'd informed them of his whereabouts. When he hadn't shown up for breakfast, Kate got the sinking feeling he was avoiding her. Why his behavior should bother her she hadn't a clue. So what if Josh O'Malley didn't like her? She wouldn't be here forever.

Glancing over her shoulder, she became aware of several people watching her with interest. Pretending not to notice, she stared straight ahead once more. Of course, the townsfolk would wonder about her. By now everyone must know she was not Josh's fiancée. She didn't like being the center of attention, however.

Maybe that's why Josh hadn't come. How difficult it would be for him to face these people—his friends and acquaintances—and admit he'd been cast off! *Father, please comfort him. Ease his hurt and disappointment.*

At last, the service began. With Mrs. Monroe at the piano, the reverend led the congregation in two familiar hymns. Its beauty was in its simplicity. Her spirit soared at the sound of the pure worship, voices lifted in praise to God.

When everyone was seated and the reverend opened his Bible, Kate sat unmoving, absorbing his every word.

Sitting in the very last row, two steps from the door, Josh couldn't tear his gaze from Kate. He studied the sweet curve of her cheek, the pink tip of her ear, the slender slope of her neck.

He should be listening to the sermon, he knew, but her rapt expression—the vulnerability and wonder he saw there—captivated him. She'd indicated faith in God, so why did she look as if this was the very first time she'd heard God's Word preached?

He tried to turn his attention to the reverend and failed. His conscience troubled him. He'd been callous and rude, and he was never rude. He prided himself on being a gentleman, yet look at how he'd treated Kate from the very moment he set eyes on her.

The fact was she scared the daylights out of him. Here he was supposed to be nursing a broken heart and instead he found himself intrigued by his former fiancée's little sister.

His instinct told him to steer clear of her. But he didn't want to hurt her. And avoiding her would not go unnoticed, not by her and certainly not by his family.

Remember, she won't be here forever.

Fall was a busy season on the farm, anyway. Hog killings, apple peelings, corn shuckings. When he wasn't helping his father and brothers, he'd be in his workshop, making furniture. The time would pass quickly.

Before he knew it, everyone was standing for the closing prayer. He'd missed the entire message because his mind had been filled with thoughts of her. Not good.

Wanting to skip the inevitable questions and looks of pity from the congregation, Josh ducked out the door and headed home ahead of his family. He waited for Kate in the shade of her front porch.

She hesitated when she saw him. What was she thinking?

"Hi." He stayed where he was, waiting for her to come to him. His parents and brothers waved but continued toward the house.

"Hello."

Kate appeared every inch the sophisticated heiress.

She was meticulously dressed, as usual, in a light brown linen suit with cutouts and dark cocoa piping on the sleeves. Her gloves and bonnet were also dark brown. With the help of his mother, she'd styled her hair differently today—the top half caught up in ribbons while the mass of dark waves tumbled about her shoulders. Sunlight glinted in the strands with each movement of her head.

"What did you think of the service?" Arms folded, he leaned back against the railing.

She climbed the three steps and stopped, her hands folded primly at her waist. "I've never heard anything like it."

That surprised him. "Francesca said your family attends church every Sunday."

"That's true. Our pastor's sermons are mostly about

helping the less fortunate. Not once have I left there feeling as I do now, convicted yet encouraged."

Interesting. "Your sister didn't care to discuss her faith. I realize it's a private topic for some people, but now I'm wondering if she didn't have a foundation to draw from."

"A couple of years ago, a friend of mine walked me through the Scriptures, showing me how to become a follower of Jesus Christ. I shared this with both my parents and Francesca." She bowed her head, her fingers now clamped tight. "They weren't interested."

A slow hiss escaped his lips. "I'm sorry."

And he was. Sorry for them, because they were missing out on a precious relationship with the God of the universe. Sorry for Kate. He, too, had loved ones who didn't know Christ and didn't care to know Him. It was tough. And he was sorry for himself. In his longing for a family of his own, he'd neglected to discover the important things about his future bride. As hurtful as it was, he was beginning to think Francesca had done him a favor.

"Me, too. I hold on to hope, however, that one day they will change their minds."

"I'll pray for that."

"Thanks, Josh. That means a lot."

In her eyes he saw sadness and something more, an emotion he himself struggled with. Loneliness. But how could *she* be lonely?

Kate was the member of a prominent, influential New York City family. Certainly she mingled with other socialites her age. Francesca had written in detail about the grand gatherings they attended each week.

Another thought struck him with the full force of a

sledgehammer. Not only was Kate lovely and sweeter than pecan pie, she was the eligible daughter of oil magnate Patrick Morgan. Single men must be lining up to court her. The image soured his stomach.

He hadn't asked if she had a steady beau, and he didn't plan to. He was *not* interested in Kate's love life.

Pushing away from the railing, he moved toward her. "Are you joining us for lunch?"

His mother and aunt had planned a picnic.

"Yes, I'm just going inside to choose a couple of books for Megan."

When he drew near, she stepped aside to let him pass. He didn't. He inhaled her citrusy scent. "Romance is her favorite."

Her long lashes swept down to hide her eyes. "I remember."

"And what is yours?"

"I prefer science and nature books."

"You surprise me, Kate."

"Why?" Her gaze shot to his. "Because socialites as a rule must only be interested in the latest fashions? Learning cross-stitch and backgammon?"

"Exactly," he drawled. "For if you women exercise your vast intelligence, you'll soon realize you have no need for men."

Kate burst out laughing. The musical sound warmed him straight through to his soul.

"You have a nice laugh," he said softly.

She blushed and looked away. He could've kicked himself. Why had he said that out loud?

"Well, I'd better change and get the wagon ready."

He did move on then, before he said something else best left unsaid.

* * *

It was a perfect afternoon for a picnic, a flawless autumn day with startling blue skies and sunshine that soothed the soul. Perched on the patterned quilt spread out across the grass, Kate was content to listen to the conversation flowing around her.

Megan and Nicole sat on her left and directly across were Nathan and Josh. While she and the girls sat primly with their skirts arranged just so, the men had removed their boots and stretched out their large frames so that they were half sitting, half lying on the quilt. Josh was nearest to her, his pant-clad leg an inch or so from her taupe linen skirt.

Kate felt the weight of his every glance as if it were a physical touch.

His classical features put her in mind of the marble statues in the estate gardens—Roman soldiers of noble beauty and strength. His skin wouldn't be cold to the touch, of course, but certainly as smooth. His trim mustache and goatee gave him a dangerous air, and it wasn't difficult to picture him as a fierce warrior, a leader among men.

The sunlight made the tips of his hair shine liquid gold. No doubt its texture was that of the finest silk… *Enough.* Like every other upstanding, morally upright man, he was out of reach. Him especially. To daydream about her sister's former fiancé was utterly unacceptable.

Wrenching her gaze away, she scanned the lush, green fields sloping gently to the stream and the trees along the bank. On distant hills stood row upon row of corn. Black shapes were some farmer's cattle grazing. The landscape's verdant beauty imprinted itself on her mind and settled deep in her soul. Never before had she been so affected by her surroundings.

As Josh had said, this place really was a slice of paradise.

Kate turned her head at the sound of Mary's laughter. She and Sam, along with Alice, Sam's late brother's wife, occupied a second quilt closer to the water. Mary had introduced Kate to the girls' mother that morning at church, and she had seemed sincere in her welcome. In fact, everyone who'd gathered around at the completion of the services had been kind, expressing their delight at meeting her. It had been as pleasant as it had been unsettling. Their lack of formality had been wholly unexpected. She couldn't picture the affluent people of her church acting in such a manner.

Megan and Nicole's younger sisters, fifteen-year-old twins Jessica and Jane, strolled arm in arm along the bank. Caleb wasn't here. He'd escaped immediately after breakfast. Kate wondered where he spent all his time.

"Kate, tell us more about New York."

Nicole's eyes sparkled with curiosity. Of all the O'Malley sisters, the seventeen-year-old wore the finest dresses, and her glossy black mane was at all times meticulously styled, not a hair out of place.

"What would you like to know?"

"How far do you live from the dress shops?"

"There are a number near our home, but oftentimes the designers come to us with new arrivals from London and Paris. If my mother, sister or I need an outfit for a special occasion, they bring sketches and materials to choose from."

Josh scowled in disapproval. She hoped he didn't assume those things were important to her.

"Can you believe that, Megan?" Nicole nudged her sister, her eyes like saucers. "I am so envious!"

Kate lifted a shoulder. "It's convenient. I'm not an avid follower of fashion, like my mother and sister. There are certain colors and fabrics I prefer, of course, but my interests lie elsewhere."

Megan looked up from the book in her lap, a volume of poetry Kate had lent her, blond curls tumbling across her forehead. "How did you come to be interested in photography?"

"My father has friends in that field—both amateurs and professionals. Whenever he visited their studios, he didn't mind my tagging along if I promised not to disturb anything. The cameras fascinated me—the different sizes and wood grains and gadgetry."

"When did you decide to try it for yourself?" Josh shifted, and his knee brushed hers.

The casual contact jolted her. Swallowing hard, she struggled to keep her voice steady. "I wanted my own camera for a long time, but my father made me wait until I was fifteen. Up until the last year or so, the process of taking a photograph and exposing the image was a daunting one. Chemicals were—and still are—involved, although now with the dry plates it isn't rushed." She addressed Megan. "I could take photographs of you and your sisters if you'd like."

"That would be wonderful! Thank you."

Nicole appeared thoughtful. "What should I wear?"

Nathan chuckled. "Clothes."

She stuck her tongue out. "Hilarious, Nathan."

"You've looked fetching in every outfit I've seen you wear," Kate assured her. "Anything you choose will do splendidly."

She blushed prettily. "That's nice of you to say."

Kate caught Josh's appreciative smile, his eyes communicating his approval. It was obvious he cared deeply for his family. Unlike the ambitious, shallow men of her acquaintance, Josh stood for honor and compassion. He was the kind of man who put the needs of others before his own and would sacrifice everything for those he loved.

"What did Kate bring for you to read, Megan?" he asked, his gaze never wavering from Kate's face. Like a moth to a flame, she was drawn to him. She couldn't look away.

"*The Count of Monte Cristo, Great Expectations* and *Mansfield Park.*"

"That should keep you occupied for two or three days." He winked at Kate.

"Maybe one day Megan and I can come and visit you in New York," Nicole said wistfully.

Kate did break eye contact then. "I'd like that," she said, meaning it.

"Honestly?"

"Yes." She laughed. "You're welcome anytime."

"Josh said Francesca is the same age as our eldest sister, Juliana. Twenty-one. How old are you?"

"Nicole." Josh's voice deepened in warning.

"Nineteen."

"The same age as Megan," she gushed. "Do you have a steady beau?"

"You shouldn't ask such things, Nicki," Nathan admonished with a nudge of his foot.

She whipped her head around. "Don't call me that!"

Kate sensed rather than saw Josh's sharpened gaze. "You don't have to answer."

"I don't mind." Nicole hadn't meant to be intrusive. She was young and in awe of Kate's life in the big city. "I don't have anyone special in my life."

"All three of my cousins are single, you know. Well, I suppose Josh isn't ready to court anyone just yet after what your sister did to him. And Caleb—" she scrunched up her nose "—is not what I'd call a catch. A bigger grump I've never met! That leaves Nathan. He's real nice most of the time."

Nathan had tugged on his boots and was hauling Nicole to her feet before anyone could utter a word. He led her, sputtering her displeasure, toward the water. The three of them sat there in heavy silence for what seemed like an eternity. Finally, Megan cleared her throat.

"I think I'll join Jessica and Jane."

Face averted, her gaze on the distant trees, Kate wished she could disappear. Her cheeks burned with humiliation.

"Kate."

"Hmm?"

"Will you look at me?"

His eyes seemed to see straight into her soul, exposing her secrets. "I'm sorry about that. My cousin rarely thinks before she speaks. I'm sure she didn't set out to embarrass you."

"Poor Nathan." She dredged up something resembling a smile. "He won't be able to look me in the eye."

"Nathan may seem shy and unassuming, but he can be tough when the need arises."

She glanced to where Nathan was walking with Nicole beside the water, his arm around her shoulders. She was a spirited girl. For any man to calm her would take a strong will and finesse.

Kate moved to rise. "Now is probably a good time to speak with your parents about arranging for another place to stay. It slipped my mind yesterday."

A tiny gasp escaped her lips when Josh took abrupt hold of her hand. She'd forgone gloves for this outing, and the sensation of his rougher skin against hers shot fiery tingles up and down her arm. His grip was both gentle and firm, anchoring her to the spot.

"There's no need to go anywhere else. Unless you want to, that is."

She bit her lip. "I do enjoy being around your family. They've been extremely kind to me."

His expression remained neutral. "Then it's settled. You're staying."

Chapter Seven

East Tennessee was weaving its way into Kate's heart.

The more she explored, the more enthralled she became. At Mary's urging, Kate had set out after lunch Monday with her camera and supplies. She'd returned to their picnic spot and spent the better part of two hours setting up the equipment and taking various shots. Though hot from working in many layers of clothing, she was satisfied with her efforts. She couldn't wait to develop the prints!

Walking back to Sam and Mary's, she soaked in her surroundings. Sunlight streamed through the trees overhead, dappling the firm, brown earth. The forest was both mysterious and peaceful and, above all, breathtaking in its beauty. A testament to God's limitless imagination.

The prospect of leaving and returning to city life saddened her.

Spotting the stream she'd tumbled into the other day, Kate decided to stop and rest. Her equipment was heavy, the tripod awkward to carry. Her neck was damp with moisture, her hair heavy and straining against the pins.

Setting everything at the base of a sugar maple, she

lowered herself onto the same rock Josh had occupied. The sparkling water meandered past. Wouldn't it feel wonderful to dip her sore feet in?

The woods stood silent and empty. No one was around to see her unladylike behavior. And her mother's voice seemed further away today.

Unlacing her boots, she tugged them off and removed her stockings, wriggling her stiff toes. Pulling her skirts up to her knees, she plunged her feet in the water. The bracing cold stole her breath at first, but she quickly adjusted to the temperature.

Leaning back, supporting her weight with her hands braced against the rock, she lifted her face to the sun. *Thank You, Father, for the gift of Your creation.*

She wondered where Josh had disappeared to after lunch. Since establishing that she would remain in his cabin for the duration of her visit, his manner had been polite yet reserved, his expression carefully neutral.

"Lily."

Startled out of her reverie, Kate bolted upright. When her gaze connected with that of Tyler Matthews standing on the opposite bank, her stomach lurched. Apprehension shot through her limbs. Her ears buzzed. What did he want with her?

Her precarious position wasn't lost on her. She was well and truly alone—far enough away from the cabins that no one would hear her if she screamed.

"Don't be afraid." He held his hand out. "I would never hurt you. You know that, don't you?"

Tyler's dark eyes pleaded with her. Judging by the expression of profound sorrow on his face, he must've loved Lily very much. A tiny part of her felt sorry for him. Still, he must be drunk to mistake her for his dead wife. And that meant he was unpredictable.

"I—I'm not Lily, remember? My name is Kate. Kate Morgan."

Expression hardening, his large hands curled into fists. "My eyes work jus' fine, Lily Matthews." He slurred his words. "I'm weary of living without you. So you can either—" Closing his eyes tight, he pinched the bridge of his nose between his thumb and forefinger. "You can—"

Her movements slow and calculated, Kate eased her feet from the water and stood up.

Opening his eyes, he stumbled forward. "Come back home of your own free will or I'll take you by force."

"I'm not going anywhere with you!"

Adrenaline pulsing through her system, she bolted. The sticks and rocks scraping her bare feet hardly registered.

"Lily!" he gasped.

She heard a splash. He was following her!

"You can't run forever!" His breathless voice was a mix of anger and desperation.

Kate's confining skirts tangled around her legs. Terror turning her blood to sludge, she yanked them up and ran faster. Her lungs burned. Her side ached under her ribs.

Where was he? She couldn't hear him behind her. Still, she expected to feel his beefy hands on her any second. Suddenly his yell rent the air and she stumbled, glancing over her shoulder in time to see him crash to the ground, his feet twisted in a thatch of overgrown ivy. Gasping, she pushed herself to the edge of her limits. She didn't see Josh until she was almost upon him.

"Kate?"

"Josh!" she gasped.

Seeing her distress, he ran to intercept her.

Shaking now, she fell against him. His strong arms closed around her, sheltering her. She was safe. *Thank You, God.*

"Is it Matthews?"

Her cheek pressed against the hard wall of his chest, she fought to catch her breath. "He appeared out of nowhere."

He eased back to peer into her face. "Are you all right?"

At her nod, he pulled his troubled gaze away to scan the forest behind her. "He's gone now, but don't worry. I'm going to have a talk with him. This has to stop." He curled his arm around her shoulders. "Let's get you back to the cabin."

She took a step and swift pain radiated across the soles of her feet. She sucked in a harsh breath.

Josh stopped. "What is it?"

She didn't want to admit to being barefoot. "Nothing. I'm okay."

His eyes narrowed. "What hurts, Kate?"

"I left my boots back at the stream. My feet are just a little scraped up."

"You ran all this way barefoot?" he demanded. Without warning, he scooped her up and strode in the direction of the cabin.

"What do you think you're doing?"

"Put your arms around my neck."

Hesitantly, she complied. Pressed against him as she was, it was impossible not to notice the strength of his chest and muscular arms. He didn't seem bothered at all by her weight, supporting her with ease as his long strides ate up the distance.

The honey-brown hair at his nape tickled her fingers, tempting her to explore the soft strands. Her gaze traveled along his temple and the sun-bronzed skin cloaking his cheekbones down to the mustache and goatee framing his firm mouth.

Josh O'Malley was the epitome of strength, confidence and masculine beauty.

And he was her sister's ex-fiancé. She had to remember that.

Thankfully no one was out and about when they arrived, and Josh headed straight for her cabin. Kicking the door closed with his foot, he deposited her gently on the sofa.

"Don't move."

He rifled through the cupboards and shelves in the kitchen and disappeared into the bedroom, returning with a bowl and a pitcher of water, and a towel draped over his wrist. When he knelt at the far end of the sofa and reached to brush aside her skirts, Kate panicked. Her mother's cold recriminations marched through her mind. This was not proper in the least!

"What are you doing?" she exclaimed.

His expression was calm and controlled. "Your feet need attention." His voice deepened. "I promise to be gentle."

"I can do it myself then."

Crossing his arms, he dared her with a look. "I'd like to see you try."

Kate knew with her restrictive clothing, especially the tight corset she'd barely managed to fasten that morning, it would be difficult to bend and doctor her feet. Josh knew it, too. He was too much of a gentleman to voice that fact out loud, however.

When she broke eye contact, he pressed her shoulders back against the cushions. "Close your eyes and relax. Think of something pleasant. It'll be over before you know it."

Mortified, certain her face would burst into flames, Kate squeezed her eyes tight and clenched her hands. Her body tensed at the first brush of his fingertips on her tender skin. Gradually though, she relaxed. True to his word, his touch was gentle and efficient as he cleaned off the dirt and applied a medicinal cream to the scrapes and scratches.

"All done."

Kate opened her eyes. Face averted, he smoothed her skirts back down and stood to clear the coffee table. She eased her feet to the rug and sat up, watching as he washed his hands and folded the towel into a neat square. Bright red stained the back of his neck, indicating that he wasn't as unaffected as he pretended.

"Tell me about Tyler," she said, partly to ease the sudden tension in the room and partly to satisfy her curiosity.

Leaning a hip against the cabinet, he leveled an inscrutable look at her. "What do you want to know?"

"You said he hasn't always been the town drunk. What was he like before his wife died?"

His lips turned down. "A good man. He and I grew up together, though he was two years behind me in school." Stroking his goatee, he appeared lost in thought. "Tyler was never happier than the day he wed Lily. He was crazy about that girl."

Kate didn't hold out much hope that a man would ever love her like that.

"Do I resemble her that much?"

His gaze shot to her face. "You share similar features

and hair, although she was taller and her eyes spaced farther apart. You could certainly pass for sisters."

Kate digested that information. She looked remarkably like Tyler's dead wife. The one he'd loved and tragically lost. How could she ever convince him she wasn't Lily? When would his obsession with her end?

"What do you think he wants with me?" her voice wobbled.

Josh crossed the room and lowered his large frame to the cushions. Sliding one arm behind her along the sofa's edge, he leaned in close and cupped her cheek. "I won't let him hurt you, Kate. I'll protect you."

Kate's expressive eyes revealed her innocent trust in his ability to uphold that promise. He meant it. He would do everything in his power to keep her safe.

Silence thick with expectation hung between them. Josh stroked her silken skin with his thumb. His gaze dropped to her parted lips, and he could no more deny his wish to kiss her than stop breathing.

He lowered his mouth, brushing her lips with the slightest pressure. His heart lurched and took off like a runaway wagon. *Easy. Don't rush it.*

Sliding his hand beneath her thick tresses to curl around her nape, Josh settled his mouth on hers, testing and tasting her sweet offering. Her hand came between them to press against his chest, directly over his heart, not pushing him away yet not allowing him any closer. The heat of her fingers seeped through the cotton fabric of his shirt, branding him.

Josh inhaled deeply her subtle, pleasing scent. She clung to him with timid devotion, and his heart swelled with a fierce protectiveness. Never before had he experienced such a sure, swift thrust of emotion. Not even Francesca had made him feel this way.

Francesca! He broke off contact and, ignoring her whimper of protest, set her away from him. Surging to his feet, he began to pace, thrusting his hands through his hair. What had he done?

He was recently jilted, a man on the rebound. Kissing Kate was the last thing he should be doing!

"Josh?"

"I shouldn't have done that. I don't know what I was thinking." He continued pacing. "I apologize."

"Right," she said on a shaky breath, "I'm not Fran."

He jerked to a stop and shot her a dubious look. "You think I don't know that?"

"Hard to ignore the differences between us." Hurt bloomed in her eyes. "You regret kissing me because you love her."

"I don't—"

There was a knock at the door. Talk about bad timing. With a long look at Kate, he went to open it. Nathan stood on the other side, her belongings in his hands.

"My camera!"

Moving toward the dining table, Nathan's gaze darted between Kate and Josh. "I was out walking and spotted your things. Is everything all right?"

He set her boots on the floor and placed her equipment on the tabletop.

"Did you see Matthews out there?" Josh said.

"No. Why?"

"He was on our property. And he frightened Kate."

"Are you okay?" Nathan's face clouded as he assessed her.

"Fine. Thanks for bringing my things." Her gaze connected with Josh's. "I'd forgotten."

Because they'd been too wrapped up in each other and that kiss. *A kiss he wouldn't be repeating.*

"What are you planning to do?"

"It's time I paid Matthews a visit."

"I'm coming with you," Nathan said.

"Fine." Josh paused in the doorway and turned to Kate. "Take it easy. Try to stay off your feet."

Eyes troubled, she nodded. "Be careful."

Pulling the door shut behind him, he followed Nathan down the steps. "You're prepared, right?"

He touched a hand to the gun in his holster. "Yep."

Josh hoped there wouldn't be trouble, but a man had to be ready just in case. Entering the barn, they saddled and mounted their horses. The first half of the ride was made in silence. Josh's thoughts weren't on the coming confrontation, however. They were centered on Kate.

He growled low in frustration. He'd hurt her feelings. The apology had made things worse.

Nathan edged his mount closer. "You gonna tell me what's going on between you two?"

No use denying it. Try as he might, he'd never been able to hide anything from Nathan.

He shifted in the saddle. "If I knew, I'd tell you."

"She feel the same way about you?" Humor laced his words.

Josh whipped his gaze to Nathan's face. "I was engaged to her sister up until a few days ago."

"I'm aware of that," he drawled.

"I have no business thinking about any woman," he stated with force, as much for his own benefit as for his brother's. "I should be heartbroken."

"And the fact that you're not bothers you."

"This attraction to Kate doesn't make sense."

"Matters of the heart rarely do."

Josh fell silent, forcing his attention to the task at hand. They were nearing Matthews's spread. Emerging from the trees, he noticed details he missed that first trip out here. Then he'd been too distracted to notice the overgrown yard, the sagging barn doors, the chickens roaming free. Apparently Matthews had more important things to do than tend his property.

"Do you think he's home?" Nathan came to stand beside him.

"Hard to tell." His narrowed gaze scanned their surroundings. The place appeared to be deserted. "Keep your wits about you."

Adrenaline surged through him. "Matthews! It's Josh O'Malley." He pounded on the door, one hand resting on his weapon. "Open up!"

Standing at the base of the steps, Nathan continued to eye the outbuildings.

Josh waited another minute before trying again. When no response came, he moved to peer through the single window. It was coated with grime to the point of being opaque. He could only make out bulky shapes. Moving back to the door, he tested the latch. Unlocked.

"Josh." Nathan's voice held a note of warning.

"I'm just gonna see if he's in there. Knowing him, he's probably passed out on the bed."

He pushed the door open and the stench of old grease and stale food filled his nostrils.

Quickly he took stock of the interior. Matthews was nowhere to be seen. If Charlotte were to see how her son had let this place go, she'd be fighting mad.

"He's not here. Go on home. I'm gonna wait for him."

"You said yourself he's dangerous. Why don't we come back tonight after supper?"

He had work to do, but this was important. Matthews was threatening Kate, and it had to stop.

"I'm staying. And I need you to go check on Kate for me."

Frowning, Nathan turned and mounted. "If you're not back by eight o'clock, I'm coming to check on you."

Kate pushed the food around her plate in hopes that no one would notice her lack of appetite. Sam and Mary were doing most of the talking. Caleb was his usual reserved self, and Nathan hadn't uttered a single word. His uneasiness only added to her disquiet.

Josh's empty chair mocked her. Had he confronted Tyler and met with trouble? What if he was hurt? The prospect of him lying injured somewhere, helpless and bleeding, set Kate's nerves on edge.

His kiss haunted her. He'd been both gentle and possessive, a curious combination that had simultaneously comforted and thrilled her. For a brief moment, she'd allowed herself to pretend she deserved a man like Josh.

That she wasn't a woman who'd been used, found wanting and cast aside.

And then reality had reasserted itself. He'd pulled away because *she* wasn't the one he wanted. She wasn't Fran.

What had he been about to say just when Nathan arrived? "I don't." "I don't" what? Regret kissing Kate? Or still love Fran?

But of course Josh loved Fran, Kate chided herself. Everyone loved Fran. And he'd been all set to marry her, hadn't he?

The clock on the sideboard chimed, startling her. Eight o'clock. On the other side of the window stood impenetrable darkness—the one thing about the mountains she didn't like. She hadn't imagined she'd miss the sometimes annoying sounds of the city as it settled into evening and the streetlamps warding off shadows.

Across the table, Nathan stood so abruptly his chair nearly toppled over. Conversation ceased as all eyes turned to him.

"Excuse me," he said over his shoulder before depositing his dishes in the basin that served as a sink. "Ma, thanks for the meal. Sorry to rush off, but I've got things to take care of."

Grabbing his jacket off the hook near the back door, he tugged on his hat and slipped out into the night. The door clicked softly behind him.

He was no doubt going to Tyler's homestead to check on Josh. Clenching her hands beneath the table, it took every ounce of self-control not to rush outside and demand that he take her along.

Mary slid a plate with a fat slice of chocolate cake her way. "Dessert, Kate?"

He was fast losing patience. Not only did the rundown cabin reek, but the rapidly cooling wind gusting outside whistled through the missing chink in the walls, making him regret not grabbing his jacket. So far Matthews was a no-show.

Rising from the lone chair in the room, he resumed his pacing. If Matthews didn't return within the next half hour, Josh would have to try again tomorrow. Nathan was probably already on his way.

His gaze settled once again on the amber-hued bottles scattered across the table, and he grabbed the oil lamp he'd lit earlier to get a better look. At first glance, they appeared to be empty bottles of alcohol, but the labels said otherwise. Dr. J. Collis Browne's Chlorodyne claimed to heal asthma, bronchitis and catarrh. Hostetter's Celebrated Stomach Bitters warded off rheumatism.

In the wagon accident that had claimed Lily's life a year earlier, Matthews had suffered severe injuries. He'd spent a month at the home of Dr. Owens, teetering between life and death. The townsfolk had called it a miracle when he'd finally pulled through.

Somehow Josh had the feeling the man didn't share their sentiments.

He sniffed one of the bottles and reared his head back. Disgusting. Setting it down, he wondered why Tyler would need medicine after all this time.

A muffled sound outside drew his attention. Muscles tensing, he snuffed out the lamp, crept to the window and, rubbing a spot clean with the threadbare curtain, peered out at the front yard. In the shadows stood a horse, its owner sliding to the ground and stumbling toward the cabin. Matthews.

One hand on his holster, Josh walked out of the cabin. "Had a bit too much to drink tonight?"

"What?" He brought his head up fast, squinting in the darkness. Then he moaned, his hands gripping the sides of his head. "What'd ya want, O'Malley?"

"What I want is for you to stay off my property. Leave Kate Morgan alone."

His hands dropped to his sides. "Kate," he mumbled, staring down at the dirt. "I dunno any Kate. Do I?" He started for the stairs. "Need sleep."

Watchful, Josh stood motionless. When Matthews's

foot caught on the bottom step and he went sprawling, Josh rushed forward to haul him upright. And when the man didn't struggle, he decided it wouldn't do a bit of good warning him off Kate. At least not tonight. He was just about passed out.

Resigned, Josh helped him inside and guided him toward the bed in the corner. He landed facedown and was snoring before his head hit the pillow.

He shook his head. What a wasted life.

"Josh?"

Nathan. He strode for the doorway and jerked his thumb over his shoulder. "He's out for the night."

"Let me guess," he said from the saddle, he thumbed his hat up. "You didn't get to have that discussion, did you?"

"Nope. Sure didn't." Josh rounded the cabin to where he'd left Chestnut. Nathan's horse, Chance, followed. "But he hasn't seen the last of me."

They rode at a brisk pace through the darkness, Josh eager to get inside and get warm. As soon as they reached the yard, he looked toward Kate's cabin. Light in the window told him she was still up, and for a moment he thought about going to her.

Nope. Too risky.

That kiss was still fresh in his mind. He'd be a fool to go anywhere near her.

Chapter Eight

Kate couldn't breathe. Darkness pressed in on her. Panic rose up to claw at her throat. She must not scream, must not make the tiniest noise. Nanny said so. Else something much worse would happen to her.

The musty odor merged with the acrid tang of mothballs, burning her nostrils. She hated it in here! But there was no one to rescue her.

Father and Mother were at the seashore and wouldn't be back for another month. Fran was with her tutor in the opposite wing of the estate. And the other employees were scattered throughout, tending their chores.

Nanny Marie had sole charge of her. She would decide when Kate could come out, when her punishment was over. Not that she knew exactly what she'd done to anger Nanny. Kate tried to be on her best behavior, but she ran afoul of her nanny nearly every day.

Suddenly, she wasn't in the closet anymore. The darkness remained, but now the walls were lined with wine bottles. It was the estate's wine cellar. A pleasant, earthy smell hung in the still air. Wesley's handsome, shadowed face appeared, his eyes gleaming and his voice coaxing.

No! This was all wrong. And yet…he was so confident and reassuring. Everything would be fine. He wanted to show her what love was really like.

She didn't have to drink a drop of wine to be intoxicated. His touch drove all reason from her mind. With every fiber of her being, she yearned to be loved.

Wesley? The shadows morphed and he was gone. Shame stained her heart. What had she done? Tears spilled down her cheeks.

Gradually, Kate woke to wetness on her pillow. It took a minute for her mind to grasp her surroundings. She wasn't in New York, but in Tennessee. Josh's cabin. His bedroom.

The horrible reality of the dream lingered, and she couldn't help but think of that night with Wesley. No matter how much she wanted to despise him, she couldn't, for the burden of guilt didn't rest entirely on him.

Kate could've stopped him at any moment. She hadn't. His words, like blessed rain, had fallen on the parched soil of her soul. She hadn't been able to resist.

Fumbling in the dark, she crossed to the window and pushed the curtains aside. The moonlight, though weak, enabled her to see enough to light the lamp's wick. The golden flare soothed her somewhat.

She'd gone to bed troubled. Worried about Josh and Nathan, she'd stared at the low ceiling—unable to sleep until she heard the sound of horses entering the lane. Careful to conceal herself, she'd watched from the edge of the glass the brothers riding tall in their saddles, relief filling her at the sight of them safe and sound.

Tonight's emotional upheaval had stirred up disturbing memories of the past, hence the dreams.

Cold through to her soul, Kate rubbed her arms, hugging herself against the whirlpool of gloom and shadows tugging her down. Her gaze fell on her Bible on the bedside stand.

Remember the truth, Christ forgives us because of His faithfulness and goodness. We don't have to do anything to deserve it—nor can we. He chose to love each and every one of us, despite our failures.

Her old friend Danielle's voice echoed in her head. A young ladies' maid working at the estate at the time of Wesley's betrayal, Danielle had seen Kate's misery and, flouting protocol, befriended her. Told her about God's love. Talked to her about the Scriptures. It was because of Danielle that Kate had turned to God.

God knew her inside and out—her fears and dreams, strengths and faults—and loved her anyway.

That truth had the power to drive out her uncertainties and worry.

Sliding the Bible into her lap, she turned to the book of Psalms and began to read.

Hard at work in his shop the following night, Josh was still kicking himself. Kissing Kate, allowing himself to feel things for her, was reckless. Against his will, she affected him. Not only had she captured his thoughts, she'd enslaved his senses, sharpening his awareness of her every move. He felt her every sigh like a soft caress. Her tender smiles weakened his resolve.

Hers was the face he saw in his dreams. Not Francesca's. And that bothered him. Was he really that shallow? Or worse, had he mistaken admiration and affection for love? The romance with Francesca had happened so fast—that initial meeting at the Meades' and then picnics beside the river, strolls through the park, shopping excursions. Three whirlwind weeks of shucking his work in order to spend time with her.

He'd been in awe of her classic beauty, her coy playfulness and breezy confidence. Francesca was fun. That last night before she left for New York, he'd blurted out a proposal. She'd laughed outright. Then, realizing he was serious, she'd smiled in that carefree way of hers and said sure, she'd be happy to.

His heart ached from the loss of her. Or was it the loss of his dream?

Unsettled, he concentrated on measuring out the chair legs for the walnut dining set he was making for Mr. and Mrs. Calhoun. After that he had a pie safe to build for their daughter, who was getting married next month and setting up her own house. He had six more pieces on order. It was enough work to keep him busy from dawn until dusk. And he had furniture yet to build to showcase in his shop once he bought it.

Bent over his worktable, he'd barely acknowledged the quiet knock before the door scraped open and in stepped the object of his turmoil. Kate. The smell of fried chicken reached him before she did.

Laying aside the cloth tape measure, Josh grabbed a towel and wiped the sawdust from his hands.

As she approached, her wide-eyed gaze surveyed the workshop with interest. She stopped a footstep away, the plate of food held out as an offering. Her eyes brimming with questions connected with his. Her finely etched brows arched up.

"I take it you're the local craftsman?"

Feeling exposed, he jerked his head. "Did Ma send you out here?" Careful to avoid touching her, he accepted the plate and utensils. "She knows I'll eat when I have time."

He ground his teeth in irritation. This wasn't the first time he'd skipped supper. His family understood his heavy workload and knew he'd be in to eat as soon as he could. So he was suspicious now. Was his ma trying to push them together?

He hoped not. He was still wrestling with Francesca's decision. And he was smart enough to know not to fall for her little sister.

"Why didn't you tell me?" She folded her hands at her waist and waited for his explanation.

Focusing on the meal, he tried not to notice how beautiful she looked in the yellow light of the oil lamps. She was dressed casually in a filmy green blouse that matched her eyes and a simple, unembellished black skirt. Her brown hair, caught up in a French twist, gleamed like the rich walnut wood he often worked with.

Swallowing, he said offhandedly, "I didn't see the need. You're a visitor here, Kate. You'll take your photographs and go back to New York. What does it matter what I do?"

Out of the corner of his eye, he saw her stiffen. "You're right, of course. You don't owe me any explanations."

Josh winced at the hurt in her voice.

"I'm sorry I bothered you," she exhaled. "Good night."

Her whole body rigid, she swept toward the door. He willed himself to be silent. Only when it closed behind her did he let out a ragged breath.

His appetite gone, he pushed the plate aside and went back to measuring. Only, he couldn't concentrate. He kept picturing the wounded look about her eyes. He'd hurt her feelings, and that made him feel like an insensitive boor.

Kate didn't deserve his harsh attitude. She couldn't know that whenever she was near, a warning hammered in his skull. If he wasn't careful, she would be his undoing.

One agonizing hour later, he gave up. It was no use. No matter what the reasons, he couldn't excuse his churlish behavior.

Tossing aside the tape, he untied his apron and hung it on the nail. He washed his hands in the basin and extinguished all the lamps but one, which he carried with him out into the night.

Time to apologize.

There was a nip in the night air, and clouds like stretched cotton obscured the stars. Angry, deep-throated yowls echoed off the barn walls, and he could make out two shapes tussling in the grass. Cats fighting over territory. Or a female.

He rapped on the cabin door and waited, not sure exactly what he planned to say. He heard the scrape of a chair, then her faint footsteps on the planks.

"Who is it?"

Not expecting her to speak through the closed door, he hesitated. "It's me. Can we talk?"

Quiet. "I'm tired, Josh. Can it wait until morning?"

Even though her voice was muffled, he could make out the defeated undertones punctuating her words. Laying his palm flat against the wood, he resisted the urge to bang his head in frustration. Fool. In protecting himself, he'd hurt her.

"What I have to say won't take long."

"I—I'm not dressed to receive you."

Sighing, Josh pushed away from the door and stuffed his hands into his pockets. "Good night, then. Rest well, Kate."

"Good night."

Discouraged, he stopped in the shop to get the forgotten plate of food. Back inside the house, he placed the leftovers in the icebox for tomorrow and walked into the living room. His father, relaxed in his chair, looked up from the Bible in his lap.

"Late night again, son?" Sam pushed his spectacles farther up the bridge of his nose.

"Yes." Josh moved to stand near the hearth, where his father had built the first fire since early spring. The heat seeped through his pants legs to warm his skin. The thought struck him that Kate needed a fire.

He turned to go. "I'll be back. I forgot to start a fire in Kate's fireplace."

"Already done." His father's voice halted his progress. "I showed her how to let it die down before she retires for the night."

Darn, he'd hoped for a solid excuse to see her. "Thanks, Pa."

His mother sat on the far end of the sofa piecing quilt squares. "What did she think of your workshop?"

"She didn't say." Not that he'd given her a chance to say much of anything.

Pulling a cushioned stool nearer to the fire, he sank down and rested his hands on his knees. Exhaustion overwhelmed him. He resisted, pushing aside the need for sleep for a little while longer.

While he loved his work and the hours passed quickly, the heavy workload took its toll on him physically. And he missed his family's lively conversations around the supper table. If the shop proved successful, he'd be forced to hire help. A good problem to have, he supposed.

"What's bothering you?" his father regarded him thoughtfully. "Is it too difficult? Having her here?"

"No, it's fine."

"She seems like such a sweet girl." Ma peered at him.

"She is."

Kind and generous, she didn't use her status and wealth as an excuse to act superior. A forgotten moment from his time in Sevierville slid unbidden through his mind.

He and Francesca had been dining in a finer dining establishment than he could reasonably afford, and the young waitress, nervous and unsure, had accidentally tipped a glass of water over into his lap. Much of it missed him, wetting only a small part of his pants, but Francesca was livid. She'd been ready to demand that the "unskilled peasant," as she'd called her, be relieved of her job. It had taken some fast talking, but he'd managed to calm her.

He couldn't fathom Kate ever acting that way. She'd shown nothing but kind regard for everyone she'd come in contact with. The way she'd taken to his cousins pleased him. Anyone who could meet Nicole's sassy, and, at times impertinent remarks with patience and even understanding was a rare person in his book.

"Do we have any more pie left over from supper, Mary? Maybe Josh would like a slice."

Setting the fabric aside, Ma rose. "Would you like one, too, dear?"

"Yes. Thank you, dearest wife."

"You're welcome, sweet husband."

He winked at her, and she blushed. All those years together and his parents loved each other more than on the day they married. It was the kind of love he craved for himself.

At twenty-four years old, he was ready to settle down and start a family. Maybe that's why Francesca's decision to marry another man chafed so. She'd cheated him out of his dream.

When Ma had left the room, his father closed his Bible and folded his hands on top. His wise gaze settled on Josh's. "What's on your mind, son?"

"I want what you and Ma have. Now that the wedding has been called off, it's not likely to happen anytime soon. Francesca is with another man and Kate…" He stroked his goatee, unable to voice his concerns. His forbidden, mixed-up feelings for her.

"Choosing a bride is one of the most important decisions a man will ever make. Did you consult God about your decision?"

Wincing, he shook his head. "Everything happened so fast. She was leaving, moments away from boarding the train, and I panicked at the thought of never seeing her again. I wanted her connected to me somehow, so when she went back to her glittering world she wouldn't forget me."

He'd made a mistake. Should've prayed about the matter first. God, in His ultimate wisdom, would've led him to the right choice.

Of course, his father didn't condemn him, only nodded in understanding. "I realize it's difficult for you to accept her decision, but maybe it was God's way of saving you from a regrettable marriage."

Was it difficult? He'd thought so at first. His pride had certainly taken a beating. Now, he realized the harder part was sorting through his unforeseen reaction to Kate.

Restless, he stood. Laying one arm across the mantel, he leaned against it, staring into the popping, hissing flames. If he didn't get this attraction sorted out, it could very easily burn out of control and he'd wind up making another rash mistake.

Kate was off-limits. An heiress to a vast fortune. Soon she would return home and, in time, marry a man possessed of a vast fortune. Together they would live a life of untold luxury.

"Something else besides the canceled wedding is bothering you."

He passed a tired hand over his face. "It's Kate. I can't think straight whenever she's near. She's very different than her sister, you know."

"Funny. Your mother had the same effect on me."

He straightened and met his father's level gaze. "I'm confused, that's all. I'll get it sorted out."

"With God's help, right?"

"You can count on it." Sometimes, instead of taking his problems to God right away, he tried to figure things out on his own. Not a wise course of action. "I'm going up to bed. Will you explain to Ma about the pie?"

"Sure." He chuckled. "I'll eat yours, too, if I have to."

"Thanks."

"I'm proud of you, son."

Josh dipped his head, grateful beyond words for the wonderful man who was his father. "Thanks, Pa. Good night."

He may as well have been invisible for all the attention she was paying him.

Seated across the breakfast table from Kate, Josh had yet to catch her gaze. Having overslept, he'd come downstairs last. She hadn't looked up at his family's chorus of greetings, nor had she acknowledged his presence once he sat down.

He didn't blame her. After his cold rebuke last night, he deserved the cool reception.

He hoped she'd go along with his idea to make it up to her. First, he had to get her attention. Shifting his boot beneath the table, he nudged the toe of her shoe.

Her green eyes shot to his over the rim of her teacup. Lowering it to the saucer with a clink, she gazed at him with uncertainty. Now what? He really didn't want to have this conversation in front of his family, did he?

In lieu of words, he smiled at her. She didn't reciprocate. Instead, she shifted her gaze to her plate, brow furrowed.

Thwarted but not defeated, he shoveled in the last of his breakfast and drained his coffee mug. He took his dishes into the kitchen and, placing everything on the counter, went out to the front porch to wait.

He didn't have to wait long. She emerged ten minutes later. When she didn't immediately notice him, he called out to her.

Kate's footsteps faltered at the sound of Josh's low drawl from the far end of the porch. Framed by the multihued forest behind him, arms crossed and one hip propped against the railing, he watched her with an expression akin to regret.

She hadn't wanted to face him today. It had been difficult, that meal, with him sitting so close and her trying to pretend his presence didn't affect her. She'd failed miserably.

Somehow this man had become important to her, and that gave him the power to hurt her.

Straightening, he slowly approached her spot near the steps, his boots scuffing the planks. His woodsy scent clung to his clothes. "I'm sorry about last night." In a familiar stance, he slipped his hands into the pockets of his brown trousers. "I know I haven't been the best host. With everything that's happened, I—" he hitched a shoulder "—I've been out of sorts lately. That's not an excuse to take it out on you, though. Forgive me?"

"There's nothing to forgive. You were right. I'm just passing through."

You're a visitor here, Kate. What does it matter what I do?

She'd been unable to push his words from her mind. His flippant remark had cut deep, flaying open her innermost fears. Not belonging. No one to love. No one to love her.

Even if she did fall in love, what man would want her?

"That doesn't mean we can't be friends. Right?"

"Friends?" She was fairly certain friends didn't kiss each other. But that wouldn't happen again. Friends is all they could ever be. "I'd like that."

"Well, then, friend, what've you got planned for the rest of the day?"

"Nothing. Why?"

"There's a place I'd like to show you, but it's a little ways from here. We'd have to take the horses. Do you ride?"

"Yes. Sidesaddle."

"I happen to have one of those in my barn." He grinned. "Oh?"

"You'll need your camera."

Curious, she cocked her head to one side. "Where is this place?"

"Uh-uh. You have to come with me if you wanna find out."

Chapter Nine

Her horse followed close behind Josh's through the brightly hued forest, which to Kate seemed like a golden sanctuary. The moist, still air, scented with moss and decaying leaves, filled her lungs. It was not unpleasant. Merely different.

They didn't speak. The only sounds stirring the silence were the plodding of the horses' hooves on the soft ground and the snap of branches that their hulking bodies brushed aside. When she wasn't studying their surroundings, she was admiring the ripple of muscle evident beneath Josh's brushed cotton shirt. His was controlled strength, ready to be unleashed at a moment's notice.

She felt utterly safe with him. Physically, at least. Her emotions were another matter.

They'd been riding about an hour and a half, the terrain growing ever steeper. She was glad for the frequent rides back home, else she might've had trouble maintaining her seat. It must be nearing noon. She couldn't see the sun for the treetops, but the hollow feeling in her stomach was a good clue.

When the sound of water reached her ears, Josh slowed Chestnut to a stop. "We'll dismount here."

Tugging gently on the reins of her mare, Kate waited for him to come and assist her. Striding toward her, his eyes sparkled with anticipation beneath the brim of his brown hat. He'd lost the brooding expression, and in its place was one of contentment. Seeing him this way pleased her. Was it possible he was slowly coming to terms with Fran's decision?

Reaching up, he spanned her waist and lifted her down with ease. He grabbed her hand to lead her in the direction of the water. "Wait! What about my camera?"

"I'll come back for it."

Hearing the eagerness in his voice, she hurried to keep up with him. She was out of breath by the time they reached the clearing. Fifty feet above their heads, water rushed over the side of the mountain to cascade in a brilliant white stream to the dusky green pool below. Framed by sleek, slate-gray boulders and thick green overgrowth, it was a glorious waterfall.

Still holding her hand, Josh assessed her reaction. "Well?"

"It's amazing," she breathed, her gaze on the massive, moss-covered tree trunks lying sideways across the mouth of the fall. "Does it have a name?"

"Hidden Oak Falls." He gave her hand a tug. "Come, there's more."

His pace more sedate this time, they circled around the pool, stepping carefully over sharp-edged rocks. From this angle, Kate could see a rock overhang and a dark, open space behind the falls. And Josh was headed straight for it.

Delighted, she grinned with pleasure. What a discovery!

He paused at the opening. A knee-high log blocked the entrance. "I'll go over first, okay?" His long legs made it easy for him. Turning back, he held on to her hand. "Just step up on it, and I'll help you down."

Glancing down at her outfit, a petal-pink shirtwaist and brown-and-pink paisley skirt, Kate regretted her choice. While her wardrobe may be fitting for city life, it was highly unsuitable for the great outdoors.

"Don't look," she warned, knowing her pantaloons would show.

"I wouldn't think of it," he shot back with a grin, then dipped his head so that she was staring at his hat's brim.

Scooping up the voluminous material with one hand, she tightened her grip on his with the other and levered herself up. Immediately he curled his free hand around her waist and swung her to the ground. The sound of thundering water masked all other sounds, and water droplets splashed against the hem of her skirts. The air was much cooler here. Goose bumps raced across her skin.

When he started to lead her farther into the dark space, Kate resisted. It wasn't enclosed like a closet, but the rock ceiling hung low and light didn't reach very far into the opening. The last thing she wanted was to become distraught in front of him again.

"What's wrong?"

"I don't like the dark, remember?" she said lightly.

"All right. We can stand right here and still have a spectacular view."

Releasing her hand, he tugged off his hat and set it on the log. He thrust his fingers through his hair, giving him that mussed look Kate found irresistible. With effort, she focused on the scene before her.

She'd forgotten her hat at the cabin, a fact her mother would lament if she knew. *Ladies must always present themselves with poise and decorum,* Georgia's voice paraded through her head. *Stand up straight, Katerina. Look at how your sister comports herself, tall and graceful like a ballerina.*

"You can walk behind the waterfall and come out on the other side." Josh moved in close in order to be heard above the noise. "There's a trail leading south."

"How did you find this place?"

"As kids, my brothers and I spent much of our free time exploring these mountains. We just happened upon it one day."

"What was it like? Growing up here?"

Leaning back against the gnarled rock, he folded his arms. "These mountains are all I've ever known. Growing up, we were expected to work hard and pitch in where help was needed. When the work was finished, though, we were free to explore. Hunt. Fish. Torment our cousins." He flashed a roguish grin.

"You didn't."

"I most certainly did." Still grinning, he shook his head. "Juliana didn't take it lying down, either. She fought back."

"What about Megan and Nicole?"

He rolled his eyes. "They went home crying to momma. Most of the time, Aunt Alice and my parents let us sort things out among ourselves. They were harmless pranks."

Josh was such a gentleman Kate had a hard time imagining him as a young, infuriating prankster. "I can't see it."

"Oh, ask Megan. She'll tell you enough stories to make

you question your friendship with me." He paused. "What about you? What was it like growing up in the big city?"

Kate sorted through the memories. "I remember wishing for brothers and more sisters. Our cousins lived far away, and their visits were limited to two weeks during the summer and one at Christmas. I played with the staff's children until the year I turned ten. That's when my mother decided it was not in my best interest to fraternize with the hired help." Tucking a stray curl behind her ear, she avoided his gaze. "But I was fortunate in that there were many diversions at the estate. I split my time between the library, the gardens and the stables."

"Did you go to school?"

"We had private tutors."

"Sounds lonely."

"It was." She squared her shoulders. "But I had a roof over my head, clothes to wear and plenty of food to eat. And many luxuries not available to most people."

"Tell me, what's a typical day for an heiress?"

"Easy. Lie in bed until noon, spend much of the day ordering the servants about, fritter away money on useless frippery and consort with other heiresses who have equally meaningless lives."

His laughter echoed off the rough surfaces. "Let me rephrase that. What's a typical day for Kate Morgan?"

"If the weather's nice, I have breakfast on the terrace overlooking the gardens. Then I go in search of my mother to see if she has anything in particular for me to do that day. If not, I sometimes assist our head gardener, Mr. Latham, in the planning and upkeep of the gardens and solarium. I prefer to be outside, my hands in the soil." Her gaze followed the fairy flight of a yellow butterfly above the water. "We have many fountains and koi ponds, but they can't compare to this."

"When you're not helping Mr. Latham, you're…"

"Taking photographs. Or in my darkroom developing prints."

"What do you do with them all?"

"Frame some of them. Lucky for me, we have ample wall space." She smiled. "I have special albums for the rest."

"I'd like to see a sample of your work sometime."

"I didn't bring the chemicals or equipment with me to develop the prints. I decided to wait until I'd settled in to have everything shipped out here." She watched a pair of cardinals swirl and sashay through the air, a streak of red in the azure sky, their song swallowed up by the waterfall. "I've been considering opening my own studio."

His brows lifted. "Oh? That's interesting. Would you do mainly portraits, then?"

Pleased he hadn't outright condemned her idea, she answered, "I would split my time between the studio and the field. Clients wouldn't have to always come in for sittings. I could go to them. Some prefer the formal atmosphere of the studio, while others prefer a more natural setting. And I'd still do landscapes and perhaps have some of the finer images for sale."

Relaxed against the rock, Josh drank in the beauty of her complexion, the bloom in her cheeks and the sparkle in her jeweled eyes. Pink suited her. She'd gone hatless, and her dark tresses had been caught in a neat twist.

Because of his own love of woodworking, he was able to appreciate her passion for photography, even though he knew nothing about it. And he admired that she had set a goal for herself. Being an heiress, she didn't have to work. He somehow doubted that Francesca would put effort into anything worthwhile.

"You've obviously given this a lot of thought. What do your parents think about your plans?"

She broke eye contact. "I haven't told them."

That was odd. Again he sensed that something was off in that relationship. He opened his mouth to question her, but she headed him off.

"I'm getting chilled," she said, rubbing her arms. "Would you mind if I set up my camera now?"

"Of course." He pushed away from the wall and, grabbing his hat, took hold of her arm. "The sunshine should warm you right up."

He helped her back over the log, and they returned to where the horses stood grazing. Gathering their supplies, they selected a spot near the waterfall in full view of the sun. Kate set about readying her equipment while Josh spread a blanket on the grass and unpacked their lunch. His ma had included thick slices of ham on sourdough bread, a jar of sweet pickles, coleslaw, baked beans, lemonade and, for dessert, peach turnovers.

Hungry now, his mouth watered at the enticing smells assaulting his nose. "Would you like to go ahead and eat now or take photos first?" He waved away a pesky fly.

She looked up from attaching her camera to its stand. "Let's eat first. Once I get started with the photos, I sometimes get carried away. I wouldn't want to keep a hungry man waiting." Her mouth kicked up in a playful grin.

Her skirts sweeping the green grass, she approached and lowered herself onto the blanket with graceful ease.

"Does it take long?"

She paused in the arranging of the billowing material

about her person to give him a quizzical look. "Does it take long for what?"

Sitting cross-legged, he gestured to her skirts. "To learn to maneuver in those fancy getups."

"Every young lady is given instructions in deportment and manners. Besides, I've dressed like this since I was a little girl, so I'm accustomed to it."

"Don't get me wrong—your clothes are beautiful. I mean, you look beautiful in everything you wear."

He clamped his lips together. He shouldn't be saying this. And yet, it was true.

"Thank you." A blush tinting her cheeks, she lowered her gaze to her lap.

Unlike Francesca, who'd preened whenever he'd complimented her, Kate was modest and shy in the face of praise.

There was so much about her that he found appealing. Her beauty wasn't only skin-deep. She had a beautiful soul, as well.

She'd make some lucky man a fine wife one day. If circumstances were different—*if* she wasn't his former fiancée's little sister and a wealthy, privileged city girl— then just maybe he'd let himself feel something for her. But they weren't. And he wasn't about to make the same mistake twice.

When he did decide to seek out a wife, he'd choose a young lady with an upbringing similar to his. Someone who loved the Lord and who strived to live each day with honesty and integrity. Never again would he allow himself to be involved with a woman who harbored secrets. Secrets destroyed people. Relationships suffered.

If Francesca had been honest with him, he'd have avoided much grief and embarrassment.

Placing bread and ham on a plate, he handed it to Kate, along with utensils. Aware of her small appetite, he allowed her to serve herself from the other containers. As suspected, she took only minimal amounts and didn't touch the turnovers. But she ate everything on her plate, and her smile was one of satisfaction.

"I like picnics. There's something refreshing about eating outdoors, especially with a view like this."

Taking a swig of his lemonade, he nodded. "I agree."

Soon she rose and went to her camera. Feeling lazy from the heat, his stomach full, he was content to recline on the blanket and watch her work. In between shots, she told him about the recent advancements in photography. She was well-informed on the topic, and her enthusiasm was evident.

Not only was Kate a joy to watch, she was easy to be with. He wouldn't mind spending the entire day out here. But projects awaited him back in his workshop. And after an hour, she was ready to pack up and go home, so they did.

After tending to the horses in the barn, he walked with her to the cabin, somehow reluctant for the outing to end.

"I had a wonderful time today." She smiled over at him. "Thank you."

"You're welcome. I enjoyed it, as well."

"Will you work in your shop now?"

He nodded. Wanting to tell her more, he said, "You know, I have plans to expand my furniture business."

Her face lit up. "Josh, that's wonderful! I have no doubt you'll be successful. Perhaps you can give me some pointers."

Her enthusiasm warmed his insides. "Well, I'm not quite there yet. But close. It's something I've wanted for a while, and now that an opportunity has come along, I feel it's the right time. In fact, there's a place—" Spying something on her porch, he broke off. "Looks like someone left you flowers."

Her finely arched brows met in the middle. "What?"

A niggling feeling of unease settled deep in his gut. He scooped up the bouquet of yellow daisies tied with a ribbon and handed them to her. Lifting them to her nose, she inhaled their fragrance. Then he spotted the folded paper.

He picked it up and, handing it to her, waited for her to read it, even though it was none of his business. The color drained from her face, and her eyes darted to the woods and the yard.

He stepped closer and gripped her arm. "What is it, Kate?"

"Tyler."

Anger seizing him, he took the paper she held out.

You are my life. I won't rest till you're home where you belong.

Crushing the note into a ball, he paced away from her. The audacity, the boldness of Matthews's actions— coming onto O'Malley property in broad daylight for the purpose of scaring Kate—spawned outrage and fury in his chest.

Had no one seen him? Obviously not. His family wouldn't have left this here for her to find.

How was he supposed to keep her safe?

He pivoted back. "From now on, I don't want you going anywhere alone."

"But—"

Going to her, he settled his hands on her shoulders. "I'm serious, Kate. If you need to go somewhere, let me or one of my brothers know. Or my father. The last thing I want is for you to encounter Matthews unprotected."

Her expression troubled, she stared up at him with trusting eyes. "All right."

"I have to make some deliveries in Sevierville next week. I'll be gone for a few days."

He'd feel a whole lot better if she knew how to protect herself. Maybe he should teach her how to handle a weapon. "I just want you to be careful."

"I know," she murmured. "The thought of being alone with him…" She trailed off, shuddering.

Without thinking, hc pulled her close and wrapped his arms around her. She came willingly. Pressing her cheek against his chest, she looped her arms about his waist. Her hair smelled fresh and clean beneath his chin.

He didn't speak, simply held her and rubbed her back in a soothing gesture. He felt her soft sigh deep in his bones. The world around them faded. The birds' chirping and the cattle's lowing receded. Holding Kate made him forget everything else.

Like how dangerous it was to care for her.

Later that evening, she was penning letters to acquaintances back home when she heard a thump on the porch.

"Hello? Kate, are you in there?"

Recognizing Mary's voice, she set aside her fountain pen and rushed to open the door.

"Mary! Can I takc that for you?" She indicated the tray in her hands.

"I brought tea." The older woman brushed past her only to hesitate at the table. "Am I interrupting your correspondence?"

Kate hurried to clear the tabletop of her stationery.

"Not at all. My hand was beginning to cramp, so a break is most welcome."

Mary poured the steaming liquid into two cups and, placing one in front of Kate, settled into the chair opposite. Her expression was one of motherly concern. "Nathan let slip what's been happening with Tyler, and I wanted to see how you're faring."

Absentmindedly she stirred the honey into her tea. "I'll admit it's unsettling. I never would've expected Charlotte's son to behave this way." Setting her spoon aside, she sipped the bracing brew. "I've heard it said that everyone has a twin. Did you know his wife?"

"In passing. Lily was a shy sort." Sighing, Mary fingered the cross at her neck. "We were all shocked to hear about the accident. And poor Tyler. He may have recovered from his injuries, but he's not been the same since."

"I wish he'd realize I'm not her."

"Don't worry." Mary patted her hand. "My boys will do everything in their power to keep you safe. More important, you're never out of the Lord's sight. He's promised not to abandon you."

"Yes, I know you're right."

God was faithful. Not like people who promised forever, then left. People like Wesley. And, yes, even Fran.

"You're not thinking of leaving anytime soon, are you? I'm enjoying having another female around. You're like the daughter I never had."

The sweet acceptance shining in Mary's eyes brought tears to her own. Not once had her mother looked at her like that. What would it have been like to grow up with a mother like Mary? To revel in the knowledge that she was special. That she was *enough*.

Swallowing the emotion clogging her throat, she shook

her head. "I still have a lot of work to do here. On the other hand, I don't want to burden your family. Not only have I displaced Josh, I'm adding extra work for you—"

She held up a staying hand. "One more mouth to feed hardly matters. And Josh has admitted he'd rather be in his old room for the time being. So, please, no more talk of being a burden. It's a pleasure to have you here."

"Thank you." She lowered her gaze, emotions near the surface. "You don't know how much that means to me."

Sensitive to her mood, Mary guided the conversation to safer topics, asking questions about her life in New York and answering Kate's questions about Gatlinburg and its history. The town was originally called White Oak Flats—that surprised Kate. Mary pointed out that it was named after all the white oak trees in the area.

She was preparing to leave when Josh arrived.

Standing tall and broad-shouldered, hat in his hands, Josh was more handsome than any man had a right to be. "Evenin'."

"Hi."

"Got a minute?"

"Certainly." She moved back to give him room to enter.

His gaze swung to Mary. "Want me to take that back to the house for you, Ma?"

"No, I can manage." Her smile encompassed them both. "Did you find your supper?"

"I did. As always, it was delicious."

"Thanks again for the tea," Kate said as Mary passed by. "And the conversation."

"Anytime, dear. See you in the morning."

"Good night, Ma."

"Good night."

Tossing his hat on the cupboard, he took a step forward. Kate's pulse picked up speed. She couldn't help but remember what had happened the last time he was here. Would he kiss her again? Should she let him?

Her inner voice of reason gave a resounding "No!" Look at what happened the last time she allowed a man to take such liberties! Her heart argued that Josh was nothing like Wesley. He would never in a million years overstep the moral boundaries. Josh O'Malley loved God and lived to honor Him.

"I came to tell you that I've decided to teach you to shoot a firearm."

What? Kate tried to make sense of his words. "Excuse me?"

"Tomorrow morning, you and I are gonna take a little walk out to where I have my targets set up. I have a gun picked out for you. It's not all that difficult. Just takes practice, is all."

Laughter bubbled up. "Me? Fire a gun? You must be joking."

His brows lowered. "Why would I do that?"

"A lady does not speak of weapons, much less handle one." The mere idea was preposterous. Who did he take her for—Annie Oakley?

"Besides, where do you propose I conceal this weapon on my person?" She spread her hands wide. "In my reticule?"

Clamping his lips together, Josh said, "I'll get you a holster to wear around your waist."

Kate blushed. "That's hardly fashionable."

"This isn't about fashion, it's about safety."

"I understand your point, Josh, but it simply isn't proper."

"This isn't New York City," he bit out. "Out here, survival is more important than propriety. Matthews was bold enough to come here in the middle of the day. There's nothing stopping him from coming back. What happens if he catches you alone? What will you do then?"

She didn't have an answer.

"Look, I'd rest a whole lot easier knowing you have a way to protect yourself."

"But—"

"No 'buts.'" Snatching up his hat, he moved to the door. "I'll stop for you bright and early. Be ready."

Chapter Ten

Standing in the thick grass, dew wetting her ankle boots and fog blanketing the meadow, Kate listened as Josh explained how to use the gun, which he'd described as a nickel-plated .44 Schofield revolver. But no matter how hard she tried to focus on his words, her attention was caught by the movement of his firm lips framed by the neat, golden-brown mustache and goatee. His quiet, confident voice resonated in the hushed silence of the early morning.

They were alone in what seemed like a magical place, cut off from the rest of the world. Even the animals had yet to stir. Her entire being focused on the man before her.

Josh O'Malley was a fine, honorable man. A family man. Hardworking. Caring.

Money and material gain weren't important to him. Neither was climbing the social ladder. Serving God and others was.

Her lungs squeezed with regret as she watched him now. She could not have him. Even if he wasn't in love with her sister, he wouldn't want her. Not if he knew her secret.

"Are you ready to try it out?" His voice broke into her thoughts.

His serious gaze was pinned to her face, questioning. Could he tell she hadn't been paying attention? He'd shown up at her door just after dawn, all business, looking as if he carried the weight of the world on his shoulders.

Clearing her throat, she nodded, despite her sudden nervousness. "I'm ready."

One brow quirked up, but he didn't comment. Moving to stand beside her, Josh transferred the gun to her hand, his warm fingers closing over hers as he demonstrated how to hold it. Her mouth went dry. Was it the fact that she was holding an instrument of death for the first time or was his nearness making her feel light-headed?

"Do you see the target there?" Letting go, he pointed to the trees not far distant.

Again, she nodded.

"Hold your arm steady, aim and pull the trigger."

He sounded so matter of fact about the process. Could it really be that simple?

Raising her arm, she pointed the gun barrel forward. It was heavier than she'd expected. Trembling, she squeezed her eyes shut and pulled the trigger. The blast startled her, and, gasping aloud, she opened one eye to see where the bullet had gone.

"Kate." He sighed, his breath stirring her hair. "You're supposed to keep your eyes on the target. How do you expect to hit it if you can't see it?"

"This may be second nature to you," she said, hiking her chin up a notch, "but the only weapons I've seen up close are the ones behind glass displays at the museum.

I never imagined I'd be holding one, much less learning how to shoot someone."

"If it makes you feel any better, I taught Megan and the girls to shoot."

Her mouth fell open. "Nicole, too?"

His lips lifting in a slight grin, he gently tapped her chin closed. "Like you, Nicole had her reservations, but she turned out to be a good shot. I have every confidence you will be, as well."

"I haven't seen any of them carrying a gun."

"Gatlinburg is a relatively safe place. We all know and look out for each other. The girls do carry weapons if they leave sight of their house for any length of time. Strangers travel through this area on a regular basis, and I feel better knowing the girls have a way to protect themselves."

But Kate wasn't worried about strangers. Tyler's face flashed through her mind, and, remembering the desperation carved into his features, she shivered. He wanted her. She couldn't help wondering what he might do once he had her.

"Don't worry," Josh murmured as if reading her thoughts. "I'll make sure you feel confident using this thing."

Positioning himself behind her, his arms came around her, his hands closing over her wrists. "I'll steady your aim, and then you pull the trigger."

Encircled by his arms, close enough to feel the rise and fall of his chest, Kate couldn't think.

Slowly he lifted her arms until they were even with the target. "Okay." His mouth hovered near her ear. "I'm ready whenever you are."

With all the concentration she could muster, her eyes wide open this time, Kate squeezed the trigger. The shot veered too far to the left. After several failed attempts, she lowered the gun.

"It's harder than it looks."

"Don't give up. It takes a lot of practice." He moved back. "We can come out here every morning until I leave."

Examining the gun in the palm of her hand, she said absentmindedly, "My parents will never believe this." Her mother would be appalled. This was one aspect of her trip best kept private.

Josh took the gun from her. "Tell me about them."

She raised alarmed eyes to his. "My parents?"

"Yes."

"What do you want to know?"

"I want to know why they didn't invite you along on their trip. And why is it Francesca spoke so fondly of them and yet you appear sad, almost regretful when the subject is brought up?"

The blood in her veins turned sluggish, and dread spread through her like poison. How could she admit the truth? That she was an outcast? Unwanted? What would he think of her then?

But his eyes held a wealth of kindness, a subtle knowing, as if he'd guessed the source of her unhappiness. Perhaps she should tell him. Shatter any illusions he had about her so-called charmed life.

Unsettled, she started walking, slowly, haltingly. He fell into step beside her, his quiet, solid presence a comfort in itself.

"Francesca's relationship with our parents is vastly different than my own. She fits their idea of the perfect daughter."

Walking beside Kate, Josh noted the dejected slump

of her shoulders, the resignation in her voice. Her words confused him. "And you don't?" he asked, disbelieving.

"Not at all." Her attempt at laughter falling flat.

"I don't understand."

"Fran does everything right. She's their pride and joy. I, on the other hand, am a source of consternation. Father is mostly indifferent, but my mother and sister can't understand why I'd rather read a book or tend flowers than pore through fashion magazines and dissect the latest gossip." Apprehension wrinkled her brow. "Now that Fran is settled, my mother will convince Father it's time to search for a suitable husband for me."

A hard knot formed in his gut at the idea of softhearted, lovely Kate being paraded before a string of fortune hunters. Something suspiciously like jealousy surged through him. "You're an adult. Surely they don't plan to choose your husband for you?" His jaw hardened. "After all, Francesca married her heart's desire, didn't she?"

Kate threw him a measuring glance. "Percy has all the right credentials. Besides, they've been attached since the year she turned seventeen. My parents had no reason to launch a manhunt. As I have no such attachments, I'm certain they'll take it upon themselves to *assist* me."

Francesca and that man attached? For years? Josh went numb. He'd had no clue.

"They'll be relieved to marry me off." She sighed. "In their eyes, I've always been trouble."

He stopped short. Kate? Trouble? Never! "No, Kate—"

"Yoo-hoo!" a familiar voice called from the trees. "Josh! Kate!"

Megan. He swallowed back his frustration as they both turned to greet her.

She arrived at their side, winded but smiling. "Aunt

Mary said you'd gone for a walk. I'm glad I found you," she said, as she shoved unruly curls out of her eyes. "I was on my way to town and wondered if Kate would like to join me."

Josh looked at Kate. "Go if you want. I've got a pie safe to finish before the day is out. We can practice again tomorrow morning."

"Practice?" Megan's gaze volleyed between them. "You're teaching her to shoot?"

"I am."

"Why?"

"Kate needs to know how to protect herself, don't you think?" It wasn't often he kept things from Megan, but he didn't want to unduly alarm her or her sisters.

Her steady gaze left his to probe Kate's. "I suppose." She didn't look convinced, but she said no more about it.

"Where are you headed?" he said.

"Momma asked me to deliver ointment to Mrs. Irving, and she gave me a list of things we need from Clawson's." She turned to Kate. "So what do you say?"

Her pretty lips lifted. "I'd like that."

"Great. My errands will go so much faster if you're along." She tugged on his sleeve. "Have you told her about the barn dance coming up?"

He'd forgotten all about it. "No, I haven't."

"Barn dance?" She looked intrigued.

"They're great fun." Megan linked her arm through Kate's. "There's music and dancing, of course. Lots of food. A chance to visit with neighbors and friends. We always have a great time."

He could just imagine the attention she would attract. A beautiful, unattached young lady didn't stay that way for very long in these parts. If he accompanied her, there'd be no end of speculation. The fact that his wedding had recently been called off would be fresh in the townspeople's minds.

Was he ready to endure that level of scrutiny? Furthermore, did Kate even realize what she was in for?

"Kate's accustomed to celebrations on a much grander scale, Megan. I doubt she'd be interested."

Kate's eyes flashed, reminding him that beneath her gentle manners lay determination. This was a lady who knew her own mind. "As a matter of fact, I think it sounds like fun."

"So you'll come?" Megan grinned from ear to ear. "You'll escort us, won't you, Josh? Nathan already has a date, and Caleb avoids social functions as a rule."

He wanted to refuse, but with both women staring up at him expectantly, it was difficult—if not impossible—to do so. "You do realize your name will be on everyone's lips, don't you? Especially if you arrive with me."

A tiny wrinkle appeared between her brows. "If it's going to be trying for you, then of course we won't go."

Touched, his words came out as rough as sandpaper. "I can handle it. It's you I'm worried about."

Megan looked thoughtful. "Most folks around here are kind, God-fearing folks. It's not their intention to make you feel uncomfortable, but, of course, they'll be curious about you, as they would be about any newcomers. You should go, and if it's awkward for you, then I'm sure Josh or Uncle Sam would take you home. Right, Josh?"

"Of course."

Tucking a stray curl behind her ear, she grinned shyly. "What time shall I be ready?"

Josh felt the impact of that grin clear down to his toes. He was in big trouble.

* * *

Walking with Megan on the well-worn path through the woods, sharing thoughts on their favorite authors and books, Kate felt content. This is what life could be like, she thought. Spending time with friends who weren't constantly comparing themselves to you, wondering whose clothing and jewels cost more or whose suitor was a better prospect. How refreshing not to be in competition!

It wasn't just Megan who made her feel this way. Megan's mother, Alice, and her sisters, Nicole, Jessica and Jane, had all welcomed her with genuine kindness. And, of course, Josh's family, except for Caleb, had treated her as one of their own from the first day. Even Josh, who'd had every reason to resent her, had gone out of his way to make her life pleasant.

It wasn't his fault she couldn't think straight when he was near. Or that her heart melted with each unexpected smile. Or that her soul yearned to knit itself with his, to be his helpmeet the rest of her days.

A deep sigh ripped from her chest. Odd how one man could represent her dreams come true yet still cause her such upheaval. A future with him was impossible. The sooner she accepted that, the better.

"Is something bothering you?"

Swinging her basket at her side, Megan maintained an easy pace. The sun had burned off the fog and chased away the nip in the morning air, the brilliant rays now warming her skin.

Not ready to share her most private thoughts, Kate shrugged. "Nothing I can speak of at the moment."

She flashed a sympathetic smile. "Well, if you ever need someone to talk to, I'm here. I've been told I'm a good listener."

Pointing to a break in the trees, she said, "Here's our first stop—Mrs. Irving's place. She's a widow, like Momma. Sweet lady. I'm dropping off some ointment for her."

Kate followed her onto the narrow footpath. Unlike Sam and Mary's neat lawn, the grass here was nearly as high as her knees.

"I'll have to ask Josh or Nathan to come by and tend this overgrown mess." Megan sighed. Approaching the small, squat cabin, she said over her shoulder, "Whatever you do, do *not* eat her green tomato pie. It's revolting!"

Crybabies. Tomato pie. Southerners sure had some peculiar-sounding foods. Smothering a giggle, Kate pressed her lips together in a tight line. She wouldn't dream of offending a friend of Megan's.

Having announced their arrival with a hard knock, it wasn't long before a short, plump, snow-haired lady appeared in the doorway. She surveyed them both.

"Miss Megan, did you bring your mother's special ointment? I've been waitin' since Sunday, you know." She aimed a stern glance in Kate's direction. "Who might this fancy young thing be?"

Swallowing a smile, Megan gestured with her hand. "This is my friend from New York City, Miss Kate Morgan."

Sparse brows descended over alert blue eyes. "Kate Morgan, is it?"

"It's a pleasure to meet you," she smiled.

"I can't say it's a pleasure to meet you—" she paused to stare hard at her "—'cause I don't know you from Adam."

Kate glanced at Megan. Sweet old lady? For certain?

Mrs. Irving's stern expression eased. "But we can remedy that, can't we? Come on in, both of you." Shuffling back, she beckoned them inside. "I've a loaf of banana bread already sliced and a pie cooling on the cupboard. It's a favorite of yours, Megan! Tomato."

Megan sucked in a harsh breath, and Kate was hard put not to laugh. Surely it couldn't be that bad!

One hour later, having said their goodbyes and heading toward town, Kate gratefully accepted the peppermint stick Megan fished out of her pocket and held aloft. Perhaps it would settle her stomach.

"I simply don't understand—" Kate wrinkled her nose in disgust "—why anyone would think to combine tomatoes with sugar."

"It's a mystery," Megan groaned and clutched her stomach. "If Mrs. Irving wasn't such a kind soul, I'd tell her the truth about that pie."

Laughter bubbled up and spilled over. Kate couldn't help it. The whole situation struck her as funny. It wasn't long before Megan joined her, and they were still laughing when they reached the edge of town.

A tall, dark-haired man she'd seen at church was out on the boardwalk polishing the barbershop window. Glancing up from his work, he grinned and nodded a greeting.

"Mornin', Miss Megan." His gaze switched to Kate. "Miss."

"How are you, Tom?" Megan stopped and Kate did the same.

Still clutching the wadded-up cloth, Tom rested his hands on his hips. "Oh, fair to middlin'. You ladies out for a stroll this fine morning?"

"Just running some errands." Megan slipped her arm through Kate's. "Tom Leighton, this is Kate Morgan.

She's newly arrived from New York. Kate, Tom owns the barbershop. He's a friend of Josh's."

"It's a pleasure to meet you, Miss Morgan. Welcome to Gatlinburg."

"Thank you."

"I hope I'm counted among your friends, as well," he teased Megan.

"Of course you are."

"And as a friend, you won't mind my asking if you have an escort to the barn dance?"

"Oh, well, Josh has agreed to escort both Kate and me," she hedged.

"He's a lucky man. I wonder if you all would mind if I tagged along? Make it an even foursome?"

"That would be wonderful."

Kate wondered at her friend's lack of enthusiasm. Didn't she like him? He seemed friendly enough.

"It's settled then."

They were making arrangements for Friday night when Kate happened to glance down the street. There, in a heated discussion with another man, stood Tyler. Alarm spread through her limbs, rendering her weak and breathless. Clutching the base of her throat, she pulled away from Megan.

She should run before he spotted her.

"Kate? What's wrong?"

"H-he's there. I have to go."

"Who?" She whipped her head around to scan the street.

"Tyler," Kate whispered, afraid to say it too loudly. Although surrounded by people, the last thing she wanted was to face him again. His desperation frightened her.

Tom stiffened. "Matthews is giving you trouble, Miss Morgan? Does Josh know?"

She could only nod.

Megan gasped, "What? Why didn't anyone tell me?"

"How about I take the two of you ladies home?" Tom suggested quietly.

"Would you mind?" Megan said, visibly upset.

"I'd actually feel better knowing you got home safely." Turning to the door, he flipped the sign to indicate the shop was closed. Extracting a key from his pocket, he locked it. "Let's go."

Chapter Eleven

Josh tested the cabinet doors to make sure they opened and closed smoothly. Standing back, he surveyed his work. All that was left to do was to stain and polish it.

A sense of accomplishment filled him. Not every man was fortunate enough to do what he loved. He was so close to achieving his dream. Three more orders—one cedar hope chest for Mrs. Calhoun, one dining set for the Millers, another display shelf for the mercantile—and he'd have the money to buy the store.

He was fairly confident the shop would be his. To his knowledge, no one else had come forward to buy it. Fulton would've spoken up if another prospective buyer had shown an interest.

A shadow darkened the open doorway, and Josh was surprised to see Tom Leighton standing there. Apprehension winged through him. His friend had a business to run, so the only reason for him to be here was if something was wrong.

When he moved aside to let Megan and Kate enter, Josh's pulse jumped. His gaze locked onto Kate's face, and he noticed her pallor right away. She looked shaken.

"What's happened?" Stepping around the pie safe, he strode to her side and took her slender, cold hand in his.

"I saw Tyler." She sought to reassure him. "In town. But he didn't see me, thank goodness. I was simply startled."

"Will someone explain to me what's going on?" Crossing her arms, Megan jutted out her chin. Most of the time, his cousin was easygoing and sweet as molasses. But she was an O'Malley. And every one of the O'Malleys possessed a stubborn streak. "Is Tyler the reason you're teaching Kate about guns?"

Catching Tom's pointed glance at his and Kate's joined hands, Josh dropped hers and slipped his into his pocket. "Look at her, Megan. Does she remind you of anyone?"

Frowning, her eyes full of questions, she studied Kate. "I don't—"

"Lily Matthews," Tom spoke up, incredulous.

Megan gasped and, covering her mouth, stared wide-eyed at Kate, who was beginning to look embarrassed from all the attention.

"Now you understand his fascination with her. His brain is so muddled with alcohol and cure-alls, he can't separate fantasy from reality."

"Cure-alls?" Tom said. "Is he sick?"

Megan lowered her hand. "I've read those can contain addictive substances. Cocaine is only one of them."

"I don't know if he's sick or not, but his place is like an apothecary shop. Bottles everywhere."

"I wonder if Charlotte is aware of all this," Kate murmured.

"I'm sorry you have to endure this." Megan laid a hand on Kate's arm. "Are you thinking of going home sooner than you'd planned?"

Josh held his breath, suddenly feeling as if he were standing at the edge of a deep ravine. He shouldn't care one way or another. Stay or go. Kate meant nothing to him. Or did she?

Squaring her shoulders, her gaze sought his. "No, I'm not leaving."

Releasing his pent-up breath, he ignored the way his heart danced a jig in his chest.

Tom settled his hat on his head. "We'd best get going, Megan. I need to get back." Tugging on the brim, he said, "Good day, Miss Morgan. Josh."

"Thanks for seeing them home safely," Josh told his friend.

"Anytime."

"I'll see you soon." With a final squeeze, Megan released Kate's arm and turned to follow Tom outside. Poking her head back inside, she smiled. "I'm glad you're staying."

"Me, too."

When she'd gone, Josh studied Kate. "Are you sure you're all right?"

"I'm fine except for a small headache. I think I'll go rest for a bit."

"I hate that he's doing this to you." He slid his knuckles down her cheek, then pivoted away to retrieve his hat from the hook by the door.

"Where are you going?" Unease crept into her features.

Putting it on, he paused in the open doorway, right hand resting on his pistol. "To end this once and for all."

"Please don't." She put a restraining hand on his arm.

Her concern touched him. "I have to."

"Not for me, you don't. I don't like the idea of you putting yourself in danger on my account. He didn't approach me today. He didn't even see me."

"I refuse to stand by and wait for him to make his next move." He held up a hand as she started to speak. "Don't worry, Kate. I'm just gonna talk to the man."

If he could find him, that is. And if he was sober.

Josh didn't hold out much hope, but he had to try.

He left her with the admonishment to get some rest, then mounted Chestnut and headed into town. There was no sign of Matthews, and when he asked around, no one had any idea where he'd gone.

He wasted an entire afternoon searching. No sign of him anywhere. Frustrated, Josh headed home.

Riding into the yard, he noticed Kate waiting for him on her porch. Her face lit up the moment she saw him, her generous mouth curving into a smile of relief and happiness.

He felt the effect of that smile clear down to his toes. A man sure could get used to a welcome like that. He allowed himself to pretend, only for a moment, that he was important to her. Wouldn't it be nice to see this exact expression on her face each time he returned home?

It would, if this were a fantasy world. But he lived squarely in reality.

He wasn't important to her, not in the way he was imagining. They were friends, that was all. And that was the way it had to stay.

Every morning for the following week, Josh took Kate out to practice shooting. Not an expert by any means, she managed to hit the target one out of every three attempts. He was a patient teacher, praising her progress, slow though it might be.

So the morning he left, Kate not only missed their time together. She missed him.

434 · *The Bridal Swap*

His smile. His laugh. The careful way he watched her when he thought she didn't notice.

It was wrong and foolhardy, she knew. But they were friends, and it was perfectly acceptable to miss a friend.

One thing she refused to do was sit around and mope about the situation.

After breakfast, she volunteered to help Mary with the week's supply of baking. Instead, Mary asked if she'd mind picking up some items at the mercantile. Eager to stay busy, Kate agreed. Too late, she remembered Josh's warning not to go anywhere alone.

She decided to seek out Nathan. Naturally, he was in the dairy barn.

"I'm sorry, Kate." He paused in forking hay into the stalls. "I can't spare the time now, but I'm free after lunch. Can you wait until then?"

"Sure."

She left him to his work, uncertain if she should put off the errand. Perhaps Mary needed those things as soon as possible. And if she took the main road, the walk to town would take all of ten minutes.

It was early. Tyler kept late hours at the saloon. He was probably still passed out in his bed.

Her mind made up, she retrieved her reticule and a shawl. A cool breeze swept through the trees, raising goose bumps on her skin despite her long sleeves and multilayered skirt. On her way out the door, her gaze fell on the holster belt and firearm lying on the side table. Josh's doing. The man actually expected her to wear the contraption around her waist with a loaded gun strapped in. Inconceivable!

With a shake of her head, she shut the door and headed for town.

* * *

Josh slapped his hat against his thigh in frustration.

They'd been making good time. The weather was clear, the dirt roads dry in most places. Now this. A downed tree blocked the road, its trunk the span of his outstretched arms. Dense forest lined either side, so they couldn't go around it.

He and Caleb frowned at each other. What now?

His glance flicked to the furniture packed neatly in the wagon bed. The sooner he delivered it, the better. Two tarps covered the table and chairs in case of rain, but the protection wasn't foolproof.

A lot hung on this delivery. The money from the sale would make it possible for him to buy the empty store. His dream was so close to becoming reality.

Digging in his supplies in search of a saw or an ax, he imagined Kate's response the first time she entered his furniture shop. Judging from her comments, she admired his work.

"I have a feeling we're gonna be here awhile," said Caleb as he joined the search, rifling through the satchels on his side of the wagon.

"I hope not. We're wasting valuable daylight."

"This is all I got." He held up a handsaw.

Josh sighed, feeling a headache coming on. "If that's true, we'll be here a week." His fingers closed around the handle of a large ax. "Aha. I don't remember packing this, but it sure is gonna come in handy. I wonder how it got there."

"The memory is the first thing to go in old age, I've heard." Caleb shot him a mocking smirk.

"Is that so? Since you think you're so clever, I'll let you have the first shot at that monster."

Holding out the ax, he suppressed a grin at the resulting scowl on his little brother's face. If nothing else, this trip was going to give them some uninterrupted time together.

Kate strode briskly down the lane, bonnet ribbons whipping in the breeze, heels clomping on the leaf-strewn bridge leading into town. Her walk had proved uneventful. Nevertheless, she was grateful when the church spire came into view. People meant safety.

Turning the corner of the barbershop, she bumped into someone and was knocked backward. A man's hand seized her arm. She gasped.

"Watch where you're goin', missy," a wizened voice complained.

Hand pressed against her chest, she glanced at the speaker and tried to place his face. Her heartbeat thundered in her ears. For a split second, she'd thought of Tyler...

"I'm sorry, sir. I didn't see you—"

"Of course you didn't," he snapped, straightening his bowler hat. "How could you with your eyes on the clouds?"

"I'm afraid I haven't had the honor of your acquaintance. I'm Kate Morgan."

He ignored her outstretched hand. "Fulton. Chadwick Fulton."

Tugging down his suit jacket with a harrumph, he stomped past her. Lips parted in surprise, she lowered her hand and turned to watch him go. Interesting.

With a shrug, Kate continued toward the mercantile, taking in the length of Main Street. Her mother and sister would be scandalized at the lack of boutiques and shops in this town. She didn't mind, however. The only time she truly liked to shop was at Christmastime, when she would get a list of needy children's names from the church secretary and spend days searching for just the right gifts. Her only regret was not being there to watch them open their packages on Christmas morning.

A big For Sale sign directly across the street caught her eye. It was propped in the picture window of what looked like an unoccupied store. Waiting until a wagon passed by, she lifted her skirts and hurried to the other side. She glanced up and down the boardwalk. People milled about, but she didn't recognize anyone.

With one hand over her eyes to block the light, Kate peered inside. A wide, spacious room stood empty. Dust coated the floorboards and the bare shelves lining the back wall. Images flashed through her head—a curtained off area for taking portraits, a back room for developing prints, more shelving to hold her camera equipment.

She gasped aloud and stepped back. A portrait studio? Here? In Gatlinburg, Tennessee?

It wouldn't work. She wasn't that brave. Oh, she'd toyed with the notion for a year or more, but fear of her parents' reaction had held her back. A Morgan heiress working as a common laborer? The mere thought of the resulting uproar made her feel slightly ill.

Her parents expected her to be home by the time they returned from Europe. They had already informed her of their intentions to find her a suitable husband—someone educated and wealthy who traveled in the same social circles. Someone like Percy, Fran's husband.

In her mother's mind, their money and connections would more than compensate for Kate's lack of purity.

Georgia's cold words haunted her to this day. *Tell no*

one of what you've done, Katerina. No man will accept a young woman of loose morals. Wesley obviously wasn't impressed. We'll have to find someone else. Once you're married, it will be too late for the hapless fool to back out.

Her mother expected her to hide the truth until it was too late.

Kate's conscience balked at such a prospect. An omission like that had the potential to destroy the trust between husband and wife.

No, if she couldn't have a family of her own, then she'd pursue a career.

If she stayed in East Tennessee, she'd be free to choose her own path. Make her own choices.

Of course, she couldn't live in Josh's cabin forever. She'd have to start fresh, find a permanent place to live. She had a sizable amount of money at her disposal, enough to sustain her for a year or more, and that wasn't including the inheritance she'd receive on her twenty-first birthday. Imagine, a home of her very own. And a profession she loved.

As she walked back to the cabin, the basket of goods in her hand, thoughts of the future filled her mind. The way she saw it, she had two choices—return to her old life or stay here and create a new one.

The decision was simple.

Josh and Caleb rolled into Gatlinburg midmorning on Saturday. The downed tree had cost them half a day's travel time, delaying their return. Josh was tired, hungry and in need of a bath and a shave. But he was glad to be back.

As eager as he was to pay a visit to Chad Fulton, first

he had to see Kate. Knowing her, she was worrying about his prolonged absence. And he needed to see for himself that she was safe.

When the wagon came abreast of his future furniture store, he glanced over and got the shock of his life. What was Kate doing in there?

Yanking on the reins, he guided the team to the side of the street. Caleb shot him a sharp look.

"I need to speak with Kate." He leaped down. "Would you mind waitin' a spell?"

"Never mind." He climbed down the other side. "I'll walk the rest of the way."

Josh made it to the door in four long strides. She glanced up at the sound of the bell, her eyes widening at the sight of him. A bell? Since when had Fulton installed a bell?

"Josh!" Straightening from her spot in the midst of a mountain of trunks and crates, she approached him with a welcoming smile.

"I'm so happy you're back! When you didn't return last night, I started imagining all sorts of terrible things."

He hesitated, his befuddled brain trying to make sense of what he was seeing. "What are you doing here? Are you lost?"

She laughed. "No, I'm not lost."

"Were you looking for Mr. Fulton? Do you need to speak to him about something?"

"My business with Mr. Fulton is complete."

"What business?"

She splayed her hand wide. "I'm a new business owner."

As her words penetrated, his gaze shot to her face. She looked nervous. Expectant.

"I don't understand."

"I bought this place. You are standing in what is now my portrait studio."

Josh floundered for a response. Was he having a nightmare?

"I thought you were going back to New York in a couple of weeks."

She crossed her arms in front of her like a shield, making her appear small and vulnerable. "I've decided to make Gatlinburg my home."

Arms at his sides, he wandered past her farther into the room. The room that was supposed to have held his furniture was instead piled with camera equipment.

His heart felt heavy, like a lead weight in his chest. Each breath was painful. So much for his grand plans.

First Francesca had crushed his dream of a family. And just when he was about to realize his dream of a business, Kate stepped in to rob him of it.

A sigh ripped from his chest. He plunged his hands in his hair, mussing it further.

No. She wasn't to blame. She'd had no clue what his intentions were regarding this place. It was his fault for not sharing them with her.

When she spoke, he had to strain to hear her quiet words. "I've already spoken with the Copelands. They will have a room to let next week. You'll soon have your cabin back."

Pivoting, he regarded her downturned face. "How am I supposed to honor my promise with you living in town?"

"Your promise?" Her head came up.

"To protect you."

"I suppose I'll have to release you of it. It isn't your job to protect me."

"I can't accept that."

Shrugging, she returned to the trunks. "What's done is done. I've already made the arrangements."

Rubbing the itchy bristle on his jaws, Josh said, "Look, I'm not in the best frame of mind right now. I'm in dire need of a decent meal and strong coffee. We'll finish this conversation later."

He needed time to sort through the implications of her decision. To figure out where to go from here.

"Fine." She didn't look up when he left, and it wasn't until he reached the barn that he realized he'd left her there alone. What if Matthews waited till she started down their lonely lane to make his move?

Spying his brother already mounted on Chance, he waved him down. "Nathan, I need a favor."

Chapter Twelve

That did not go well. Hurt by Josh's cold reaction to her news, Kate stared unseeing out the plate-glass window overlooking Main Street. Weren't friends supposed to celebrate each other's good fortunes?

Perhaps he'd been merely tolerating her presence here. After all, she'd indicated that her stay was temporary. And she was Fran's sister. When Josh looked at her, he must automatically think of the grief Fran had caused him. The thought saddened her.

The bell jingled. In the doorway stood Nathan, looking more solemn than she'd ever seen him. Sweeping off his hat, he nodded in greeting.

"Mornin'."

"Nathan." She tried to muster up a smile, but couldn't. "What can I do for you?"

"Josh wanted me to check on you and ask when you planned on coming home so one of us could escort you."

"Why does he pretend to care?" she blurted out, blood rushing to her face. "I already told him not to bother."

She turned her back, blinking fast to fight back tears

and the unexpected rush of emotion. Nathan's boots clomped on the weathered planks as he moved closer.

"Kate," he began hesitantly, "I, uh, think there's something you should know. Something Josh would never tell you himself."

She wiped the moisture from her eyes and turned back. "What is it?"

Nathan's kind eyes held a hint of regret. "He's been making plans for quite a while to expand his business."

"I know. He told me."

"When Mr. Fulton decided to retire and close up his law practice, Josh approached him about purchasing this place. Fulton knew he was close to having the full amount, but refused to hold it. My father offered to lend Josh the money, but he wouldn't accept it." He sighed heavily. "I don't know what is going on between you two, but I know my brother. He cares about you."

Closing her eyes, Kate pressed her palm over her heart. Oh, no. It couldn't be.

He must despise her! First Fran's betrayal and now this…

"Wh-why didn't he tell me?" she whispered.

"He wouldn't want you to feel bad."

No wonder he'd reacted the way he did! He must've been in shock. Seeing his dreams fall to the wayside a second time. Now both Morgan sisters had dealt him a cruel blow.

"Please, I need to be alone," she managed, not daring to meet his gaze.

"He wouldn't want you to blame yourself. You couldn't have known."

She stared at the floor, unable to come up with a response.

His boots shifted. Clearing his throat, he said, "I'll be in town for a while. I'll stop back by later and see if you need anything."

The door closed behind him. The resulting silence was oppressive.

Kate sank to the floor and, burying her head in her hands, burst into tears.

Kate locked up the studio three-quarters of an hour later. She rushed down the street, head down, in an effort to avoid eye contact with passersby. No doubt her eyes were red-rimmed and bloodshot, and she wasn't in the mood to answer questions her appearance would surely spawn.

Determination fueled her long strides. She had bought the store from Mr. Fulton. There was no reason why she couldn't turn around and sell it to Josh.

He had his heart set on opening a furniture store. She would not stand in his way.

She found him in his workshop, standing idly behind his worktable and looking as if he hadn't a clue what to do next. He'd changed out of his rumpled travel clothes and into a pair of pressed jeans and a shirt that matched his eyes. He'd shaved, his goatee neat as ever, and his hair was damp from a recent wash. The pleasing scent of soap mixed with the pungent odors of pine and varnish.

His awkward attempt at a smile brought a fresh wave of tears.

"You've been crying." A wrinkle forming between his brows, he came around the table but didn't move to touch her. "Matthews didn't—"

"I know about your plans for the furniture store," she said, hiking up her chin. "Nathan told me."

A shutter descended over his expression. "He shouldn't have done that."

"He shouldn't have had to. Why didn't *you* tell me?"

"It doesn't matter now. It obviously wasn't meant to be."

"You're wrong." She pulled the bill of sale out of her reticule and held it out. "I'm going to sell the space to you."

His eyes widened. Palms face up, he shook his head. "Sorry, not interested."

Planting one hand on her hip, Kate ignored his assertion. "You've been working toward this for a long time. I wouldn't have bought it, had I known. Surely you believe that?"

"I do. And just as you don't want to stand in the way of my dreams, neither do I want to keep you from yours." He jerked his head at the paper she dangled in front of him. "Put that away. The place is yours."

"Don't be stubborn. I refuse—"

She broke off when he snatched the document from her fingers and, carefully refolding it, tucked it back inside her reticule hanging from her wrist. Hands on his hips, his eyes challenged her. "Does your studio have a name?"

"You will not have the final say in this."

"I'm not buying the space from you, Kate."

They stood nearly toe-to-toe, gazes locked in a silent battle of wills. Her mouth thinned with displeasure, a darker emotion similar to desperation lurking beneath the surface. This conversation was not going the way she'd planned. Why was he being so stubborn?

How could she enjoy her new venture, knowing she'd denied him his dream?

"This has been an upsetting morning for both of us."

Pivoting away from him, she stalked to the door, only to turn back at the last moment. "I'm not accepting this as your final answer. Take some time to think it over."

She swept out the door before he could respond. Chances were she didn't want to hear what he had to say anyway.

Not in the mood to return to her studio, Kate decided to take a stroll around the farm. Her focus was turned inward, and she didn't look up as she usually did to drink in the beauty and majesty of the mountains towering above her. When she tired of walking, she entered the orchard and sank down at the base of an apple tree to rest. She'd brought a copy of Jane Austen's *Emma* along, and, pulling it from her pocket, attempted to read.

But she couldn't concentrate.

The defeat in Josh's eyes tormented her. Somehow, someway, she had to make him agree to her suggestion.

"Kate?"

Twisting to look up the low rise, she spotted him. "I'm here."

Josh came to her, bending at the waist to peer at her beneath the low branches. "You missed lunch. I was worried."

Setting her book aside, she folded her hands in her lap. "I lost track of time. Besides, I'm not hungry."

He slipped his hat off and, crouching low, moved to sit opposite her. He skimmed his hair with an impatient hand and dropped his hat in his lap. "I know my reaction to your new studio wasn't what you'd expected. I was surprised."

"I know. And I'm sorry for that. But I meant what I said earlier. I want you to have the store. This is your birthplace. Your family and friends are here." She hitched a shoulder. "I can go anywhere to open a studio."

"Tell me something." His blue eyes quizzed her. "Why Gatlinburg?"

"I love it here. These mountains speak to my soul. I see God's fingerprint everywhere I look." She spread her hands wide. "There's a feeling I have when I'm in the forest that I haven't experienced anywhere else. When I'm surrounded by endless trees and hushed stillness, I don't ever want to leave. You probably think that's ridiculous." She laughed self-consciously.

"Not at all. In fact, I feel the same way. Still, life is different here."

"I'm aware of that."

He stared hard at her. "I think, after a time, you'd miss the creature comforts of city life."

"I'm not Francesca."

"I know that," he responded evenly. "But you and she had the same upbringing."

"Simply because we are siblings doesn't mean we share the same values. Do you and your brothers all have the same opinion about everything?"

He set his jaw. "No, we don't."

"You see?"

"I don't think you comprehend the reality of living without servants to cater to your every need. Out here, dinner doesn't just appear on the table every night. If you want something to eat, you gotta go out to the garden and pick it yourself. You have to choose one of your livestock or hunt down a wild animal and, once you've killed it, bleed it dry, skin, carve and cook it. *Then* you get to eat." His serious gaze challenged her. "Do you know how to cook?"

Lifting her chin, she retorted, "As a matter of fact, I do."

"Honestly."

Kate had made friends with the head chef, who'd agreed to teach her the basics. While her skills weren't those of a professional, those staff members who'd sampled her food said she had talent. Her mother wasn't told, of course. The daughter of Patrick Morgan doing menial work? Perish the thought!

"You think I'm lying?"

"Of course not." Shifting, he stroked his goatee. "Look, I'm sorry. It's not my intention to upset you. All I'm trying to do is make you see reality."

"This conversation is pointless. I'm not staying here because you are going to buy the store back from me."

"That's not going to happen."

Exasperated, Kate threw up her hands. "You're not making any sense! You don't want me to stay and yet you won't buy the building so that I can leave."

He stilled. "I never said I didn't want you to stay."

Her heart paused midbeat, then thudded wildly. "What do you mean?"

"I'm concerned that you won't ultimately be happy here. This is all brand-new and different from the city. For you, Gatlinburg might be a nice place to visit, but not to live in."

"Perhaps you're right."

"Really?"

"But there are no guarantees in life. Who knows? I might never get tired of country living."

Presenting her with his profile, he stared off into the distance.

"All I know is I'm no longer satisfied with my life in New York. I'm ready for a change."

"I just can't believe you'd be happy here."

"You have no idea what my life is like."

He looked at her then. "I know you're surrounded by luxury. You saw the way people stared at you the day you arrived. They only see clothes and carriages like that in magazines or when wealthy folks like you pass through these parts, which isn't often. You honestly think you'd be happy living in a two-room cabin the rest of your life?"

"You didn't doubt Francesca's ability to be happy here, so why do you doubt mine? What makes me so different?"

Kate gazed at him, a wounded look in her eyes. Her lower lip trembled, and he itched to smooth it with his thumb. If he rattled off the many wonderful qualities she possessed that Francesca lacked, she might think he harbored feelings for her. Which was ludicrous. He'd learned his lesson—no more foolhardy decisions.

"It didn't occur to me how much I'd asked her to give up until you arrived. Watching you at the supper table that first night…how out of your element you were… We come from different worlds, you and I."

"You're speaking of material wealth. Yes, we have ladies' maids and butlers and kitchen staff. Fine art lines the hallways. Bohemian crystal bowls and vases grace Italian marble tables. My mother has fresh-cut roses delivered to her suite every day of the year. It's an extravagant lifestyle. Do I enjoy the delicious meals and having an entire library at my disposal? Of course. Does it make me happy? No." Her voice dipped. "I'm lonely there, Josh. I don't have many friends."

Her words came out in a quiet hush, yet there was no disguising their sadness.

He almost reached out and tugged her close for a hug. Somehow, he held back. "I can't imagine why not," he murmured, his voice thick.

"It's an issue of different values and interests." She sighed. "Spending time with your family and cousins has given me a glimpse of what home and family should be." Her green gaze settled on his with confidence. "I can live without the extras. I don't want to live without the things that really matter."

"Are you sure about this?" Megan regarded her with wide eyes. "You have such exquisite clothes. Why would you want to wear one of my dresses? Not that I mind, of course. I simply don't understand."

Standing in her bedroom, Kate smoothed the lightweight cotton material, then pressed her hands against the flat of her stomach. She inhaled, expanding her lungs as far as they would stretch. Her stiff, confining corset lay abandoned on the bed.

"Believe me, if you had to wear that tortuous article day after day, you'd understand." She twirled in a circle to watch her skirt flare like a bell. With a wide grin, she said, "I feel so free!" Sobering, she sought her friend's gaze. "But how do I look?"

Moving behind her, Megan gathered the excess material around Kate's waist and pulled it taut. "I'm taller than you."

"And not top-heavy." Kate grimaced.

"Don't complain about the blessings God gave you," she chided gently. "You have an attractive figure."

The simple compliment brought tears to her eyes. All

she'd ever heard from her mother and sister were derogatory comments. Could it be that her figure wasn't as unbecoming as she'd been led to believe?

"The length needs to be hemmed, as well," Megan observed, unaware of Kate's reaction. "We need Aunt Mary's help. She's a much better seamstress than I am."

"I wonder if she'll have time." Today was Wednesday. Only two more days until the dance.

"She'll make time." She whirled around. "I'll see if she has a free moment now to take measurements. Be right back." She was out the door before Kate could blink an eye.

Moving to the kitchen window, she pushed the curtain aside and watched as her friend crossed the yard. When she paused to wave at someone, Kate followed the direction of her gaze and spotted Josh standing in the doorway of his workshop, long apron wrapped around his waist and one arm propped against the doorjamb.

Her breath caught. Since their conversation in the orchard, they'd spoken only in passing. He'd hardly left his workshop, even taking his meals there. There'd been no mention of resuming shooting lessons and absolutely no references to the studio.

He was avoiding her. If only he'd stop being so stubborn and agree to buy back the store.

Josh disappeared from view, and Kate let the curtain fall back in place.

No doubt he regretted his promise to escort her and Megan to the dance.

Megan's soft footfalls on the porch sounded a moment before she glided inside. "She'll be here in fifteen minutes." Perching on the edge of the sofa cushion, she looked up and frowned. "What's the matter? You look sad."

Kate sank down beside her. "Maybe I shouldn't go. After all, Josh agreed to take both of us, and now that Tom is going, it's more like a pairing off."

"What's wrong with that?"

"What if Josh doesn't like the idea of being paired with me? He did try and talk me out of it, remember?"

"Josh is a private person, that's all. He's afraid showing up with you is going to stir up a hornet's nest of speculation. I'm sure he's trying to shield you from that possibility."

"Then we shouldn't go."

"No!" Megan leaned forward and covered Kate's hands with her own. "You have to go. You'll see, it's great fun! And don't worry about anyone else. The O'Malleys stick together. There'll be enough of us there to form a buffer against curious bystanders."

"I don't know."

"What else is bothering you?"

"I don't blame him for not wanting to spend time with me. I ruined his life—" her voice wobbled "—and now he despises me."

"That's not true!" Megan curled an arm around her shoulders. "You had no idea of his plans. He may be disappointed, but I know him. He's smart. And he doesn't give up easily. He'll figure out another way to achieve his dream."

Kate sniffed. "I wish he would just agree to take it back. Why does he have to be so obstinate?"

Megan threw back her head and laughed. "He's an O'Malley."

Miserable, Kate urged her friend, "Perhaps you should

talk to him. If he wants to back out, I'll honor his wishes. The last thing I want is to force my company on him."

"Don't be ridiculous," she scoffed. "As if any man wouldn't be thrilled to spend time with you! He likes you, Kate. I can tell."

"How can you say that? My sister betrayed him. Instead of welcoming his blushing bride to town, he got me—the bearer of bad tidings. And now I've single-handedly destroyed his dream of a business all his own. He must rue the day he heard the Morgan name."

Leaning against the side of the wagon, Josh tipped his head back and watched as the last remaining rays of the sun bathed the distant mountain peaks in pale pink and peach. He silently thanked God for the sight.

It had been a long, tiring day. He'd delivered the cedar hope chest right after breakfast, then got to work on his next project, not stopping until late afternoon when Nathan had poked his head in the shop and asked if he was still going to the dance tonight. And even though he hadn't eaten since early morning, he wasn't hungry. He was too wound up to think about food.

Kate dominated his thoughts.

He'd rehashed the events of the past week a thousand times. She hadn't been aware of his plans to buy the store. He knew her. She wasn't the type to deliberately hurt others.

Kate wasn't at all like her sister. She was an honest, caring woman with a heart as big as the forest.

Still, it hurt to have his dream snatched away like that. All his planning and hard work—the late nights, missed suppers, aches and pains—had been for naught.

Oh, he still had his clients and a long list of projects. But the furniture store he'd envisioned would have to wait.

He'd spent a lot of time on his knees the past few days, asking God why. He'd had such peace about his plans. Now he was confused and upset.

Hearing movement from inside her cabin, he tossed the sliver of hay to the ground and settled his black hat on his head.

Kate emerged and all thoughts of his failed plans scattered like leaves on the wind.

Josh swallowed hard. Gone was the stiff, extravagant clothing. In its place was a simply made dress that showed off her curves to perfection. Her hair only partially restrained by forest-green ribbons that matched the color of her dress, the remainder flowed down past her shoulders in thick, glossy waves. She could've been any girl in town. A country girl.

Seeing her this way was a hard blow to the gut. His breath hissed out from between his lips. In a near stupor, he approached and extended his hand to help her down the steps.

She placed her soft, bare hand in his, and he detected the slightest hint of a tremor. His fingers tightened in response. When she was standing directly in front of him, he could only stare.

Her jewel-like eyes held a thousand mysteries. "Is something the matter?"

"Uh-uh." He shook his head, feeling suddenly like a timid youth. "You're beautiful."

Her curled lashes swept down to hide her eyes, dark half-moons against her pale skin. A light breeze teased the tendrils around her face, and he resisted the urge to smooth them back.

Clearing his throat, he said, "It will get cooler as the night progresses. Do you have a shawl I can fetch for you?"

"I forgot to lay one out. I'll get it."

Slipping her hand from his, she hurried back inside and returned a few minutes later with the desired article. "Where are Tom and Megan? I thought they were going with us."

"Nathan stopped in his shop for a haircut this afternoon, and Tom was running behind. He passed along a message that he will pick up Megan. They'll meet us there."

His friend had had a crush on Megan for years, but he'd wanted to wait until his business was up and running to make his move. No doubt he wanted to spend a few minutes alone with her.

Megan could be tough to read, though. Friendly to everybody. No telling if she viewed Tom as a romantic interest or merely a friend. Time would tell, he supposed.

He gestured to the wagon. "Shall we?"

"Wait, we don't have to do this. I won't be offended if you'd rather not."

"And deny myself the honor of escorting the most beautiful lady in town?" he challenged.

Her cheeks bloomed with color. "But after what I did—"

"Let's agree not to discuss the topic for tonight. This is your first barn dance, and I want you to have a good time."

She was quiet as they approached the wagon.

The sun dipped behind the mountains, blotting out much of the daylight. Another cool breeze rustled the leaves in the trees, and Kate shivered, her gaze darting anxiously to the shadowed woods behind the cabin.

"It's getting dark."

He wondered if there was more to her fear than she was letting on. Instead of questioning her, however, he helped her up onto the wagon seat and circled around the back to climb up on the other side. When she'd wrapped her shawl securely around her shoulders, he signaled the team to head out.

Kate sat quietly beside him, apparently content to survey their surroundings. With each passing minute, black swallowed up the sky. Here and there a star flickered on as if lit by a match. The kerosene lamps swung from their hooks, lighting their way.

Night had taken hold by the time they arrived at the Fosters' farm three miles west of town. People were still arriving, unloading baskets of food and jugs of lemonade and sweet tea from their wagons. His parents had come early to help with the setup, and since Nathan's date was Elijah Foster's daughter, he'd ridden over with them.

A lively tune drifted on the cool breeze, with snatches of conversation and laughter mixed in.

"Isn't Caleb coming?"

"Doubt it." She accepted his outstretched arm. "My little brother tends to keep to himself. Always avoids large crowds."

"Why do you think that is?"

"He's self-conscious about his scar."

"How did it happen?"

He didn't answer right away, his attention caught by the thick tangle of trees. Nothing seemed out of the ordinary. Still he couldn't shake the sensation someone was out there watching.

"Josh?"

"Sorry. What were we talking about?"

She looked at the trees. "What is it? Did you see something?"

"No, nothing. Must've imagined it."

She stiffened. "You don't think—"

"No, I don't," he said firmly. "He's not that bold. I'd say he's not that dumb, but alcohol tends to cloud reason."

"But—"

He touched a finger to her lips. "Remember my promise?"

Girlish giggles erupted to their right. A glance over his shoulder revealed three girls in pigtails watching their every move. The oldest girl's red hair shone in the moonlight.

He dropped his hand. "We should go in."

"Why the frown?"

"See the one on the far right? She reminds me of Juliana at that age. Still hard to believe she's gone. I never dreamed she'd leave Gatlinburg."

He missed their talks. Juliana had a lot of insight into relationships and wasn't afraid to share her opinion. He remembered how at her wedding reception she'd voiced her doubts about his choice of a city girl for a wife. She'd been right.

"The two of you are very close, aren't you?"

"Like brother and sister." He glanced at Kate. "You know, I have a feeling the two of you would hit it off."

"I would like to meet her someday."

"Maybe you will."

The barn doors had been thrown open to let fresh air circulate. A crush of people encircled the dance area and musicians. Lamps had been strung from post to post, suspended from inch-thick ropes high above the crowd. The Fosters and the setup crew had done their job well. There wasn't a trace of animal odor in the air, only fresh hay and a potent mix of men's cologne and women's perfume.

The women wore their finest dresses, the men their cleanest clothes, hair and beards trimmed for the occasion.

Beside him, Kate's expression was one of shy curiosity. She surely wouldn't be impressed with this backwoods gathering.

"Howdy, Josh." Ed Wilcox walked up, a pipe dangling from one corner of his mouth. His gaze switched to Kate. "Ma'am."

Josh made the introductions. "Nice to meet ya," Ed said. "Josh, the wife is mighty pleased with the new table. Impressed the in-laws, too." He grinned, setting his pipe to wobbling precariously.

Josh experienced a rush of pleasure at the compliment. Satisfied customers meant repeat business. "I'm glad to hear it."

The older man's grin grew even wider, and the pipe slipped free. He caught it before it hit the ground. "Say, when you plannin' on settin' up your store? Your pa told me all about your big plans. He's right proud of ya."

Kate stiffened beside him. Sensing her sudden anxiety and afraid she might dart off, he reached over and threaded his fingers through hers. With the other hand, he clapped the man on the shoulder. "I'd love to discuss my plans with you, but this is the young lady's very first barn dance. I don't think it'd be right to talk business. Let's talk later, okay?"

"Certainly." His eyes twinkled knowingly.

Before he could say anything else to upset Kate, Josh nodded a farewell and tugged her in the opposite direction.

"Would you like something to drink?"

"Maybe later."

She sounded dejected. Great. Why did the first person they ran into have to be Ed Wilcox? Pa shouldn't have told him. Or anyone else, for that matter. But Pa *was* proud of all three of his sons. He guessed it was natural for a father to brag about his offspring.

He just wished Ed had chosen another time to bring up the sore subject.

"I'm sorry about that. The good thing is that not many people know about the store, so I don't think we'll have any more questions." He squeezed her hand. "Remember, we're here to enjoy ourselves."

"All right." She gave him a small smile, and he knew it was for his benefit.

Spying his parents, he led her through the crowd to their side.

His mother leaned forward with a smile. "Kate, you look beautiful. How do you feel?"

"Wonderful." She blushed. "Thanks for all your help."

"If you'd like, we can go to Clawson's next week and buy some material. It wouldn't take long to sew two or three more dresses."

Josh thought the suggestion unnecessary. Wasted money and energy, in his opinion. Kate's wardrobe was of the finest quality. Why would she want to wear home-made dresses?

"I'd like that."

He could tell by her earnest tone that she wasn't simply placating his mother. She was sincere.

Nicole appeared then, an eager bounce to her step. With a quick hello to his parents and himself, she focused her attention on Kate. "Do you have a free moment? I'd like to introduce you to some friends of mine."

"Would you mind?" She turned to him.

"Not at all."

Her wide smile conveyed her gratitude, her sparkling eyes her anticipation. Josh watched as, arm in arm, the pair wove a path through the throng to the refreshment table, where a cluster of young ladies stood chatting. They welcomed Kate with eager smiles, pressing in close to be introduced to her.

His mother excused herself to check on the refreshments. His father stared after Kate and Nicole.

"That gal looks right pretty, don't you think?"

"She does at that, Pa."

Kate was laughing, pearl-white teeth glinting in the lamplight, her face glowing with happiness. Watching her, his heart yearned to be the one to make her laugh. To bring her joy. To thrill her.

Whoa! Josh shook his head to dislodge the thought.

"Kate seems happy here," Pa continued. "I had my doubts at first, but she fits in just fine."

"Yep." How long would her contentment last, however?

"I have to commend you, son. You're handling this whole situation better than most men would have."

He let loose a slow sigh. "I'm still trying to figure out my next move."

"Trust in the Lord's guidance," Pa said. "He has a plan for your life."

"I know. It's just that sometimes I'm impatient for Him to reveal it to me."

He felt a tap on his shoulder. "Evenin', O'Malley."

Noah Townsend stood beside him. The same age as Josh, he'd been married and widowed in the past year.

A hardworking man, he didn't come to town often. Josh was surprised to see him.

"Good to see you, Townsend. How ya been?"

"Can't complain. The harvest has been plentiful this year." He glanced across the room. "I heard you have a lady visitor out at your place. That her?"

Josh's mouth tightened. He didn't like the direction this conversation was headed in. "Her name's Kate Morgan."

"Beautiful girl." Noah's tone warmed with appreciation. "You think she'd agree to dance with me?"

"She's an adult. You'll have to ask her."

Noah pinned him with a serious gaze. "Am I overstepping my bounds, O'Malley? I know you were engaged to her sister, but if there's something between you two…"

Yes, he wanted to say, Kate was off-limits. But he couldn't.

He had no claim on her.

"To the best of my knowledge, Kate's not attached to anyone."

"Good. I believe I'll go on over there before someone else gets the jump on me. Evenin', gentlemen."

His stomach a hard knot, he watched Townsend approach Kate, singling her out from the rest of the group. Her expression revealed her initial surprise, quickly masked by polite acceptance. Good manners instilled from birth, he thought, wondering if she truly wanted to dance with the man or had agreed because politeness dictated it.

He watched as the pair joined the other couples on the dance floor. When Townsend took her in his arms, Josh felt ill. A sour taste coated his mouth. Heaving a sigh, he turned away from the disturbing sight.

"Want something to drink, Pa?"

"No, thanks. I believe I'll join that group of old married men over in the corner. Catch up on the latest gossip," he said with a wink.

Josh made his way to the makeshift table in the corner near the door and helped himself to a Mason jar filled to the brim with sweet tea. He took a long chug of the full-bodied brew, his gaze once again drawn to the couples whirling to the music.

Kate moved with grace and elegance. Although she was surely unfamiliar with the rustic, enthusiastic music, she followed Townsend's lead without a single misstep. She was a natural.

Josh noticed she kept her gaze downcast, but that didn't deter Townsend. His mouth was moving a mile a minute and, on occasion, his words elicited a laugh from Kate. He wondered what the widower's motives were. Surely he wasn't already in the market for another wife!

At last the song came to an end. Straightening, he started forward only to stop when another man—Carl Howard—intercepted the couple leaving the dance floor. The music started up again, and Josh watched with dismay as Howard led Kate into a lively number. A glance around revealed a number of single men focused on his date.

The acid in his stomach churned with frustration. He wasn't a dancer. Never had been. He hadn't planned on asking her to dance. It hadn't occurred to him that he'd be standing on the sidelines watching her whirl away the night with every young buck in town.

Chapter Thirteen

Her toes ached. Her throat was as dry as the Sahara. And if she had to dance with one more stranger, her cheeks would surely crack from the strain of her pasted-on smile.

Where was her supposed escort? Irritated and confused, Kate glanced surreptitiously about for the tall man with short, tousled hair the color of wheat. Yet there was no sign of him.

Why had he agreed to bring her, only to abandon her?

Feeling a light touch on her sleeve, she whipped her head up, expecting to see him. But it wasn't Josh. Masking her disappointment, she greeted Megan with a simple nod. She couldn't bring herself to smile.

"Kate! You sure are a popular dance partner!" Her skin was flushed, eyes bright with excitement. "Are you having fun?"

She couldn't bring herself to spoil her friend's mood. "The music is wonderful."

"I believe you've cast a spell on all the single men below the age of forty, Kate Morgan. You're the belle of the ball!"

All except one, she thought. "You're exaggerating. And what about you? I haven't seen you sitting out any of the dances."

She shrugged. "I've known most of these men my whole life. It's not exactly romantic to dance with someone who used to sneak frogs into my lunch pails."

"I noticed Tom has hardly left your side. Where is he, anyway?"

"Getting us something to drink." She glanced over her shoulder. "He's a good man. A good friend."

"A romantic friend?" Kate dared to ask.

"Not exactly." Her lips quirked. "Josh tells me I read too much. That I have fanciful notions of what a man should be."

"Do you agree with him?"

Tilting her head to the side, she considered the question. "Yes and no. I do know I don't wanna settle for less than God's best. He knows my heart. What or who will complete me. Does that make sense?"

Kate nodded, thinking it made total sense. She'd settled for less than God's best when she'd allowed Wesley to take her virtue. And now she carried around with her the shameful realization that no honorable man would want her for his wife or the mother of his children.

Megan peered closer. "Has all the dancing worn you out? There's some empty chairs against the wall. We can sit and rest awhile if you'd like."

"No, thank you." The heat was suddenly too much to bear. "If you don't mind, I'm going to step outside for some fresh air."

She turned away before Megan could protest, shouldering her way through, gaze locked on the door and the darkness beyond.

Just as she was about to leave the building, a hand caught her wrist. "Where do you think you're going?"

Kate would know that voice anywhere. She slid her gaze up to his face. Judging by his expression, he wasn't any happier than she was at the moment.

"I'm going outside for some fresh air."

Josh quirked a sardonic brow. "You do look flushed. Must be from all that dancing."

How dare he sound perturbed! She tugged on her hand, and he released it. "Isn't that what people are supposed to do at a barn *dance?*"

Folding his arms across his chest, he narrowed his gaze. "My assumption was you're supposed to spend time with the one who brought you."

"Hah!" Jamming her hands on her hips, she glared at him. "And my assumption was the one who brought me wouldn't abandon me to a procession of strange men!"

His lips parted in surprise. She didn't give him a chance to reply.

Stomping out into the night, Kate strode the length of the wooden structure and turned the corner, too angry to be intimidated by the darkness. Crisp air brushed her heated skin. Crickets chirruped. Muted music and laughter passed through the wall at her back.

Glancing up, she gazed at the fat, pearlescent moon, floating in the blue-black expanse. Not a cloud marred the view. Hundreds of stars twinkled above her.

A wide clearing bordered the Fosters' barn. Then the forest took over. The shadows were so thick there, the trees merged together.

"Kate." Josh had rounded the corner and was advancing toward her. He held a kerosene lamp aloft, the golden light sharpening the planes and angles of his face. He looked wary. And a bit sheepish, which wasn't like him. Josh was ever-confident, unwavering, a pillar of strength.

He set the lamp in the grass. "You're right. I shouldn't have left you to fend for yourself. I assumed you were enjoying the attention."

"Enjoying the—" she huffed. "If that's your attempt at an apology, you're not doing a very good job."

"What?"

"You honestly think I like being passed around like that?" Pivoting, she swung away from him.

He seized her upper arm, halting her retreat. "That's not what I meant—"

"Why didn't *you* ask me to dance?" She whirled back. "I gave you a chance to back out, remember? But no. You insisted on coming. Why?"

He grimaced. "I'm sorry. I should've explained before now that I'm not much of a dancer. I enjoy the music, but I'm horrible at keeping time. I tend to botch the steps, and I'd hate to put either of us through the embarrassment."

"Oh."

The strains seeping through the wall changed tempo, the instruments strumming a sedate, melancholy tune. The air between them stilled, stretching taut with unvoiced awareness.

In one smooth movement, Josh slid an arm around her waist and tugged her against him. His voice a mere whisper against her hair, he said, "There aren't any spectators out here. And I really would like to dance with you, Kate. Will you do me the honor?"

Overwhelmed by the moment, she could only nod.

His large hands spanning her waist, they swayed as

one to the sweet melody. Back and forth, feet barely moving, they danced beneath the stars.

Light-headed, Kate rested her cheek against his chest. His heart beat steady and sure beneath her ear. Josh held her reverently, as if she were made of fine porcelain. He was good at this. Making her feel cherished. His solicitous nature led her to believe he cared for her. *Just as you believed Wesley cared. You were wrong then, and you're wrong now.*

Easing back, his blue eyes, aflame with need, hungrily roamed her face. "I want to kiss you again," he breathed.

"Did you kiss Fran?"

He reared his head back. "No."

"But you wanted to." She didn't know why she was bringing this up now, but Fran hovered like a ghost between them. "Of course you wanted to." She grimaced, pulling away. "You asked her to marry you."

He didn't try to stop her retreat. "It's complicated."

"No, it's not. You fell in love with my sister and wanted her for your wife."

Presenting him with her back, she rubbed her palm over her heart in a vain effort to stop the stabbing pain that truth inflicted.

"That's what I thought, too," he said quietly. "Until you came."

She didn't move. Couldn't. "What are you saying?"

He circled to face her. "Our time together was brief. I got to know her facade, not her heart." Sliding a finger beneath her chin, he tipped her face up, forcing her to look at him. "Family is everything to me. Marrying her meant the start of my own, a partnership for life. All this time, what I thought was love was simple longing. Do you understand how it feels to want to belong to someone?"

His question scraped raw the wounds inside. Her eyes smarted with tears. "I do."

"I'm drawn to you, Kate."

"Y-you are?" *He wouldn't be if knew the truth about you,* an ugly voice inside her head said accusingly. *No!* Dread slithered through her. *Josh can never find out.*

"You're the sweetest woman I know. Intelligent. Honest. Above reproach."

Honest. Above reproach. The words reverberated through her brain like continued striking of a gong.

After his ordeal, of course he would place an even higher importance on these particular qualities. He couldn't know she was neither of those things.

"I'm not—"

A movement on the edge of her field of vision registered a split second before Josh was hauled backward. She heard the crack of bone striking bone as a balled-up fist connected with his face.

"Josh!" she screamed, her mind scrambling to make sense of the scene being played out in front of her.

Landing hard on the ground, he rolled away before the man's boot could find its target. He scrambled upright and rushed his attacker. They fell in a heap not far from her feet, limbs flying, grunts terrorizing the night.

The stranger's hat went flying. One look and Kate knew his identity. Tyler.

Cold fear constricted her lungs, slowing her blood flow, making her heart flounder. Help! She had to get help!

Her feet like lead, she hurried to find someone—anyone—who could stop Tyler from harming Josh. What if he had a gun? she thought frantically.

A group of men had congregated near the wagons. "Please! Come quick!" she yelled, chest heaving.

"What's the matter, Miss?"

"Josh. He's being attacked!"

They ran past her, warning her to stay put. Instead, she stumbled after them, skidding to a stop at the corner of the barn. *God in Heaven, please let him be all right.*

All she could see were Josh and Tyler scuffling in the grass near the tree line.

More men were streaming from the barn, passing her and crowding around the dueling pair, blocking her view. Nathan rushed past, shouting at her. "Go inside, Kate! Find Ma and stay with her!"

Megan appeared at her side. "Nathan's right." Putting an arm around Kate's shoulders, she urged her to leave. "It's safer inside."

"But what if he's hurt?"

"Josh can hold his own. Besides, look at all those men," she said soothingly. "They'll have it broken up in no time."

Kate reluctantly allowed herself to be led away. Sam and Mary met them outside the door. Once she explained what had happened, Sam insisted on taking the women home. Upset, but not willing to argue with her hosts, she found herself sandwiched between the two on the bench seat of their wagon.

As Sam led his team away from the Foster farm, she craned her neck in an attempt to see any sign of Josh. Mary patted her knee. "He'll be just fine, dear. Don't you worry."

"She's right," Josh's father echoed. "By now I'd wager they've got Matthews under arrest, and Josh is giving his account to the sheriff."

* * *

Adrenaline pulsed through Josh's body. He fought to free himself from the hands restraining him, preventing him from finishing what Matthews had started. His enemy lay prone on the ground, face in the dirt, hands tied behind his back. Unlike Josh, he wasn't struggling.

"Calm down," Nathan growled in Josh's ear. "Unless you wanna join him in the jail tonight."

Chest heaving, he closed his eyes and concentrated on slowing his breathing. His pulse thundered in his ears. His jaw ached from that first blow, and he suspected he might have a busted rib or two.

He twisted his head around to skewer his brother with his gaze. "Where's Kate?" he grunted.

"Safe."

Sheriff Timmons strolled over. His hand resting near his gun handle, he leveled his gaze at Josh. "You boys can let him go now."

They released him. Reaching up, he rubbed his sore jaw.

"What happened here, O'Malley?"

"Matthews ambushed me. I defended myself."

"Why would he do that?" He spit a stream of tobacco juice.

Aware of all the curious ears listening in, Josh said, "Can we speak in private, Sheriff?"

He studied Josh a long moment before waving the crowd away. "All right, go on about your business, gentlemen." To his deputy, he said, "Take Matthews and load him in the wagon."

The deputy hauled him to his feet. Matthews glared at Josh as he was led past. "Stay away from my Lily, or else," he snarled.

Josh clenched his hands in tight fists to keep from lunging at him. He reminded himself that the man was not in his right mind.

When everyone had gone, only he and Nathan were left behind.

The lawman cocked a brow.

"It's okay," Josh said. "My brother already knows what's going on."

"And what's that?"

"Matthews believes our guest, Kate Morgan, is his dead wife." He went on to explain the encounters Kate had had with him. "She and I were out here talking when he appeared out of nowhere and punched me."

He spit again. "You know I can't hold him based on your word alone. I'll keep him overnight for disturbing the peace, but he'll be free by noon."

Josh hadn't expected anything more. "I understand."

"I suggest you keep your eyes and ears open, gentlemen."

"Will do, Sheriff."

"G'night." He tipped his hat and walked toward his wagon.

Nathan turned to him. "You okay?"

"I will be as soon as I figure out what to do about Matthews."

"Tough to reason with a drunkard."

"I can't stand by and do nothing." Spotting his hat on the ground, he picked it up and slapped it against his leg to dislodge the dirt. "This man has lost all sense of reality. Kate's not safe with him walking around loose."

"So what's your plan?"

"I don't know yet. But I'll figure something out. You can count on it."

* * *

Alone in her cabin, Kate paced from one window to the next, flicking the curtains aside to peer into the darkness. Where was he? Edgy with nervousness, she was ready to jump out of her skin. Not knowing where or how he was doing was driving her mad!

Sam and Mary had volunteered to wait up and keep her company, but she'd declined their offer. Riding away from the Foster farm, she'd been sorely tempted to cast aside ingrained notions of polite behavior and demand they take her back. Somehow she'd managed to maintain an air of tranquility.

Her imagination conjured up torturous images of Josh, hurt and bleeding.

Pressing her fingers against her throbbing temples, her eyes squeezed shut, she attempted to block out the horrifying image of Tyler's fist slamming into Josh. Over and over again. Josh's grunts as he defended himself against the blows.

A light step on the porch had her running for the door. Yanking it open, she fell into his arms and sobbed. "I was so worried."

His fingers trailed lightly across her back, but he didn't return her embrace. "Please don't cry." His voice was soft.

She tightened her hold, and he sucked in a painful breath. Immediately she released him, gasping at the sight of his face.

Blood trickled from an inch-wide gash on his right cheekbone. His lower lip was busted. There were bits of grass and hay in his hair and a rip in the shoulder of his shirt. His left hand cradled his ribs.

"Oh, Josh," she whimpered, knowing this was all because of *her*. Tyler wanted her. And Josh was standing in his way.

"It's not as bad as it looks."

Taking his free hand, she led him inside and closed the door. "Have a seat at the table."

Removing his hat, he laid it aside and fluffed his hair. He pulled out a chair and eased into it, his gaze following her every move.

When she'd gathered a bowl of water and hand towels, she told him, "I have no nursing experience, but I found a stray dog once. I doctored his injured leg for him."

His mouth curled in response, reopening the cut in his lip. "Ouch." He went to touch it, but she captured his wrist before he could.

"Let me clean it." She folded the white towel into a square, submerged it in the water and squeezed out the excess.

"Wait."

Standing over him, she held the towel aloft and looked into his impossibly blue eyes. His hair was rumpled, his jawline darkened by a day's growth of stubble. The top buttons of his shirt were undone, revealing a light patch of hair beneath his collarbone.

"Before you proceed, I need to know how the dog fared."

She hid a smile. "I'm happy to say he did quite well."

"All right, then," he drawled. "Go ahead and do what you gotta do."

She studied the gash on his cheek. "I'll be as gentle as I can, okay?"

She cleaned it the best she could and applied a thin layer of ointment. Josh sat with his eyes closed the entire time.

"I think you need stitches."

"Not a big fan of needles."

"Me, either, but it might scar without them."

"Can you bandage it?"

"Sure." She did as he asked, then turned her attention to his other injury.

Bending closer, her hair swinging forward, she carefully pressed a clean cloth against his lower lip. Opening his eyes, he stared at her from beneath heavy lids, revealing a curious mix of pain and longing.

They remained that way, he sat motionless and she bent over him, her free hand braced against the back of his chair. Then he eased her hand away from his mouth. The cloth fell to the table.

Reaching up, he twined her hair around his finger. "You have beautiful hair," he rasped, "like chocolate. And so incredibly soft…"

Kate swallowed hard, afraid to breathe. He was going to kiss her. His words scrolled through her mind… *I'm drawn to you, Kate.*

He brought her mouth down to his. Fireworks exploded behind her eyes. Clinging to his shoulders, she tentatively returned the pressure of his lips, careful of his injury.

In a move that startled her, Josh shoved to his feet without releasing her. Holding her close, his hands spanning her back, he kissed her tenderly. She held tight to him, lost in a swirl of emotions.

You're playing with fire, Kate. Allowing him to kiss her, to hold her, only fanned the flames of her feelings. This man was a dream come true. He was everything she'd ever wanted in a husband. Yet he was out of reach.

Josh eased the pressure of his lips. With a shuddering

sigh, he folded her in his arms and buried his face in her hair. "My sweet Kate," he whispered.

Pulling away, she touched a trembling hand to her mouth.

"Everything all right?"

Gathering her courage, she blurted out, "Don't do that again."

"What? Kiss you?" Stiffening, his eyebrows slammed together. "I didn't exactly plan it. But I got the feeling you enjoyed it as much as I did."

"It's not wise." She stared down at the smooth floor-boards. "You and I aren't courting. We're friends. That's all. There's no future for us."

He was quiet so long, she at last looked up. His expression was one of acceptance tinged with regret. "You're right. I apologize. It won't happen again."

Grabbing his hat, he dropped it on his head. "It's late. I should go."

Heart heavy, she stayed rooted to the spot as he strode across the room and slipped out the door. Why did doing the right thing have to hurt so much?

Chapter Fourteen

The next morning, Josh woke to someone nudging his shoulder.

"Wake up, Josh." Nathan stood over him. "Time to get up and get your Sunday clothes on."

"It's Saturday," he grumbled, pressing his face farther into the pillow. Saturday was the only day of the week he allowed himself an extra half hour of sleep and his brother was ruining it.

"Kate's taking portraits today."

He came instantly awake at the sound of her name. Scooting up in the bed, he leveled a look at his brother. "Who decided this?"

Nathan shrugged. "I'm not in on the decision making around here. I just do what I'm told."

Josh quirked an eyebrow. They both knew that wasn't entirely true. His younger brother was easygoing, yes, but he was definitely his own man.

"What about Caleb? Did he agree to be in it?"

His youngest brother's accident had changed him from a fun-loving jokester to a quiet, embittered loner. Nothing they did or said seemed to make a difference.

Slathering the shaving soap on his face, Nathan turned down his lips. "He agreed only because Ma pleaded with him."

Caleb's behavior troubled both his parents, but Ma was taking it especially hard. It was tough not to get frustrated with his stubbornness, but all they could do at this point was pray for God to change his heart.

Swinging his legs around, Josh planted both feet on the floor. His ribs ached something terrible. Pain radiated through his chest with every breath. "Can you wrap me up?" He grimaced.

His brother regarded him through the mirror. "Yep. Give me a minute."

Josh reached up and touched the bandage on his cheek. "How am I supposed to be in a portrait with a busted-up face?" Had they forgotten what happened last night?

Nathan shrugged. "Don't ask me."

Wondering why they couldn't have simply waited, he glanced out the window at the gray, overcast day. He hoped it didn't rain and ruin Kate's plans.

Was she still upset with him? He'd acted foolishly, allowing his attraction to her to overrule his common sense, and she'd stopped him from going any further.

Thankfully it was merely infatuation driving him and not true feelings. Kate was a sweet, intelligent, lovely woman. Any man would be tempted to care for her. And he did like her…as a friend.

How could he not? She was sunshine in winter, a rainbow in the midst of thunderclouds. When he was with her, worries faded and all he could think about was making her smile.

But he couldn't allow himself to fall in love with her. It would only mean heartbreak for them both.

By the time Nathan had wrapped his ribs, Josh was dizzy with pain. Sweat beaded his brow. Bracing himself against the dresser, he waited for the searing pain to pass.

"You don't look so good," his brother stated flatly. "I'm going downstairs to tell Ma you're not up to this."

"Wait." He didn't want to ruin Kate's day.

"No," Nathan said, already heading for the door. "At this rate, you'll pass out before you get one leg in your pants."

Shuffling to the bed, Josh eased down onto the feather-stuffed mattress. Between his facial injuries and his cracked ribs, he felt as if he'd gone head-to-head with an angry bull. Matthews had been furious, all right. But at least Josh had held his own.

The fight had given townsfolk even more to gossip about. Frustrated and physically weak, he drifted back to sleep. It was nearing noon when Ma entered his room with a tray bearing a bowl of vegetable soup and two dinner rolls shiny with melted butter. His stomach rumbled. He couldn't remember when he'd last eaten.

Placing it on his bedside table, she straightened and looked at him with concern. "How are you feeling?"

"Better." And he did, as long as he didn't move.

"Do you need help with this?" She touched his shoulder.

"No, thanks, Ma. I can manage."

She gazed down at him a long moment, assessing him. "All right. If you need anything just holler." She turned to leave.

"Ma?"

She turned back. "Hmm?"

"Was Kate terribly disappointed?"

The wrinkles fading from her brow, she gave him a

gentle smile. "Not at all. She was very concerned about you."

"Oh?"

"Yes. I shouldn't have insisted on doing them today anyway. I didn't get a good look at your face last night. Are you hurting? I can get you something for the pain."

"It's not so bad."

"Eat something," she urged on her way out the door. "You'll feel better."

"Yes, Ma."

He managed to eat it all before lying back down and sleeping the day away. It was dusk when he finally awoke. Muscles stiff, he moved cautiously as he first sat, then stood to his feet. Not thrilled at having wasted an entire day in bed, he went downstairs in search of a cup of coffee and a bite to eat.

His parents were in the living room. "Feeling better, son?" Pa looked up from his newspaper.

"A little."

Ma looked up from her mending. "Are you sure you should be up walking around?"

He wasn't sure at all. But he wasn't one to lie around. "I'll be fine."

"I set aside a plate for you. Want some coffee?"

"I'll get it."

Once he'd eaten his fill, he went to retrieve his fiddle from the hutch in the corner, careful not to jar his ribs. His soul was in need of soothing, and music never failed to do that.

"Are you playing outside tonight?"

"Yeah. Are you gonna sit out there for a spell?"

"I don't think so."

His mother worked from sunup to sundown. She

needed to take more breaks, in his opinion. "Are you sure? The weather will be turning cold before long." He looked to his father. "What about you, Pa?"

He pushed his spectacles up his nose. "You go on ahead. I think I'll sit right here and keep your ma company."

"Want me to prop the door open then?"

"That would be nice, dear." His ma smiled over at him.

Nudging the footstool against the door, he stepped out into the dark night, lit up from one end of the sky to the other by thousands of twinkling stars. It was a pleasant night, the air sweet with the curious mix of apples and mums. His gaze went immediately to the cabin at the edge of the woods. Lamplight shined through the windows, which meant Kate was still awake. He wondered what she was doing, if she was perhaps reading or penning letters or some other pastime well-to-do young ladies indulged in.

With a sigh, he rested his weight against the railing and, tucking his instrument beneath his chin, brought the bow up and slid it along the taut strings. His eyes drifted shut. The music flowed from somewhere deep inside, and he played without conscious thought.

He played songs his father and grandfather had taught him as a child. Bit by bit, his muscles relaxed, the tension seeping from his body.

He played for nearly an hour. When he lowered his instrument and stared up at the stars, he heard soft clapping from the direction of the cabin. Squinting through the darkness, he could just make out Kate's silhouette. His heart tripped.

"You make beautiful music, Josh O'Malley," she called in her cultured, warm voice.

"I'm glad you enjoyed the impromptu concert," he answered, walking to the edge of the porch.

"I did. Very much."

He held up a finger. "Wait there. I'll be right back."

Returning his instrument to the hutch, he went back outside and crossed the yard with long strides, stopping at the base of the steps.

Standing in the shadows of the overhang, she studied him. "I'm glad to see you up and around."

With one hand on the railing, he settled a boot on the bottom step. "I'll have to take things a little slower than usual, that's all."

"I'm sorry, Josh," she said solemnly. "If it weren't for me, none of this would've happened. You wouldn't have been hurt."

"Don't say that. Your resembling Lily Matthews is an unfortunate coincidence. We'll have to find a way to deal with this."

Stepping forward into the moonlight, he could see the fear written plainly across her features. "What if he has a gun next time?"

"I'll be armed from here on out."

She worried her bottom lip with even, white teeth.

"Hey—" he climbed the steps and took hold of her hand "—remember we have a Heavenly Father who's promised never to leave us or turn His back on us. 'Where can I go from Your Spirit? Where can I flee from Your presence? If I go up to the Heavens, You are there. If I make my bed in the depths, You are there.'"

"'If I rise on the wings of the dawn,'" she continued softly, "'if I settle on the far side of the sea, even there Your hand will guide me, Your right hand will hold me fast.'"

Kate found comfort in the reminder of God's care and protection. There was nowhere she could go where He wasn't. She had to believe He would protect Josh.

She studied his dear face. His split lip didn't look too bad, but the angry gash on his cheek was edged with bruises. Seeing him battered and bruised hurt her heart.

She hadn't wanted to acknowledge the truth, but Tyler's attack had forced the issue.

What she felt for this man was not a mere passing fancy. These were not shallow feelings. No, what had started as an infatuation had taken root and blossomed into a deep, abiding love.

A love she could never express or give free rein to.

Feeling ill, she tugged her hand free and pressed it against her roiling stomach. It was a struggle to maintain an air of calm. "I'm suddenly very tired. I think I'll turn in early."

Unaware of her inner turmoil, he descended the steps. "Sweet dreams, Kate."

Clutching the post to keep from falling in a heap, she watched his tall form as he walked away, her heart aching with the knowledge he could never be hers.

Kate's dreams that night and the nights following were not at all sweet. An angry Tyler chased her through the woods. Josh was there, too, just out of reach. He called to her, but no matter how hard she tried, she couldn't run fast enough.

She awoke Thursday morning with a heavy feeling in her chest. The sound of rain spattering across the roof promised a gray day to match her mood. Her plans to take photographs of the town would have to be postponed.

There was a chill in the air, the floor cold against her

bare feet. She dressed quickly in an unadorned brown skirt and sunny-yellow shirtwaist in defiance of the gloomy weather. Pulling on a pair of brown leather ankle boots, she dashed through the rain to the main house.

She'd managed to avoid Josh all week and hoped to do the same today. How could she act normal around him? Pretend to be happy when her heart ached at the sight of him?

So far, no one had noticed anything amiss. Or if anyone had, no one had commented on it. Josh had kept himself busy in his workshop, so she hadn't had to endure his presence during mealtimes.

Seeing only Mary in the house, she let out a sigh of relief. But her relief was short-lived. After a simple breakfast, Mary asked if she'd mind taking a biscuit and jug of milk out to Josh's workshop. She did mind, but she couldn't refuse her hostess's simple request. Not without offending her or raising suspicions.

Praying for strength, she entered his workshop. Bent over a waist-high table with a chisel in his hand, he didn't see her at first. A half-assembled chair stood nearby.

She seized the chance to steel her resolve. *Think of him as a friend. A confidant. A buddy.*

Looking anywhere but at him, she surveyed his shop. A cozy space, well-lit with kerosene lamps, he kept it neat and orderly. Tools of all shapes and sizes hung on pegs on the wall beside him. Farther back stood saws and machines she hadn't seen before. The scents of pine and wood stain hung in the air.

"Good morning." He noticed her presence and set aside his tools.

As he straightened, his quick smile slipped into a frown.

The careful way he moved was unmistakable. "Your ribs are still hurting, aren't they?"

"They're much improved, but still a bit sore." He spied the things in her hands. "Ma sent breakfast, did she? All I had this morning was a cup of coffee."

Wiping his hands on a towel, he came around the table and took the jar and bundled napkin from her. "Thanks." Taking in the wet spots on her blouse, he said, "Doesn't look like it's gonna let up anytime soon, does it?"

"No." She grimaced. "I'd planned to take photographs of the church today."

He was standing too close. *Do not think about his tender kisses.*

The door scraped open. "Josh, I need—" Caleb stopped and stared at the two of them, his mouth firming in disapproval. Sweeping off his hat, he dipped his head. "Miss Morgan. Pardon the interruption." His gaze swung to Josh. "I need to borrow your hammer. Mine broke."

"Here you go." Josh slipped the tool off its peg and handed it to Caleb. "What are you working on?"

"Building more shelves in the barn." He turned and left without another word.

"I'm curious about something."

"What's that?"

Kate moved away from him and pretended interest in the chair he'd been assembling.

"How come you don't work in the dairy with your father and brothers?"

With a poignant smile, he carefully leaned back against the table and put his hands in his pockets. "My grandfather was a master woodworker. Every summer during our visits to his house, I'd beg to help him build something. The summer I turned ten, he decided I was old enough to help without hurting myself. He was a good teacher. Patient. Taught me everything I know.

"Soon I started collecting tools. I cleared out a space in our barn where I could work after my chores were done." He shifted his weight. "My dad was great. He gave me the freedom to choose my path. And I'm fortunate my brothers didn't mind the dairy business. Nathan's a natural animal lover, and Caleb likes the solitary nature of the job."

Glancing at the stacks of lumber in the corner, she murmured, "So you're doing what you love and making a living at it."

And I'm the reason your dream of expanding fell apart.

"I'm a fortunate man."

How could he stand to look at her after what she'd done? Flouncing into town and invading his home, his family and, ultimately, his business. In that instant, she knew she couldn't stay. If he didn't want to purchase the store from her, she'd give it to him. He'd be angry, of course, his pride wounded, but she'd be long gone before he found out.

"Josh," said Nathan, as he shoved open the door, his face and hair dripping wet. "Bess is terrible sick, and Pa's getting the wagon ready for deliveries later today. Can you lend me a hand?"

"Sure." He untied his apron and hung it on the wall. When he stopped in front of Kate, his eyes held a touch of disappointment. "In case you forgot, Bess is the brand-new momma cow. I'm not sure how long I'll be. This may take a while."

Relieved at the interruption, she managed, "I'll go and see if Mary needs my help with anything."

"I'll see you later." Plucking his hat off the table and settling it on his head, he followed Nathan out into the downpour.

Kate didn't move for the longest time. As soon as she had a chance, she'd pen a letter explaining everything. Then she'd make preparations to leave Gatlinburg.

Sorrow squeezed her heart. Unable to face anyone, she decided against returning to the main house and dashed across the soggy yard to her cabin.

In an effort to push aside thoughts of leaving, she wrote her parents a letter. She also wrote to her sister, careful to keep it impersonal. If Francesca guessed Kate's feelings for Josh, who knew how she'd react.

The remainder of the day passed slowly. The rain continued through the afternoon, and eventually she grew drowsy from the unrelenting pitter-patter against the roof. Stretching out on the sofa, she pulled the quilt up to her chin and drifted to sleep.

The dream started innocently enough. Another party at the estate. Couples dancing and laughing. Soon the bright, cheerful colors dimmed. The guests disappeared. Now it was just her and Wesley. Walking down the long, dark corridors of the basement in search of the wine cellar. This was a maid's or butler's job, she mentioned. He wanted to see her father's celebrated collection for himself, he said. And glorying in his undivided attention, she happily led the way.

Inside the low, brick-walled room, Wesley stood very near. He held her hand. Told her she was beautiful. The candle flame flickered out, utter darkness descended and her childhood fears overtook her. Terror caught her in its grip. Shaking uncontrollably, she reached out frantically for Wesley.

His voice soothed her as he pulled her into his strong embrace.

"No." She shook her head. "We mustn't."

His hands gripped her shoulders. "Kate, wake up."

"No." She twisted her head away. "Wesley, stop!"

"Kate!" He gently shook her, his voice very near her ear.

But it wasn't Wesley's voice. It was Josh's

Slowly she became aware of her surroundings. She was lying on the sofa in the cabin. And Josh was there, sitting on the edge of the cushion, leaning over her.

His eyes were dark with concern. "Kate, you were having a bad dream."

Shoving her hair out of her eyes, she scooted up into a sitting position. "I must've dozed off."

As he stood to his feet, his gaze remained fixed on her. "Who's Wesley?"

Josh watched the tumble of emotions on Kate's face. She turned her gaze away.

"He's, um, a friend of the family's."

Her reaction to a simple question had his senses on high alert.

"And you were dreaming about him?"

She stood to fold the quilt, smoothing it into a tidy square. "People dream about friends and acquaintances all the time, don't they? Even those they don't see on a daily basis."

Her effort to remain casual told him there was something more to this than she was letting on. "It wasn't a pleasant dream. Did he hurt you?"

She hesitated a second too long. "No."

When she made to move past him, he caught her arm.

Her shadowed eyes flew to his face. "Your sister deceived me. Don't do that to me, Kate."

The color drained from her face. "I would never hurt you the way she did," she insisted, anguish underscoring her words.

He believed her. Still, doubt wormed its way into his mind. She was keeping something from him.

He dropped his hand, unsettled by the entire exchange. He'd come to bring her a plate of food, since she hadn't shown up for supper. When he'd walked in and seen her asleep on the sofa, he hadn't been able to resist watching her for a moment.

She'd looked so peaceful—a sweet smile on her lips, her dark hair spread out in a curtain across the pillow. In an instant, her sleep had become troubled. And when she'd starting calling out, he'd decided to wake her.

He stoked up the fire, gritting his teeth at the pain shooting up his sides. It had been an exhausting day. Pushing and prodding a sick cow hadn't helped his injured ribs. "Your supper is on the table."

She didn't respond. He heard the scrape of chair legs on the floor and assumed she was eating. When he turned, she was sitting at the table all right. But she wasn't eating. Hands resting in her lap, she was staring out the window. Her dejected expression wrenched his heart.

Blowing out a breath, Josh went to her. Crouching down, he covered her hands with his.

When she angled her face down, her pale eyes shimmered with unshed tears.

"Please don't be upset. I wasn't comparing you to your sister. You have a sensitive, caring heart. I know you wouldn't willingly hurt anyone."

"Oh, Josh—" her lower lip trembled "—have you ever done something you later regretted?"

"Of course." He gave a sardonic laugh. Asking Francesca to marry him ranked at the top of the list.

"Me, too." Her gaze skittered away. "I believe the Bible when it says God forgives me when I mess up. My head believes it, but at times I have a tough time convincing my heart."

"Sometimes you have to set aside your feelings and make the conscious decision to trust in His promises. 1 John 1:9 says, 'If we confess our sins, He is faithful and just and will forgive us our sins and purify us from all unrighteousness.' He forgives us, not because we deserve it, but because of His goodness and the love He has for us."

"You're right," she said softly. "I have to keep reminding myself."

"Is there something bothering you? I've been told I'm a good listener."

"I've no doubt about that." She pressed her fingertips to her temples. "Actually, I have a headache. I think I might retire for the night."

"It may be you need to eat something." Josh stood. "I'll leave you to eat your supper in peace. See you in the morning?"

"Sure." She seemed distracted.

She made to rise, but he stopped her with a hand on her shoulder. "Sit. I'll let myself out. Just remember to lock it before you go to sleep."

Walking across the damp yard, he couldn't shake the feeling of unease. Francesca had been involved with another man throughout the duration of their courtship. She'd been toying with him. Using him to make another man jealous. Any man would be distrustful after tangling with a deceitful woman.

Kate's different, he reminded himself.

Why, then, had she acted so strangely when he'd inquired about the man in her dreams?

Face facts, O'Malley. You want her for yourself, and the idea of any other man having a claim on her doesn't sit well with you.

No, that wasn't true. He'd been careful to guard his heart.

Kate Morgan wasn't the woman for him.

Keep telling yourself that, O'Malley. You just may start to believe it.

Chapter Fifteen

Something was bothering Kate.

He could see it in the slight slump of her shoulders and the sadness tingeing her smiles. Her gorgeous green eyes no longer sparkled. And she was eating even less than usual.

Despite various attempts to get her alone, he hadn't succeeded. She was deliberately avoiding him, and he couldn't figure out why.

Perhaps today he'd get answers.

Reaching into the wardrobe cabinet, he slipped his gray suit off the hook and dressed with care. She was taking photographs of their family today. The gash on his cheek had healed enough so that it wouldn't show.

"See ya downstairs," said Nathan, shaved and dressed in his dark brown suit, as he disappeared through the doorway.

Five minutes later, Josh descended the steps in a hurry, only to jerk to a stop at the bottom. Kate was there in the living room gazing out the window, a vision in a creamy yellow confection of a dress that complemented her lustrous brown hair and green eyes. She turned at the sound of his footsteps.

Was it his imagination or had he seen a flash of longing on her face before she'd schooled her features?

"Good morning, Kate. How did you sleep?"

"I slept well, thank you."

Her polite smile wedged beneath his skin like a splinter. "I don't believe you."

Startled, her composure slipped. "Excuse me?"

Reaching up, he lightly touched a fingertip to the bruised skin beneath her eyes. "Your face tells another story."

Sucking in a breath, she stepped back. "I—I don't know what you're talking about."

His patience snapped. Closing the distance between them, he clasped her hands. "What's wrong, Kate? I know something's bothering you. I—"

"We're ready if you are, Kate." His mother, wearing her favorite pink floral dress and the pearl necklace his father had given her on the day of their wedding, bustled in from the kitchen.

Dropping her hands, Josh paced away from her.

"I have everything set up on the front lawn."

"Lead on, then," said Mary, smiling with enthusiasm.

Out front, his father and Caleb waited beneath the branches of a hundred-year-old oak. Pa, still fit and in good health, looked dapper in his pin-striped suit. Caleb paced in his gray trousers, black brocade vest and burgundy dress shirt, his expression clearly stating he'd rather be anywhere else.

Kate approached her camera perched on its stand, removed the lens cover and peered into the viewfinder. Straightening, she moved with careful steps to survey the area, all intense concentration and focus.

The first portrait was to be of the entire family. With an easy manner and pleasant yet firm tone, she directed everyone into position, all the while avoiding eye contact with Josh.

"All right, everyone." She circled behind her camera, scalloped lace underskirts catching on the blades of grass. Framed against the dreary skies, she was a burst of sunshine. "I need for you to stand very still until the exposure is complete. It takes approximately sixty seconds."

Stooping to peer through the viewfinder, she recapped the lens only until she'd removed the cover from the dry plate. "Ready? Here goes." Then, snatching off the lens cover, she held up her hand to remind them not to move.

"Got it!" She beamed after a minute. "Now, Sam and Mary, how about one with just the two of you? Then I can take one of your sons by themselves."

Josh and his brothers stood off to the side while Kate maneuvered their parents into place. He didn't miss the love in his mother's eyes as she glanced up at his father, nor the tender way he held her close. Life on a working farm and raising three rambunctious boys couldn't have been easy. They'd faced their share of hardships, but it had only made them stronger as a couple. And they'd learned to find joy in the simple things.

He wanted that same loving partnership for himself. He studied Kate. If only things were different…

"Josh? Hello?" Nathan snapped his fingers in front of his face. "It's our turn."

Embarrassed to be caught woolgathering, he was quiet as he headed toward the desired spot. Passing by her, he inhaled her citrusy scent and, unable to resist, tugged on a lemon-hued ribbon entwined in her dark locks. The backs of his fingers brushed against her nape.

She sucked in a breath, turned wide, questioning eyes on him. The air between them shimmered with unspoken longing. Okay, he shouldn't have done that.

Nathan cleared his throat. Josh dropped his hand. *Get a grip, O'Malley.*

"You, ah, had a ribbon out of place," he murmured. "It's fixed now."

Cheeks blazing, she nodded and turned to direct his brothers. Her voice was not as steady as before, but she maintained her businesslike approach.

When she'd taken the photograph, Caleb groused, "Are we done? I've got work to do."

Before anyone could answer, he stomped off toward the house to change. The door slammed behind him.

"Wait—" Mary clasped her hands together "—we don't have a picture of you, Kate. Do you think you could show Samuel what to do so that you can have your picture made with the boys?"

Kate appeared uncertain. "I suppose so. Are you positive you want one?"

"Of course, dear." She patted Kate on the shoulder. "You're part of the family now."

She dipped her head, but not before Josh caught sight of the sudden tears springing to her eyes. He yearned to hold her then, to ease her loneliness. Anger rose hot and swift in his chest at the way her parents and sister had alienated her, made her feel inadequate. How could they not see how kindhearted and special she was?

When she'd finished showing Pa how to work the camera, Mary suggested, "Why don't you stand over there with Joshua and Nathan?"

Nathan settled a hand on Josh's shoulder and addressed her. "Sorry, Ma, I've got a barn full of cows waitin' to be milked. Kate, I hope you understand."

With a parting squeeze, he strode away. Josh made a mental note to take both of his brothers to task later on. While Caleb had been just plain rude, Nathan had bailed in a sly attempt to push the two of them together.

Ma linked an arm with Kate and him and guided them to the tree. "I suppose it's just the two of you, then." She sounded much too cheerful to his ears.

Flushed with embarrassment, Kate glanced over at Josh and caught his intense scrutiny. Did this make him uneasy? It certainly made her feel that way. The knowledge that she was leaving made being near him difficult.

Mary urged them closer until their shoulders touched, then went to stand beside Sam. "Look and see if that's gonna be a good shot," she urged.

"I'm curious," Josh said softly without turning his head, "how many portraits you've had taken of yourself. Since you're usually behind the camera, that is."

Still staring at the camera, she replied, "Very few. I'm sorry you've been placed in this position. Don't feel compelled to ask for a copy of the print if you don't want one."

"Why would you say that?" He did turn his head then. "Of course I want one."

Though she knew it was irrational, his vehemence pleased her deep inside.

"All right, you two," Mary called, "we're ready. Joshua, unless you want to be caught forever mooning at Kate, look over here."

Kate heard his heavy sigh and almost smiled. Hardly daring to breathe, they stood unmoving until Sam replaced the cover as she'd instructed him to do.

"I guess that's it," Mary announced with satisfaction. "Thank you so much, Kate."

"It was my pleasure," she assured her, moving to gather up her equipment. "I'll develop these as soon as possible and make sure you get a copy of each one."

Josh's hand closed over hers. "I'll help you with this."

She released the tripod stand with reluctance. "Thank you."

Mary and Sam headed for the house. Beside her, Josh was quiet as they walked across the yard. When he'd deposited her gear on the table, he slipped his hands into his pockets and regarded her with questioning eyes.

"Well?"

"Well what?"

"Are you going to tell me what's wrong?"

"Josh." She sighed.

"Is it me? Have I done something to anger you or make you upset?"

"I'm leaving."

His head jerked back. "Gatlinburg?"

Gripping the top rung of the chair rail, she nodded. "It's time."

"I don't understand," he ground out. "What about the studio? And your book?"

"I can't get over the fact that I'm standing in the way of your dream. If you don't want the store space, I'll put it up for sale. As for the book, I'm shelving that idea for the time being. Perhaps in the future…"

"You didn't do it intentionally."

"My intentions are irrelevant."

"What can I do to convince you that I don't blame you for any of this?"

"Simply put—I can't enjoy it. Every time I step foot

in there, I think of you and your furniture and all the hard work you've done to achieve your goals. I've made up my mind, Josh. Nothing you can say will change it."

The next morning, Josh was in that drifting state between sleep and wakefulness when his mother poked her head in his room. "Joshua? Are you awake?"

"Not exactly," he mumbled into the pillow.

"Are you going to be around today?"

He struggled to open his eyes. "Yeah. I'll be in the workshop. Why?"

"Your father and I have some business to attend to. Caleb is accompanying us."

That got his attention. Pushing upward, he peered at her. "Oh? What did you use to bribe him?"

Ignoring his remark, she said, "Nathan is headed over to the Foster farm, and I'm not sure what time he plans to be back. I don't want Kate left alone. Can you keep an eye on her?"

"Sure. I'll be around all day."

"Oh, good," she said, relieved. "I'm going down to fix coffee."

When she'd left, Josh cradled his head in his hands and stared up at the ceiling.

Kate's announcement yesterday had sent him reeling. While he was touched by her concern for his happiness, he couldn't comprehend her reasoning. He'd seen her in action—it was plain as day that she loved her work. Owning a studio would not only give her an avenue to pursue her passion, it would also grant her independence from her family. She had a chance at a new life here.

She had new friends. And his family had practically

adopted her. Not only that, but she loved these mountains as much as he did.

After all the sorrow in her life, she deserved this.

It also struck him as odd that he wasn't jumping at the chance to take possession of the store. Here she was, offering to hand it over, and all he could think about was her happiness.

He may not have a store to stock, but he still had customer orders to fill.

There'd be other opportunities for him to expand, but apparently God had other plans at this time. So he'd just keep doing what he'd been doing. Taking individual orders and doing his utmost to please his customers.

Lord, I'm so confused. The thought of her leaving kills me. Help me, Father. I must keep my wits about me. Remember all the reasons we can't be together.

Downstairs in the kitchen, he asked, "Have you seen Kate this morning?"

"She stopped in earlier." Ma wrapped her shawl around her shoulders. "All she wanted was a cup of tea. Said she wasn't hungry."

"Hmm." Brows pulled together, Josh glanced out the dining room windows. Had she been eating at all the past few days? Worried, he debated going over there.

Then he noticed the sky's odd color. "Are you going far? Looks like it might rain."

"No. And I'm sure your father will keep an eye on the weather. See you later, dear."

She went to join his father and brother in the barn, and he heard the team pull out not long after. He ate his breakfast with haste, not lingering to savor his coffee as he would've if Kate had joined him at the table.

Outside, a stiff breeze raised goose bumps on his arms.

Holding on to his hat, his boots ate up the distance between the main house and the cabin. Music greeted him on the front steps. One foot on the porch, his hand gripping the railing, he paused to listen.

The delicate, ethereal notes put him in mind of angels and cherubs, of lush flower gardens and flowing waterfalls. Kate's harp, he mused. Lovely music suited to a sophisticated, talented young lady.

Would she let him watch her play? he wondered.

A raindrop splattered on his hand, then another. Eyeing the rain-swollen clouds hanging low in the pale yellow sky, he realized with a pang of disappointment that he'd have to wait for another time. He was in for a soaking if he didn't get to his shop soon.

With one last glance at Kate's door, he pivoted on the step and sprinted away.

Kate discovered that weathering a thunderstorm in a solidly constructed mansion was vastly different than in a two-room, built-by-hand cabin. Huddled on the sofa beneath a mound of quilts, she winced at each flash of lightning and the resounding boom of thunder that shook the cabin's foundation right afterward. Dark clouds had rolled in about an hour earlier and the storm didn't show signs of abating.

Unceasing rain thundered against the roof. Gusts of wind rammed into the walls.

She hugged her Bible to her chest and prayed. She'd never lived through a tornado and so didn't know what to expect. What if one raged outside her door? What would she do? Where would she go?

The door flew open then, slamming back against the wall. Kate screamed.

Josh stood on the porch, water sluicing off his hat and poncho.

"The storm's getting worse," he shouted above the din. "Put your boots on. And a warm jacket. We're gonna take cover."

Spurred by the urgency in his voice, Kate did as she was told. While she didn't relish the thought of venturing outside, she'd rather ride out the storm in Josh's company than alone.

When she joined him on the porch, he reached past her to close the door.

"Ready?"

His concerned gaze searched hers, and it took all her willpower not to throw herself in his arms.

"I'm as ready as I'll ever be, I guess," she told him.

"Let's go then."

Her hand tucked safely in his, they hurried down the steps and dashed across the yard. Soaked to the skin in the space of a minute, she regretted not taking a hat to shield her face. The rain pelted her tender skin. The wind whipped her dripping hair in her eyes.

As soon as they reached the orchard, Kate realized their destination. The apple house.

She wanted to rail at him for his insensitivity! How dare he bring her *here* of all places?

Surely he hadn't forgotten her fear of dark, cramped spaces!

Shoving open the door, he put an insistent hand against her lower back, silently urging her inside.

Kate resisted, digging her heels in the wet soil. The sound of her heart roaring in her chest drowned out his words and the storm raging all around them. She would not, *could* not go in there.

* * *

Josh noticed at once the change that came over her. All color drained from her face, and she raised stricken eyes to his.

"I can't!" Terror radiated off her in waves. "I'm going back to the cabin!"

Thunderclouds roiled like boiling soup directly above their heads. Caught in the storm's fury, tree limbs thrashed wildly about. Tornados weren't a common occurrence in these parts, but he didn't want to chance being out in the open. And her cabin was surrounded by trees that could potentially be uprooted.

As much as he hated to cause her distress, he had to put her safety first.

"This is our best shelter," he said as he urged her forward. "I'll light one of the oil lamps before I close the door. You'll see—there will be plenty of light."

Her fingers dug into his arm, her expression begging him to find another alternative.

"You don't understand!" Her voice was high and shrill. "I'd rather be anywhere else! I'd rather stay right here than go in there."

"I'm sorry, sweetheart. This is our only choice." He hated to see her so upset, but what other option did he have?

An abandoned milk pail flew past their heads, missing them by mere inches. That settled it.

Snaking his arm around her waist, he propelled her inside. He had the door shut before she had time to resist.

There were no windows here. The darkness inside the low, squat building was complete. He couldn't make out her shape.

"Josh, no!" She gasped and lunged past him in a desperate bid for the door.

Stunned by her response, it took a split second for him to react. He darted forward and hauled her back against him, hugging her trembling body close.

"Hey," he murmured against her ear, "it's all right. You're safe here."

Something was terribly wrong. This was no ordinary fear of the dark. Josh determined right then and there he was going to find out the reason behind it. But first he had to calm her down.

"Let me go!"

Struggling against his hold, she attempted to pry his arms away, her fingernails scraping his skin. He held firm. She was crying in earnest now. The pitiful sound broke his heart.

"Kate, my love," he said as he pressed his face close to hers. "Remember my promise? You're safe with me. Remember? Safe."

He continued to murmur words of encouragement while praying furiously for help from the Almighty above. Gradually she ceased struggling, her sobs abating to hitched breaths.

She was silent for an eternity, the sound of their ragged breaths loud in the enclosed space.

"Kate?"

"Y-yes?"

"I'm going to light a lamp, okay?"

It seemed like a lifetime in coming, but at last she jerked a nod.

When he eased his arms from around her, he didn't move away until he was certain she wasn't going to bolt again. Or slide to the floor in a heap.

Jaw clenched tight enough to crack his teeth, he crouched low and swung his hand in a wide arc in search of the lamp he'd brought. His fingers brushed the glass and it toppled beyond his reach.

"Don't move, okay? I'm gonna open the door so I can see to light the lamp."

He could hear nothing but the wind howling outside.

"Kate?"

"O-okay."

Scuffing his boots along the dirt, he moved forward until he encountered the door. He eased it open. Caught up by the violent wind, leaves swirled in funnels about the yard. The chickens squawked in the confines of their house.

He'd lost precious time rounding up the skittish animals and securing the barn doors. But everyone else was gone, so it fell to him to do it alone.

Lord, please spare us. And the farm, too. Protect my family.

Working quickly, he located the lamp and fished the match out of his pocket. His fingers shook when he tried to light the wick. He grimaced. He must've transferred all his calm to Kate and in turn assumed her nervousness.

The wick flared to life, casting a golden glow in a wide circle. Setting it in the dirt near Kate's feet, he sucked in a deep breath. "I'm going to close the door. Is this enough light?"

She kept her face averted. "I think so."

He hurried to do the task, getting a face full of rain as the wind changed direction. He slipped off his hat and poncho, hanging them from a nail protruding from the shelf on the wall, then turned to stare at her bedraggled form.

"You're soaked. Would it help to take off your jacket?"

After a moment's thought, she undid the buttons and slipped it off. Her fingers were like ice when they brushed against his. Hanging her jacket on top of his poncho, he returned to her side. She rubbed her arms in an effort to get warm.

Uncertain as to what to do to comfort her, he sat down on the low bench. "Come sit with me. I'll warm you."

When she lifted her head, Josh nearly gasped at the pain and vulnerability in her expression. "I shouldn't."

"Why not?"

Her gaze slipped to the floor. "Never mind."

"Kate, please." He needed to comfort her as much as he needed to be comforted. Her outburst had rattled him as nothing else ever had.

With hesitant steps, she came and sat a good six inches away, her back ramrod straight. Feeling like a youth, he curled his arm around her shoulders and scooted in close.

"You can rest your head on my shoulder if you want," he said.

About five minutes passed before he felt her relax, her head shifting against him. He recognized it as a small victory. They sat together listening to the storm rage over their heads.

When he could stand the silence no longer, he voiced the question on the tip of his tongue. His fingertips lazily stroked her arm. "What happened to make you fear the dark?"

"It was a long time ago," she said haltingly, her muscles tensing up again. "I haven't told anyone. Ever."

"Talking about it may lessen the power it has over you."

She lifted her head but didn't move away. "Or it could make the nightmares worse."

His fingers stilled. His own body tensed. Whatever had happened, it was going to be hard to hear.

"My parents traveled quite frequently when we were young. We were left in the care of nannies and, as we got older, governesses. The spring I turned six, Mother hired Nanny Marie."

Her voice dipped so that he had to strain to hear her. "She was an angry woman. I never could figure out what I'd done to make her angry…"

Josh steeled himself, dreading her next words, yet knowing she needed to find release.

Her features twisted in hurt bewilderment. "Nearly every day for six months, she locked me in the supply closet. Left me there for hours in the dark. Common, everyday items took on a life of their own. From an adult's perspective, there was nothing in there that could've hurt me, but for a small child—" She broke off, shivering.

Rage burned in his gut at the vicious stranger who'd done this. Ruthlessly he pushed it down to deal with later. Kate had her hands full coping with her own emotions. She didn't need to deal with his, too.

"Did your parents prosecute this woman?"

"They never knew what happened. She resigned her position without warning, and we never heard from her again."

"You didn't tell them because she threatened you."

Releasing a shaky breath, she jerked a nod.

"All these years you've shouldered this burden alone. No more." He pulled her close, stroking her damp hair when she relaxed against him. "May I pray for you?"

"I'd like that."

"Lord Jesus, I ask You to heal Kate's wounds, the secret hurts she holds inside only You can see. Release her from the fear that binds her. In Christ's name, Amen."

Swiping at her eyes, she straightened. "Thank you, Josh."

"I didn't do anything."

"That's the first time anyone has prayed for me besides Danielle, my friend who showed me how to follow Christ. It means a lot to me."

His heart aching for what she'd endured, he covered her slender hand with his. "I hate that you were forced to suffer in that way. The nanny should've been sent to prison for what she did to you—an innocent child. If I could, I'd gladly wipe away every memory that torments you."

I'd kiss away each nightmare, the pure beauty of our love chasing away every shadow until no darkness remained.

Love? No, that was too strong a word. He cared deeply for Kate, but that wasn't the same as loving her. Or was it?

"I wish you could," she whispered mournfully.

Caressing her cheek, he murmured, "I can help you make new memories. Happy ones."

She encircled his wrist and leaned her cheek into his palm. Her black lashes fluttered down to rest against the translucent skin beneath her eyes.

Tenderness flooded him. He longed to take her into his arms and kiss her, but aware of her vulnerable state of mind, he held back.

Impatient pounding on the door broke them apart. Josh bolted to his feet.

The door flung open. "Josh? You in there?"

Striding the length of the space, his heart jerked at the lines of anxiety in Nathan's face. Behind him, the sky had lightened and the rain had abated. "I'm here. Kate, too."

"Come quick! Ma's been in an accident."

Chapter Sixteen

Fear flashed across Josh's face. He quickly masked it with grim determination. Their conversation forgotten, worry for Mary's well-being gnawed at Kate's insides. How bad was it? Would Mary be all right?

"I want to go with you," she said.

Eyes dark with worry, he held out his hand and she took it, relieved to be out of the dark, damp structure. Already the clouds were dispersing. Thunder rolled in the distance. Water dripped from the leaves and roof edges, pitter-pattering onto the soggy earth.

They sprinted to the front of the house, where Nathan had left the wagon, mud splattering the men's pants legs and the hem of Kate's dress. Josh lifted her with ease onto the seat and jumped up beside her. Nathan climbed up on the other side and, seizing the reins, ordered the horses forward.

The ride into town was a tense one. No one uttered a word. Kate waited for Josh to ask what had happened and what injuries Mary had sustained, but his jaw remained clenched in silence. Reaching over, she clasped his hand. His fingers gripped hers as if they were a lifeline.

He'd be devastated if… No, she stopped her mind from wandering down that path. It was too painful. Kate had grown to care a great deal for the kind, generous, loving woman. She hated to think of her in pain.

For everyone's sakes, she prayed for a positive outcome.

The lane was littered with leaves and branches snapped off by the storm. In town, the post office window was broken, and the barbershop's wooden sign was gone.

She prayed no one else had been injured.

At last they reached the doctor's home, which doubled as an office, located at the edge of town. A hand at the small of her back, Josh ushered her inside. Nathan brought up the rear.

Sam looked up from his pacing, his features softening with relief at the sight of his sons.

"How is she, Pa?"

The older man's cheek was bruised and there was a scratch on his chin, but otherwise he appeared to be fine. "Doc Owens is checking her now, but he's fairly sure she has a broken leg."

"What happened?"

"We got caught out in the storm. The horses spooked, and the wagon overturned."

Kate gaze wandered past the three men. That's when she noticed Caleb sitting in one of the parlor chairs, his head in his hands. His posture spoke of utter defeat. Despite the uneasiness he inspired in her, Kate's heart went out to him. He was obviously hurting.

Gathering her courage, she went and sat in the chair next to him. He didn't look up or acknowledge her in any way.

"Are you all right?"

"Go away."

The words were spoken without malice. In fact, she wondered at his complete lack of emotion.

"Were you with your parents when it happened?"

He was silent, utterly still for so long she assumed he'd drifted off to sleep. When he finally spoke, his words took her by surprise.

"It's my fault."

"I don't understand."

His head whipped up, his eyes spearing hers. Raw grief and bitterness burned in the dark depths. "I was leading the team when the accident happened. I couldn't control them. I'm the reason Ma is lying in there hurt."

"No, son." Sam must've overheard Caleb's remarks. He came and settled a hand on the young man's shoulder. "You're not to blame. The outcome would've been the same if one of your brothers or I had been holding the reins."

"You're wrong." Shaking off his father's touch, Caleb lunged to his feet and stalked outside, the door slamming behind him.

Sam's shoulders slumped. Nathan came up behind him, his expression sad. "Don't worry, Pa. I'll talk to him."

When he'd left, Josh crossed to the hutch where a tray was arranged with a pitcher and empty glasses. He filled one with water and handed it to his father.

"Thanks," he said absently, his gaze glued to the closed door at the end of the hall.

Josh crouched down beside Kate, balancing himself with a hand on the chair's arm. "I'm glad you're here."

"Me, too."

When the door opened and the doctor emerged, both father and son advanced on him.

"How is she?" Sam spoke first.

"As far as I can tell, her only injury, other than minor scrapes and bruises, is a broken leg. She doesn't appear to have any internal injuries, but I'd like to keep her overnight just for observation."

"I want to see her."

"Certainly." He nodded at Sam. "One visitor at a time, though. I've given her some laudanum for pain and she's drowsy."

While Sam went to see his wife, Josh asked the doctor more questions. Nathan returned without Caleb, which didn't surprise Kate. He'd been extremely upset, feeling the weight of misplaced guilt.

While she was relieved that Mary would be okay, she couldn't help worrying about the youngest O'Malley. Perhaps Josh would seek him out later. Make him see reason.

Once Josh and Nathan had peeked in on their mother and seen for themselves that she was all right, it was decided that Sam would stay the night. Back at the house, the threesome ate a simple supper of sandwiches and warmed-up soup from the day before. Lost in their own thoughts, it was a quiet meal.

The exhaustion on Josh's face mirrored how Kate felt—emotionally and physically drained.

Lying in bed not long after, Kate tossed and turned in the dim light, her mind buzzing with all that had occurred that day.

The storm. Mary's accident. The scene in the apple house.

Josh had been incredibly tender and understanding. Recalling how he'd held her, calmed her, *prayed* for her, tears spilled over onto her pillow.

It had been difficult, divulging her childhood secret. Now there were only three people on this earth who knew—Nanny Marie, Kate herself and Josh. He'd been right. Somehow, sharing that horrifying piece of her past with him had eased the grip it had on her.

But what of your other secret? His reaction to that would be drastically different, I'd guess.

A chill gripped her heart. Curled on her side beneath the covers, her skin was warm but her insides suddenly felt encased in ice.

He couldn't find out.

Don't worry. Josh hasn't professed his love to you. And he certainly isn't going to propose to you.

He may not have come right out and said it, but he believed she belonged in New York, not Gatlinburg. There would never be a reason to tell him.

The moment Kate opened her eyes, she knew she'd slept considerably past her usual wake-up time. Blowing out an exasperated breath, she slipped out of bed and dressed as quickly as she could in a serviceable black skirt, the plainest one in her wardrobe, and a burgundy blouse. Not bothering with jewelry, she captured her thick waves in a simple bun at the base of her head and slipped her black boots on over her stockings.

She'd planned to cook breakfast for the men this morning. Too late for that.

Crossing to the main house, she noticed downed tree limbs scattered across the yard. Yesterday's fierce winds had stripped a number of trees of their leaves. The air was clean and crisp this morning, the sky stretching a grayish-white above her—a reminder that winter hovered around the corner.

She knocked on the front door and waited, her stomach protesting the long hours since her last meal. Goose bumps racing along her skin, she anticipated a steaming cup of tea.

Josh opened the door, his gaze warming when he saw her. "Mornin', sleepyhead. Come in."

Closing the door behind her, he remarked, "You don't have to knock, ya know. Feel free to come and go as you please. You're not a visitor anymore."

"I hadn't planned on sleeping in."

He slipped his hands into his pockets. "Nathan left about an hour ago to check on Ma."

"You didn't stay behind on my account, did you?"

"I didn't want to leave you here alone."

She opened her mouth to protest, but he rushed ahead. "Besides, there's not much I can do there anyway. Aunt Alice and Megan are there, too. I'm sure Doc doesn't want his office overrun with visitors."

"But—"

He stepped close and pressed his finger to her lips. "Shh." His blue eyes darkened with emotion. He dropped his hand but didn't move away, his broad shoulders filling her vision. "How did you sleep?"

"Better than I have in a long time." For the first time in weeks, she'd slept a dreamless sleep.

"No nightmares?"

"No."

"I'm glad." Looking pleased, he nodded in the direction of the kitchen. "How do biscuits with apple butter sound? I'll even throw in a cup of your favorite tea."

Since her arrival, Kate had grown to love Mary's fluffy "cathead" biscuits, so called because of their size. The biscuits, with their light-as-air layers of pure delight, slathered with butter and jam, were now her breakfast of choice.

In the kitchen, she stood off to the side while he stoked

up the fire in the cookstove and set the kettle on to boil. She'd seen both Josh and Nathan in action in here. They seemed capable and completely at ease doing what was considered women's work.

"Do you think your mother will be able to come home today?"

"I sure hope so."

As he arranged the tea service, Kate studied his hands. Strong and tanned, his lean fingers handled the delicate china with care. She knew from experience the tenderness those hands possessed.

He frowned. "Our biggest challenge is going to be keeping her from doing too much, too soon. She's used to taking care of all of us. I'm not sure how she's going to handle being on the receiving end."

"I can help with that. I've decided to hold off on my travel arrangements."

"You're staying?" Hope lit up his features.

"Only until Mary is back on her feet." She looked away. "Starting with today's lunch, I'm taking over kitchen duty."

"Is that a fact?" One brow quirked up, mocking her, as he folded his arms across his chest.

"I do know how to cook."

"So you said. I'm just having a hard time believing it."

"Believe it. Immediately after breakfast, I'd like for you to bring me a chicken."

He dipped his head in mock seriousness. "Of course."

Kate wasn't surprised at his reaction. Josh saw her as a pampered, helpless heiress. Let him laugh. He would soon see that he was wrong about her.

Josh bit the inside of his cheek to keep from laughing as he deposited the squawking chicken on the floor.

Looking domestic with her sleeves rolled up to her elbows and one of Ma's aprons tied about her waist, Kate stood at the dry sink peeling carrots.

Her fine brows shot up to meet her hairline. "What is *that?*"

"You mean you don't know?"

She edged backward as the hen strutted closer. "Of course I do! But what is it doing in here?"

"You asked for a chicken. I delivered."

She planted her fist on one hip. "I meant a slaughtered one, and you know it."

He smiled at the undisguised tremor of laughter in her voice. Wayward tendrils had slipped free of her loose knot to frame her face, her cheeks tinged pink from the warmth of the cookstove heating the kitchen. Her rose-petal lips beckoned him to discover their soft fullness. It seemed like a lifetime since he'd sampled their sweet promise.

She looked completely at home in Ma's kitchen. He didn't want to think how much he'd miss her once she left. They likely wouldn't cross paths again. Trips to New York didn't happen every day.

Should he try to convince her to stay? What would that mean for his business plans? More importantly, what would that mean for his personal life?

Having Kate around wouldn't be easy. Not only was he attracted to her, he cared about her. How would he find it in him to resist falling in love with her?

There were plenty of questions banging around in his mind, but few answers. Heading outside with the bird, he wondered when and if his life would ever go back to normal.

* * *

When Josh slapped the headless bird on the counter, Kate attempted to keep her expression blank. She'd never prepared an animal for cooking, but she'd seen it done many times. It couldn't be *that* difficult.

He stood near the back door, a silly grin on his face. His eyes sparkled with mischief, and she could almost read his thoughts. *Let's see how the heiress handles this one.*

She squared her shoulders, not about to let him guess at her uncertainty. He'd argued that she couldn't make it on her own. He was about to see how wrong he'd been.

"Don't you have a project to work on?"

"Nope." His grin widened, his even, white teeth flashing.

He apparently had every intention of watching her prepare lunch.

"What would you normally be doing right now?"

He shrugged. "Reading. Fishing. Playing chess."

"How about you go read something then?"

"I can help, you know. I have lots of experience. Despite Pa's objections, Ma taught us how to cook more than the basic eggs and flapjacks. Her reasoning was simple—you can't always count on a wife to cook. After a baby comes, for instance."

Kate's cheeks burned at the mention of childbirth. It wasn't acceptable to speak of such things with a man, especially if that man was single and happened to have kissed you on more than one occasion. The way his gaze caressed her face didn't help.

Being alone with Josh in his childhood home, sharing simple, everyday tasks, stirred up daydreams of him and her as husband and wife. Every fiber of her being longed for the dream to become reality.

Impossible. I'm not good enough for him.

Conflicting emotions tore at her, cutting up her peace. She loved Josh, loved his family and this town. She desperately wanted to stay forever, but being near him, knowing he was out of reach, would be bittersweet torture.

Her mother's features, twisted in cold fury, flashed in her mind. *How dare you risk our family name...the Morgan reputation! You'd better hope Wesley doesn't breathe a word of this to anyone. No man will want you now, Katerina! You understand you must never tell a living soul. And if you are with child, I will send you away. You will cease to exist in my mind.*

Turning away, she blinked fast to stem the threatening tears, scooping up the carrot peelings and tossing them in the waste bucket. "Thanks for the offer," she said, clearing her muddy throat, "but I'd feel more comfortable working on my own."

"All right. I'll be in the living room if you change your mind."

"Okay."

Wanting to avoid his perceptive gaze, Kate purposefully kept her back to him as he left the room. *Oh, Lord, I made a mistake coming here. I lost my heart to a man I can never have.*

But no matter how difficult it would be to say goodbye, she'd rather live without him than see the expression on his face when she told him the truth.

Chapter Seventeen

The mouthwatering aroma of fried chicken wafted into the living room, eliciting an impatient growl from Josh's stomach. Setting aside his book, he drifted into the dining room and surveyed the bounty. Sliced bread and a crock of butter, pickled beets, a white ceramic bowl of steaming carrots and green beans topped with what appeared to be chopped almonds.

Reaching out, he nabbed a carrot and stuck it in his mouth just as Kate turned the corner, a platter full of chicken in her hands. She cocked an eyebrow in his direction. He'd been caught.

Grinning, he swallowed the morsel glazed with honey and a spice he couldn't identify. It was surprisingly tasty. Maybe he'd underestimated her abilities.

"Can I help you with anything?" he asked, rounding the table to pull out her chair.

"No, everything is ready."

When she was seated, he returned to his chair opposite her. After they bowed their heads, he gave thanks for the meal and prayed for quick healing of his mother's injuries. She was quiet as they dished out the food.

Josh bit into the chicken and closed his eyes in ecstasy. He'd been wrong. And he wasn't too proud to admit it.

"This is delicious, Kate. You're an excellent cook."

"I'm glad you like it."

"How did you learn to cook like this?" he said between bites.

He watched as she touched the corners of her mouth with her napkin and smoothed it onto her lap. Even with her tousled hair and flour-smudged blouse, she managed to retain her regal air. Her perfect manners went bone-deep.

"In the estate kitchens. The staff took time out of their busy schedules to instruct me."

"I'm guessing your parents weren't told about this?"

Her lashes drifted down. "No."

She didn't seem inclined to talk, so he concentrated on his food. When a team leading a wagon entered the lane, Josh dropped his napkin on the table and went to the door. It was his mother's good friend, Betty Stanley, along with her youngest son, Leroy.

"Afternoon, Josh!" Betty greeted him anxiously. "Reverend Monroe announced what happened to Mary, and I wanted to check in on her."

"That's mighty nice of you, Mrs. Stanley, but Ma's not here. Doc Owens kept her overnight for observation." Spying the basket in Leroy's arms, he stepped back. "Would you like to come in for a cup of coffee? Kate and I were just finishing up lunch."

"Oh, I'm sorry I missed her. We won't stay, but we brought some loaves of bread and jars of my apple butter your ma is so fond of." Elbowing Leroy, she nodded toward Josh. Startled, the twelve-year-old handed over the basket.

"Thank you kindly, ma'am. I'm sure she'll be home later today if you'd like to stop by again."

"I'll wait until tomorrow. She'll need her rest." She elbowed the boy again. "Let's go, son."

When he placed the basket on the end of the table, Kate's brows rose in question.

"Mrs. Stanley dropped off fresh bread and apple butter."

"How thoughtful."

"I'd wager this is only the first contribution. People tend to wanna help each other out around here."

Her eyes warmed with appreciation. "I like that tradition."

He glanced out the window behind her and spotted his aunt and cousin coming down the lane. They'd just been to see his mother. Going to the door, he searched their faces as they approached, muscles loosening when he didn't detect concern or worry in their expressions.

"Josh." His aunt greeted soberly as she climbed the steps. Megan trailed behind her.

"How's Ma?"

Alice stopped to catch her breath, her kind eyes peering up at him. Five years older than her sister-in-law, her brown hair was streaked with silver and there were more pronounced worry lines on her forehead.

"A little pale for my liking, but she insists she's fine. She wants to come home this afternoon."

"Is Doc Owens going to allow it?"

"He's leaving that up to your ma and pa."

Megan piped up. "I think Uncle Sam wants her to stay another night, but she's certain she'll rest better here."

Alice shrugged. "That's probably true. And it's at most

a ten-minute ride, so as long as they take it slow and keep her leg steady it shouldn't cause any harm."

Josh opened the door wide for them to enter. "Do they need me over there?"

"I don't see why. Between the three of them, they should be able to get her into the back of the wagon without any trouble. Sam can sit with her while Nathan leads the team."

While Josh was conversing with his aunt, Kate entered the living room. A tentative smile hovered about her mouth, but her manner was subdued. What was she thinking? Was she reconsidering her decision to leave? He knew how much Megan and the girls meant to her.

Megan's gaze strayed to the dining room. "It smells delicious. Josh, did you cook all this?"

"Actually, Kate prepared it." Meeting her shadowed gaze beyond Megan's shoulder, he said, "Turns out she's an excellent cook."

"Oh? You've been keeping secrets from us?"

Megan's voice was full of teasing, so Kate's reaction confused him. Her body jerked, as if startled, the color leeching from her face. "That wasn't my intention—"

"Relax." Megan patted her shoulder. "I was teasing."

Josh interrupted. "If neither of you have eaten, I'll bring extra plates. There's plenty."

"That would be wonderful," said Megan. "I'm eager to try your cooking, Kate. Who taught you?"

Her knuckles showed white where she clenched her hands together at her waist. "The estate chefs."

"That sounds like an amazing experience." She went around to sit beside Kate's empty place. "Are you hungry, Mother?"

A smile brightened the older woman's face. "Even if

I wasn't, the smells alone would tempt me." Moving toward the table, she said, "I see we've interrupted your meal. Kate, come and finish. You look like a stiff wind would blow you away."

Kate's face felt like a frozen mask. How much longer she could maintain this facade of contentment she hadn't a clue, but it felt dangerously close to slipping. She'd somehow managed to get through the excruciating meal by taking frequent small bites. Her rationale? With a full mouth, she wouldn't be expected to contribute to the conversation.

Only, she hadn't been even slightly hungry to begin with. And now it felt like a rock had been wedged beneath her rib cage. Perched on the sofa beside Megan, she sat straight and tall and resisted the urge to press a hand against her upset stomach.

Megan's comment about secrets had rattled her. Megan had no way of knowing the truth, of course. Only a handful of people knew about Kate's indiscretion and not one of them was here in Tennessee.

This only confirmed her decision to leave. Her secret, if it should be revealed, would splinter Josh's good opinion of her. No longer would he look at her with kindness and admiration but with scorn and disgust. Kate wasn't certain she could survive that.

Across from her, Josh looked tense. He couldn't seem to sit still. First he'd lean forward, resting his elbows on his knees and fingering his goatee. Then he'd slump back against the cushions. When he rose to pace near the front door, his aunt commented on his apparent unease.

"What's bothering you, dear?"

"Just restless is all."

"You're going to give me indigestion," she scolded

good-naturedly. "Where is your brother Caleb? I haven't seen that boy in ages."

Kate watched Josh's expression closely. The corners of his mouth turned down in a worried frown.

He stopped to stare out the window, his fingers gripping the sill. "I haven't seen him since yesterday. He left as soon as he learned the extent of Ma's injuries."

"I hope he hasn't gone and gotten himself into trouble."

"Me, too."

His gut-deep sigh spoke volumes. This obviously wasn't the first time the youngest O'Malley had been a source of concern. Kate offered up a quick prayer for Caleb's safety and the mending of his internal wounds, both past and present.

"They're here."

Straightening, Josh breezed through the door. Kate followed, eager to see Mary for the first time since the accident. Nathan, in his extraordinary way with animals, coaxed and cajoled the team to move with extra care. It was as if the horses understood they were carrying valuable, fragile cargo.

Vaulting to the ground, Josh was in the yard and striding toward the wagon even before it eased to a stop. Kate hung back.

She was struck by Mary's vulnerable appearance. This energetic, full-of-life matriarch who toiled dawn to dusk, taking care of her family without complaint, was being tended to by grown men as if the slightest movement might break her. Seeing the older woman's pale face, the pain she tried so valiantly to mask, Kate battled back tears. She loved Mary like a mother.

Her gaze sought Josh's face. His lips were pressed in

a grim line, jaw rigid with emotion. How she longed to press her hand there, to smooth away his worry. He was a man of deep feeling and sensitivity to others' suffering.

But already she'd begun to withdraw, to dam the tide of love flowing from her heart. She'd stay until Mary didn't need her. Then she'd return to New York City.

"How's that, Ma?" Josh tucked the quilt around her shoulders and dropped a kiss on her forehead before standing back to study her. Color bloomed once again in her cheeks, and the lines of pain bracketing her mouth appeared less often. Thank God, she was on the mend.

In the six days since she'd been home, she had yet to leave her bedroom. Not that she hadn't protested that fact. But the O'Malley men were a stubborn lot. Overly protective, too, of their loved ones. His mother was being coddled by all of them. Kate, too.

"I'm warm now that you've stoked up the fire." She settled more firmly against the pillows. "You look tired. Why don't you go downstairs and rescue Kate from the kitchen? The two of you have been working yourselves to death ever since the accident. You deserve to relax. Play a card game. Go for a walk if it isn't too cold."

He massaged the back of his neck. "Good suggestions, but she's not one to leave work undone." *Besides, I'm fairly certain she's avoiding me.*

"She surprised us all, didn't she?"

"If you mean that she's practically stepped in and taken your place, then yeah. Don't be surprised if she approaches you to teach her how to sew. I heard her asking Nathan today if he had any mending he needed done."

He'd walked in on their conversation that morning before breakfast. Nathan had greeted him as usual. Kate, on the other hand, had barely acknowledged his presence. Apparently she preferred his brother's company to his now. He'd kept his expression blank, unwilling to let her see the depth of his hurt.

Strangely, he didn't have a clue as to what he'd done wrong.

Mary chuckled. "Sam told me she's becoming quite the laundress."

"I offered to help her, but she waved me away."

Her humor faded. "I wish she would stay. I'm going to miss her sweet spirit and ready smile. For a time, I'd hoped…well, that the two of you would end up together."

Her words pierced his heart. "It wouldn't work, Ma."

"Why not? Is it because she's wealthy? Is that what's bothering you?"

"Kate is accustomed to a far different lifestyle than we have here. A month in the mountains isn't enough time for her to make a sound decision about whether or not she wants to make this her permanent home."

"I don't know. She's an intelligent woman. I trust her to know her own mind. And besides, if she loved you, it wouldn't matter where she lived as long as it was with you."

Kate? Love him? The idea settled like a warm blanket over his soul.

No. He was positive she saw him only as a friend. As Ma said, if she loved him, she wouldn't leave.

"Well, she doesn't, so it doesn't matter." He moved toward the door. "Do you need anything else? More water? A snack?"

"I can see you aren't in the mood to discuss it," she said drily. "Can you find your pa and send him up here?

I'd like for him to read the Scriptures to me, if he has time."

"He always has time for you."

His hand on the doorframe, she spoke softly, "Your father and I have been blessed with an extraordinary marriage. We want the same for all three of you."

"I know."

"I'm praying for you. And Kate, too."

He turned back with a grateful smile. "Love you, Ma. Good night."

"I love you, Joshua. Good night."

He took the stairs two at a time, pausing in the living room long enough to relay his ma's message to his father before heading for the kitchen. Kate stood at the dry sink washing the supper dishes, her back to him. At the sound of footsteps, she glanced over her shoulder. Did her eyes brighten at the sight of him or was it a trick of the light?

Whatever the case, it didn't last. Her expression quickly sobered.

"How's Mary?" She turned her attention back to her work. "Does she want anything else to eat? If so, it wouldn't take me long to fix something."

He drew alongside her in order to have a clear view of her face. "No, she's still full from supper."

Eyes downcast, she shifted away from him. "She seems to improve every day. I'm relieved to see it."

The action disturbed him. Every day since the accident, he sensed her withdrawing from him a little more.

Crossing his arms, he leaned a hip against the counter. "Knowing you're here has been a huge comfort to her. We're all grateful for everything you've done to help out."

"It's nice to be able to repay your family's kindness."

Unable to stand the small talk a moment longer, he

touched her sleeve. "You've been putting in long hours. You deserve a break. Take a walk with me."

The hand holding the washcloth stilled on the plate. "I've got all these dishes to finish."

"Forget the dishes. I'll do them later."

"It's dark out."

"We'll stay near the house where the light can be seen through the windows. I'll take a lamp." His voice dipped. "Trust me to keep you safe."

He waited, barely breathing, as she silently debated. Her eyes shimmered with uncertainty. "Okay."

"I'll get my jacket."

Grabbing it off the hook by the back door, he slipped it on while she dried her hands. She approached and accepted the shawl he held out to her. Head bent, she wrapped the dove-gray material snuggly around her shoulders, slender fingers fastening the row of silver clips. The lamplight glimmered off the chocolate tendrils that had escaped her chignon. He clenched his fists to keep from tucking the wayward strands behind her ear. She no longer welcomed his touch.

Outside, he held out his arm for her, and she tucked her hand in the crook of his elbow. The action brought her close to his side. He inhaled the faint scent of soap and citrus clinging to her clothes.

There was a nip in the night air, but not cold enough to be unpleasant. Kate was no doubt used to much lower temperatures than this. The stars sparkled in the velvet sky.

Walking in the direction of the barn, quiet spanned between them.

He tried to memorize everything about this night—her scent, the feel of her close to him, the whisper of her skirts brushing against his pants. Soon there'd be no more reason for her to stay. She would pack up her things and return to New York.

"What are you thinking?" he asked.

"How much I'm going to miss Tennessee and all the wonderful people I've met." Wistfulness marked her words.

"Have you told the girls?"

"No, not yet."

"Nicole will no doubt pester you for an invitation to visit."

"I would love for all of you to visit. Will you?"

He stopped and faced her. "You know I can't do that. Seeing Francesca and her husband would be awkward at best."

Shadows obscured her eyes. "I understand."

"Do you understand I don't expect you to give up your studio for me? I want to make it clear that I don't hold what happened against you. And I don't begrudge you your dream. It hasn't been easy to accept, but apparently God has other plans for me. If you want to stay, I'll support you. I'll even be your first customer."

Eyes going wide, she pressed a palm over her heart. "That means a lot to me, Josh." Her voice was wobbly. "But I can't."

"I'm going to miss you, you know," he blurted out.

Before he knew what she was doing, Kate pressed her lips to his in a tender, whisperlike touch so sweet it made his chest ache. Then she was pushing out of his arms and racing across the yard. What—

"Kate!"

Her cabin door slammed shut. He jerked as if slapped. It sounded like goodbye.

Chapter Eighteen

Kate flung herself across the bed, sobs racking her body.

She'd been a fool to come here! What had she truly hoped to accomplish? To satisfy her curiosity? To see for herself the man in the photograph? Or had she come hoping for something else entirely? His eloquent letters—filled with passion for his family, his home, his mountains—had touched her lonely soul and sparked dreams of an altogether different life.

A fulfilled life. One with sincere friendships, a sense of belonging and acceptance, and that most crucial of all emotions—love.

She'd found it all right here.

From that first day, the O'Malleys had welcomed her with open arms. Sam and Mary treated her like the daughter they'd never had. Here she had brothers. Sisters. Friends.

And then there was Josh. He was a gentle, compassionate, honorable man. Aware of her feelings and sensitive to her needs. With him, she felt cherished. Safe. And, yes, loved.

Reaching up, she pressed trembling fingers to her mouth, where her lips yet tingled from the spontaneous kiss. She would savor forever the memories of his embrace. There wouldn't be another.

After what happened tonight, Kate knew she couldn't stay another day. Her emotional retreat was hurting them both.

Her mother was right. Honorable men desired virtuous wives. And while she believed God had forgiven her, she understood that a man like Josh would be hard-pressed to look past such an indiscretion.

She'd known full well that what she was doing was wrong. Believing herself to be in love with Wesley, and he with her, she'd ignored the inner warnings. Now she was paying the ultimate price—giving up the one man who could offer her the future of her dreams.

Desolate, Kate fell into a fitful sleep and awoke the next morning with a lingering headache, a dull throbbing behind her eyes. Her stomach a hard knot, she couldn't fathom facing Josh across the breakfast table. Tears threatened even now. How could she maintain her composure in his presence?

The sound of wagon wheels on the rutted ground outside startled her out of her reverie. It was early for visitors. At the sight of Alice and the twins, she uttered a soft cry of disbelief. Their arrival was like a gift.

She wouldn't have to worry about Mary or the men. Between the church people and Alice and the girls, they'd be in good hands.

Over the next hour, she carefully repacked her clothes and other belongings and tidied up the cabin. Then she dressed with care in the same outfit she'd arrived in—

the seafoam-green ensemble. How long ago that day seemed…

Fighting a fresh wave of tears, she folded up the store's bill of sale, tucked it in an envelope and penned Josh's name across the front. She placed in the middle of the table where he'd be sure to see it. He'd be angry at first, she thought, but he'd soon come to realize it was for the best.

With only her camera and reticule, she stood in the doorway and glanced back at her temporary home. Yes, it had been built for her sister. Somehow, though, she'd come to think of it as her own.

God help me. Give me the strength to do what I have to do.

Turning, she closed the door behind her.

He couldn't get that kiss out of his mind. She'd done it without thinking, spurred by emotion that had rocked him to the core. Was Ma right? Did Kate feel something beyond friendship for him? And, if so, what was he supposed to do with that?

Father God, my emotions are all mixed up. I don't want her to go. On the other hand, I'm afraid of what might happen if she stays. Above all, I don't want to hurt her. She's endured enough sadness in her life.

He descended the stairs, lost in thought. When he heard a gaggle of feminine voices coming from the kitchen, he paused on the bottom step. It was early for visitors.

Then he recognized his aunt's voice and those of the twins.

"Morning, ladies," he greeted, scanning the room for Kate.

She must still be in bed.

Alice paused in unpacking her basket of baked goods and jars of preserves. "We're here to keep your ma company and give Kate a break. She's been working from dawn to dusk ever since the accident, and we thought we'd take over for a day."

"Kate isn't here," auburn-haired Jessica announced.

All eyes turned to where she stood in front of the woodstove. Josh was the first to question her. "What do you mean?"

"I saw her walking to town."

That didn't make any sense. "When was this?"

The young girl lifted a shoulder. "Half an hour ago, maybe?"

Jane admonished her twin. "You should've said something."

Jessica's eyes widened. "Why? What's so unusual about Kate going to town? Maybe she needed something from Clawson's."

Grabbing his hat off the hook, he opened the back door. "Never mind. I'll go check on her."

Striding across the yard, Josh tried to ignore the sinking sensation in his stomach. There could be a simple explanation for her going to town on her own. Except, she hadn't done it before as far as he knew. And she knew there was the risk of running into Matthews.

His knock was followed by silence. Were her trunks already packed?

"Kate?" He waited. "It's me, Josh. I'd like to talk to you."

Again, nothing. Opening the door, he peered inside. "Hello?"

His gaze landed on the envelope with his name on it. Dread settled deep in his bones. His steps measured, he took his time opening it, not wanting to see the contents. And then he saw the bill of sale.

An inventory of the bedroom confirmed his suspicions. The wardrobe stood empty, and her trunks were lined in a neat row on the far side of the bed.

She was gone.

She couldn't resist one last look around the studio.

It was just as she'd left it. Crates and trunks dominated the center of the room, a good majority of them unopened. Before coming here, she'd stopped by the mercantile and arranged for Mr. Moore to repack everything and ship it back to New York for a small wage. When he'd expressed his regrets at her leaving, she'd come near to weeping and rushed out the door.

Walking in the direction of the livery, she'd managed to stem the tide of emotion. Later, when she was alone, she'd deal with her grief.

It hadn't been easy to find someone willing to take her to Sevierville on such short notice, but, as in most situations, money made all the difference. From there she'd have no trouble finding a private carriage for hire. She was to meet the man back at the livery in exactly one hour, enough time to stop here and dream about what might've been.

Light from the plate-glass windows illuminated the front room, but the windowless back room was sheathed in shadows. She lit a lamp. In the corner sat a trunk full of portraits she'd taken of the city and the estate. Josh had expressed interest in seeing her work, so she'd had them sent along with the other supplies.

Sighing, she crouched down to rifle through the prints.

Perhaps she'd leave one or two for him and his family to remember her by.

The creak of the rear door startled her. Straightening, she crossed the room and peered to her left at the entrance. A gust of wind caught the door and it swayed, creaking again. She didn't see anyone.

"Hello?"

A floorboard groaned somewhere in the front room. Her neck prickled with unease.

"Is anyone out there?" she called.

The air was still, quiet. Must've been a trick of her imagination. Still, she didn't have a lot of time to waste. Turning back, she returned to the trunk and hunkered down once more. She lifted out the first portrait.

"Hello, Lily."

Her stomach dropped. No. It couldn't be.

Not him. Not here.

She was alone. Without defense.

Whirling to face him, the print slipping to the floor, she gasped at the determination carved in Tyler's features.

"Here we are, alone at last." He stepped inside and, without breaking eye contact, shut the door behind him. "You can't run from me anymore."

Her heart slammed against her rib cage, her lungs constricting with fear. "I—I don't want to run."

She had to bide her time. Appease him until she could figure out a way of escape.

Oh, God, please help me!

"Good." He advanced slowly, his eyes unnaturally bright. "Cause I'm tired. Tired of chasing you. A husband shouldn't have to chase his wife."

Her mouth cotton-dry, she tried to swallow. Her fists

curled into tight balls, her fingernails dug into her palms. She forced herself to stand completely still, to mask her distaste, as he ran the pad of his thumb across her lips. Alcohol practically oozed from his pores.

Built like a prizefighter, Tyler could overpower her without breaking a sweat.

How could she defend herself?

"I've missed you, Lily."

Invading her space, he cupped her neck and yanked her against his unkempt body.

Please, no! Suddenly she couldn't stifle the instinct to fight.

Struggling, she shoved against his chest. His fingers dug into her neck. She cried out. They scuffled, and his boot connected with the lamp, sending it flying. The sound of glass breaking dimly registered in the back of her mind.

"Stop. Fighting. Me," he huffed.

Her arms began to buckle beneath his superior strength. Desperate to evade his advances, she angled her face away from his. When she felt his rough mouth scrape the sensitive skin on the column of her neck, bile rose in her throat.

The smell of smoke and flames gradually penetrated her senses. "Fire," she gasped.

"Huh?" The moment his hold slackened, she surged backward. Her foot slipped. She felt herself falling, and then her forehead struck the corner of the trunk and everything faded to black.

Josh was angry. How could she leave without saying goodbye? His family, especially Megan and Nicole, would be deeply hurt. He wouldn't have expected such callous behavior from Kate.

Crossing the bridge into town, he glimpsed a thin stream of kettle-black smoke spiraling into the sky. He rubbed a hand over his eyes. Was he seeing things?

He urged his horse to go faster. Apparently, no one else had noticed it, for the handful of people on the streets were going about their business as usual.

He shouted to get their attention. "Something's on fire!"

Jerking to a stop, he slid to the ground, scanning the businesses to see which ones were involved. He couldn't see a thing from this position, but smoke didn't lie.

"I'm going around back," he yelled at Mr. Moore, who'd run into the street behind him. "Pass the word."

He passed frightened women clutching children to their sides. More men came out into the streets.

"Josh!"

Tom rushed outside. "What's wrong?"

"I saw smoke," he yelled, not hesitating. If a fire were to get out of control, the whole town could go up in a matter of minutes.

"Wait!" Tom called. "I saw Kate inside her studio earlier. Do you think she's still in there?"

Josh stumbled, alarm spiraling through him. His throat closed up. "Are you sure?"

At his affirmative nod, Josh pointed to the front door. "Go in that way! I'll go around back."

Please, God, let him be wrong.

Rounding the corner, he nearly stumbled at the sight of Tyler Matthews dragging an unconscious Kate out of the burning building. When his brain finally processed what his eyes were seeing, rage claimed him. He flew at the other man.

"Get your hands off her!"

Tyler's eyes went wide. He released her and, spinning around, sprinted into the forest.

"Kate!"

He fell to his knees in the dirt beside her and hauled her half onto his lap. Her head lolled to the side, revealing a jagged gash at her temple. Blood trickled down her too-pale cheek.

"Please talk to me, my love." He pressed his face in close, his fingers stroking her soot-streaked hair. Her eyes remained closed, her breathing shallow.

Seeing her like this struck a chord of fear deep within his soul. What if…

It was then that the truth slammed into him.

He couldn't lose her! Life without Kate—

Shaking now, he couldn't bear to finish the thought. *I love her.*

He could deny it no longer. His love for Kate burned brightly inside him, the intensity rivaling the noonday sun, filling the empty spaces until he could see nothing but her.

He didn't hear Tom running up behind them. "The place is consumed in flames! You need to move away before the whole structure collapses." He skidded to a stop. "What happened? Is she all right?"

"I'm taking her to Doc Owens," Josh murmured grimly.

"Stay with me, sweetheart," he whispered in Kate's ear.

Cradling her in his arms, he walked as quickly as he could without jarring her. By the time he stumbled into the doctor's house, his muscles were strained from the exertion.

"Doc! I need your help!"

The middle-age man emerged from his office, his sharp gaze quickly taking stock of the situation. "Take Miss Morgan in here." He held the door open to the same room his mother had occupied a week earlier.

Josh deposited her with care on the examination table and gently brushed the hair off her face. "There's a fire in town. She was pulled unconscious from one of the burning buildings. I don't know how she got that gash."

But he had an idea. Fear for her safety was the only thing keeping him from hunting Matthews down like the swine he was and making sure he never harmed Kate again. Not to worry. He'd deal with Matthews in due time.

"I need you to wait outside." He rinsed his hands in a basin of water.

"I can't leave her."

The doctor stared at him. "You are not her husband. I can't allow you to stay here while I examine her."

"But—"

"Josh, the longer we stand here arguing, the longer she has to wait for medical attention."

He didn't want to leave her. Taking hold of her limp hand, he tried to convey his strength to her, willing her to hear him. "I'm not leaving, Kate. I'll be right on the other side of that door," he whispered. "Doc's gonna take good care of you."

Ignoring him, the doctor lifted her right wrist to check her pulse.

He was being dismissed. Feet dragging, Josh left the room, closing the door behind him. Slumping into the nearest chair, he buried his face in his hands.

All he could think was that the woman he loved was lying unconscious in the next room, and he was powerless to do anything to help her.

Pushing to his feet, he paced the length of the parlor, his mind returning again and again to the mental image of Matthews dragging her out of the studio. Gut churning, he forced his thoughts away from what might've transpired in the moments before the fire. No use working himself up until he knew the facts. But if he found out Matthews had laid a finger on her...

When his father came through the front door, Josh felt a little less alone. They embraced briefly.

"How is she?"

Sam's gaze darted to the closed door, his face reflecting understanding. He knew exactly what Josh was enduring, had been in this very same position.

"I don't know. Pa, what if—"

He held up a hand. "Let's not borrow trouble."

"But I feel so helpless," he said, shoving a hand through his hair.

"There is one thing you can do for her. Pray."

Pa settled an arm on his shoulders and, bowing his head, prayed for Kate and the safety of the men working to put out the fire. Josh seconded the petition.

Dr. Owens emerged from the examination room. "Miss Morgan is awake. You may see her now."

Pulse jumping, Josh searched his features for clues. "How is she?"

"It appears her only injury is the head wound. Her lungs are clear, and she's not complaining of anything other than a headache."

The knot in his stomach eased as relief flooded him. "Thank you."

With a grateful nod, he entered the room and, approaching the bed, sank into the straight-backed chair beside it. Lying flat on her back, a crisp white quilt tucked around her, her chest rose and fell with even breaths. Her cheek nestled in the pillow, lips parted and drawing in air.

Resting one arm above her head, he leaned forward and covered her clasped hands with his own.

"Kate?" Not wanting to startle her, he spoke in a hushed voice.

Her lashes fluttered, then slowly lifted. Peridot-green eyes focused on his. "Josh?"

"Hey." His hand tightened on hers, heart swelling with compassion at the sound of her scratchy voice. "How are you feeling?"

Her lids drifted shut. "I've been better."

Her body needed rest, he knew, but the questions couldn't wait. He phrased them as best he knew how. "You were pulled from the fire. Do you remember what happened before that?"

Her lids snapped open, anger sparking in the luminous depths. "Of course I remember. Tyler cornered me in the back room. We struggled. He overturned a lamp. That's how it started."

Josh sucked in a breath. She was irate, not scared. Did that mean he hadn't succeeded in harming her?

Quashing his own fury at the man, his gaze roamed her face. "Did he hurt you?"

She shook her head, then winced. Slipping one hand free, she gingerly fingered the bandage at her temple. "No, thank God. I guess, in a way, the fire was a blessing in disguise. If it hadn't started, I don't know what he might've done."

"He pulled you out, you know."

Her brow furrowed in disbelief. "What?"

"I saw it with my own eyes."

Her expression turned thoughtful. "He wouldn't leave Lily to die."

Reminded of the terror of that moment, he ran a knuckle down her cheek. "I was terrified I was going to lose you. My lovely Kate—" his voice cracked with emotion "—I can't imagine life without you. I love you."

He held his breath, waiting for her reaction.

Joy leaped in her eyes. Her lips curled upward. Then, like a cloud eclipsing the brilliant sun, her delight vanished.

Closing her eyes tight, she turned her face away. "Please, don't."

Confused, hurt, he sank back. "Don't what? Tell you the truth?"

A single tear slipped from beneath her lashes. "You were right, after all. I—I've discovered I miss the city. I wouldn't be happy here long-term." Her pitiful, ragged breath gouged his soul. "I'm leaving as soon as I can arrange a ride to Sevierville."

"So you're saying you don't return my feelings?" He strove to maintain his composure, to hide his pain.

Oh, God, this is so much worse than I could ever have imagined. How could I have misinterpreted her behavior?

Covering her eyes with her hand, she murmured, "I care for you a great deal, but we're from different worlds, you and I. My place is in the city."

"What about your studio?"

She was quiet a long time. "It wasn't meant to be."

She was using words he himself had used to describe their situation.

"Kate—"

"Please, Josh—" her voice shook "—the pain in my head is worsening. Can you get the doctor?"

"Of course." He stood looking down at her, committing her features to memory.

So this was it. She didn't want him. Like her sister, she was captivated by the city and all its pleasures. How could he have ever thought an heiress would throw away a life of luxury to be with him? Fool. That's what he was. Worse than Megan with all her romantic notions.

He wouldn't stay where he wasn't wanted.

"Goodbye, Kate."

Chapter Nineteen

Against the doctor's advice, Kate got out of bed the following morning and, unable to find her clothes, dressed in the outfit she'd placed in her overnight satchel. She'd refused to take the pain medicine he'd offered, and so had passed an agonizing night in the stark examination room.

Moving around wasn't helping. Her temple throbbed beneath the bandage, her head unnaturally heavy and her neck stiff. Her eyes felt gritty, though from smoke or lack of sleep she wasn't certain.

When she straightened from pulling on her boots, the room tilted and she flung out a hand to steady herself. Thankfully, the chair was there to grab onto.

How am I going to survive a wagon ride through the mountains? she wondered.

She couldn't afford to stay. The sooner she left, the better—before her heart overruled her better judgment and she begged Josh's forgiveness.

She'd done the unthinkable. She'd come here to right a wrong, to do the decent thing and deliver the news face-to-face. Her self-righteous anger at Fran's duplicity mocked her now.

Fran's actions seemed insignificant compared to Kate's treachery. Josh had offered her his heart, and she'd callously rejected him. Rejected by yet another Morgan sister.

The conversation replayed inside her head, the stunned sorrow in his voice echoing in her ears. How she'd longed to blurt out the truth, to say, *Yes, of course I love you! How could I not?*

*Better a tiny, white lie than the truth…*a voice reminded. But was it? Was it really?

Honestly, Katerina, how could you be so naive? Fran's disdainful expression flashed in her mind's eye. *Why would Wesley Farrington want anything to do with you? He's suave and sophisticated and you, well, you are nothing a man of his worth would desire. Imagine, my own sister willing to give herself to the first man who winks at her!*

The shame flooded her anew, firming her resolve. Josh could never know.

Standing slowly in hopes of warding off the dizziness, she slipped her reticule over her wrist and carefully reached for her satchel.

"Kate! What are you doing out of bed?" Megan appeared in the doorway, eyes widening at the sight of her travel costume and luggage. "You look awful. Where do you think you're going?"

The sight of her friend threatened the tentative hold she had on her emotions. "I thought you'd have heard by now. I'm going back to New York."

"Nathan told me. I just couldn't believe it." Her gaze was full of sadness. "Why, Kate?"

"First, tell me. How is Josh?"

"I haven't seen him since before the accident."

Kate bit her lip. She desperately needed to know whether or not he was all right.

"Do you think he went to confront Tyler?"

"It's possible. After what he did to you, Josh would want to make sure his actions didn't go unpunished."

She gripped Megan's arm. "Why would he go alone? What if something's happened?"

"If you care so much for him," she asked gently, "then why are you leaving?"

Kate broke eye contact. "I need to go home. Let's just leave it at that."

"Are you planning on returning?"

"I don't think that would be wise." She took her hands in hers. "Please say you'll come and visit me. You, Nicole and the twins. I can't bear the thought of not seeing you again."

Her smile was tremulous. "I'd like that."

Grateful that she didn't pursue the issue, Kate hugged her friend. "You'll send Nathan or Caleb to find Josh, won't you?"

"I'll go straight there. Try not to worry. He can take care of himself."

Easier said than done. "And you'll give everyone my love? Tell them I—" her voice hitched "—I'll never forget their kindness."

She hated to leave without saying goodbye, especially to Sam and Mary, but it couldn't be helped. When she got to the city, she'd purchase appropriate gifts to send back as a token of her thanks. It wasn't ideal, but it was the best she could do given the situation.

She pulled her shawl more tightly around her shoulders. "My escort is probably outside waiting. Will you walk me out?"

Megan sniffled. "Of course."

After informing Dr. Owens of her departure and thanking him for his services, the pair walked arm in arm through the parlor and out onto the front porch. The man she'd hired was indeed there with his team and wagon. For propriety's sake, his wife was accompanying them.

"Good afternoon." He tipped his hat and took her satchel, placing it in the wagon bed.

This was it, she thought, her gaze sweeping the familiar street. Time to say goodbye to this town that had stolen its way into her heart.

When she glimpsed the burned-out shell of her studio, bittersweet sadness settled in her soul. Her dreams, and Josh's, too, had gone up in smoke.

Sensing Megan's perusal, Kate said, "I hope he rebuilds. Opens the furniture store he wanted."

"It seems to me he'd rather have you than any ole furniture business."

Gritting her teeth, she battled back the tears. She could not speak about this, her greatest heartache. Not now. Maybe not ever.

With one last, hasty hug, she murmured, "I'll write as soon as I get there. Take care, Megan."

"Kate."

There was no mistaking his voice. Why had he come? Releasing her friend, she met his intense gaze with trepidation. How could she endure this? Saying goodbye to him a second time?

"I need a word with you."

He looked as miserable as she felt. Her heart twisted with regret and longing for what might've been.

Megan slipped away without a word. Josh spoke to

her driver, instructed him to give them a few minutes to speak in private.

When he neared, she saw the misery in his eyes. She alone bore the responsibility for that pain.

"I've been thinking." He measured his words carefully. "Does it have to be New York City? Knoxville isn't nearly as large, but it has a lot of the comforts you're used to. You could have your studio. I could have my furniture store. We could give it a go, don't you think?"

She gasped and pressed a hand to her heart, stunned by his offer to move to the city. "Gatlinburg is your home! Everything you love is here."

His eyes darkened. "Not everything. Not if you leave."

"I couldn't—"

"Kate Morgan—" he gently grasped her hands "—you mean the world to me. I want to share my life with you. Where we live doesn't matter as long as you're with me. You said you care for me. Enough to marry me? To be my wife?"

Overcome with emotion, Kate couldn't speak. How she'd dreamed of this day! Josh loved *her*. He wanted to marry *her*.

But her joy was short-lived.

Tears streaming down her cheeks, she looked him full in the face. "I'm no better than my sister, Josh. I lied to you."

His brow furrowed in confusion. "About what?"

"I told you last night that the reason I'm leaving is because I miss the city. That was a lie. I also said that I don't—" she broke off on a shuddering breath "—that I don't l-love you. That, too, was a lie. I do love you, Josh, with everything in me."

His expression cleared and, smiling like a child on

Christmas morning, he gripped her hands a fraction tighter. "You love me? Then why not tell me straight-out? Were you afraid?"

"Yes, I was. I am." *Lord, help me. This is the hardest thing I've ever had to do.* Heart racing, limbs trembling, she slipped her hands free of his. "I'm not the virtuous woman you believe me to be. When I was seventeen, there was a man. A very charming man who came along when I desperately needed to feel loved. And he and I… that is, one night we—" She stumbled around for words to express what she'd done, but there was no simple way to put it. "We were intimate."

"It was the man you were dreaming about, right?" Josh's face was pale beneath his tan, his eyes cool. His fingers curled into tight fists. "Wesley?"

Kate flinched. "Yes."

"I see."

His words resonated with disappointment. He passed a hand over his face and, with a guttural sigh, turned his back on her.

The slight was like a physical blow. His rejection couldn't be clearer.

"I know this hurts you and I never meant for that to happen. I'm sorry."

Swallowing back tears, she swept up her skirts and walked with as much dignity as she could muster to the wagon. Mr. Furley appeared and, at her request, helped her into the back. The jarring movement was almost too much for her. Her head swam. She closed her eyes and waited for it to pass.

Help, Lord. Sinking down, she rested against the wagon directly behind the driver's seat, legs stretched out before her in a most unladylike position. It hardly mattered.

His back to the street, Josh didn't move to stop her or wave goodbye.

As the wagon jerked and rolled out onto the street, her gaze didn't waver from his familiar form. Heart ripping in two, she bit her lip until it bled. She'd known it would be like this. *I'm sorry, Josh. So sorry.*

The wagon rounded the bend, and she could see him no more.

His whole body was numb. His mind. His limbs. His heart.

Kate's revelation had hit him with the full force of a cannon blast.

Walking without seeing where he was going, Josh battled anger and bitter disappointment. She'd seemed innocent. Pure. And yet, she'd given herself to a man who was not her husband.

Jealousy surged hot and fast at the thought of her with Wesley. Gritting his teeth, he rid his mind of the images. How could she do it? Didn't she know how amazing and precious she was?

First Francesca. Now Kate. He'd had enough secrets to last a lifetime.

"Josh!" Blond curls falling in her eyes, Megan rushed up. "I passed Kate's wagon. She was crying her heart out. What did you say to her? Couldn't you convince her to stay?"

"Not now, Megan," he warned, his long stride even.

"Are you the reason she's crying?"

"I'm not discussing this."

Spotting the burned-out studio, he changed direction

and strode toward it. He needed to assess the structural damage and decide if any of it could be salvaged. His brothers had offered to help him rebuild. Staying busy was the key to survival.

The front entrance was impassable. He'd have to go around back.

"Aren't you going to go after her?" His cousin hurried to keep up. "She didn't seem happy about leaving. In fact, she looked miserable. You don't look much better."

What could he say? Of course he was miserable. The woman he loved wasn't who he'd thought she was.

The back door was missing. With his gloved hand, he tested the sturdiness of the frame.

Megan sighed. "This isn't the ending I'd imagined for the two of you."

Whirling around, he growled, "This is real life, Megan, not one of your novels. You can't always count on a happy ending."

Hurt flashed across her face. "Despite what you might think, I do know the difference between reality and make-believe."

"I'm sorry." He applied pressure to his temples where a headache was starting. "I shouldn't have snapped at you."

Huddling into her wrap, she shivered. "It's all right."

"Maybe you should go on home," he suggested in a gentler tone. "I've got business to tend to and it may take a while."

"I did promise Nicole I'd help her sew a dress this afternoon." Her expression had a forlorn quality. She was hurting, too.

He touched her sleeve. "See you later, then?"

"Of course." She tacked on, "I'm not giving up on you two."

"Megan," he warned.

"That's all I'm going to say. For now."

He sucked in a breath, but she flounced off before he could utter a word. Minx.

Navigating the burned-out structure wasn't easy. Kate's belongings had all succumbed to the fire. His heart was heavy with the knowledge of all she'd lost.

He glanced in the back room where the fire had started, expecting to find nothing left. His gaze lit on one of her trunks. The outside was singed, and one of the bottom corners was warped by the heat. But overall it appeared to be in one piece.

The ceiling here was intact. He advanced carefully into the room and, hefting the heavy trunk outside, deposited it in the grass.

Prying the lid open, he sat back on his haunches. Kate's pictures.

Not from here, from her life in the city.

One by one, he sifted through the stack of images. Shot at interesting angles, she'd made clever use of shadow and light to create not pictures, but works of art. This was not the work of an amateur. Kate had talent.

Replacing the prints, he shut up the trunk and hefted it into his arms. He'd make sure she got these back.

The piercing wind battered Josh's reddened cheeks and tore at his hat as he, Nathan and Caleb hefted another hundred-pound log into place. The early November weather had turned bitter practically overnight. Sweating beneath his undershirt, he knew it was only a matter of time before one of them became sick working in these conditions. At least the end was in sight. A day or two more and they'd start on the roof.

"Hey, fellas." Megan and Nicole smiled up at them, baskets held aloft. "We brought lunch."

Josh didn't want to stop, not even to eat, but he couldn't be selfish. His brothers needed a break. "We'll be right down," he called, watching as the girls went around to the side and entered the open doorway.

The four walls provided shelter from the wind, but their breaths puffed white in the chilly air.

"What brings you two out on a day like this?" Nathan asked around a mouthful of sandwich.

Watching as Megan extracted a long envelope from her pocket, Josh stopped midchew, anticipating her words. His pulse accelerated.

"I got a letter from New York." Her gaze speared his. "Kate sends her regards."

Swallowing hard, he tossed the sandwich back into the basket and stalked outside. He didn't want to talk about Kate, or even think about her. While he couldn't prevent her from haunting his dreams, he could at least try to harness his waking thoughts.

A month had passed since she left. One long, lonely, miserable month.

He missed her so much it was a physical pain. He walked around with a hollow, aching, cavernous sensation inside that nothing could ease.

Her presence lingered everywhere he looked. The breakfast table. The apple house. His workshop.

He avoided the cabin at all costs. Sensing his turmoil, his parents hadn't asked when he planned to move back in. Caleb hadn't been as sensitive. His offer to take the cabin had been met with stony silence from Josh and a word of admonishment from Nathan.

"Josh, wait." Megan came up behind him. "I didn't

mean to upset you. I just thought you'd want to know how she's doing."

Unable to resist, he turned to face her. "So? How is she?"

She held out the letter. "Would you like to read it for yourself?"

He stuffed his hands in his coat pockets. "No. Thanks."

She pursed her lips. "Fine. I'll give you the highlights. In every other sentence she asks about you. In the rest of it, she says how much she misses us. All of us."

"Those feelings will lessen over time."

As his would, he prayed. Living like this wore a man down. He couldn't remember the last time he'd smiled. Or enjoyed a good meal. Or played his fiddle. The music, the joy, was gone from his life. All because of Kate and her secrets.

"I don't agree. It's clear to me that she loves you, Josh, and regrets leaving. I think you should go to New York."

"That's not gonna happen."

She stamped her foot. "Don't be stubborn! It's plain for all to see you're a mess without her." The wind whipped her hair around her face, and she shoved it aside. "What will it hurt to go and see her again?"

"Listen, I know your intentions are good, but there are some issues here you aren't aware of. Issues that can't be overcome."

"Tell me. Maybe I can help."

He crossed his arms over his chest. His affection for his cousin was the only reason he was standing here discussing what was a private matter. "In the books you love so much, what happens when someone turns out to be vastly different than you thought she was?"

A line formed between her brows. "How is Kate different than what we thought? Isn't she an heiress?" She clapped a hand over her open mouth. "Is she not Francesca's sister? You said they looked nothing alike."

"Of course she's an heiress and, yes, she's Francesca's sister. You didn't answer my question."

"All right, all right. If a person keeps important information hidden, it's usually for a good reason—at least in her mind."

What was Kate's reason?

Megan studied him. "Are you going to forgive her for whatever it is she lied about?"

"She didn't outright lie, exactly." *What did you expect her to do? Introduce herself and then blurt out her indiscretion?*

"The particulars are none of my business, but I want to remind you that everyone makes mistakes. Kate has a good heart. She wouldn't deliberately hurt you, not if she could help it. I know that as sure as I know my own name."

Beneath the disappointment, his heart recognized her words as the truth.

If he stepped back from his own hurt long enough to study the situation, he could see how she'd be terrified to tell him. *She didn't have to. She could've kept her secret to herself and married you anyway.*

"Put yourself in her shoes," Megan suggested, "and try to figure out the reasons driving her actions."

Kate had lived a privileged yet lonely life. Her family had made her feel as if she were less than she was, had made it clear she didn't measure up to their standards. He could only imagine how hungry she'd been for love, for acceptance. For a man without morals, Kate would've been an easy mark.

His heart spasmed painfully in his chest. *Oh, God, she chose the honorable path by telling me about her mistake. She laid bare her heart, made herself vulnerable and I turned my back on her. Another rejection in a lifetime of rejections.*

He bowed his head. "What have I done?" he groaned.

He felt Megan's hand on his arm. "It's not too late to repair things."

He had to go to her! To beg her forgiveness.

Movement registered on his left. "O'Malley?"

He'd know that voice anywhere. *Matthews.* The sound ignited a flame of fury in Josh's gut. The knowledge of all he'd done to torment Kate, the image of him dragging her unconscious from a fire his actions had started, combined to drive rational thought from his mind.

He didn't question why Matthews had approached him. He didn't care. All he could think about was Kate.

In the blink of an eye, he had the villain in a crushing throat hold and had slammed him back against the wall. Megan gasped.

Struggling for air, his eyes bulged and he clawed at Josh's fingers.

"How dare you show your face around here?" Josh growled through clenched teeth, barely registering Megan yelling for his brothers. He wanted answers.

"Hey!" Nathan seized his shoulder. "What are you lookin' to do? Kill him?"

Caleb appeared on his other side, but he didn't try to restrain him. He glared at Matthews. "He's not worth it, Josh."

Matthews glanced wildly between the three men, obviously terrified, chest heaving. Josh only tightened his grip. This sorry excuse of a man deserved to pay for hurting the woman he loved more than life itself.

"Josh, don't!" Megan cried.

Let him go, an inner voice urged. *Vengeance is Mine, says the Lord. Let Me handle him.*

Matthews's face had a chalky hue. His hands were growing limp.

With a disgusted noise, Josh released him. Blood roared in his ears. What had he almost done?

Matthews staggered a couple of steps in the opposite direction, eager to put distance between himself and the others.

"Why did you come here?" Nathan prodded.

When Josh finally looked at his enemy, he noticed the sorry condition he was in. He looked visibly weak, his eyes sunken and his skin pasty. He'd lost weight, too. But he appeared to be sober.

"I—" His dark, pained eyes settled on Josh. "I came to ask your forgiveness for what I did to your friend. Kate, I think her name is. I never meant to hurt her—"

"You expect us to believe you?" Josh couldn't stand to hear her name on his lips.

Nathan put a restraining hand on his chest, just in case Josh decided to have another go at Tyler.

Matthews hung his head. "It's true. I— My mind was so mixed up. The alcohol. The elixirs. After the fire, I threw it all out. I, ah, have been pretty sick."

Josh could see that. Still, it didn't excuse his behavior. But at least he'd come to his senses, was no longer in the clutches of whatever substances had been fueling his fantasy that Kate was his dead wife.

"I'll be moving on." He lifted his head again and looked at Josh, misery and regret in the harsh lines of his face. "Too many memories here. I can't—" He broke off, covering his eyes with one hand and rubbing his temples as if his head pounded.

Against his will, Josh experienced a shred of compassion for the man. He'd lost the light of his life, his beloved wife. How would Josh react in the same situation? How would he survive if anything ever happened to Kate? His stomach lurched.

He surprised them all by blurting out, "I gotta go."

Nathan's brows slammed together. "Go? Go where?"

"I think I know." Megan's eyes lit up with hope.

He addressed Matthews. "I accept your apology. Take my advice—stay off the booze. And I'm warning you now—stay away from my family."

Caleb piped up. "Kate isn't—"

"Not yet." Josh clapped his brother on the shoulder. "But I hope she will be. Soon."

Twenty-four hours later, he was on a train bound for New York. It couldn't go fast enough, in his mind. He'd let her leave believing he no longer cared for her, that he condemned her for her past actions. When he thought about the misery she must've endured these past weeks, his eyes grew suspiciously wet and he ducked his head so his hat's brim shielded his face.

Forgive me, Lord, for being a stubborn fool. He only hoped Kate would give him a second chance.

Chapter Twenty

"Miss Katerina, you've been summoned to the lower-level drawing room."

Standing at the library window, she tore her gaze from the barren gardens below to answer the footman. "Thank you, Mr. Crandall."

With an abbreviated bow, he slipped from the room.

Her deep sigh fogged the polished glass and with a shiver, she turned and started for the door. *What now?* she wondered. Was she to be taken to task yet again for her unapproved sojourn to the wilds of Tennessee?

Her parents had arrived home a week earlier, and her mother had yet to stop berating her for her foolishness. Kate had listened without emotion. It was as if she'd cried out all the tears she possessed and was capable of no more. Now all she felt was numb.

As she swept through the wide corridors, Kate's green satin skirts rustled and the heels of her shoes tapped against the marble floor. On this gray, overcast day, weak light filtered through the floor-to-ceiling windows, barely chasing away the gloom.

The weather suited her mood.

Life without Josh was like a day without sunshine. Without joy or laughter.

Not for the first time, she wondered how he was doing. Did he miss her at all? Did he think of her? The look in his eyes in the moments before she left was burned into her consciousness.

As she descended the grand staircase and neared the drawing room, voices filtered into the hallway.

Francesca and Percy.

Her mood sank even lower. Her sister would no doubt have plenty to say about her decision to stay with the O'Malleys.

Squaring her shoulders, she held her head high as she made her entrance. There would be no avoiding this meeting. Better to get it over with so she could return to her self-imposed solitary confinement.

"Ah, here is your sister at last." Georgia's face radiated disapproval. "Katerina, come here. Francesca and Percy have arrived home from Italy."

Kate noted that Fran looked refreshed after her extended honeymoon, her golden hair and skin kissed by the sun. On the other hand, Percy appeared unchanged, his dour expression much the same as ever.

Rounding on her, Fran's blue eyes sparked fire. "Mother tells me you stayed in Gatlinburg for over a month. What, pray tell, did you find to occupy your time?"

"Good morning, Fran," she responded drily. "Nice to see you, as well. How was your honeymoon?"

"It was fine," she snapped. "I would much rather hear about your trip."

"Just fine?" Percy's face darkened.

"You know what I meant, darling." She shrugged off his protest. "I'm trying to find out what my dear little sister has been up to." Folding her arms, she swung her gaze back to Kate. "Well?"

"It was a wonderful trip. I made many friends while I was there."

Moving past the grouping of sofas and wingback chairs, she made her way to the French doors to stare out at the gardens, wishing it was instead the lush Tennessee forests and valleys she'd come to love.

From her place on the sofa, Georgia lamented, "What I can't understand is what possessed you to undertake a trip of that magnitude without our approval. And without a chaperone! Honestly, Katcrina, where is your sense of decorum?"

"Personally I think she was adopted!" Fran exclaimed.

Ignoring the comment, Georgia demanded, "Answer me, young lady!"

Kate faced her mother. "I don't have an answer for you, Mother. I've apologized more times than I count. I do not know what else I can do or say to please you."

At that moment, Kate realized she was finished apologizing for the woman she'd become. She would never fit into this family or their high-class world.

"I will not tolerate such insolence from you, daughter—"

"I think I've heard about enough."

Kate gasped at the sound of the familiar voice. It couldn't be! Yet there he stood in the doorway, black hat in hand, heartbreakingly handsome in the same gray pin-striped suit he'd worn to greet her that first day.

"Josh!" Her palm covering her galloping heart, she gaped at him. "What are you doing here?"

He stepped inside the room, his gaze hungrily roaming her features. "I had to see you again. Kate, we need to talk."

Georgia rose to her feet. "Who are you? How did you get in here?"

"Joshua," Fran said breathlessly, "it's wonderful to see you again."

Percy shot to his feet, his face a thundercloud. "Is this the backwoods hick you were engaged to?"

He ignored them all, his attention on Kate alone. An odd mix of contrition and impatience marked his features. "Is there somewhere we can talk privately?"

"Why are you looking at my sister like that?" Fran demanded suddenly, her gaze volleying back and forth between the two.

"If you must know, I'm in love with her. I've come to ask her to marry me. Again."

Wary, Josh watched Kate's expression closely. Her green eyes widened, glistening in the soft glow emitted by the ornate wall sconces. The longing he glimpsed on her face fanned the flames of hope within his chest. Would she find it in her heart to forgive him?

"Again? What—" his former fiancée sputtered. "You must be joking!"

Francesca stalked over to stand halfway between him and Kate. Hands fisted on her hips, Francesca looked about ready to explode, her beauty marred by jealousy and plain mean-spiritedness. She'd hidden it well those short weeks they'd spent together. Looking back, there'd been hints of her true personality, but he'd been too besotted to spot them.

He could've been shackled to this woman for life. *Thank you, God, for sparing me.*

"This isn't a joke." He frowned at her.

She rounded on Kate. "You planned this all along,

didn't you? Don't think I didn't notice you mooning over his picture! How could you do this to me?"

Kate lifted her chin. "You're forgetting that you're a married woman, Fran. You chose Percy over Josh. I didn't *do* anything to you."

"Joshua," Fran began, sounding like the cat who caught the mouse, "did Katerina ever mention a man by the name of Wesley Farrington?"

"Fran, no!" The color drained from her face.

"I know everything." He injected frost into his voice. "And it doesn't change the way I feel about your sister."

Francesca's husband wore a smirk. "It doesn't bother you that she's damaged goods?"

Josh took a menacing step forward, keeping a tight rein on his emotions. "I won't allow you or anyone else to say such things about Kate."

"Josh, please. You don't have to do this."

Crossing the room to stand before her, he drank in her appearance. After the misery of living without her all these weeks, the sight of her was a gift in and of itself. "Yes, I do. There are things I left unsaid back in Gatlinburg. Things I hope will change your mind."

"Mother," Francesca wailed, "aren't you going to call the footmen to remove him? This is outrageous!"

Kate motioned behind her. "Come with me."

With graceful movements, head held high like a queen, she led him through the French doors onto a maze of brick pathways, sculpted bushes standing like sentinels on either side. They walked past manicured lawns, empty fountains, and fallow flowerbeds to another wing of the mansion. The Morgans' wealth hadn't been exaggerated.

She paused outside a door to tell him shyly, "This is my studio. We'll have privacy in here."

Once inside, his boots sank into the plush Oriental rug. It took a moment for his eyes to adjust to the dim light, but once they did, his gaze was drawn to the wallpapered walls where photograph after photograph of the mountains, the town of Gatlinburg and his family were displayed.

What struck him most were the number of pictures of just him. The one of him fishing the day she'd fallen in the water. Lounging next to a picnic basket. Dressed in his suit before church services.

She avoided his questioning gaze, but the pink staining her cheeks was a telltale sign of her embarrassment.

"You have talent," he said, bypassing the photos of himself to study the ones of the town. "These are amazing. They shouldn't be locked away in here. People should see them."

"You're too kind."

"No." He turned back. "No, I'm not. I was wrong to let you go the way I did. I acted like a fool. Can you forgive me?"

"I don't blame you. After what I did—" She broke off with a helpless gesture.

"Can you tell me about it?"

"I was a foolish young girl." Her eyes darkened with shame.

Going to stand before her, he gently took her hands in his.

"There's more to the story than that," he prompted quietly, dreading her words yet needing to hear them.

"Wesley was the first boy to notice me. I was lonely. When he began to pay attention to me, I was flattered. Here was someone my parents approved of, a promising young man from an upstanding family, and he was interested in *me*.

"During one of our parties, he asked to see my father's wine collection. I didn't see any harm in it." She shrugged. "But then the candle was somehow extinguished and the room was plunged into darkness. I panicked…" Her voice trailed off.

"Let me guess," Josh inserted, "instead of leading you out of there, your young man took full advantage of the situation."

"I allowed it to happen."

"My darling." He reached out and gently lifted her chin, forcing her to meet his gaze. Her eyes were large in her pale face. "He lured you down there for a reason. You were young and vulnerable. A prime target for a lustful young man without morals or any sense of decency."

He couldn't fathom how anyone could be so callous as to abuse her trust in such a way and then abandon her. A fierce protectiveness rose in his chest.

"We've all made mistakes we wish we could take back. All we can do is ask for forgiveness and move on. What happened in the past doesn't define who you are today. I'm sorry it took me so long to realize that. I've been miserable without you."

"What are you saying?" she breathed.

"You know what I admire about you?" He trailed a knuckle down her silken cheek.

Capturing her bottom lip with her teeth, she shook her head.

"After the disappointments and trials you've endured, you could've easily become bitter. Hardened your heart. Refused to trust or love others. But you didn't do any of those things. You, Kate Morgan, are a woman of integrity. A woman whose capacity to love humbles me." He slipped his hand beneath her hair to cup her neck. With his thumb, he made lazy circles on the soft skin. "I love you."

Kate let the precious words sink in. Her past hadn't destroyed his love for her.

Cradling her face with his hands, he stared deep into her eyes. "I want you for my wife. I want us to start a family of our own. We can make new memories, joyful ones to replace all that's happened in the past. We can start new traditions that we'll teach to our children and grandchildren. What do you say?"

Since childhood, she'd yearned for love and acceptance, a family who genuinely cared for one another. And here was the man she loved and admired offering her that very thing. Josh was offering himself to her. As his wife, she'd have a kind, thoughtful husband to love and share life with. To start a family with.

"Are you certain that's what you want?"

Leaning in, he brushed his lips across hers in silent declaration. "I love you. Nothing will ever change that."

Her fears laid to rest, she basked in the unconditional love shining in his eyes.

"I love you, Josh," she uttered softly, a blush stealing into her cheeks. "I would be honored to become your wife."

With a whoop that startled her, he encircled her waist and whirled her about, his husky laugh delighting her. Balancing herself with her hands on his shoulders, she couldn't help laughing right along with him. Then he lowered her feet to the floor and kissed her soundly.

"You've made me the happiest of men."

Caressing his cheek with her palm, she smiled at him. "And you, my love, have made all my dreams come true."

Epilogue

Two weeks later

Placing the last candle on the window ledge, Kate adjusted the bough of greenery and turned to survey the decorated church. Bouquets of orange and pink mums, yellow marigolds and goldenrod clustered around the podium, a burst of autumn colors against the white walls. Greencry entwined with cheerful orange ribbons adorned the pews.

It was a scene reminiscent of the season of bounty and harvest. Of Thanksgiving.

The perfect time for a wedding.

Her gaze settled on her fiancé. Looking handsome and relaxed, he stood in the far corner with his cousin Juliana and her husband, Evan Harrison. All three had silly grins on their faces, happy simply to be in each other's company once again.

Kate watched as Evan held his wife close, his manner loving and protective, his eyes full of love. How many times over the past week had Kate glimpsed him placing his hand tenderly over the slight swell of Juliana's abdomen where their first child nestled? Seeing them together, she found it difficult to believe the story of their meeting, of how he'd been masquerading as an outlaw and had kidnapped Juliana when she'd interrupted the robbery of Clawson's Mercantile.

Juliana had merely laughed at Kate's shocked reaction. The gorgeous redhead laughed a lot, no doubt giddy with joy to be among her family once more.

Megan appeared at her side looking radiantly happy. "I just love weddings—" she sighed dreamily as she surveyed the room "—and yours and Josh's is going to be beautiful, don't you agree? Are you happy with the way everything looks?"

"It's perfect." Grinning, she looped her arm through Megan's. "I can't wait until tomorrow."

The past two weeks had been a whirlwind of activity. They had lingered in New York only long enough for Kate to repack her traveling suitcase and arrange for her personal maid to act as chaperone on the return trip to Tennessee. Saying goodbye to her parents and sister had been more difficult than she'd anticipated, regardless of their disdainful attitudes. They were her family, and she loved them. Who knew if she'd ever return to the city of her birth?

Without Josh's support and the prospect of a new life, she might've crumbled. But God was faithful. The Healer of all wounds. He'd provided a brand-new family just for her.

Tomorrow she would walk down this aisle and join her life to his. She would be an O'Malley. An official member of the family.

As if reading her thoughts, Megan declared, "I'm so gloriously happy the two of you worked things out. Soon you and I will be family! And we'll get to see each other every day. I'll come and visit you in your new studio. I wonder who will be your first customer?"

The mention of Josh's wedding gift made her smile. Shortly after their return, he'd approached her with a blindfold and mischief in his eyes. Ignoring her questions, he'd driven her into town and, standing on the boardwalk, revealed his surprise.

Hanging above the door of the new store he'd rebuilt with his brothers was a carved sign with the words K. O'Malley Photography and J. D. O'Malley Furniture.

"Well? What do you say?" He'd tipped his head, a smile quivering about the corners of his mouth. "Partners?"

Overwhelmed by his thoughtfulness, she'd thrown her arms around in his neck. "You're too good to me!" she'd exclaimed, words muffled against his shirt collar.

First he'd stunned her with the announcement that he and his brothers were going to build a new, larger cabin just for them. And now this!

He'd held her tight, his face pressed against hers. "Is that a yes?"

She'd eased back to stare into his dear face. "Since we are to be partners in life, it makes sense for us to be partners in business, as well. I'm not sure how I can ever thank you properly."

His lazy smile and the flare of heat in his eyes had made her insides go all quivery. "Oh, I think we can come up with something." He'd brushed a too-brief kiss across her lips. Releasing her, he'd gestured toward their combination store and studio. "For now, would you like a tour?"

"I'd like nothing better."

"Kate—" Megan nudged her "—are you listening?"

She blinked to clear her mind of the pleasant memory. "Sorry, what were you saying?"

"Never mind—" she chuckled "—as the bride-to-be, you have an excuse to daydream."

Kate spotted Tom off to the side with Nathan and Nicole. His gaze seemed to follow Megan around the room. "I'm curious—did you ask Tom to come and help decorate?"

The sparkle in her eyes dimmed as she shook her head. "No, Josh did that."

"He can't keep his eyes off you, you know."

Regret pulled at her generous mouth. "I was hoping… that is, while he's a kind, upstanding man, there's just no spark between us."

"Spark?"

"Yes, spark. Don't pretend you don't know what I mean." She gave her a look. "Whenever you and Josh are in the same room together, the air practically hums. I can see it in the way you two look at each other. It's the same with Evan and Juliana."

Kate couldn't deny it. "So you're saying there's no magic with Tom."

"Exactly."

She tugged her friend close. "One day soon you'll meet the man of your dreams."

"That's what I keep telling her," Juliana piped up, her forest-green eyes brimming with happiness and humor. "She's got her heart set on a romantic hero come to life."

Megan grinned. "That's right. No ordinary man will do for me."

Kate sought out Josh. Her heart skipped a beat when she encountered his ardent gaze. Even from this distance, the look in his eyes made her knees go weak. Yes. There was a spark all right.

"I already found my hero," she said softly, smiling at him.

With a parting word to Evan, he started toward her.

Seeing the looks exchanged between the couple, Juliana gave her a grateful smile. "You've made him more happy than I've ever seen him, Kate. And that makes *me* happy. Welcome to the family."

Her kind words meant a lot to Kate. In the few, short days she'd spent in Juliana's company, she'd become fond of the young woman and would be sorry to see her leave.

"What are you three whispering about over here?" Josh curled an arm around Kate's waist and tucked her against his side. He dropped a kiss on her cheek, something he did with pleasing regularity these days.

She had delighted in discovering his affectionate side. He was quick to hug and hold her, and he liked to steal kisses. Simply holding hands seemed to please him. Having lived in a loveless household for much of her life, she treasured his each and every touch.

"We were saying how thrilled we are to have Kate," Megan said.

"Yes, indeed." His smile was tender as he gazed down at her. "I think we'll keep her."

Evan strolled up at the same time Juliana smothered a yawn. "I think it's time we head back to the cabin." He rested a hand on her shoulder. "Little momma here needs her rest."

"I do get tired more easily these days." To Kate, she said, "I'll see you in the morning. Sleep well."

Taking their cue from the expectant couple, everyone left except for Josh and Kate.

Their arms wrapped loosely about each other's waists, he groaned good-naturedly, "I wish it was tomorrow already. I can't wait to make you my bride."

"I have a feeling the day will go by faster than you think."

And it did.

In an emotional, romantic ceremony that next afternoon, with family and friends looking on, she and Josh exchanged vows to love and cherish each other the rest of their lives. The evening passed in a blur of well-wishes, gift-opening, cake-cutting and, for the bride and groom, longing glances and stolen kisses when they thought no one was watching.

At long last alone in their cabin, Kate's stomach fluttered with nervous excitement. With one final glance in the mirror, she emerged from the bedroom wearing a lace and satin nightgown, handmade specially for her wedding night.

A soul-satisfying contentment filled her. Her past, so riddled with pain and regret, no longer haunted her. She'd let it go. What was important was the here and now, and learning to savor each moment of her new life.

This was a day of new beginnings.

At the whisper of luminous material, her husband glanced up. His eyes widened, then darkened as he took in the sight of her. He stood slowly to his feet and walked toward her.

Still dressed in his black suit pants, the top buttons of his white dress shirt undone and the sleeves rolled up to reveal muscular forearms, he was devastatingly handsome. His honey-brown hair was mussed, giving him a rakish look.

Her pulse quickened.

Reaching up, he removed the pins from her hair one by one, watching as her tresses fell in waves about her shoulders. "You are ravishing, Mrs. O'Malley."

Kate's eyes drifted shut, and she smiled. How she treasured the sound of her new name!

"Thank you, Mr. O'Malley."

"I'm a fortunate man to have you as my bride."

She looked at him then. "I'm not the bride you initially picked out."

"True." His smile was loving and wise. "But you're the bride God wanted for me. And we all know His choices are best."

Josh enfolded her in his embrace and kissed her then, expressing his love and adoration for her with tender touches and earnest whispers.

He loved her, and she loved him. They would spend the rest of their lives celebrating the gift God had given them.

* * * * *

SPECIAL EXCERPT FROM

❧

LOVE INSPIRED
INSPIRATIONAL ROMANCE

When a charming rodeo cowboy comes home,
will he make amends to an old sweetheart?

Read on for a sneak preview of
The Prodigal Cowboy,
the next book in Brenda Minton's miniseries
Mercy Ranch.

Holly saw him enter but she didn't believe it, not at first. It couldn't be Colt, looking rugged but handsome, a few days' growth of whiskers on his too-attractive face as he leaned heavily on a cane and announced his arrival like she might have been waiting for his return.

He removed his hat and pushed a hand through dark hair. For a moment she was eighteen again, meeting up with a guy and not realizing the combined power of attraction and loneliness.

Just like that day twelve years ago she felt it again, hitting her hard, taking her breath for just an instant before she reminded herself that he was a two-timing, no-good piece of work that she wanted nothing to do with.

She couldn't let herself get pulled in by his looks and charm. Not again.

"Holly," he started.

She shook her head and took a step back.

"What are you doing here?" she asked. It wasn't the first time he'd come home. Nor the first time she'd seen him in the past eleven years.

It's just that he never came here, not to the café.

"I just need a few minutes of your time."

"Why?"

He had moved closer and was suddenly in front of her, smelling too good. She nearly groaned at her own weakness for this man.

"Spit it out, Colt."

He motioned her toward a table, even pulled out a chair for her.

She took the seat and he sat across from her. "Get it over with, please. I can't take much more of this. Are you sick? Did that bull hurt you worse than everyone said?"

He grimaced as he leaned back. "I'm not sick. I would tell you not to worry but I doubt worry is the first thing you feel for me."

"I would be upset if something happened to you," she admitted, her voice faltering.

"This isn't about the accident. I'm healing up fine." He leaned back in his chair and studied her face. "You're still beautiful."

"Don't. I don't want your compliments. You're obviously here on business. So why don't we cut to the chase?"

He didn't smile. "Of course, right to the point. Holly, it's about Dixie. That's why I'm here."

Dixie.

He wasn't here about the café or about them. He was here to tell her something concerning Dixie.

Their daughter.